Betsy Byars

Betsy Byars

The Eighteenth Emergency

The Cartoonist

The TV Kid

The Cybil War

WHSMITH
EXCLUSIVE
· BOOKS ·

The Eighteenth Emergency first published in Great Britain
by The Bodley Head in 1974
The Cartoonist first published in Great Britain by The Bodley Head in 1978
The TV Kid first published in Great Britain by The Bodley Head in 1976
The Cybil War first published in Great Britain by The Bodley Head in 1981

This edition produced exclusively for W.H. Smith in 1986 by
Octopus Books Limited
59 Grosvenor Street
London W1

ISBN 0 7064 2777 7

Printed at The Bath Press, Avon

Contents

THE
EIGHTEENTH
EMERGENCY

1

THE pigeons flew out of the alley in one long swoop and settled on the awning of the grocery store. A dog ran out of the alley with a torn Cracker Jack box in his mouth. Then came the boy.

The boy was running hard and fast. He stopped at the sidewalk, looked both ways, saw that the street was deserted and kept going. The dog caught the boy's fear, and he started running with him.

The two of them ran together for a block. The dog's legs were so short he appeared to be on wheels. His Cracker Jack box was hitting the sidewalk. He kept glancing at the boy because he didn't know why they were running. The boy knew. He did not even notice the dog beside him or the trail of spilled Cracker Jacks behind.

Suddenly the boy slowed down, went up some stairs and entered an apartment building. The dog stopped. He sensed that the danger had passed, but he stood for a moment at the bottom of the stairs. Then he went back to eat the Cracker Jacks scattered on the sidewalk and to snarl at the pigeons who had flown down to get some.

Inside the building the boy was still running. He went up the stairs three at a time, stumbled, pulled himself up by the banister and kept going until he was safely inside his own apartment. Then he sagged against the door.

His mother was sitting on the sofa, going over some papers. The boy waited for her to look up and ask him what had happened. He thought she should be able to hear something was wrong just from the terrible way he was breathing. 'Mom,' he said.

'Just a minute. I've got to get these orders straight.' When she went over her cosmetic orders she had a dedicated, scientific look. He waited until she came to the end of the sheet.

'Mom.' Without looking up, she turned to the next page. He said again, 'Mom.'

'I'm almost through. There's a mistake some –'

He said, 'Never mind.' He walked heavily through the living-room and into the hall. He threw himself down on the day bed.

His mother said, 'I'm almost through with this, Benjie.'

'I said, "Never mind."' He looked up at the ceiling. In a blur he saw a long cobweb hanging by the light fixture. A month ago he had climbed on a chair, written UNSAFE FOR PUBLIC SWINGING and drawn an arrow to the cobweb. It was still there.

He closed his eyes. He was breathing so hard his throat hurt.

'Benjie, come back,' his mother called. 'I'm through.'

'Never mind.'

'Come on, Benjie, I want to talk to you.'

He got up slowly and walked into the living-room. She had put her order books on the coffee table. 'Sit down. Tell me what's wrong.' He hesitated and then sat beside her on the sofa. She waited and then said again, 'What's wrong?'

He did not answer for a moment. He looked out of the window, and he could see the apartment across the street. A yellow cat was sitting in the window watching the pigeons. He said in a low voice, 'Some boys are going to kill me.'

'Not *kill* you, Benjie,' she said. 'No one is –'

He glanced quickly at her. 'Well, how do I know what they're going to do?' he said, suddenly angry. 'They're chasing me, that's all I know. When you see somebody chasing you, and when it's Marv Hammerman and Tony Lionni and a boy in a black sweat shirt you don't stop and say, "Now, what *exactly* are you guys planning to do – kill me or just break a few arms and legs?"'

'What did you do to these boys?'

'What did *I* do? I didn't do anything. You think I would do something to Marv Hammerman who is the biggest boy in my school? He is bigger than the eighth graders. He should be in high school.'

'I know you did something. I can always tell. Now, what happened?'

'Nothing, Mom. I didn't do anything.' He looked down at his shoes. With his foot he began to kick at the rug. A little mound of red lint piled up in front of his tennis shoe.

'They wouldn't be after you for nothing.'

'Well, they are.' He paused. He knew he had to give an explanation, but he could not give the right one. He said, 'Maybe Hammerman just doesn't like me. I don't know. I'm not a mind reader.'

'Look at me, Benjie.'

Without looking up he said, 'Mom, just listen to what Hammerman did to this boy in my room one time. This boy was in line in the cafeteria and Hammerman came up to him and –'

'What I want to hear is what happened *today*, Benjie.'

'Just *listen*. And this boy in the cafeteria was standing in line, Mom, doing absolutely nothing, and Hammerman comes up to him and –'

'Benjie, what happened *today*?'

He hesitated. He looked down at his tennis shoe. There was a frayed hole in the toe, and he had taken a ballpoint pen and written AIR VENT and drawn a little arrow pointing to the hole.

'What happened?' she asked again.

'Nothing.' He did not look at her.

'Benjie –'

'Nothing happened.'

She sighed, then abruptly she looked up. 'The beans!' She walked to the kitchen, and he lay back on the sofa and closed his eyes.

'Benjie?' He looked up. His mother was leaning around the door, looking at him. 'Why don't you watch television? Get your mind off yourself. That always helps me.'

'No, it won't help.'

'Well, let's just see what's on.' She came back in, turned on the television and waited for the set to warm up. He closed his eyes. He knew there was nothing on television that could interest him.

'Tarzan!' his mother said. 'You always have loved Tarzan.'

He opened his eyes and glanced at the screen. In the depths of the jungle, a hunter had stumbled into quicksand, and Tarzan was swinging to the rescue.

'All the hunter has to do,' he said with a disgusted sigh, 'is lie down on the quicksand and not struggle and he won't sink.'

'That wouldn't leave anything for Tarzan to do though, would it?' his mother said, smiling a little.

'Oh, I don't know.' He closed his eyes and shifted on the sofa. After a minute he heard his mother go back into the kitchen. He opened his eyes. On the screen the hunter was still struggling. Cheetah was beginning to turn nervous somersaults. Tarzan was getting closer.

Once he and his friend Ezzie had made a list of all the ways they knew to stay alive. Ezzie had claimed he could stay alive in the jungle forever. Ezzie said every jungle emergency had a simple solution.

Lying on the sofa, he tried to remember some of those old emergencies.

A second one came into his mind. Emergency Two – Attack by an Unfriendly Lion. Lion attack, Ezzie claimed, was an everyday occurrence in the jungle. What you had to do to survive was wait until the last moment, until the lion was upon you, and then you had to ram your arm all the way down the lion's throat. This would choke him and make him helpless. It was bound to be a little unpleasant, Ezzie admitted, to be up to your shoulder in lion, but that couldn't be helped.

'Is the Tarzan movie any good?' his mother asked from the kitchen.

'No.' He reached out with his foot and turned off the television. He sighed. Nothing could take his mind off Marv Hammerman for long.

'If it makes you feel any better,' his mother said, 'Teddy Roosevelt had the same problem. I saw it on television. Boys used to pick on him and chase him.'

'No, it doesn't,' he said. He waited a minute and then asked, 'What did Teddy Roosevelt do about it?'

'Well, as I remember it, Teddy's father got him a gymnasium and Teddy exercised and got strong and nobody ever picked on him again.'

'Oh.'

'Of course, it wasn't the same as –'

'Don't bother getting me a gymnasium.'

'Now, Benjie, I didn't –'

'Unless you know of some exerciser that gives instant muscles.' He thought about it for a minute. He would go out, exerciser in his pocket, and say, 'Here I am, Hammerman.' Then, just when Hammerman was stepping toward him, he would whip out the exerciser, pump it once, and muscles would pop out all over his body like balloons.

'Well, you'll handle it,' his mother said. 'In a few weeks you'll look back on this and laugh.'

'Sure.'

He lay with his eyes closed, trying to remember some more of the old ways he and Ezzie knew to survive life's greatest emergencies.

Emergency Three – Unexpected Charge of an Enraged Bull. Bulls have a blind spot in the centre of their vision, so when being charged by a bull, you try to line yourself up with this blind spot.

'Fat people can't do it, Mouse,' Ezzie had told him. 'That's why you never see any fat bullfighters. You and I can. We just turn sideways like this, see, get in the blind spot and wait.'

He could remember exactly how Ezzie had looked, waiting sideways in the blind spot of the imaginary bull. 'And there's one other thing,' Ezzie had added. 'It will probably work for a rhinoceros too.'

Emergency Four – Crocodile Attack. When attacked by a crocodile, prop a stick in its mouth and the crocodile is helpless.

At one time this had been his own favourite emergency.

He had spent a lot of time dreaming of tricking crocodiles. He had imagined himself a tornado in the water, handing out the sticks like party favours. 'Take that and that and that!' The stunned crocodiles, mouths propped open, had dragged themselves away. For the rest of their lives they had avoided children with sticks in their hands. 'Hey, no!' his dream crocodiles had cried, 'Let that kid alone. He's got sticks, man, *sticks!*'

Abruptly he turned his head toward the sofa. The smile which had come to his face when he had remembered the crocodiles now faded. He pulled a thread in the slip cover. The material began to pucker, and he stopped pulling and smoothed it out. Then he took a pencil from his pocket and wrote in tiny letters on the wall PULL THREAD IN CASE OF BOREDOM and drew a little arrow to the sofa.

The words blurred suddenly, and he let the pencil drop behind the sofa. He lay back down. Hammerman was in his mind again, and he closed his eyes. He tried hard to think of the days when he and Ezzie had been ready to handle crocodiles and bulls, quicksand and lions. It seemed a long time ago.

2

'HEY Mouse!' It was Ezzie.

He got up from the sofa quickly and went to the window. 'What?' he called back.

'Come on down.'

His mother said in the kitchen, 'You've got to eat.'

'I've got to eat, Ezzie.'

'Well, hurry up. I'll wait.'

He stood at the window and watched Ezzie sit down on the steps. The dog had finished with his Cracker Jacks and was now sitting in front of Ezzie, looking at him hopefully. The smell of chicken and noodles was coming from one of the windows, and the dog thought it was coming from Ezzie. The dog wanted some chicken and noodles so badly that his nose had started to run.

Ezzie patted the dog once. 'I haven't got anything,' he told him. 'And quit looking at me.' Once the dog had looked at Ezzie so long that Ezzie had gone in the house and fixed him a devilled egg sandwich. 'I haven't got anything,' Ezzie said again and turned his head away. Ezzie had named the dog Garbage Dog because of his eating habits. 'Go *on*.' Slowly Garbage Dog got up. He circled once like a radar finder and then began slowly to move in the direction of the chicken and noodles.

'Come to supper,' Mouse's mother called. He went into the kitchen where his mother was putting the food on the table. She sat down, spread a paper napkin on her lap and said, 'Why doesn't Ezzie help you with those boys?'

'What?'

'Why doesn't Ezzie help you fight those boys?' she repeated, nodding her head toward the window.

'Oh, Mom.'

'I mean it. If there were *two* of you, then those boys would think twice before –'

'Oh, Mom!' He bent over his plate and began to smash his lima beans with his fork. He thought about it for a moment, of stepping in front of Marv Hammerman and Tony Lionni and the boy in the black sweat shirt and saying in a cool voice, 'I think I'd better warn you that I've got my friend with me.'

'Who's your friend?'

'*This* is my friend.' At that Ezzie would step out from the shadows and stand with him.

Marv Hammerman would look at them, sizing them up, the two of them, this duo his mother had created for strength. Then with a faint smile Hammerman would reach out, grab them up like cymbals and clang them together. When Hammerman set them down they would twang for forty-five minutes before they could stumble off.

'Well, I know what I'm talking about, that's all,' his mother said. 'If you could get Ezzie to help you –'

'All right, Mom, I'll ask him.'

He ate four lima beans and looked at his mother. 'Is that enough? I'm not hungry.'

'Eat.'

He thought he was going to choke. Emergency Five – Being Choked by a Boa Constrictor. When you were being strangled by a boa constrictor, Ezzie had said, what you had to do was taunt the boa constrictor and get him to *bite* you instead of *strangle* you. His bite, Ezzie admitted, was a little painful but the strangulation was worse.

This had seemed a first-rate survival measure at the time. Now he had trouble imagining him and Ezzie in the jungle being squeezed by the boa constrictor. He tried to imagine Ezzie's face, pink and earnest, above the boa constrictor's loop. He tried to hear Ezzie's voice taunting, 'Sure you can strangle, but can you bite? Let's see you try to bite us!'

'Hey, Mouse, you coming?' Ezzie had opened the door to the hall now, and his voice came up the stairs as if through a megaphone.

'I'll eat the rest later,' Mouse said. He was already out of his chair, moving toward the door.

'Oh, all right,' his mother said, 'go on.'

He ran quickly out of the apartment and down the stairs. Ezzie was waiting for him outside, sitting down. As soon as he saw Mouse, Ezzie got up and said, 'Hey, what happened? Where'd you go after school?'

Mouse said, 'Hammerman's after me.'

Ezzie's pink mouth formed a perfect O. He didn't say anything, but his breath came out in a long sympathetic wheeze. Finally he said, '*Marv* Hammerman?' even though he knew there was only one Hammerman in the world, just as there had been only one Hitler.

'Yes.'

'Is after *you?*'

Mouse nodded, sunk in misery. He could see Marv Hammerman. He came up in Mouse's mind the way monsters do in horror movies, big and powerful, with the same cold, unreal eyes. It was the eyes Mouse really feared. One look from those eyes, he thought, just one look of a certain length – about three seconds – and you knew you were his next victim.

'What did you do?' Ezzie asked. 'Or did you do anything?'

At least, Mouse thought, Ezzie understood that. If you were Marv Hammerman, you didn't need a reason. He sat down on the steps and squinted up at Ezzie. 'I did something,' he said.

'What?' Ezzie asked. His tongue flicked out and in so quickly it didn't even moisten his lips. 'What'd you do? You bump into him or something?'

Mouse shook his head.

'Well, what?'

Mouse said, 'You know that big chart in the upstairs hall at school?'

'What'd you say? I can't even hear you, Mouse. You're muttering.' Ezzie bent closer. 'Look at me. Now what did you say?'

Mouse looked up, still squinting. He said, 'You know that big chart outside the history room? In the hall?'

'Chart?' Ezzie said blankly. 'What chart, Mouse?'

'This chart takes up the whole wall, Ez, how could you miss it? It's a chart about early man, and it shows man's progress up from the apes, the side view of all those different kinds of prehistoric men, like Cro-Magnon man and Homo erectus. *That* chart.'

'Oh, yeah, I saw it, so go on.'

Mouse could see that Ezzie was eager for him to get on to the good part, the violence. He slumped. He wet his lips. He said, 'Well, when I was passing this chart on my way out of history – and I don't know why I did this – I really don't. When I was passing this chart, Ez, on my way to math –' He swallowed, almost choking on his spit. 'When I was passing this chart, Ez, I took my pencil and I wrote Marv Hammerman's name on the bottom of the chart and then I drew an arrow to the picture of Neanderthal man.'

'What?' Ezzie cried, '*What?*' He could not seem to take it in. Mouse knew that Ezzie had been prepared to sympathize with an accident. He had almost been the victim of one of those himself. One day at school Ezzie had reached for the handle on the water fountain a second ahead of Marv Hammerman. If Ezzie hadn't glanced up just in time, seen Hammerman and said quickly, 'Go ahead, I'm not thirsty,' then this sagging figure on the steps might be him. 'What did you do it for, Mouse?'

'I don't know.'

'You crazy or something?'

'I don't know.'

'Marv Hammerman!' Ezzie sighed. It was a mournful sound that seemed to have come from a culture used to sorrow. 'Anybody else in the school would have been better. I would rather have the principal after me than Marv Hammerman.'

'I know.'

'Hammerman's big, Mouse. He's flunked a lot.'

'I know,' Mouse said again. There was an unwritten law that it was all right to fight anyone in your own grade. The fact that Hammerman was older and stronger made no difference. They were both in the sixth grade.

'Then what'd you do it for?' Ezzie asked.

'I don't know.'

'You must want trouble,' Ezzie said. 'Like my grand-father. He's always provoking people. The bus driver won't even pick him up any more.'

'No, I don't want trouble.'

'Then, why did you –'

'I don't *know.*' Then he sagged again and said, 'I didn't even know I had done it really until I'd finished. I just looked at the picture of Neanderthal man and thought of Hammerman. It does look like him, Ezzie, the sloping face and the shoulders.'

'Maybe Hammerman doesn't know you did it though,' Ezzie said. 'Did you ever think of that? I mean, who's going to go up to Hammerman and tell him his name is on the prehistoric man chart?' Ezzie leaned forward. 'Hey,

Hammerman,' he said, imitating the imaginary fool, 'I saw a funny thing about you on the prehistoric man chart! Now, who in their right mind is going to –'

'He was right behind me when I did it,' Mouse said.

'What?'

'He was right behind me,' Mouse said stiffly. He could remember turning and looking into Hammerman's eyes. It was such a strange, troubling moment that Mouse was unable to think about it.

Ezzie's mouth formed the O, made the sympathetic sigh. Then he said, 'And you don't even know what you did it for?'

'No.'

Ezzie sank down on the steps beside Mouse. He leaned over his knees and said, 'You ought to get out of that habit, that writing names and drawing arrows, you know that? I see those arrows everywhere. I'll be walking down the street and I'll look on a building and I'll see the word DOOR written in little letters and there'll be an arrow pointing to the door and I know you did it. It's crazy, labelling stuff like that.'

'I never did that, Ez, not to a door.'

'Better to a door, if you ask me,' Ezzie said, shaking his head. He paused for a moment, then asked in a lower voice, 'You ever been hit before, Mouse? I mean, hard?'

Mouse sighed. The conversation had now passed beyond the question of whether Hammerman would attack. It was now a matter of whether he, Mouse Fawley, could survive the attack. He said thickly, remembering, 'Four times.'

'Four times in one fight? I mean, you stood up for four hits, Mouse?' There was grudging admiration in his voice.

Mouse shook his head. 'Four hits – four fights.'

'You went right down each time? I mean, POW and you went down, POW and you went down, POW and you went –'

'Yes!'

'Where did you take these hits?' Ezzie asked, straightening suddenly. Ezzie had never taken a single direct blow in his life because he was a good dodger. Sometimes his mother chased him through the apartment striking at him while he dodged and ducked, crying, 'Look out, Mom, look out now! You're going to hit me!'

He asked again, 'Where were you hit?'

Mouse said, 'In the stomach.'

'All four times?'

'Yeah.' Mouse suddenly thought of his stomach as having a big red circular target on it with HIT HERE printed in the centre.

'Who hit you?'

'Two boys in Cincinnati when I was on vacation, and a boy named Mickey Swearinger, and somebody else I don't remember.' He lowered his head because he remembered the fourth person all right, but he didn't want to tell Ezzie about it. If he had added the name of Viola Angotti to the list of those who had hit him in the stomach, Ezzie's face would have screwed up with laughter. 'Viola Angotti hit you? No fooling, Viola Angotti?' It was the sort of thing Ezzie could carry on about for hours. 'Viola Angotti. *The* Viola Angotti?'

And Mouse would have had to keep sitting there saying over and over, 'Yes, Viola Angotti hit me in the stomach. Yes, *the* Viola Angotti.' And then he would have to tell Ezzie all about it, every detail, how one recess long ago the boys had decided to put some girls in the school trash cans. It had been one of those suggestions that stuns everyone with its rightness. Someone had said, 'Hey, let's put those girls over there in the trash cans!' and the plan won immediate acceptance. Nothing could have been more appropriate. The trash cans were big and had just been emptied, and in an instant the boys were off chasing the girls and yelling at the top of their lungs.

It had been wonderful at first, Mouse remembered. Primitive blood had raced through his body. The desire to capture had driven him like a wild man through the school yard, up the sidewalk, everywhere. He understood what had driven the cave man and the barbarian, because this same passion was driving him. Putting the girls in the trash cans was the most important challenge of his life. His long screaming charge ended with him red-faced, gasping for breath – and with Viola Angotti pinned against the garbage cans.

His moment of triumph was short. It lasted about two seconds. Then it began to dim as he realized, first, that it *was* Viola Angotti, and, second, that he was not going to be able to get her into the garbage can without a great deal of help.

He cried, 'Hey, you guys, come on, I've got one,' but behind him the school yard was silent. Where was everybody? he had wondered uneasily. As it turned out, the principal had caught the other boys, and they were all being marched back in the front door of the school, but Mouse didn't know this.

He called again, 'Come on, you guys, get the lid off this garbage can, will you?'

And then, when he said that, Viola Angotti had taken

two steps forward. She said, 'Nobody's putting *me* in no garbage can.' He could still remember how she had looked standing there. She had recently taken the part of the Statue of Liberty in a class play, and somehow she seemed taller and stronger at this moment than when she had been in costume.

He cried, 'Hey, you guys!' It was a plea. 'Where are you?'

And then Viola Angotti had taken one more step, and with a faint sigh she had socked him in the stomach so hard that he had doubled over and lost his lunch. He hadn't known it was possible to be hit like that outside a boxing ring. It was the hardest blow he had ever taken. Viola Angotti could be heavyweight champion of the world.

As she walked past his crumpled body she had said again, 'Nobody's putting me in no garbage can.' It had sounded like one of the world's basic truths. The sun will rise. The tides will flow. Nobody's putting Viola Angotti in no garbage can.

Later, when he thought about it, he realized that he had been lucky. If she had wanted to, Viola Angotti could have capped her victory by tossing his rag-doll body into the garbage can and slamming down the lid. Then, when the principal came out onto the playground calling, 'Benjamin Fawley! Has anybody seen Benjamin Fawley?' he would have had to moan, 'I'm in here.' He would have had to climb out of the garbage can in front of the whole school. His shame would have followed him for life. When he was a grown man, people would still be pointing him out to their children. '*That*'s the man that Viola Angotti stuffed into the garbage can.'

Now he thought that Marv Hammerman could make Viola Angotti's blow seem like a baby's pat. He wanted to double over on the steps.

Ezzie said, 'You ought to watch out for your stomach like a fighter, protect your body. There's a lot of valuable stuff in there.'

'I know.'

'The trick of it,' Ezzie said, 'is moving quickly, ducking, getting out of the way.' Ezzie did a few quick steps, his feet flashing on the sidewalk. 'You dance, Mouse, like this.' Mouse suddenly remembered that Ezzie had once told him that if you were ever bitten by a tarantula (Emergency Six) you had to start dancing immediately. Ezzie said you were supposed to do this special Italian folk dance, but any quick lively steps would probably do.

Mouse had a picture of himself doing this lively dance in front of Hammerman. Hammerman would watch for a moment. There would be no expression on his face. The dance would reach a peak. Mouse's arms and legs would be a blur of motion. And then Hammerman would reach down, a sort of slow graceful movement like he was bowling, and come up effortlessly right into Mouse's stomach.

Mouse leaned forward, shielding his body with his arms. He cleared his throat. 'Did anybody ever hit you, Ezzie?'

Ezzie stopped dancing. 'Sure.'

'Who?'

'Well, relatives mostly. You can't hardly walk through my living-room without somebody trying to hit you – for any little thing. I accidentally step on my sister's feet – she's got long feet, Mouse, she can't hardly buy ordinary shoes, and she takes it as an insult if you step on one of them. She's fast too, Mouse. That's how I learned about getting out of the way.'

'But nobody like Hammerman ever hit you?'

'No.' He sounded apologetic.

Mouse sighed. Above him his mother called, 'Benjie, come up now. I want you to do something for me.'

'I got to go.' Mouse still sat there. He hated to leave the warmth of Ezzie's understanding. Ezzie didn't want to leave either. Mouse had taken on a fine tragic dimension in his eyes, and there was something about being with a person like that that made him feel good.

Ezzie had felt the same way about their teacher last fall when he had told them he had to go to the hospital. For the first time, Mr Stein in his baggy suit had seemed a fine tragic figure, bigger than life. Ezzie would have done anything for Mr Stein that day. But then, when Mr Stein came limping back the next week – it turned out he had had some bone spurs removed from his heels – he had been his normal size.

'Benjie, come up now,' his mother called again.

'I'm coming.'

'Did you tell your mom about Hammerman being after you?' Ezzie asked.

'Yeah.'

'What'd she say?'

He tried to think of the most impossible statement his mother had made. 'She said I'll laugh about it in a week or two.'

'Laugh about it?'

'Yeah, through my bandages.'

Ezzie's face twisted into a little smile. 'Hey, remember

Al Armsby when he had those broken ribs? Remember how he would beg us not to make him laugh? And I had this one joke about a monkey and I would keep telling it and keep telling it and he was practically on his knees begging for mercy and –'

Mouse got slowly to his feet. 'Well, I better go,' he said.

Ezzie stopped smiling. 'Hey, wait a minute. Listen, I just remembered something. I know a boy that Hammerman beat up, and he said it wasn't so bad.'

'Who?'

'A friend of my brother's. I'll find out about it and let you know.'

'All right,' Mouse said. He did not allow himself to believe it was true. Sometimes Ezzie lied like this out of sympathy. If you said, 'My stomach hurts and I think I'm going to die,' and if Ezzie really liked you, he would say, 'I know a boy whose stomach hurt worse than that and *he* didn't die!' And if you said, 'Who?' Ezzie would say, 'A friend of my brother's.' Ezzie's brother only had one friend that Mouse knew about, and this friend would have had to have daily brushes with death to fulfil all of Ezzie's statements.

Still, it made Mouse want to cry for a moment that Ezzie would lie to spare him. Or maybe he wanted to cry because Hammerman was going to kill him. He didn't know. He said, 'Thanks, Ez,' in a choked voice. He turned and walked quickly into the apartment building.

3

MOUSE was just starting up the stairs when his mother and Mrs Casino from across the hall came out of the apartment. 'Wait a minute, Benjie,' his mother said. 'Mrs Casino wants to know if you'll walk up to Margy's and get Mr Casino. She'd do it but she's keeping the baby for Agnes tonight.'

Mrs Casino's round face was worried. She was holding her apron up in both hands. She said, 'You mind, Benjie?'

He minded and he wanted them to know it. He sighed and looked down at his feet, at the vent hole in the toe of his shoe. Then he glanced up at the wall. There was a long crack in the plaster, and two months ago Mouse had written TO OPEN BUILDING TEAR ALONG THIS LINE and drawn an arrow to the crack. He turned his head away. He thought suddenly that Ezzie was right. He shouldn't draw those arrows everywhere.

'Well?' his mother said.

'Oh, all right.' Mouse turned and started down the stairs, his shoulders hanging. He knew this gave him a dejected look because his mother was always telling him in such a stern way to hold up his shoulders.

'You're a good boy, Benjie,' Mrs Casino called, then she said loudly to his mother, 'You got a good boy there. That's one boy we don't have to worry about in this world.'

His mother called, 'Just go right straight there and back, Benjie.'

'All right.'

'And don't rush Mr Casino.'

'He won't rush him,' Mrs Casino said confidently.

Mouse went out the door, slamming it behind him, and started up the street. The sun had disappeared in the few minutes he had been inside, and now the street was darker, colder. Pigeons were going to roost over the grocery store, their wings pale against the dark brick. Mouse zipped up his jacket.

A block ahead he could see Ezzie running. Ezzie and his five sisters and brother had to be there when Ezzie's father got home from work. It didn't matter what they did during the day as long as all seven of them were there waiting at the day's end.

Mouse called, 'Hey, Ez! Ezzie!' Ezzie turned and Mouse said, 'Wait up.'

Ezzie pointed to his arm where a watch would have been if he had had one. Mouse nodded and waved him on and then walked slowly up the street.

He started thinking again about Marv Hammerman. In his mind he could see Hammerman exactly as he had looked after school that afternoon. Mouse hadn't gotten around to telling Ezzie about that.

Mouse had come out of school so fast he had almost pushed two girls down the steps. He wanted only to get home before Hammerman saw him.

'Watch it, Benjie,' the biggest girl, Rebecca, had said, straightening angrily.

He had muttered, 'Sorry,' and had run ahead of them a few steps. Then he came to a halt. At the bottom of the steps was Marv Hammerman, waiting.

There was something animal-like about Hammerman with his long limbs and careless grace, his clothes that fitted as if they were an extra skin, the shaggy hair that appeared never to have known the pull of a comb. Hammerman had been watching for Mouse, and his eyes got a little brighter when he saw him.

'I thought you were in such a big hurry,' Rebecca said scornfully, nudging him in the back with her books as she passed. Mouse hardly noticed.

Hammerman's face was already the way it would be when he was a man. When Mouse read of boys having to go to work in the coal mines and cotton mills at age twelve and thirteen in the old days, it did not seem possible until he had seen Marv Hammerman.

Hammerman's face did not change expression when he saw Mouse, just sharpened a little. Mouse thought his own face might have been made of thin rubber, it was changing expression so rapidly. His face twisted into shock as he saw Hammerman, then into fear. Then, quickly, awkwardly, Mouse pantomimed that he had forgotten something. He turned and ran back into the school. Once inside, he had run through the halls, down the back stairs, out the side exit and twenty-five blocks out of his way to get home.

To take his mind off Hammerman, he tried to think of another of Ezzie's emergencies. These emergencies were the only things that could make him feel better.

Emergency Seven – Seizure by Gorilla. If this happens, you relax completely and make soothing noises deep in your throat. Ezzie claimed this was foolproof, but Mouse had never been convinced.

'I tell you it's a sure thing, Mouse,' Ezzie had said. 'You make the soothing noises, and he lets you go.'

'I still don't think it would work.'

'All right,' Ezzie had said, 'when a gorilla gets *you*, you scream and kick and holler. When one gets *me*, I'm making soothing noises.' Ezzie had been sensitive about the success of his emergency methods.

Emergency Eight – Attack by Killer Whale. This is one of life's most serious emergencies. When this happens, you swim away from the whale as rapidly as possible. Do not try to get swallowed because, Ezzie said, there isn't as much air in those whales as you'd think. If you do get swallowed by accident, take small measured breaths and try to get coughed out. Then you start swimming away rapidly again.

Mouse passed Margy's apartment he was so busy thinking about the killer whale. Then he turned around. He went up the stairs, entered the apartment and knocked at the first door. When Margy, Mrs Casino's daughter, opened it, he said, 'I came for Mr Casino.'

'Oh, yes.' She turned. 'Papa, the Fawley boy's here for you.' She went over and said, 'Papa, you ready to go home?'

Mr Casino was staring at the television with eyes that seemed to have pulled back into his head a little. He did not look up. She touched his shoulder.

'Papa, you ready to go?' She got him to his feet. He had once been an enormous man but was bent over now so that she could put his overcoat on and button it with ease. 'He's ready, Benjie.'

Mouse was waiting at the door, and she brought Mr Casino over. She put his hand on Mouse's shoulder, and the two of them went outside and down the stairs. Mr Casino moved slowly, shifting his weight noticeably with each step, favouring his left leg, rocking back and forth.

Mr Casino had been like this for as long as Mouse could

remember, but Mrs Casino was always talking about the time, before his illness, when he had been the strongest man in the town. He was so strong, she said, that the cry, 'Get Mr Casino!' would bring everyone in the neighbourhood running to see what feat of strength he would do this time. His skill as a furniture mover had been such a legend, she said, that people would stand on the sidewalk like it was a parade to watch Mr Casino lift armchairs over his head as if they were basketballs.

Then came the stroke that would have killed another man. Mr Casino had lived, but all that was left of his strength was the iron jaw which jutted out from his face. Mouse walked along beside Mr Casino, keeping his steps in rhythm. He said, 'Mr Casino, some boys are going to kill me.'

There was no reaction. Mr Casino's huge hand on Mouse's shoulder did not even tighten in sympathy. It made Mouse sad because he wanted a great reaction. He wanted Mr Casino's old strength to return, Samson-like. He wanted Mr Casino to roar with rage, to stretch out his long arms and threaten to pull down whole buildings if those boys were not brought before him.

Mouse said, 'Did you hear me? Some boys are going to –'

Suddenly he heard a shout behind him. He stopped walking, turned and saw Ezzie running toward him. Ezzie was waving his hands in the air, shouting, 'Hammerman! Hammerman!'

Mouse said, 'Wait a minute, Mr Casino,' in a voice so low it seemed to come from the bottom of a well. He said louder, 'Wait! Stop, Mr Casino.' Mr Casino walked a few more steps and then stopped. Mouse ran back toward

Ezzie, and then Ezzie grabbed his arm and swung them both around with his momentum.

'Hammerman's coming,' Ezzie gasped.

'What?'

Ezzie pointed behind him. 'Hammerman's coming,' he said. He panted for breath and tried to swallow air into his lungs. 'He's in front of the news-stand, he and the black sweat shirt. I saw them – they were coming this way – and I had to run all the way around to –' He gave up trying to speak, hung his head and gasped.

It seemed to Mouse that while Ezzie was having the most terrible trouble getting breath, he, Mouse, had stopped breathing altogether. Actually, the whole world seemed to have stopped. It had ground down like an enormous, overworked machine. 'In front of Hogan's news-stand?' he asked.

'Yeah.' Ezzie pointed, jabbing his finger in the air. 'Right *there*.'

Mouse said in a rush, 'Look, Ez, could you take Mr Casino home for me. Just walk with him – that's all you have to do – because if I run I can probably get home before Hammerman sees me.'

'I can't, Mouse, I got to get home myself.' Now Ezzie seemed to have stopped breathing too.

'Ezzie, listen –'

'My dad will kill me, Mouse, you know that.' Ezzie was not as afraid of his father as he pretended, but he *was* afraid of Mr Casino. He had once come upon Mr Casino unexpectedly on the landing outside Mouse's apartment. In that dark spot, Mr Casino had seemed with his huge body and sunken eyes a terrifying figure. Ezzie had gasped and stood there, flattened against the wall, too frightened to raise his voice above a squeak. Even when Mouse had come out and said, 'Oh, that's just Mr Casino,' Ezzie had still been frightened. 'Oh, yeah,' he had said, *just* Mr Casino,' and he had done a Frankenstein-like imitation of him to cover up his fear.

Now he said, 'I got to go. Hurry, and you'll get home, Mouse. You can make it.'

Mouse said, 'Wait a minute, Ezzie. Look, if you'll –'

Ezzie was already running, pointing to his imaginary watch. 'I got to go.'

'Ezzie –'

'I *got* to.'

Ezzie ran backward for a few steps, and then he turned and crossed the street. He waited for a car to pass, then ran faster. Mouse could see from the way Ezzie was running that he was not going to change his mind.

'Come on, Mr Casino,' he said quickly. He hesitated for a moment, torn between whether he should try to return to Margy's or get home. He put one arm around Mr Casino's huge waist and pushed him forward. 'Let's go home.' Slowly Mr Casino began his rocking steps.

Mouse glanced over his shoulder. The sidewalk was empty. 'Let's *go*, Mr Casino.' He turned and looked back again. 'Let's *go*.'

His head was pounding with fear. He could not even swallow. He expected his legs to fold up at any moment like the legs of an old card table.

The street was deserted now. That was another thing that frightened him. There was no one who could help him. He glanced back over his shoulder again. And then abruptly he felt that he could not bear the suspense any longer. He knew that Hammerman would be coming around the corner at any second – it was the instinct that comes to the hunted occasionally. He knew that Marv Hammerman was at this moment ready to round the corner of Fourth Street and catch sight of him and Mr Casino making their endless way home. Then he would be lost. Mr Casino, too.

He said, 'Come in here, Mr Casino. Quick!' Mouse went in the first door he came to and found himself in the dark entrance hall of an apartment. He put Mr Casino back against the wall where the mailboxes were. He said, 'Stand there.' Then he opened the door a crack and looked out.

The street was still empty. Mouse waited at the door with his hands in his jacket pockets. He said without looking around, 'We'll go in just a minute, Mr Casino. This won't take but a minute.' He opened the door again. There was no one in sight, and he opened the door wider. He stuck his head out this time, and at that moment Marv Hammerman and the boy in the black sweat shirt came around the corner.

Mouse drew back quickly against Mr Casino, clutching Mr Casino's coat. He felt Mr Casino's huge body stirring beneath the cloth and he took his hand. 'We'll go in a minute.' He wondered if Hammerman had seen him glance out the door. If so, all was lost.

Mouse reached around Mr Casino and tried the door that led to the apartments. As he had feared, it was locked. He and Mr Casino were trapped in this musty smelly entrance hall. A person could be beaten and left for dead in a hall like this, Mouse thought. No one would even come out of his apartment to see what all the yelling was about.

Mr Casino took a step toward the front door and Mouse

said, 'No, no, Mr Casino. Wait a minute.' He held Mr Casino's arm with both hands and drew him back against the mailboxes. Mr Casino remained beside him for a moment and then made a movement toward the door again.

'Just a minute, Mr Casino.' Mouse dared not lean forward and look out the door for fear Marv Hammerman would be glancing at the door at the same moment. 'We'll be all right, Mr Casino. Don't worry. We're just going to wait here a minute.'

Mr Casino's overcoat smelled of dry tobacco even though he had not smoked his pipe for years. It was a smell that Mouse associated with his own father. He lost the smell suddenly in the musty odour of the cold hall and he put his face against the overcoat.

Mr Casino started toward the door again. Mouse said, 'Not yet, Mr Casino, please.' He held his arm, trying to draw him back. This time Mr Casino was determined and there was no stopping him. 'Mr Casino, *please.*' Mouse tugged his arm. '*Please!*' He remembered Mrs Casino telling about a time during their courtship when ten men had tried to keep Mr Casino from entering a dance hall where she was doing the polka with another man, and Mr Casino had toppled all ten men as easily as if they had been bowling pins.

Mr Casino pushed open the door and started out. Mouse hesitated. He remained against the wall. He was sick. He thought that he shouldn't have eaten those beans for supper. Even four lima beans could be a terrible burden for a stomach under conditions like these.

He swallowed and waited a minute more in the dark hall. He pressed his face against the cold metal mailboxes to see if that would keep him from being sick. Then in a rush he tore himself away from the wall and went out the door after Mr Casino.

As he came through the door, he had a moment of dizziness. It was as if he had just stepped off one of those rides at the amusement park that Ezzie was so fond of and that made Mouse sick. 'You want to get your money's worth, don't you?' Ezzie would say. Mouse wished that Ezzie was there to stumble around with him, moaning with pleasure at his dizziness. 'Where am I, Mouse, where am I?'

The world was spinning so rapidly that for a minute Mouse couldn't see anything. Marv Hammerman could have been right in front of him, and Mouse wouldn't have been able to see him.

He held onto the banister, leaning on it, and then suddenly everything cleared. Mouse looked up the street and there was Garbage Dog coming toward him with an old Lorna Doone cookie box in his mouth. He looked the other way and there was Mr Casino making his way back to Margy's. In the distance were two strange boys walking along with a basketball, bouncing it back and forth between them.

Marv Hammerman was nowhere in sight. With an almost sickening sense of relief, Mouse knew that Hammerman had not seen him and had gone on across the street and up Fourth to where he lived.

'Wait a minute, that's the wrong way, Mr Casino,' he called quickly. 'Wait, Mr Casino.'

He ran after Mr Casino and caught up with him just as the two boys stopped bouncing the ball. The boys were looking curiously at Mr Casino in his long dark overcoat.

'This way,' Mouse said. He turned him around, and with the same slow rocking steps they started for home. 'We'll be all right now.'

4

MOUSE entered the apartment and went directly into the hall and sank down on his bed. In the living-room his mother was still going through her cosmetic orders. She called, 'Did you get Mr Casino home all right?'

He said, 'Yes.' He waited, but she did not say anything else. He turned over on his bed and looked at the wall. His heart was still beating so loudly he could hear it. It seemed to him that he had passed through the most dangerous moment of his life. He wanted to call out, 'I was just almost killed in case you are interested,' but he did not. He knew the loud strange way his voice sounded when he was frightened, and he knew that his mother would not be concerned, but only tired, a little disgusted. 'Don't start on that again,' she would say. She never seemed to take danger seriously.

He thought of taking out a pencil, writing on the wall ALIVE AND WELL BY A MIRACLE and drawing an arrow to his collapsed body, but he didn't have the strength to look for a pencil. He lay without moving.

He recalled the time he had had his tonsils out, how lightly his mother had treated that. She had said, 'Look, it's just your tonsils – those little things on the back of your throat. Don't make a big deal out of it.'

But it had been a big deal to him. He could still

remember the feeling of being in the hospital, of lying in a strange bed. The only reason he had been able to survive that night at all was because, at the last minute, his father had gone down to the car and brought up his flashlight. It was a big, heavy metal flashlight that his father kept in the car in case of an emergency on the road. His father had brought the flashlight out from under his jacket and quickly poked it under the covers. 'There, now you'll be all right.'

The flashlight *had* made Mouse feel better. The cold metal against his leg had calmed him. And when all the other children had gone to sleep and he alone had lain there awake, he had turned on the flashlight and shone it on the faces of the other children in the ward. He could remember right now the way their faces had looked in the pale circle of light. He thought that if he saw one of those children on the street right now today, he would recognize him and go up and say, 'Hey, weren't you in the hospital one time?'

Marv Hammerman came back into his mind and Mouse shifted onto his other side. He tried to think of something else.

Emergency Nine – Approach of Mad Elephants. When a herd of mad elephants is stampeding in your direction, quickly climb the nearest tall tree and wait. According to Ezzie there was nothing as pleasant as lying coolly on the limb of a huge tree while a herd of mad elephants passed beneath you like a noisy, dusty river.

'Do you have any homework?' his mother called from the living-room.

'No.'

'Well, there's a horror movie on channel fifty-three.'

'I might be in in a minute,' he said. He unzipped his jacket and stared up at the ceiling.

Emergency Ten – If attacked by a vampire, make the sign of the cross.

Emergency Eleven – If attacked by a werewolf, draw a six-pointed star and get in it.

The phone rang, and his mother answered it. She came into the hall where he was lying on the day bed. There had been a lot of talk at one time of moving into a larger apartment where he could have a bedroom of his own, but Mouse thought he would feel funny in a bedroom now. The hall with the day bed and the bookcase at the end for his things suited him just fine.

'Your dad wants to talk to you.'

Mouse got up quickly because his father's understanding about the flashlight was still in his mind. Mouse's father had been driving a truck for the last two years, and Mouse hardly ever got to see him. He ran to the phone. 'Hello.' He looked down at the table. On the cover of the telephone book he had written ALL THE NUMBERS IN HERE ARE TO BE DIALLED ON THIS, and then had drawn an arrow to the telephone. 'Hello,' he said again, louder.

'Benjie?'

'Yes, this is me.'

'Well, how are you, son?'

'Fine.' He paused and added with a loud laugh, 'For *now* anyway.' It was his scared voice, but his father did not recognize it over the telephone. Mouse waited for his father to say sympathetically, 'Oh, is there something wrong?'

Suddenly he wanted this more than anything. He began

to twist his finger into the telephone cord. He wanted his father to beg. '*Tell* me, Benjie,' he wanted his father to say. 'Whatever the trouble is, I want to know. I demand to know. *Tell* me.'

'Oh, all right,' he would then answer as casually as possible. 'Three boys are going to kill me – Marv Hammerman, Tony Lionni, and a boy in a black sweat shirt.'

His father said, 'I'm in Kentucky and, boy, is it raining. How is it there?'

'Well, the *weather's* all right.'

'Fine, listen, I was just thinking maybe we might do something next weekend. It looks like I'm going to be in town after all.'

Mouse hesitated, holding the phone against his cheek. His mother was not looking at her orders now, but was sitting up straight listening to his conversation. She said, 'Speak up, Benjie, talk to your father. This is long distance.'

'I know, Mom.'

'Well, how about it, Benjie? You want to do something next weekend?'

'Sure,' Mouse said, 'that would be fine.' Then he laughed again and said, 'If I'm still *able* to do something.'

'Don't start on that, Benjie,' his mother said in a low voice.

'How does the baseball game sound?' his father said.

'What?'

'The baseball game.'

'Fine, that sounds fine,' Mouse said, looking at his mother.

'Sound excited,' his mother suggested from the sofa.

41

'He's making a special effort to do this.'

'Yeah, that sounds *very* fine,' he said. He gave up on his father. One by one, the people who could help him were falling away, leaving him to face his trouble alone. It was like one of those western movies.

'And now let me speak to your mom for a minute,' his father was saying.

'Sure.' He held out the phone. 'He wants to speak to you.' His mother came over quickly, and Mouse went back and lay on the day bed. He heard his mother saying in a low voice, 'No, no, there's nothing wrong with him. No, nothing.' There was a pause. Her voice got lower. 'He's just got the idea that some boys are after him, that's all. It's nothing.'

He waited, thinking he might be called back to the telephone. Then he heard his mother say, 'No, we can have supper here. You have to eat out too much. No!' She laughed. 'Besides I've got a new recipe I want to try – a lady served it at one of my parties.' There was a silence. Then she laughed and said, 'Napoleon's hot dogs.'

Mouse turned over. The covers were twisting beneath him like a rope. He looked at the wall and he remembered another dangerous thing that had happened to him, a second crisis survived, like the tonsils.

In September he had got the idea that he would like to climb up the cliff behind the new shopping centre at Hunter's Square. There was a large rock on top with a button-like rock in the centre, and Mouse wanted to climb up, write PRESS FOR SERVICE and draw an arrow to the button. The idea, once it had entered his mind, would not leave; and finally he had persuaded Ezzie to go over to the shopping centre with him.

42

Ezzie had not been enthusiastic. As Mouse was purchasing a can of spray paint in the dime store, Ezzie had stood there saying, 'What do you want to do this for, Mouse? That's forty-nine good cents you're wasting!' Ezzie never had any money. His father pretended to be deaf when the word allowance was mentioned.

'It's not a waste.'

'We could buy pretzels with that money. You get three pretzels for thirty-nine cents which would leave a dime for –'

'Ez, I'm going to do it.'

There was a deep sigh from Ezzie at this persistence. He followed Mouse out of the store and spoke only when they were facing the solid wall of the cliff. 'Where is it you're going to write this, Mouse?' he asked scornfully. He already knew because Mouse had told him a dozen times.

'There.'

They looked up together. Mouse was squinting into the sun, but Ezzie's face had a flat look. He said, 'Why can't you just write your name over there under the peace sign like any normal person. That's what I'd do.'

'No.'

'Sometimes you're stupid, Mouse.' Ezzie sat down on the ground. 'Well, go on, get it over with.'

Mouse hated Ezzie to be disgusted with him. He was the only good friend Mouse had ever had. He looked at Ezzie who was staring at his feet.

'All right, Ezzie, I'm going to start now if you want to watch.'

'I've seen disasters before,' Ezzie said in a bored voice.

'Here I go anyway.' Climbing up the cliff was easy at first. A lot of boys had climbed and left footholds, but

43

Mouse went slowly anyway. The can of spray paint was tucked in his belt pressing against his stomach.

The higher he climbed, the harder it got. By the time he reached the halfway mark he was winded, and his arms and legs had started to ache. Every minute began to seem like ten.

'I'm still going,' he called to Ezzie, but Ezzie did not answer. Mouse wanted to look down, but he had had to stop doing that a long time ago because of dizziness. 'I'm still going, Ez.'

He had to find little ways to climb now because there did not seem to be any footholds at all. He used roots and crevices and toeholds, and finally he was there. Gasping from exertion and nervousness he panted out, 'I made it, Ez.' Ezzie did not answer.

Holding onto a root with one hand, Mouse took out the spray can. He shook it and began to write. P. 'How does that look, Ez? Can you read it?' He made an R and an E. He leaned to the side to continue with the two S's and suddenly his foot slipped. It was a terrible sickening sensation.

One minute he was painting an S, the next he was hanging by a root with one knee balanced on a sharp rock. His whole life, it seemed, depended on whether this root was going to hold or not.

'Hey, watch it!' Ezzie called.

Mouse couldn't speak. His leg was digging against the cliff, running as if it were in a race by itself. For a moment, Mouse thought it was all over. His leg started going slower. The root began to pull out of the earth. And then miraculously his other hand found a little ledge and his foot found a rock. The root held; his other foot found a toehold.

Ezzie called, 'Hey, don't do that, will you? It makes me nervous.'

Mouse inched his way back to the ledge. '*You!*' he managed to gasp.

'Yeah, me.'

Mouse clung for a moment. He was so weak he thought he might slip down the cliff like a blob of grease.

Ezzie said, 'You dropped your spray can, did you know it?'

'No.'

'It's busted.'

'Oh.'

'The whole nozzle's gone.' Ezzie shook the can. 'It's full of paint but the nozzle's gone. I told you we should have got pretzels.'

'Well, I might as well come down then.'

Lying on his bed now, Mouse thought that that particular emergency, falling off a cliff, had been avoided by one of those simple survival tricks. Brushes with nature were simple. Emergency Twelve – When you are falling off a cliff, grab a root with one hand, a ledge with another, put your foot on a small rock and then coolly climb down.

His mother came to the doorway and said, 'What are you and your dad going to do next weekend?'

'We're going to the baseball game.'

'Well, that will be nice, won't it?'

'Yes.'

'Your father's making a special effort to get home.'

'I wish he could be home all the time,' Mouse said.

'Well, I do too.' She stood there a minute, looking at him. 'Your father doesn't like this either. It's no fun for him to be driving all the time. Anyway, it won't be forever.' She waited a minute and then said, 'Well, better put on your pyjamas and get to bed.'

He got up quickly as if he had just been lying there waiting for someone to tell him what to do. He went into the bathroom, took his pyjamas from a hook behind the door and got ready for bed.

He lay there for a while. In the living-room, his mother had put out the lights and was watching television. He could see the light flickering as the picture changed. He tried to think of another emergency he could handle.

Emergency Thirteen – Octopus Attack. This was one emergency measure everyone agreed upon – John Wayne, Tarzan, Jungle Jim, everybody. It had worked in every South Sea movie Mouse had ever seen. When attacked by an octopus, you stab the octopus in the eye with the knife you have tucked into the waistband of your bathing suit.

He lay without moving. In the living-room, his mother switched channels.

Emergency Fourteen – Parachute Jump. If you are called upon to make an unexpected parachute jump from a plane, you must relax your body completely. Ezzie had learned this from a talk show on television. The natural thing, Ezzie had learned, is for the parachute jumper to start making climbing movements with his arms and legs, trying unconsciously to get back up to the safety of the plane. Ezzie said everybody does this, but what *he* would do would be hold his body in a relaxed position, count to ten, and pull the rip-cord.

While Mouse was waiting to think of Emergency Fifteen, he fell asleep.

5

MOUSE came slowly down the stairs in the morning. There was a small round hole in the plaster by the front door, and Mouse had once drawn an arrow to the hole and had written DROP COINS HERE BEFORE EXITING. He went out the door, looking down at his feet, taking the steps one at a time. He was trying to be late for school now that his efforts not to go at all had failed.

'Mom, I'm sick, hear? I'm really sick,' he had said at breakfast. He had been sick too. 'I can't even eat, I'm so sick.'

'All right, if you're sick, show me some fever,' his mother had said, getting up from the table and going into the bathroom for the thermometer. 'If you don't have fever, you aren't sick enough to stay home.'

He had sat at the table while she went for the thermometer, thinking of how much he missed his father. Breakfast had been a different meal before his father started driving a truck.

Mouse remembered suddenly the way his father used to tell his dreams at breakfast, fantastic dreams that would have Mouse hanging over his plate, too engrossed to eat.

'Did you dream about the little people last night?' would be the first thing he would say to his father in the mornings. The dreams about the little people had been Mouse's all-time favourites. They all ended with the little people, a hundred and eighteen of them, lifting his father and bearing him down the street with such speed that his father appeared to be on roller skates. His father got out of a lot of tight places that way, and the puzzlement of his father's dream enemies as he slipped past them in this manner never failed to delight Mouse.

Now that Mouse was older and had dreams of his own to remember, he thought that the dreams of the little people were just stories his father had made up to amuse him. Still, he wouldn't mind right now, as big as he was, hearing another of those little people dreams.

His mother returned with the thermometer and he said, 'There are lots of illnesses that you don't have fever with, Mom. Didn't you ever hear of food poisoning?'

'Put this in your mouth.'

He had known it was hopeless, but he had kept the thermometer in his mouth, rubbing it with his tongue just in case the friction might somehow cause the mercury to rise.

His mother waited by the table. Then she removed the thermometer and looked at it. 'Normal. Get your books and go to school.'

'Mom, I am *sick*.'

'Go.'

Slowly Mouse left the apartment and walked in the direction of the school. He knew that he would have to be very late in order to miss Marv Hammerman, because Hammerman never went into the school until the last possible minute. He just lounged outside with his friends.

The street was empty except for two ladies talking, and Garbage Dog who was standing by the ladies looking up at them. There was the faint aroma of bacon grease about one of the ladies. 'Go on,' one of the ladies said, kicking at him.

Garbage Dog moved back a few steps and continued to stand watching them. On his short legs he appeared to be lying down. Mouse remembered that he had once measured Garbage Dog's legs as part of an arithmetic assignment about learning to use the ruler. Each student had had to measure ten things, and the first thing Mouse had measured was Garbage Dog's legs. They were not quite three inches long.

It had been an impressive way to start out the list of things he had measured. Garbage Dog's legs – two and seven-eighths inches.

At least half the people in the class had not believed that figure. 'Hey, no dog's got legs that short,' one boy had cried.

'This one does.'

'Two and seven-eighths inches?'

'Yes, two and seven-eighths inches.'

'That's just *that* long.'

'I know. Listen, I can bring this dog to class if you want me to, Miss Regent. I can catch him and we can –'

'No, Benjie,' Miss Regent had said quickly, 'I don't think that will be necessary. Some dogs do have very short legs.'

'But two and seven-eighths inches!' the boy had cried again, holding up his paper ruler. 'That's just *that* long.'

Mouse knelt and scratched Garbage Dog behind the ears. He must have hit the spot where it really itched, because Garbage Dog leaned back, his nose pointing to the sky, and started making a moaning noise.

'That feel good?' It was surprising, Mouse thought, that a dog like this who had never known soap or flea powder could smell so nice and fresh. It was a kind of dairy and dry leaves smell. 'There? Is that where it itches?'

The quiet of the street made Mouse think he was late enough. 'I better go.' Still kneeling, he took out his pencil, wrote SCRATCH ME on a smooth spot on the sidewalk and drew a little arrow to Garbage Dog. Then he rose.

As he walked, Hammerman came back into his mind. It seemed to Mouse that everything, everybody, had suddenly shrunk in importance, making Marv Hammerman a giant. Hammerman towered over the street in Mouse's mind so that the buildings were toys around his ankles, and the pigeons that roosted on the roofs flew around Hammerman's knees.

Mouse walked slower and when he got to the school, it was deserted. The late bell was ringing. Mouse took the steps two at a time and then ran down the hall to his room.

'You're late, Benjie,' Mr Stein said, looking up at Mouse from his desk.

'Yes, sir, my mom thought I was sick.'

He sat at his desk, pulled off his knitted hat and stuffed it in his pocket. He was taking off his jacket when Dick Fellini nudged him in the back. He turned and Dick said, 'Ezzie wants you.'

Mouse glanced at Ezzie, and Ezzie's mouth formed the words, 'Did you see Hammerman last night?' Mouse nodded. 'What happened?' Ezzie asked.

Mr Stein said, 'Ezzie have you got something to share with the class?'

'No, sir.'

'Then why are you talking?'

'I don't know.'

'You don't *know*?'

'No.'

'Then if you don't know, I suggest that you stop,' Mr

Stein said.

'Sure.' Ezzie waited until Mr Stein was busy with some papers, and then he punched the boy in front of him and whispered, 'Tell Mouse that Hammerman was looking for him this morning. Pass it on.'

Four seats up, Mouse could hear what Ezzie had said perfectly. Then he had to listen to it being passed down the row of seats. To Frankie. To Louise. To Dick Fellini. He waited, and Dick said in his ear, 'Ezzie says Hammerman was looking for you this morning.'

Mouse nodded. He wished suddenly that he could be part of this chain of whisperers. He wished he could nudge the boy in front of him and say, 'Hammerman's looking for Mouse. Pass it on.' What it came down to, he supposed, was that he wished he wasn't Mouse.

'What did you do to Hammerman anyway?' Dick Fellini asked in his ear.

Mouse lifted his shoulders and let them fall. He felt terrible. He wondered how anybody could feel this sick and not have fever. It didn't seem possible.

Mr Stein was saying, 'Let's see now. I had some announcements. Did anybody see a pink mimeographed sheet?'

'Is that it on the floor, Mr Stein?'

'Yes, thank you, Rose. Now let's see what confusion the office has arranged for us today.' He glanced up and said, 'Yes, Benjie, what is it?'

Mouse cleared his throat and said, 'Could I go get a drink of water?' He paused and then added, 'I don't feel very good.'

Mr Stein looked at Mouse. Mr Stein didn't rely on thermometers. Over the years he had developed an eye for

51

the faker. He looked, judged and said, 'I guess so, Benjie.' Mouse got up quickly and started for the door. Then Mr Stein added, 'Only I wish you kids wouldn't come to school when you're sick.'

'I didn't have any fever.'

'Most people don't early in the morning.'

'Oh.' Mouse wished he had had this piece of information earlier.

'You come to school, infect everyone and go home. *Then* you get the fever. And where does that leave the rest of us?' Mr Stein had gotten mumps two winters ago from a boy named Beanie Johnson, and Mr Stein had been cautious ever since.

Wanting to reassure Mr Stein that this was not a similar case, Mouse said in a low voice, 'I think this is more like food poisoning, Mr Stein.'

'Well, let's hope so. Go on and get some water and see if that helps.'

Mouse went out into the hall. As he closed the door he heard Ezzie say, 'Could I go get a drink of water too, Mr Stein?'

Mr Stein looked him over. 'No.'

Mouse walked on down the hall. When Ezzie was smaller, Mouse remembered that he used to keep a tooth in his pocket for emergencies like this. Then he could always go for a drink. He would hold up the tooth and say, 'My tooth came out. Can I go get a drink, Miss Regent?' It used to work all the time. It was the only good he ever got out of his lost teeth, because Ezzie's parents had never heard of the tooth fairy. They claimed it was something Ezzie had invented to get money out of them.

Ezzie had even made Mouse go home with him once.

Mouse had stood there in the kitchen in front of Ezzie's mother, while Ezzie, pink-faced and earnest, had said, 'Go on, Mouse, tell her. Is there a tooth fairy or not? All I'm asking for is the truth.'

Mouse had waited a moment for Ezzie's mother to look at him, but she continued to baste something in the oven.

'Mrs Weimer?' She had glanced up at him then, her face red and shiny with heat. 'Mrs Weimer,' he had said, 'there *is* a tooth fairy.'

'A what?'

Ezzie had shoved him aside. 'A tooth fairy, Mom.'

Mouse had stepped around Ezzie. 'What the tooth fairy does, Mrs Weimer, is leave money under people's pillows when they lose a tooth.'

Mrs Weimer finished basting the meat and put it back in the oven.

'Mrs Weimer,' Mouse had continued, even though the smell of failure was mingled with the odour of meat, 'Mrs Weimer, *you* are the tooth fairy, you and Mr Weimer.'

'Did you hear that, Mom?' Ezzie had said. 'Did you hear who the tooth fairy really is?'

'I don't think it's going to work,' Mouse had said under his breath.

'It's *got* to.' If it didn't, Ezzie was not going to be able to go to dawn-to-dusk science-fiction day at the Rialto on Saturday. 'It's *got* to.'

But it hadn't. The next morning when Ezzie looked under his pillow, there was no money. There was only his tooth still wrapped in a little piece of toilet paper.

Mouse walked down to the water fountain and took a few swallows of water. It was warm and tasted of iodine. Ezzie had once said he thought that the teachers were putting a chemical into the water to make them all behave.

Mouse stood at the water fountain. Overhead the hall clock counted out a minute. The school clock didn't just click like other clocks, it jerked out the minutes. There had never been enough noise in the hall, not even between classes, to drown out the sound of the clock. Mouse waited for another minute to be sounded, and then he turned and went back to his room.

'Do you feel any better, Benjie?' Mr Stein asked.

'Yes, I'm fine now.' He took out his pencil, drew an arrow to himself and wrote FINE on the pale wood of his desk. Then he rubbed it away with his thumb and waited for Mr Stein to tell them to take out their English books.

He was still sitting there fifteen minutes later, staring at his desk, when he realized with a start that everyone else had their English books out and open to the story about King Arthur. Mouse looked around in astonishment. Dick Fellini was trying to explain a knight's honour. At the back of the room, Ezzie was swinging his hand in the air like an upside-down pendulum so that he could get Mr Stein's attention and tell the class the plot of a movie about knights he had seen recently on television. Ezzie got tired of waiting to be called on. 'Mr Stein! Mr Stein!'

Mr Stein ignored him. He said to Dick Fellini, 'Do you think, Dick, that honour and truth and the things the knights stood for have changed, or do you think they still hold true today?'

'Let me think,' Dick said.

Ezzie could wait no longer to join in the discussion. Still waving his hand in the air he made a generous offer. 'Ask me anything you want to about honour, Mr Stein, and I'll tell you.'

6

It was right after history class when Mouse saw Hammerman for the first time that day. All morning he had been running from one class to another, pushing people aside in his haste, bumping into others, darting around the edge of the hall. The only thought in his mind was getting to the safety of his next class.

'Watch it, Mouse!'

'Look out, Mouse!'

'Quit pushing, Mouse!'

It occurred to him as he ran that there could be no question of how he got his nickname this day. He *was* a mouse. He wished his mother was there to see him because she was always asking, 'Why do they call you Mouse?'

'Because I act like one, I guess,' he had answered, but this hadn't satisfied her.

'Well, tell them to stop.'

'Mom, you don't *tell* people what to call you.'

'A nickname like that can stick with you.'

'I don't care.'

'Well, you will. If you get to be president of a college or a company some day, people will still be calling you Mouse.'

'I don't think you have to worry. I'm not planning to be president of anything.' But the idea had stuck with him. 'I, Mouse Fawley, do hereby swear that as president of this great company...' It did sound bad. 'And now we take great pride in presenting the distinguished and honourable president of our university – Mouse Fawley!' Very bad.

By lunch time Mouse began to think he was going to make it through the day without seeing Hammerman at all. Then after history he came out of class on the run. He was the first person out of the room and he started quickly down the hall. He had been out of his seat so fast that the hall was deserted. Even the library had not started to empty yet. Feeling safe, Mouse had glanced down at his books, which were slipping, and when he looked up he saw Marv Hammerman standing by the door to the boys' rest room. It was as sudden as a feat of magic.

Mouse spun around abruptly. His math class was just down the hall, but he would have to pass Hammerman to get to it. He decided instead on a safer route. He would run down the stairs, cross the first-floor hall and then run up the other stairs to math. He no longer cared how it looked to run like this. He only wanted to avoid a meeting with Hammerman at all cost.

By the time he was coming up the other stairs, the crowd in the hall and on the steps was beginning to thin. Mouse was running. He was dodging the remaining people as if he was playing a strange game. He was almost to the landing when he looked up and saw that Hammerman was waiting at the top of the stairs. While Mouse had been making this long, frenzied run, Hammerman had coolly walked down the hall and waited, catlike, for him.

Mouse stopped. All day he had been hearing the phrase, 'Hammerman's after Mouse,' and now the people on the steps began to walk more slowly, casting glances at them. Mouse knew that the whole school was waiting for the slaughter.

He couldn't run now and so he came up the stairs slowly, pulling himself along with the aid of the banister. He was aware that he was not safe even in the hall. He remembered hearing that one time Hammerman had hit someone in front of the auditorium, and a teacher was standing right there and didn't see it. The boy had been knocked off his feet, Mouse remembered hearing, a huge knot parting his hair, and the teacher had thought the boy had fainted from lack of air.

That's how slick Hammerman was, Mouse thought. It would not have surprised him if Hammerman had leaned over and with the most casual of blows sent Mouse reeling backward down the stairs. Hammerman would be able to do this so skilfully that the few stragglers who saw it would swear that Mouse had tripped. But then, in fear, they would probably do that anyway.

The late bell rang, and Mouse slowly kept coming up the stairs. When he got to the top, all the stragglers were gone except a boy on the landing below who was pretending to straighten his books. Mouse felt that there was nobody in the world but him and Hammerman. He said, 'I'm late for math,' and kept looking at his shoes.

Then he glanced up, squinting at Hammerman, and Hammerman moved his face as if he had chewing gum or a Life Saver in his mouth.

Mouse said, 'Did you say something?'

Hammerman shook his head, and with the sun coming in the window behind him, his hair seemed to fan out like feathers. His face didn't change expression but his eyes were very bright. Mouse thought that this was because he was doing the one thing he was really good at.

Hammerman's nostrils widened a little, and Mouse wondered if Hammerman could smell fear the way animals could. He had read somewhere that animals become disgusted by the smell of fear and this causes them to attack. Mouse was sure the whole stairway reeked with his fear now. He felt as if he was going to choke on it himself. Emergency Fifteen – When you are afraid, don't let your body know it.

'I really didn't hear what you said, if you said anything,' Mouse said, stuttering a little.

'I'll see you after school.' Hammerman took his finger and touched Mouse on the chest and then passed him and started down the stairs.

'What?' Mouse asked.

Hammerman let the air come out of his nostrils in a sigh of disgust. Still, Mouse knew, a little thing like not having a worthy opponent wasn't going to cause Marv Hammerman to give up the fight.

Without turning around Hammerman said, 'After school.'

Mouse said, 'Oh, sure.'

Hammerman went down the steps so smoothly he might have been sliding. Mouse went to his math class and sat down. He could still feel the place on his chest where Hammerman had touched him. He thought that if he opened his shirt he would be able to see a red dot there, marking the spot.

Across the room Ezzie was waving his arms to get Mouse's attention. Mouse looked and watched Ezzie's mouth form the question, 'Did anything happen with Hammerman?' Mouse nodded. 'What?'

Mouse said, 'I'll tell you later,' beneath his breath. He

started turning through his notebook as if he were searching for an important paper.

A moment passed, and the boy next to Mouse touched his arm. 'Ezzie wants you.'

Mouse nodded but continued looking through his papers. The boy nudged him again and jerked his thumb toward the far side of the room. 'Ezzie.' With a sigh Mouse stopped looking in his notebook for the imaginary paper. He looked at Ezzie.

'What happened?' Ezzie asked again, pouncing on each word. 'What happened with Hammerman?'

The teacher opened her book, looked up at the class and said, 'Ezzie, could I have your attention please?'

Ezzie was beyond hearing the teacher. He leaned over the aisle. '*What happened?*'

'Ezzie!' the teacher said. Now he heard and looked up, startled. 'Take your book and go to the board, will you?'

Ezzie stood up quickly, found his book and walked slowly up the aisle, holding the book in one hand. As he passed the teacher's desk he said, 'I didn't have time to study much last night because my sister was sick. She made me put out the light.'

'Put the first problem on the board, please.'

Ezzie picked up the chalk and looked carefully at his book. Mouse also opened his book and tried to concentrate. It was amazing how difficult it was to get your mind *off* something, he thought.

Ezzie put the chalk to his lips. He appeared to be ready to drink a vial of white liquid, perhaps the 'smart' medicine he was always hoping some scientist would discover – one sip and instant smartness. He said regretfully, 'This was the one problem I didn't get, Mrs Romanoski, I remember now. I got all the others, but this one stumped me.'

'It's exactly like problem two.'

'It is?' His face was blanked by surprise.

'So if you got problem two, then you should be able to do problem one.'

'Yeah, I guess so.'

Mouse tried again to concentrate, but he couldn't. The thought of Marv Hammerman filled his mind completely. He thought that if doctors were running an experiment on his brain, pouring ideas in, the ideas would just flow right out because there was no room left.

Slowly, glancing frequently at the book, Ezzie began to put his problem on the board. Mrs Romanoski waited a minute and then said, 'Ezzie, this is *not* an addition problem.'

'It isn't?'

'No.'

'Are you kidding me, Mrs Romanoski?'

'It is *not* addition.'

'Oh.' Quickly Ezzie erased the plus sign with his fingers, leaving a clear round spot on the dusty blackboard. 'Wait a minute.' He hesitated. 'Are we looking at the same problem?'

'Problem one.'

'Yeah,' he said, shaking his head from side to side. 'Problem one.' He paused and then said in an enlightened voice, 'What *page*, Mrs Romanoski?'

'Page forty.'

'Yeah.' His voice sagged. 'Problem one, page forty.' He took another sip of chalk. 'Wait a minute, let me read this thing again.'

Mouse let his head drop down on his book and felt the

cool page against his face. His temperature, he thought now, was beyond being registered, rapidly approaching the point where the body shrivelled like a raisin.

'Benjie, are you all right?' Mrs Romanoski asked. He lifted his head and looked at her. 'You don't look well to me.'

'I don't feel good either,' he said.

'Then perhaps you should go to the office.'

He hesitated. 'All right.'

'I'll go with him,' Ezzie offered quickly.

'No, Ezzie, you continue with your problem.'

'But –'

'Ezzie.'

There was a silence as Mouse got up, gathered his books and walked to the door. As he went out into the hall he heard the teacher say, 'All right, Ezzie, it's a multiplication problem.'

'*Multiplication?*'

'Yes.'

'Well, that's what I thought.'

Quickly Mouse started down the deserted stairs to the office.

7

MOUSE was lying on the sofa watching a cartoon. It was the kind of old cartoon that he particularly disliked – the ones in which boxes of soap powder and tubes of toothpaste dance on little legs, but he kept watching. It was four o'clock in the afternoon, and school had been over for thirty minutes. Mouse had been lying on the sofa since then imagining Marv Hammerman standing outside the school waiting for him. He knew exactly how Hammerman would look – relaxed, watchful, his hair flowing, his hands hooked in his back jeans pockets, his eyes bright, his face expressionless. Mouse had not been able to get that picture out of his mind.

He watched some matches singing, 'I Don't Want to Set the World on Fire' in high voices, and then there was a knock at the door. Mouse got up so quickly that he knocked a glass off onto the floor. He walked silently into the middle of the room to see if the door was locked. It wasn't.

The knock came again. Mouse waited, wondering if he should try to climb out on the fire escape and hide. He imagined the door bursting open and Hammerman standing there, filling the doorway.

There was another knock. 'Hey, Mouse, you in there?' It was Ezzie, and Mouse called quickly, 'Yeah, come on in.' He went back and picked up the glass and the two ice cubes that had spilled onto the rug.

'How are you feeling?' Ezzie asked.

'Oh, all right.'

'Hammerman was looking for you after school.'

Mouse moistened his lips. 'He told me to meet him, but I was sick. They made me go home.'

'The boy in the black sweat shirt – you know which one he is?'

'Yes.'

'Well, he and Hammerman came over to me after school.'

'What did they say?'

'Hammerman just said, "Where's your buddy?"'

'Tell me every word, Ez, don't leave out a thing.'

'That *was* every word. "Where's your buddy?"'

'So what did you say? Did you tell him I had to go home sick?'

'Yeah.'

'And what did he say to that?' Mouse had the briefest hope that his having to go home sick might cause some sympathy from Hammerman.

'He didn't say anything, but the boy in the black sweat shirt said, "Yeah, *scared* sick," and sort of smiled like this.'

'What else?'

'That was the whole conversation, Mouse. First *he* said, "Where's your buddy?" Then *I* said, "He had to go home. He was sick." Then the boy in the black sweat shirt – I found out his name is Peachie – said –'

'Never mind. I remember it,' Mouse said quickly.

'Well, you were the one who wanted to hear it.'

'Once. I wanted to hear it *once*.' He sat down on the sofa. On the television screen a bottle of cough syrup was dancing with a bottle of cold tablets, and every time the bottle of cold tablets did a fancy step, the stopper would come off and the tablets would bounce up into the air and then back into the bottle. Mouse said, 'Turn that thing off, will you?'

Ezzie paused in front of the television to imitate the bottle of cold tablets. 'Hey, look at this, Mouse!'

Mouse glanced at him and then back at the table. 'I said to turn that thing off.' Reluctantly Ezzie stopped dancing, turned off the television and Mouse said in a low voice, 'My problem is that I have a *thing* about being hit, I don't know why it is, Ezzie. I just hate to be hit – or hurt in any way really, especially when I know it's coming. I just *hate* to be hurt. It's one of my personal peculiarities, Ez, and somehow I think that makes people *want* to hit me. It's strange.'

'Listen, nobody wants to get clobbered.'

'Not as bad as me.'

'Sure, it's the same with everybody.'

'I just wish you'd been in the hall with me that first day, Ezzie, and seen the look in Hammerman's eyes –' He broke off. He didn't know why he had said that. It was the moment he wanted most to forget. He added quickly, '*Then* you wouldn't be so –'

'Come on and let's play basketball,' Ezzie interrupted.

'I just don't feel like it.' Mouse wanted to get the conversation around to how unfortunate and unfair his plight was.

'Come *on*, will you? You can't ruin your whole life just because of Hammerman. Besides, if he shows up, you can just go in the grocery store and pretend to be buying something.' He paused, then added with a little smile, 'Band-Aids.'

Mouse got slowly to his feet. 'I don't feel like doing anything.' If he had had a pencil handy he would have drawn an arrow to himself and written the words FRAGILE – DO NOT BEND, FOLD OR MUTILATE.

'Come *on*.'

'Oh, all right.' Reluctantly Mouse followed Ezzie out the door, and they went down the stairs together. Once outside Ezzie ran ahead eagerly and turned into the alley by the bakery. 'Come on, will you?' He ran to the paved area behind the store where the basketball hoop had been put up on the back of the grocery.

Ezzie ran over to where Dick Fellini was idly dribbling the ball and shouted, 'Hey, Fellini!' He begged for the ball with his hands, weaving agilely about the pavement, eluding imaginary guards.

'Fellini!' he cried again. He was open now and could make the perfect lay-up shot.

Ezzie had every move of the basketball player down perfectly. He could execute those high jump shots. He could fake, pivot, and go up for a hook shot. He could make the best-looking free throws of anybody. He could dribble so close to the ground the ball seemed to be rolling. The only thing he couldn't do was get the ball in the basket.

He ran up to the net. 'Hey, Fellini, the ball, gimme the ball!'

Fellini fed him the ball, and Ezzie went up in a graceful arc, threw the ball with one hand and watched it bounce off the rim of the basket. Fellini got the ball from the doorway of the grocery store where it had rolled and began dribbling again.

'Hey, Fellini, the ball!' Ezzie spun around now, leaped into the air and caught the ball. Then in a spectacular move he managed to get the ball off before his feet touched the ground. The ball was about a foot short of the basket, and it bounced to where Mouse was standing. Mouse ignored it and let it roll.

Then Mouse walked over and sat down by the grocery. Garbage Dog was there in the doorway, and when he saw Mouse he came over.

'How you doing, boy?' Mouse rubbed Garbage Dog behind the ears. 'How are you today?' Mouse really liked this dog. He had never realized how much he liked him until this moment. He thought that Garbage Dog was the kind of animal that never actually changed in any way, just revealed new aspects of his personality from time to time. Like the event of last summer. Mouse thought about that as he continued to scratch Garbage Dog behind the ears.

Mouse and Ezzie had been patting Garbage Dog that day – this had been in August – and while they were just sitting there, patting him, Ezzie had noticed that the dog's mouth was slightly open. He had said, 'Hey, Mouse, what's old G. D. got in his mouth?'

Mouse had bent over and looked. Garbage Dog had long hair that hung over his mouth a little. 'I can't see.'

Ezzie had reached out and lifted the dog's lip by this long hair. 'What is it? Can you see now?'

'No.'

'Well, let's get his mouth open. This is driving me crazy.'

They had struggled to open Garbage Dog's mouth, while the dog sat looking beyond them at the back of the dry cleaners.

'Help me, Mouse, you think I can do this all by myself?'

'I'm helping. He doesn't want to open his mouth though. That's obvious. You can't just force –'

'Yes, you can. There's a spot that you press – it's back behind the jaw somewhere – and this spot makes the dog's mouth spring open. I've seen a lady in my apartment give her dog worm pills this way. Wait a minute. This might be it.' Ezzie pressed on both sides of Garbage Dog's face, and abruptly his mouth opened. A small green turtle fell out onto the pavement.

Mouse and Ezzie had looked at it for a moment without speaking. Then Ezzie said in a wondering voice, 'Am I going crazy, or is that a turtle?'

'It's a turtle.'

'But how could that be? Where would you get a turtle around here?'

'Out of somebody's turtle bowl maybe.'

'Let me see that.' Ezzie had picked up the turtle and looked at it, turning it over in his hand. 'This is a real living turtle.'

'I know.'

'But how could it be? How could such a thing as this be?'

'I don't know.'

'It's like "Twilight Zone," Mouse. Do you understand what has happened? Garbage Dog has come strolling up with a living breathing turtle in his mouth.'

They had sat there with Garbage Dog between them for a long time that afternoon talking about the turtle, about the strangeness of it. Ezzie kept saying over and over, 'It's a living breathing turtle. This turtle is living and breathing!' And Mouse kept saying, 'I know.' Finally they had argued a little about which one of them owned the turtle, and then they had agreed that it belonged to Ezzie because he had noticed it first.

Later that evening Ezzie had sold the turtle to a girl in his apartment building for a quarter. For weeks after that Ezzie never passed Garbage Dog without checking his mouth, the way other people check the coin return slots in telephone booths.

Now Ezzie was guarding Dick Fellini, waving his hands in Fellini's face, trying to knock the ball from his hands. Suddenly Ezzie was successful. He had the ball, bounced it once, whirled out and away from the basket and lifted his arm in a beautiful shot that missed.

Fellini caught the rebound and shot. Then with a forward dart, Ezzie scooped up the ball and dribbled over to Mouse. 'Hey, Mou-sie Boy.' Ezzie threw the ball to Mouse, and Mouse tossed it back without enthusiasm. 'Come on,' Ezzie urged.

'In a minute,' Mouse said. He did not feel like any physical activity. All his strength had to be saved. If he wasted his life force frivolously in games, he thought, there might not be enough.

'Mouse!' Ezzie threw him the ball again. This time Mouse was caught off-guard, thinking about Hammerman, and the ball landed hard in his stomach. He got to his feet quickly, holding the ball against him.

'Watch what you're doing, will you?' he said. He shifted the ball to his hip.

'I'm sorry. I —'

'Yeah, you're *sorry* all right.'

'Aw, come on, Mouse.'

Mouse stood there with the ball, looking at Ezzie as if he were seeing him for the first time. Dick Fellini, who was waiting beneath the basket, came walking over, shaking his hair out of his eyes. He said, 'Hey, what's with Mouse?'

Ezzie said, 'Nothing. Come on, Mouse.'

Mouse hesitated. Ezzie was standing with his arms held out for the ball. He said again, 'Come on, Mouse, gimme the ball. Let's play.'

Mouse pulled the ball back and fired it at Ezzie. He threw hard, aiming at Ezzie's stomach. He wanted to crumple Ezzie, to drop him to the pavement. 'Take the ball!' he said.

Ezzie drew back instinctively. The ball missed his stomach, struck him on the hand and then bounced over to Dick Fellini. Fellini took the ball, dribbled to the basket and threw it in. He caught the rebound and made another basket.

Ezzie said, 'You didn't have to hit my sore finger,' in a flat, angry voice.

'What sore finger?' Mouse asked.

'That one.'

'Boy, that really is a sore finger, Ezzie. That's some sore finger — a hangnail.'

Ezzie put his finger in his mouth to ease the pain. All the while he was looking at Mouse, and Mouse was waiting. Then Ezzie took his finger out of his mouth and looked at it.

Mouse thought then that Ezzie was going to say something funny about his finger, to try to make him laugh. Instead Ezzie turned and ran quickly to where Dick Fellini was lining up for a free throw. Ezzie leaped agilely into the air, trying to intercept the ball, and then he watched while Fellini made the rebound.

'Hey, Fellini, gimme the ball,' he cried, spinning around. 'The ball!'

'Yeah, Fellini, give him the ball so he can miss again,' Mouse shouted. He waited to see if Ezzie was going to answer, to swop insults with him. Ezzie ignored him.

Ezzie said, 'Fellini, gimme the ball.'

Mouse turned and walked toward the alley. He glanced back once, saw Ezzie dribbling in the opposite direction and then he kept going.

He walked slowly, kicking a bottle cap ahead of him. To get his mind off how bad he felt, he tried to think of another emergency he could handle. He couldn't think of anything. He went slowly over a list of the world's greatest dangers – tornadoes, earthquakes, tsetse flies, the piranha. Behind him he heard Ezzie cry again, 'Fellini, the ball, gimme the ball.'

He kept going. Cyclones, the coral snake – Then he came to sharks and he stopped.

Emergency Sixteen – Sudden Appearance in Your Swimming Area of Sharks. Ezzie had once read the way to handle that emergency in a comic book. You simply relax your body and play dead. Sharks are bored by dead bodies.

This solution left Mouse dissatisfied. Ezzie had really read that in some comic book, but it was the most unsatisfactory advice Mouse could think of. Play dead! It was impossible.

It seemed to him suddenly that what most emergency measures amounted to was doing whatever was most unnatural. If it was natural to start screaming, survival called for keeping perfectly quiet. If it was natural to run, the best thing to do was to stand still. Whatever was the hardest, that was what you had to do sometimes to survive. The hardest thing of all, it seemed to him, was not running.

He tried to imagine him and Ezzie in the ocean playing dead while the curious sharks swam around them.

'It'll work, it'll work, I tell you,' Ezzie would be muttering out of the side of his mouth. 'It worked for Popeye, didn't it?'

Mouse thought of it a moment longer. He imagined the sharks moving away and he and Ezzie floating alone in the ocean. 'I told you nothing would happen,' Ezzie would say, smiling a little. Somehow this didn't make Mouse feel any better.

Emergency Seventeen – Visit of a Cobra. When this happens, Ezzie said, you stop whatever you are doing at once and you begin to make smooth rhythmic body movements which will hypnotize the cobra.

He remembered that Ezzie had once shown him exactly how these movements should be done. 'Like this, Mouse, like this, see?'

'I don't think movements like that would hypnotize a cobra.'

'Well, I happen to know a boy who hypnotized a cobra in a zoo like this,' Ezzie had said, stopping the movements abruptly. 'And if you don't believe me, his name was Albert Watts.'

Mouse sighed. He kicked the bottle cap into the gutter. Anyway, he thought, life and death struggles with cobras and sharks and lions seemed less likely every day.

He heard a noise behind him, and he looked around and saw Garbage Dog following on his short legs. 'Good boy!' he cried. He had never been so glad to see anyone. 'Come on. You want something to eat? Come to my house.'

At the stairs to the apartment Garbage Dog hesitated, and Mouse drew him quickly forward. 'Come on, boy, food!' Slowly, with Mouse urging him along, Garbage Dog began to take the steps one at a time.

GARBAGE Dog had not been inside a house for years. He hesitated at the door, and then when Mouse pushed him, he entered. He walked around the edge of the room, avoiding the carpet, until he came to the kitchen. Then he sat uneasily by the table. There was a little hot air blowing on him from under the refrigerator, and this worried him. He moved over by the sink.

'What do you want to eat?' Mouse asked. 'Bologna sandwich all right?'

Garbage Dog's nose started to run as soon as the refrigerator door was opened. He got up, moved forward and looked into the brightly lit box. He could smell meat loaf and bologna and cheese, and then everything blended into a general food smell which was even better. He waited without moving. His eyes were riveted on the refrigerator.

Mouse gathered up bologna and cheese, shut the refrigerator door with his shoulder and got bread from the counter. 'Here,' he said.

Garbage Dog was accustomed to little titbits – crusts of bread and pieces of broken cookies and the dry ends of ice cream cones. He hardly ever got a whole sandwich. He took it in his mouth and stood for a moment, looking at Mouse. Then he went under the table and began to eat. He finished quickly and came back. He stood looking from Mouse to the refrigerator.

'How about bread with bacon grease on it?' Mouse asked. He broke bread into a small bowl and poured bacon grease over it. He was sprinkling this with grated cheese when his mother came into the apartment.

'Benjie?'

'I'm in here, Mom.' He set the bowl on the floor.

'Well, I hope you aren't eating because –' She broke off. 'What is that dog doing in here?'

'I had to let him come up,' Mouse said. 'He followed me.'

'Well, I don't want dogs in here, you should know that. As soon as he finishes, take him out.'

'*If* he'll go. He follows me every –'

'Out.' She went into the living-room and said, 'And don't *you* eat anything, because Mrs Casino's giving you supper.'

He followed her quickly into the living-room. Behind him came Garbage Dog, sliding a little on his short legs. Garbage Dog stepped on the carpet by accident, and then quickly walked over and stood by the front door, looking worried.

'Where are you going?' Mouse asked his mother.

'I've got a cosmetics party,' she said. His mother went to people's houses and showed cosmetics and people bought them. It occurred to Mouse that he had always wanted to see what went on at one of these parties.

He said quickly, 'I could go with you. I could –'

'You know that's out of the question.'

'I wouldn't be any trouble. Nobody would even know I was there.'

'No.'

'But I *want* to go.'

'I've already told Mrs Casino you would come. Now, I've got about two seconds to get dressed. Where's my new order book, have you seen it?'

73

She went into her room, and Mouse walked to the front door where Garbage Dog was waiting. Garbage Dog still looked uneasy.

'Come on, you've got to go,' Mouse said, letting his shoulders slump. Eagerly Garbage Dog went out the door and down the stairs. 'You just have to go, that's all. There's nothing I can do.'

Mouse came slowly back up the stairs as his mother was leaving. He waited on the landing for a moment, watching her go, and then he decided he didn't want to go back in the apartment and be by himself. Sighing, he crossed the landing and knocked at the Casinos' door.

'Mrs Casino, it's me – Benjie Fawley.'

'Come in, Benjie.' She opened the door. 'Come on in and don't mind me. I'm cooking.'

'I guess I'm early.'

'Well, that's good. You can play checkers with Papa. Come on in. He's so lonely these days. That man –'

Mouse interrupted. 'I'm really not very good at checkers. I've hardly played since fourth grade.'

He suddenly wanted very much to sit in the warm kitchen and watch Mrs Casino cook. She had a comforting manner about her. If he had said, 'Mrs Casino, some boys are going to kill me,' she wouldn't have wasted time asking, 'Why?' and 'What did you do?' She would have cried, 'Where are those boys? Show me those boys!' She would have yanked on her man's sweater, taken her broom in hand and gone out into the street to find them. 'Show me those boys!'

He had a brief, pleasant picture of Mrs Casino cornering Marv Hammerman in the alley and raining blows on him with her broom. 'You (*pow*) ain't (*swat*) touching (*smack*)

74

my (*zonk*) Benjie (*pow, bang, smack, swat, zap*)!' There was nothing comforting about sitting with Mr Casino. Mouse had already told him about the boys being after him and gotten no reaction at all.

Mouse could see Mr Casino sitting in the other room. He stood in the doorway with Mrs Casino. He hesitated.

As he was standing there he thought of something that had happened at school the past week. Mrs Tennent had brought movies of her Christmas vacation to school and had shown them to all her classes. And when she had shown everything that had happened to her and her sister in Mexico, then she reversed the film and they got to see everything happen in reverse. They got to see Mrs Tennent walking backward into the hotel and into the bullfight. They got to see her sister walking backward through a market place. They got to see a funny looking taxi driving backward, and people eating backward, and a man diving backward up onto a high cliff. They had all laughed because there was something about people walking backward in that bright, skilful, cheerful way that was funny.

Suddenly that was what Mouse wanted to happen now. He wanted to walk backward out of the Casinos' apartment. He wanted to walk backward to the basketball court, and then to school, reversing everything he had done in a bright, cheerful way. He wanted to move backward through Thursday too, and he especially wanted to walk all the way back to when he had come out of history class and paused by the prehistoric man chart. He wanted to stop everything right there. He would have paused a second, and in that second he would not have lifted his hand to write Marv Hammerman's name. Then the world could go forward again.

He felt Mrs Casino urging him into the room. He said reluctantly, 'I haven't played checkers in years. I'm not sure I even remember how.'

'You're good enough. Go on.' Mrs Casino took him firmly by the shoulders and pushed him into the room where Mr Casino was sitting by the window. 'Papa's just learning checkers over again anyway,' she said.

Mouse crossed the room, dragging his feet. He said, 'Hi, Mr Casino,' in a low, unenthusiastic voice because he wanted to be *with* somebody. He was lonely. I, Mouse Fawley, do hereby swear that I feel very lonely. He thought he would have to make a declaration of it to make people understand. 'How are you, Mr Casino?' he asked in the same flat voice.

'He's fine, aren't you, Papa?' Mrs Casino said. She patted Mr Casino on the shoulders as she passed behind his chair. Mouse sat down. Mr Casino was in an armchair, and the bottom had sunk so low that Mouse in his straight chair was the taller of the two.

'Here you go.' Mrs Casino brought out the checkers, the oldest set Mouse had ever seen, and set it on the table. The black and red board had been worn white where the checkers had been moved across it. When she put the set down, Mr Casino reached out slowly with one enormous hand. His fingers were trembling a little, as if the distance from the armrest of his chair to the box of checkers was long and hazardous.

'I'll set these up,' Mouse said. 'I can do it better.' Quickly, efficiently, he put the checkers in the squares, his and Mr Casino's. Then he leaned back in his chair. 'Go ahead, Mr Casino.' He could hear the impatience in his own voice.

He glanced up at Mrs Casino, who was still standing by the door, drying her already dry hands on her apron. Then quickly Mouse looked back at the checkerboard because he had seen something in Mrs Casino's eyes. It was just a flash of something, a cloud over the sun, a sadness, and it bothered him.

She said, 'He's supposed to use his left hand as much as possible.'

'Oh,' Mouse said. He wanted to explain that the reason he was acting this way was because he had the impossible burden of being chased by Marv Hammerman. He wanted Mrs Casino's sympathy.

'Mrs Casino,' he wanted to say, 'if you only knew what it's like to have Marv Hammerman out to get you.'

He felt tears stinging his eyes, and he knew he was not going to tell Mrs Casino, and that he was not going to tell anybody else either. 'Your move,' he said loudly to Mr Casino. He shifted in his chair and then abruptly he slumped.

He had suddenly thought back to that moment outside history class when he had turned and looked around and seen Hammerman. That first moment – it was what had been troubling him all along.

It wasn't entirely clear. It was as if a fog had filled the hall that day, making everything hazy. Still Mouse could remember the way Hammerman's eyes had looked in that first unguarded moment. There hadn't been enough fog to blot that out. Mouse thought again about that moment in the hall. It had been flitting in and out of his mind like a moth for two days. Now he made himself think about it.

He sank lower in his chair, because he knew now what

troubled him. He had felt somehow close to Hammerman in that first terrible moment. He had known how Hammerman felt. It had been the same way he had felt when everyone first started calling him Mouse. They had been united for a moment, Mouse and Neanderthal man.

He said in a low voice, 'You can have first move, Mr Casino.'

Mr Casino sat for a moment and then made a gesture with his fingers as if he was flicking a fly off the armrest.

Mrs Casino said, 'He wants you to go first, Benjie.' She was still patting the backs of her dry hands on her apron.

'Oh, sure.' He looked at the board as if the decision was one of the most important of his life. The checkers were thin and wooden and darker in the centre from the sweat of people's fingers. They were clear for a moment and then they blurred a little. Mouse reached out and pushed one forward before they got so blurred he couldn't find them.

He leaned back in his chair. The late afternoon sun was coming in the window, and the dust in the sunlight gave him a sad, old-timey feeling. He thought that if he closed his eyes, he would not be able to tell even what century he was in. It could be a hundred years ago and he could be sitting here in an old-timey suit with knickers and a tie. It could be a thousand years ago. It was that kind of timeless feeling.

Some things, he thought as he stared down at the checkerboard, just don't change. He remembered how he used to enjoy looking through books that showed the old and the new – the Wright Brothers' glider opposite a jet plane, or an old Victrola opposite a hi-fi set. Looking at pictures like that always made him feel superior, as if he had advanced in the same way as the machines. He felt different now. He thought of all the people who had ever lived as being run through by a single thread, like beads.

'Well, I'll get back to my cooking, if you don't need me,' Mrs Casino said.

'No, we'll be fine.'

He looked at Mr Casino who was reaching out slowly. He was still a large man, but he had once been enormous, and everything he was wearing was too big for him. The cuffs of his shirt came down over his speckled hands. The cotton pants were gathered in at the waist with his belt. Mouse waited, watching sadly, while Mr Casino pushed one of his checkers forward with a trembling hand.

Mouse said, 'My turn?' He bent forward over the board.

In the kitchen, Mrs Casino started to sing. Outside two men were arguing about baseball. A bus passed. Mrs Casino started on a western song. Mouse tried not to think of anything but the checker game. He said self-consciously, 'Oh, I've got a jump.' He took it and leaned back in his chair.

It was a long, slow game, the first game Mouse had ever played in which it didn't seem important who the winner was, or rather a game in which both players were winners.

Mouse said, 'Do you want to play again?' He waited a minute, and then he pushed all the checkers across to Mr Casino and said gently, 'You set them up this time, will you?'

9

SATURDAY was warm and bright, the first pretty Saturday they had had since Christmas. Mouse, lying on his bed in the hall, could tell it was sunny just from the brightness of the normally dark hall.

'Mom!' he called, not knowing what time it was and whether she had gone out to deliver cosmetics yet. 'Mom!' There was no answer. There used to be a boy who lived in the apartment next door when Mouse was little, and every time Mouse would call, 'Mommie!' the boy would answer, 'Whatie?' in a high false voice.

Mouse got out of bed slowly, in stages. He sat on the edge of the bed, leaned forward, looked at his feet, straightened, and then continued to stand by the bed for a moment. Then abruptly he dressed, went into the kitchen and looked at the boxes of cereal on the shelf. He tore open a box of Sugar Pops. He waited, looking at the cereal, and then refolded the box and put it back. He went into the living-room, and out of habit he switched on the television. Superman was on the screen, flying over the city in his suit and cape. Mouse watched for a moment and then turned off the television. Superman might be faster than a speeding bullet and able to leap tall buildings with a single bound, Mouse thought, but even Superman couldn't keep himself from being tuned down to a small white dot.

Mouse got his jacket from the chair by the door. Even though he knew it was going to be warm outside, he put on his jacket and zipped it up. Then he left the apartment.

The street and the sidewalks were crowded. Some girls were roller skating, and it was the first time Mouse had seen that this year. Usually he and Ezzie liked to sit on the steps and watch the girls, calling out things like, 'Congratulations,' when they slipped. This would have been a good time to sit and yell comments of this nature because the girls had lost their talent for skating over the winter.

'Help me,' the biggest girl was yelling. 'Don't let me fall.' While she was screaming, the two smaller girls, sisters in matching sweaters, began to lose their balance. 'Help me,' the big girl cried. The two sisters were now on their knees, still holding the big girl up. 'Help!' the big girl cried and then she too went down on the sidewalk.

'Yeah for Louise!' Ezzie would have cried in delight. He would have nudged Mouse as the girls struggled to their feet, anticipating more fun. 'Get this, Mouse. Keep your eye on Louise. She's the one to watch.'

Mouse passed them without comment. Louise was still sitting on the sidewalk saying, 'I think I broke something. No fooling, I think I broke something.'

Mouse kept walking down the crowded sidewalk. He knew a lot of these people, but nobody seemed to be speaking to him today. It was as if everybody in the world knew what he was going to do, and everybody knew that if they gave him any sympathy at all, if they even patted his shoulder or took his hand, he would not be able to do it. He would just fold up on the sidewalk, curled forward like a shrimp.

He crossed the street, touching both feet on the old trolley tracks because this was supposed to bring luck, and he stepped up on the sidewalk in front of the laundry. He thought that he could walk down this street blindfolded and know right where he was. The odours that came out of the different doors told him what to expect, what cracks there were in the sidewalk, who would be standing in the doorways. He turned the corner, passed the old movie theatre, the Rialto. He smelled the old musty smell. Then he stopped thinking of anything except the fact that he was now on Marv Hammerman's street.

A bus passed him, stopped to pick up an old woman with a folded shopping bag under her arm and then moved on. Mouse had started to sweat. It wasn't that warm a day, not even with his jacket zipped up, but sweat was running down his sides beneath his shirt in a way it had never done before. At the same time his throat had gone completely dry, and the two conditions seemed somehow connected.

He saw a boy who had been in his school last year and he asked, 'Have you seen Marv Hammerman?' His voice had the crackling dry sound of old leaves. He turned his head away and coughed.

'Not this morning.'

'Doesn't he live around here?'

'He lives right over there,' the boy said. 'Lots of times he's down at Stumpy's.'

'Oh.'

'If I see him I'll tell him you're looking for him.'

'I'm Mouse Fawley,' he said, looking at the boy, and the boy said, 'I know.'

Mouse glanced at his watch. It was 9:31. Slowly he walked the half block to Stumpy's, which was a pizza place that had pinball machines. The entrance was below street level, and Mouse stopped and looked inside for a moment. He couldn't see anything at first because his eyes were still accustomed to the bright light outside, but he could hear the sharp mechanical sounds of the pinball machines, the bells, the clicks, the machine-gun bursts of points being scored. He went down the steps.

'Is Marv Hammerman here?' he asked, squinting up at the man behind the counter. The man was putting packs of gum in a display stand. He glanced at Mouse and kept on straightening the gum.

'No, he hasn't been in. Hey, Steve, where's Hammerman?'

The man and Mouse waited while Steve's ball travelled down through the bright maze of the pinball machine. Steve urged the ball into the holes with gentle leaning movements of his body. When it was over he said, 'He may be in later.'

'He may be in later,' the man told Mouse.

'Thanks.' Mouse turned and walked out of Stumpy's. He lifted the cuff of his jacket and checked his watch again. It was 9:36. Slowly he began to walk up the sidewalk. This was the one thing he hadn't thought of – that he wouldn't be able to find Hammerman. He walked two more blocks, turned around and came up the other side of the street.

He thought he would not be able to bear the tension if Hammerman did not appear soon. He crossed in front of Stumpy's and started down the street again, moving a little faster. He thought he had been walking for hours. Where could Hammerman be? He looked at his watch again. It was 9:55.

The sunlight seemed blinding now, and Mouse wanted to dim it so that whatever was going to happen would not be lit up for everyone to see. He walked to the end of the block and squinted down at his watch. It was 9:57. He paused in front of the barber shop to wind his watch and found that it was already wound tightly. He could not remember winding it, but it was that strange kind of day when watches could wind themselves and a minute could become an hour and the sun could shine on one single person like a spotlight.

He started walking. He walked in the same quick way, and he was almost back to the old Rialto theatre when he saw Marv Hammerman coming toward him. Hammerman was with the boy in the black sweat shirt, and both of them were walking quickly as if they had heard Mouse was waiting. The boy in the black sweat shirt was smiling a little.

When Mouse saw them, his walking suddenly became harder. His shoes seemed to stick to the sidewalk, and his legs got heavy. He felt as if he were walking under water. He pulled down his jacket, smoothed his hair, hitched up his pants, kept his hands busy in order to keep attention from his slow heavy feet. He pulled at his ear lobe, wiped his nose, zipped his jacket higher. Foolishly he thought of the hundred and eighteen little people of his father's dreams. He wished they would appear, lift him and carry him away. 'So long, Hammerman,' he would cry as they hurried him to safety.

Mouse kept walking, and the three of them met in front of the Rialto by the boarded-up booth where Mouse used to buy tickets to the Saturday science-fiction specials.

Mouse finished working the zipper on his jacket and pulled his cuffs down. He said to Hammerman, 'I was sick yesterday and I had to go home, but I'm here now.'

It came out in a rush. Mouse hoped that he hadn't said it so quickly that Hammerman didn't hear it. It was important that this one thing be said while he was still able to talk.

'He still looks a little sick to me, don't he to you?' the boy in the black sweat shirt said, smiling. 'Course he looks better than he's *gonna* look.'

Mouse didn't say anything. He was trying to steel himself for the battle. The only thing he knew about fighting, he realized now, was that if you put your thumbs inside your fists and hit somebody hard with your hand like that, you could break your thumb. He rearranged his hands which he had instinctively folded with the thumbs inside.

He cleared his throat, wondering if he was supposed to say something else. He had had so little experience in fighting that he did not know how a fight of this kind, an arranged fight, would actually start. He remembered seeing a fist fight in an old silent movie on television one time, and the opponents had lifted their fists at the same moment, in the same position, and had circled each other in a set pattern. Still he couldn't imagine this fight starting, not in that way or any other. He could only imagine the ending.

The boy in the black sweat shirt jerked his head at Hammerman. He said to Mouse, 'He don't like anybody writing things about him.'

Mouse was so nervous he thought perhaps the boy had been talking to him for hours. He wasn't certain of anything. He said quickly, 'I know.'

The boy in the black sweat shirt nodded at Hammerman again. He said, 'He wants you to know real good.'

The sun went behind a cloud, and it was suddenly dim beneath the marquee. Mouse couldn't see for a minute. He had been looking at the boy in the sweat shirt while he was talking, and now the boy was silent. All Mouse could see was the whiteness of his smile.

Mouse looked back at Hammerman. For a moment he couldn't see him clearly either. Hammerman's face was a pale circle in the darkness, like the children's faces in the hospital ward, lit up by the light from Mouse's flashlight. Then, abruptly, everything snapped into focus. Hammerman's face was so clear there seemed to be nothing between Mouse and Hammerman, not even air. They could have been up in that high altitude area where the air thins and even distant points come into focus.

Hammerman hadn't made a move that Mouse could see. He was still standing with his hands at his sides, his feet apart. But his body had lost its relaxed look and was ready in a way that Mouse's body would never be.

Mouse raised his fists. His thumbs were carefully outside, pointing upward so that he appeared to be handling invisible controls of some sort. Then he saw Hammerman's fist coming toward him, the knuckles like pale pecans, and at the same time Mouse saw Hammerman's eyes, pale also but very bright. Then Hammerman's fist slammed into his stomach.

Mouse doubled over and staggered backward a few steps. He thought for a moment that he was going to fall to the ground, just sit down like a baby who has lost his balance. He didn't, and after a second he straightened and came toward Hammerman. He threw out his right hand.

He didn't see Hammerman's fist this time, just felt it in the stomach again. It was so hard that Mouse made a strangled noise. If he had eaten breakfast, there would have been Sugar Pops all over the sidewalk from that blow.

Choking, coughing, he staggered all the way back and

hit against the side of the theatre where pictures of man-made monsters used to be posted. He stayed there a minute, bent over his stomach, waiting for his strength to return. He could almost feel the old favourites – Gorgo, Mothro, Godzilla – waiting behind him. He tried to pull himself forward. He felt for a minute that he had become glued to the theatre, plastered there like the pictured monsters. Then he came free and took three heavy steps forward to where Hammerman was waiting. Gorgo had walked like this. Mouse thought of how Gorgo's feet had crushed whole buildings with these same heavy steps. His own feet could barely lift the weight of a pair of tennis shoes.

Mouse's hands were up. He threw the invisible controls forward and hit nothing. Then he felt a sharp stinging blow on his breastbone. He hadn't seen that one coming either. He put out his fists, to ward off blows again rather than to land them, and then Hammerman's fist was in his face. It landed somehow on his nose and mouth at the same time. Then there was another blow directly on his nose.

Mouse's nose began to gush blood. The blood seemed to be coming from everywhere, not just the nose, and Mouse wiped his face with one hand. Quickly, anxiously he got his hands back in position. He threw the right control forward.

Suddenly he couldn't see. He wiped his hand over his eyes, then wiped his nose and got set. He was leaning forward now, pressing his knees together to steady them. The blood from his nose was splattering on the sidewalk.

He waited, wondering how long he could continue to hold this position. Then he heard Hammerman say, 'You had enough?'

'No, he hasn't had enough,' the boy in the black sweat shirt said. 'He's still standing.'

Hammerman said again, 'You had enough?'

Hammerman's voice seemed to be coming from somewhere far away, but the voice wasn't asking the right question, Mouse thought. It seemed simple suddenly. He saw it now as an old-fashioned matter of honour. He, Mouse, had dishonoured Marv Hammerman; and now Hammerman had to be the one to say when his honour was restored. It was one of those things that doesn't become absolutely clear until the last minute and then becomes so clear it dazzles the mind.

Mouse could hear Dick Fellini's voice explaining honour and knighthood to the English class. He could hear Ezzie saying, 'Ask me anything you want to about honour, Mr Stein, and I'll tell you.' It was an odd thing but he, Mouse, who had felt honour, who had been run through with it like a sword, couldn't say a word about it.

He looked at Hammerman, squinting at him, and said, 'If you have.'

'If *he* has!' the boy in the black sweat shirt cried. 'Man, he can keep going like this all morning.'

There was a long pause, and Mouse suddenly feared he was going to start crying. He couldn't understand why he should want to cry now when it was almost over. The worst thing that could happen now was the big final blow, the knock-out punch that would leave him unconscious in the shadow of the Rialto. He could even take that if only he did not start crying.

Hammerman lifted one hand and opened it a little as if he were releasing something. It was a strange gesture, and it seemed to Mouse the kind of gesture a dancer might try to make, or a painter might try to put in a picture. He imagined a small statue, bronze, on a round pedestal, of Marv Hammerman with his partially raised open hand.

Hammerman said, 'Go on.'

'What?'

'Go on.'

Mouse wiped his nose with the back of his hand and said, 'Thank you.'

The boy in the black sweat shirt leaned back and hollered, 'Whoooo-eeee! You welcome.'

Mouse passed them, holding his hand over his nose. The boy in the sweat shirt laughed again. It was a loud explosive laugh, and the boy spun around to watch Mouse walk away.

'Whooo-eeee!' he said. 'You are most certainly welcome. Come around anytime.'

Mouse turned the corner and kept walking. Tears were in his eyes now, and he could not see where he was going. It was, he thought, the gesture that had weakened him. The careless ease of that opened hand – Mouse couldn't seem to get that out of his mind.

He made his way down the sidewalk with his eyes closed. He thought suddenly that if he could see where he was going it would probably not be down Fourth Street at all. He was probably walking across some dusty foreign field. If he could look up, he would not see the tops of buildings, the flat blue sky with a jet trail drawn across it. He would see gold and scarlet tournament flags snapping in the wind. There would be plumes and trumpets and horses in bright trappings. Honour would be a simple thing again and so vital that people would talk of it wherever they went.

He felt as if a vanished age had risen up like a huge wave and washed over him. Then he smelled a dry starchy smell and knew he was passing the laundry. He stopped and wiped his hand across his eyes to clear them. He stepped against the wall and then opened the door into an apartment building where he didn't know anybody. He sank down on the steps against the wall.

With a sigh he hung his head and pinched his nose shut. His nose was still bleeding. He saw that now. He noticed the other damage. His upper lip was bleeding and starting to swell. His stomach hurt so bad it might be weeks before it would accept food again. He couldn't bend over any further without feeling the pain in his breastbone. He looked at his watch. It was 10:13.

Well, he thought wryly, at least I didn't break my thumbs.

10

A lady from the lower apartment saw him when she came out to get the mail, leaned over him and asked, 'Are you all right?' She was a big woman. Mouse couldn't see her right then, but he could feel the solidness of her presence.

He nodded. He tried to get up, thinking she wanted him to get out of the hallway. Still holding his hand over his nose, he managed to get to his feet. She said, 'You come on in. Come on now.'

She pulled him forward with her strong arms and led him into her kitchen. 'What happened to you, huh?' she asked as she was wringing out a cloth at the sink. He just shook his head. 'Probably a fight – is that what it was – a fight?' He nodded. 'Either that or you got hit by a freight train. You kids.'

As she came over to where he was sitting, he looked up and was surprised to see that she was a small woman, dark and quick moving. She had a gypsy face. She said, 'You kids never learn. There's a better way to settle things than with your fists, you know that? A clever person never has to feel one single blow his whole life. Let me see your hands. I can't tell what part of you is hurt the worst.'

He held up his hands, bloody but unscarred. They were hands that hadn't landed a single blow. The woman wiped them clean, finger by finger, the way his mother used to wash his hands when he was little.

'Fighting is not the answer,' she said.

'I know,' he said, able to speak at last. 'Only it wasn't a real fight.'

'Then I'd hate to see you after a real one,' she snapped. She looked at his cleaned hands. She turned them over. 'I bet the other kid didn't get a scratch on him.'

'No.'

'You can't win.'

'I know.'

'Well, at least you've learned that.' Continuing to babble about the dangers of fighting, she stopped his nose from bleeding, gave him a piece of ice to put on his upper lip, washed his face and even, in her concern, wet his hair and combed it. She parted his hair on the wrong side and combed it straight across his forehead. This, plus the swollen lip, made his face look strange reflected in the window over the sink.

'Now, you go right home and lie down, you hear me?

Don't let that bleeding start up again, and if it does, you put wadded paper up under your lip like I showed you.'

'Yes, and thank you.'

'And don't fight any more.'

'I won't.' He tried to smile. 'If I can possibly help it.'

'You kids.'

He went outside and for the first time he knew what real relief was. It was a relief so great that the whole world looked different to him, cleaner and sharper. He had not even felt this way when he got out of the hospital after losing his tonsils. It was the kind of light feeling that might come with a lessening of the pull of gravity. He felt that if he wanted to, he could actually float up through the buildings. He imagined himself rising, moving slowly and easily, waving to the startled people in the windows, smiling to them. His body was the lightest, most unburdened thing in the world. Strings would be required in a minute to hold him to the ground.

He walked slowly back to his street, holding the ice cube, which the lady had wrapped in a little square of cloth, against his lip.

As he rounded the corner, he saw Ezzie and Dick Fellini and Dutch Richards standing by the mail-box. Ezzie had his back to Mouse. He was saying to Dutch, 'Aw, come on, gimme the ball. Don't you want to see me do the trick?'

'Frankly, no.'

'Come on, Dutch. If I had a new ball and you wanted to do a trick with it, I'd –'

Mouse came up and lowered his ice cube. He said, 'Well, I fought Hammerman.'

Dutch stopped bouncing the ball and Ezzie spun

around, his trick forgotten. 'You what? You fought Hammerman?' Ezzie asked incredulously.

Mouse nodded.

Ezzie straightened. '*You* fought Hammerman?'

'Yes.'

Mouse knew that Ezzie had had a secret fear that he, as Mouse's best friend, might be called on to participate in the fight. Mouse knew Ezzie was especially afraid that he might have to take on Peachie, the boy in the black sweat shirt. Now it was hard for Ezzie to believe that this danger had passed.

'Where was this fight?' Ezzie asked. 'What happened? Come on, tell me about it.'

'Well, it was in front of the Rialto,' Mouse said. His swollen lip made his voice sound strange, or perhaps it was the strangeness of what he was saying. He stopped and put the ice cube back against his lip.

The Saturday traffic seemed loud in the street. Two boys on motorcycles passed. Ezzie glanced impatiently at them for interrupting and then prompted eagerly, 'So? Go on.'

'Well, I went over to the Rialto looking for Hammerman and –'

'*You* went looking for *him*?' Ezzie asked.

'Let him tell it, Ezzie,' Dutch said.

'Well, I went over there looking for him,' Mouse continued, 'and we met in front of the Rialto and had a short fight and now it's over.' Mouse thought that those were the most comforting words he had ever heard.

'How short was the fight?' Ezzie asked. 'I mean, in blows. How many blows, Mouse, do you remember, or was it so many that you couldn't –'

'Five,' Mouse said.

'Five!' The hush of Ezzie's voice made five the most important number there was.

'Two in the stomach, one on the breastbone, right about there.' He put his hand over the exact spot. 'Two on the face.' There was no need to point out where those blows had landed.

'You took all those blows?'

Mouse nodded.

'Did you fall down, or what?'

'No, I didn't fall. Well,' he said truthfully, 'I would have fallen if the Rialto theatre hadn't been there, and I staggered around. But I never actually went down.'

Ezzie and Dutch and Dick were looking at him. It was a strange sensation for a minute. It was as if they were not looking at him at all, but at what was going on inside him. They had all four wanted X-ray eyes at one time or another, and now Mouse suddenly had the feeling that the other three had got them. He shrugged self-consciously and said, 'Well, I better go get another ice cube. This one's about gone.'

He started walking, and Ezzie left the others and followed him. He said, 'Listen, I want to hear some more about this fight. What was it really like? I mean, did he say anything, or what? You haven't told me *anything*.'

Mouse turned and looked at Ezzie, squinting in the sunlight. He wet his swollen lip with his tongue and said, 'It was just sort of an honourable thing, Ezzie.'

'A what?'

'An honourable thing.'

'Hammerman? Honourable?'

Mouse nodded. He knew that he was not going to be

able to explain it to Ezzie. He wasn't even sure he understood it himself now. But at the moment when he and Marv Hammerman had met in front of the Rialto, it had been clearly and simply a matter of honour.

He wanted to explain. He said, 'Hammerman's not like I thought, Ezzie, that's all I'm trying to say.'

'Are we talking about the same Hammerman?' Ezzie's face had gotten pinker with his puzzlement.

Mouse nodded. 'Marv Hammerman.' He looked down at his tennis shoes which were splattered with blood. He couldn't even see where he had written AIR VENT now. Still looking at his shoes he said, 'I don't even know what Hammerman *is* like. It's strange, Ezzie, I can't explain it in words.'

'Quit fooling now! What happened? How bad was it?' Ezzie threw out his hands in an old gesture of agitation he saw his grandfather use daily. '*Tell* me.'

'Well,' Mouse began and then he trailed off. He tried to think of something to tell Ezzie, but he couldn't. He knew how Ezzie felt, cheated at not knowing the details of the ending. He had felt that way one time when he had been watching a television show. Right at the most exciting part a news bulletin about a hijacked airplane had come on and Mouse never got to see how the story came out. His mother had said, 'Well, you know the dog rescued the boy. Even *I* can tell you that.'

'Yes,' he had said, 'but I wanted to see it happen.'

Mouse tried to smile with his swollen lip. He shrugged his shoulders. He said, 'Well, Ezzie, he could have made it a lot worse.'

Ezzie could not understand what was happening, but for some reason, even though Mouse was no longer a tragic figure, no longer marked by destiny, he had not shrunk back to his normal size like Mr Stein. Even standing there with a bloody jacket and a swollen lip and wet hair that still had the comb marks in it, Mouse seemed bigger. It was such a strong impression that Ezzie wondered if Mouse had actually gotten taller. He wanted to stand back to back with Mouse in front of a mirror and measure.

Mouse started slowly up the steps. Despite the light feeling of his body, his legs weren't working as well as usual.

Ezzie said quickly, 'I'll get an ice cube for you.'

'I'm all right, Ez, I can –'

'No, I'll get it. I want to.'

Ezzie went up the stairs, taking them two at a time. Mouse waited at the bottom, resting his weight on the metal banister. He felt strange. It wasn't the swollen lip or the new part in his hair or the lightness of his body. He had sometimes wished in the past two days that he wasn't himself, and it seemed now that this wish had come true. He almost had to remind himself who he was. I, Benjie Fawley, am alive and well. He let the air out of his lungs in a long sigh. I, Benjie Fawley, have survived.

Dick Fellini called, 'Hey, Benjie, you guys want to play ball?' Fellini was bouncing the basketball, twisting it in such a way that it came back to him as it bounced.

He said, 'Sure,' even though he was not sure his legs were going to cooperate in the plan.

'Well, come on then.'

'I'll wait for Ezzie.'

Dutch and Dick Fellini waved and started down the sidewalk. Mouse waited by the stairs. 'Ez, come on,' he called after a moment.

Ezzie appeared at the window. 'Hey, can I have a bologna sandwich?'

'Yeah, if you'll come on.'

'You want one?'

'No.' He realized suddenly he was hungry after all, and he called out, 'Yeah, Ezzie, I want one.'

Ezzie came back to the window. 'Mustard and relish? And there's some lettuce in a plastic bag and a couple of okra pickles.'

'I don't care, Ezzie, just make it and come on, will you?'

'I'm *coming*, only if you're going to make a sandwich, then you might as well make a *sandwich*.'

Mouse waited, and after a minute Ezzie came out of the apartment with the sandwiches. 'The ice cube's in my pocket,' he said. Mouse fished the ice cube out of Ezzie's shirt pocket, brushed the lint off and twisted it into the square of cloth. Then he took his sandwich and said, 'Let's go.'

'Right.'

As they walked down the street, Ezzie took a bite of his sandwich, then turned it around to make sure the okra pickles weren't going to fall out. He shook his head and said, 'And you fought Hammerman.'

A passing bus blocked out the answer, which was, 'Well, not really, Ezzie,' and anyway Ezzie was already starting to walk faster down the sidewalk, holding his sandwich in the crook of his arm for safety.

'Race you, Benjie,' Ezzie said. It surprised Ezzie for a moment that he had said Benjie instead of Mouse. Then he broke into a run.

Garbage Dog was sitting in the shadow of the steps, but

as soon as he heard the sound of running, he got up and came out quickly. He looked down the street. He saw the two boys running toward him, and after a minute Garbage Dog started running too.

Garbage Dog ran down the middle of the sidewalk. He heard the boys getting closer behind him and he ran faster. He was getting worried. The boys caught up with him, the three of them ran a few steps together, and then the boys passed. Ears back, Garbage Dog began to run faster. His wild eyes rolled to the two boys because he didn't know why they were running.

Then suddenly the boys slowed down to turn into the alley. Ezzie said, 'Here, G. D.,' and dropped the crust of his sandwich. Garbage Dog managed to stop. He came back and circled the crust.

'And here's something from me too.' Another piece of crust and a half slice of bologna.

Watching the boys, Garbage Dog began to eat. He saw the boys disappear laughing behind the bakery, and after a moment he hurried to join them.

THE

CARTOONIST

1

'ALFIE?'

'What?'

'You studying?'

'Yes,' he lied.

'Well, why don't you come down and study in front of the television? It'll take your mind off what you're doing,' his mother called.

He didn't answer. He bent over the sheet of paper on his table. He was intent.

'Did you hear me, Alfie?'

'I heard,' he called without glancing up.

'Well, come on down.' She turned and spoke to Alma. 'Who's the announcer that says that on TV? It's some game show. He says, "Come on downnnn," and people come running down the aisle to guess the prices.'

'I don't know, Mom. I don't watch that junk,' Alma said.

'But you know who I'm talking about. Alfie Mason, come on downnnnn!'

Alfie didn't answer. He was drawing a comic strip called 'Super Bird'.

In the first square a man was scattering birdseed from a bag labelled 'Little Bird Seed'. In the next square little birds were gobbling up the seeds.

In the third square the man was scattering birdseed from a bag labelled 'Big Bird Seed'. In the next square big birds were gobbling up the seeds.

In the fifth square the man was scattering huge lumps

from a bag labelled 'Giant Bird Seed'. In the last square a
giant bird was gobbling up the little man.

There was a smile on Alfie's face as he looked at what
he had done. At the top of the drawing he lettered in the
words *Super Bird*. He was going to do twelve of these
super comic strips, he had decided, one for each month.
When he got through, he would call it 'Super Calendar'.
Maybe he would get it published, and later, when he
learned how, he would animate 'Super Bird', make it into a
film. Whenever he drew something, he always saw it in
motion.

'Alfie?' his mom called again.

'I'm busy, Mom. I'm studying.'

'Well, supper's ready.'

'Oh.'

'Come down right now.'

'I am. I just want to get my papers in order. If I leave
them in a mess, sometimes I can't . . .' He trailed off.

He now had two strips for his calendar. 'Super Bird' and
'Super Caterpillar'. He didn't know which he liked best. He
looked from one to the other, comparing them.

In the first square of 'Super Caterpillar', a giant
caterpillar was happily eating New York City. In the
second square he was happily eating New York State. In
the third he was happily eating the world. In the last
square, he was unhappily falling through space, his
stomach a big round ball. Alfie was especially pleased with
the expression in Super Caterpillar's eyes as he tumbled
helplessly through space.

'Alfie!' his mother called loudly. Alfie knew she was at
the foot of the ladder now. She rattled the ladder as if she
were trying to shake him down. 'I'm coming up there to

pull you down by the ear if you don't come this minute.'

'I'm *coming*.'

He got up quickly and turned his papers face down on the table. He started for the ladder that led downstairs.

Coming down from the attic was like getting off one of those rides at the amusement park, Alfie thought. It left him feeling strange, as if he had moved not from one part of the house to another but from one experience to another without time to get his balance.

Alfie and his family had been living in this house for seven months, and when Alfie had first seen it he had thought of that old rhyme about the crooked man who lived in a crooked house. Nothing about this house was straight. It had started as two rooms, and then another room had been added. A kitchen had been made from the back porch. The roof was three different colours. The doors were crooked and so were the windows. The floors slanted. If you set a ball on the floor, it would roll to the wall. The house had been built by three different men, none of whom had ever had a lesson in carpentry.

The only thing Alfie liked about the house was the attic. That was his. He had put an old chair and a card-table up there, and he had a lamp with an extension cord that went down into the living-room. Nobody ever went up but Alfie. Once his sister, Alma, had started up the ladder, but he had said, 'No, I don't want anybody up there.'

She'd paused on the ladder. 'Why not?'

'Because . . .' He had hesitated, trying to find words to express his meaning. 'Because,' he said finally, 'I want it to be *mine*.'

Alma had nodded. She understood how important it

was to have things of your own because their mother used everything of Alma's from her cosmetics to her shoes.

Now Alfie closed the trapdoor, easing it down because it was heavy. He climbed down into the living-room.

'I don't know what you do up there,' his mom said, watching him.

'I study.'

'Well, it's not healthy – no windows, no air. I keep expecting you to smother. Mr Wilkins has an old window in his garage. Maybe I could get him to–'

'I like it just the way it is,' Alfie said quickly.

'Well, you ought to be more like Bubba,' she said, eyeing him critically. 'When he was your age he was outside every day, passing a football, dribbling a basketball–'

'Stealing a baseball,' Alma added.

His mother ignored Alma. 'You're never going to be on a team.'

'That's true,' he said.

'But, Alfie, everybody wants to be on a team!' She broke off, then said tiredly, 'Now, where's Pap? Get him, Alfie. Tell him supper's ready but don't tell him it's Sloppy Joes or he won't come.'

Alfie went out the back door. He knew his grandfather would be sitting in the yard, reading yesterday's news-paper.

'Supper's ready,' he said to his grandfather's back.

His grandfather was hunched over the paper, muttering to himself as he read. 'Look at that, will you?'

Alfie knew he wasn't expected to look, just listen. He leaned against the side of the door. 'What's happened?' he asked.

'The President of the United States,' Pap said, his voice

heavy with disgust, 'has give away twenty million bushels of grain to the Russians.'

'He didn't *give* it to them, Pap?'

'As good as. And you know who's going to pay, don't you?' He looked around, his heavy brows drawn low over his eyes. Then his brows jumped up as if they were on strings. 'You and me.'

'Yeah,' Alfie said.

His grandfather turned back to the newspaper, looking for something else that would irritate him. 'Ha,' he said, finding something. He circled the important articles with a yellow Magic Marker. 'Listen here. The state highway department is going busted. They're going to be six million dollars in debt by the end of the year if the state senate don't bail them out.'

'Pap, supper's ready,' he said quietly.

'And you know who's *really* going to bail them out, don't you?'

'You and me.'

'Yeah, you and me who don't even own a car.' He snapped the newspaper back into place. 'I built me a car when I wasn't much older than you. Did I ever tell you about it?'

'Yes.'

'Stole all the parts. It never cost me a cent.'

'It wouldn't run, though.'

'I had one ride in it. Best car ride I ever had. My brothers pushed me down the road in it, see, hoping it would start up when it got rolling. We lived at the top of a steep hill in those days, and it got rolling, all right. Oh, did it roll!'

'It didn't start, though.'

Pap ignored him. 'Wind was whipping back my hair – I didn't put no windshield in the car – I can still feel it. And my brothers was yelling and hanging on – they jumped on soon as I got going – my brother Alvin was lying on the hood – and I was steering. I felt as good as if I was at the Indy 500. That was some ride.' His grandfather sat staring into space, remembering.

'Are you two coming to supper or not?' his mother said. She was standing just inside the screen door.

'We're coming,' Alfie said. 'Come on, Pap.'

Slowly his grandfather got to his feet. 'You steal me enough parts and I'll make you a car. I can do it. We could coast down the hill on it anyways. It would be something to do.'

'I don't want to make a car.'

'If you'd been on that ride with me, you'd want to.'

'Maybe.'

'I didn't want to do nothing else for the longest time. When you find something you like to do, well, then you want to keep on doing it.'

Alfie thought of his drawings upstairs. 'That's true,' he said.

'I wish we still had the wrecking business,' Pap said sorrowfully. 'Maybe you and me can get it going again – just one or two good wrecked cars and we–'

'He's going to be a football player,' his mom said behind them.

The three of them stood without moving for a moment. Alfie looked down at his feet. His feet turned in. When he was just beginning to walk, a neighbour had told his mother that if she put his shoes on the wrong feet, his feet would turn out. His earliest memories were of women stopping his mother in the A & P and saying, 'Did you know your little boy's got his shoes on the wrong feet?' He used to stand with his legs crossed so that his shoes would look like everybody else's.

Now he tried to imagine his turned-in feet in football shoes, waiting on Astro Turf for the kick-off. He glanced back at his mom. She had a pleasant look on her face. She was in the stands again, cheering for Alfie as she had once cheered for Bubba. She was wearing her good-luck pants suit and holding her good-luck monkey's paw. She would turn around from time to time to brag to people, 'My boy's number twenty-eight, the quarterback.'

'The one with the turned-in feet?' they'd ask, leaning forward over their pom-poms.

Smiling a little, Alfie glanced at his grandfather. He was still going down the hill in his make-do car with his brothers hanging off like monkeys. His face looked younger, less lined, shoved forward slightly to meet the wind.

'Well, let's eat. I got a lot of studying to do after supper,' Alfie said. Studying, these days, meant drawing comic strips.

His grandfather blinked. Alfie could see he was back in the yard again – abruptly – old and disgruntled by yesterday's news. He put the paper in his chair and lumbered to the porch. As he entered the kitchen and saw the Sloppy Joes on the table, he let out a groan that seemed to come from the depths of his stomach.

'Now, Pap,' Alfie's mother said soothingly, 'Sloppy Joes are good for you. They build up your blood.'

'Ain't no need building up an old man's blood,' Pap said. He sat and shoved his paper napkin angrily in the collar of his shirt. 'An old man's blood gets too strong, his veins'll give way. His veins get too strong, his skin'll give way. His skin gets too strong, his mouth'll give way—'

'I guess that's the only way we'll get any peace around here,' Alfie's mother snapped. 'Pass the Sloppy Joes, Alma.'

2

ALFIE climbed up to the attic again after supper. His mother was hooting at a fat man on *Let's Make a Deal* who had on a gigantic baby diaper.

'And look, he's got a pacifier and everything. Come look at this fool, Alma.'

'Oh, Mom, those people are disgusting.'

'Pap, you want to see something funny?'

Pap didn't answer. He was making his way to the back fence, where he hoped to talk politics with his neighbour, W. C. Spivey. This was a nightly occurrence in good weather. Just after the evening news he and W. C. would meet at the back fence to curse politicians, newscasters, and the President of the United States. It was the happiest time of Pap's day.

He stopped at the back fence. 'Governor!' he shouted. It was what he called Spivey. Spivey called him the Colonel. Neither title was earned. 'Oh, Governor!'

Alfie pulled himself up into the attic and, as he always did, turned his head to the rafters. There were his drawings. They hung from every beam, every board. He never looked up without feeling better. No matter how low he was, looking up at his drawings always made his spirits rise.

He eased into his chair and turned over his papers. He looked at 'Super Caterpillar' and 'Super Bird' to see if they were as good as he remembered. He smiled. They were. He leaned 'Super Bird' against a jar of pencils so he could glance at it as he worked.

He took a fresh sheet of paper and started on another super strip. He had it all planned. The idea had come to him when he had seen his mother painting her finger-nails at the supper table.

He might have missed it if Alma hadn't said, 'Mom, don't polish your nails at the table. This isn't a beauty parlour.'

'I'm almost through.' She finished the last nail and held out her hands. 'How's that? It's a new shade called Tahiti Pearl.'

'I *know* it's a new shade. I bought it,' Alma said. She glanced at her mother critically. 'And put the top back on tight.' At some point, Alfie thought, Alma had become the parent; his mother, the child. Alma was the one who was stern, who never gave in. Alma was the one who bossed him, who told him what to do.

It was the pearl nail polish that gave Alfie his idea. In the first square a girl would be painting her finger-nails Pearl. In the second she would be painting her hands Pearl. In the third she would be painting her arms Pearl. In the fourth she would be painting her whole self Pearl. In the last square a giant would appear, pick her up, and set her in a tacky ring.

He would call it 'Super Ring', and he knew just how the girl's face would look in that last square as she sat yoga fashion in the tacky ring.

As soon as he got the idea, he wanted to tell everybody at the table about it. He looked up. His mom was waving her fingers in the air to dry them. Pap was picking suspicious-looking things from his Sloppy Joe. Alma was reading a book beside her plate.

Alfie decided to keep this idea to himself. No one would think it funny, especially his mom. He had only made her laugh once that he could remember.

His brother, Bubba, had been able to make her laugh all the time. Everything Bubba did seemed funny to her. Alfie remembered how she had laughed the time Bubba sat Dexter Wilkins on the water fountain at school and turned on the water. She had laughed at that until tears ran down her cheeks.

'You mean Dexter Wilkins whose dad owns Wilkins Hardware? I knew him in high school.'

'Yeah, and he had on a pair of new pants.'

'What kind?'

'Green double-knit.'

At that, his mom had leaned back on the sofa, holding her sides, laughing as if she would never stop. Even the fact that she had to go to the principal's office with Bubba the next day had not dimmed her enjoyment. In the principal's office she burst into laughter again – she had not meant to – she just couldn't help it. Every time the principal mentioned water fountain or Dexter Wilkins or green double-knit pants, she had laughed. She had tried to pretend she was coughing – she told them this when she got home – but she couldn't, and in the end the principal got disgusted and dismissed them both. Before they left the building, his mom made Bubba show her the water fountain.

Alfie ruled his paper into five squares. He drew the lines carefully because he had to save paper. A man at Logan's Printers and Binders had given him a box of old paper, and it was already half gone. Some of the sheets had printing on one side or smudges or letterheads, but Alfie had learned to use whatever he had. Before he discovered this friend at Logan's Printers and Binders, he had been so desperate for paper that he had torn the front and back pages out of all his school books.

The drawing went well. In the first square the girl looked as if she were really painting her finger-nails. Then he skipped to the last square. He wanted to draw that one while it was still clear in his mind.

'Alfie?' his mother called from downstairs.

He jerked, making a line across his paper. Carefully he erased it and blew away the scraps of eraser. 'What?' he called back.

'Are you *still* studying?'

'Yes.'

'Well, come on down and keep Pap and me company.'

'I will in a minute.' He bent back over his work. His pale straight hair fell over his forehead.

He sketched in the giant, looked at what he had drawn, and erased it. The card-table wobbled every time he erased. He wiped the scraps away. He tried again, erased that. He grimaced as he regarded his work. His mother had broken his concentration.

He twirled the pencil, baton-like, in his fingers. His thin fingers handled the pencil skilfully, and he began to draw again. He sketched lightly this time.

'*Alfie!*'

'In a *minute*.'

'Right *now*.'

Suddenly the light went out in the attic. Alfie knew what had happened. His mother had pulled the extension cord out of the wall below.

'*Mom!*' he protested.

'Well, I want you to come down here,' she said.

'Mom, plug my light back in.'

Silence.

Alfie sat in the dark. A patch of light slanted up from the living-room. 'Mom, plug my light back in,' he said in a sterner voice. He sounded like Alma. 'You want me to fail Science?'

'I'll give you' – she paused – 'five more minutes – no, I'll give you till the next commercial.' His mom didn't have a watch. She told time by television.

'Ten minutes,' he bargained.

Silence.

He waited in the darkness. 'All right,' he sighed, 'till the next commercial.'

The light went on, and Alfie began to draw with renewed intensity. But he was in a hurry now, trying to finish before the next commercial. And when he tried too hard, he never did anything right.

He drew the giant's face. It looked distorted. The giant's nose looked like a three-leaf clover. He erased it. The last square was getting a grey, used look. 'I'll have to do this whole thing over,' he muttered.

Below he heard the strains of a Diet Pepsi commercial. Abruptly his mom turned the volume up so he couldn't miss it. The lights in the attic went off and on, off and on.

'I'm *coming*,' he said.

He turned his paper face down on the table. He got up.

To lift his spirits he held 'Super Bird' to the light and looked at it one more time. Then he glanced up at the ceiling where his drawings hung. He began to climb down the ladder.

'Well, it's about time,' his mother said. She turned down the television. 'And I hope you're going to be better company than Pap.' She crossed to the overstuffed sofa and sat.

Pap was sitting in a straight-backed chair. He looked and was unhappy. He had not been able to discuss politics with the Governor because the Governor's wife, Bena, had a sinus headache. He sighed with discontent and indigestion.

He said, 'TV's not as good as radio used to be.'

Alfie sat down on the sofa by his mom. The springs were broken, and Alfie got the bad cushion. He sank deep. He didn't glance at his grandfather, because he knew what was coming and he didn't want to encourage it by appearing interested.

Pap said, 'I was on the radio one time. Did I ever tell you about it?'

'Only one hundred and fifty thousand times,' Alfie's mother snapped.

Pap went on as if she had not spoken. 'It was the *Major Bowes Amateur Hour*. I did eleven bird-calls and ended up whistling "Listen to the Mocking-bird". I got more applause than anybody.'

'Why didn't you win then?' Alfie asked in spite of himself.

'Because a little girl that looked like Shirley Temple did a toe-tap to "God Bless America".'

'Oh.'

'Her relatives sent in more than two thousand cards and letters. If it hadn't been for her, I would have won, either me or the boy that played "Lady of Spain" on the accordion.'

Alfie glanced at his grandfather, then back at the television. That was the story of his family's life, he thought. Almost. Almost winning the *Amateur Hour*. Bubba almost getting a football scholarship to WVU. His mom almost getting the job at Moore's Jewellery Store. Alfie wanted to be different. He wanted to be more than almost.

'Let me see if I can still remember some of my bird-calls,' Pap said thoughtfully.

'Oh, Pap, not tonight,' Alfie's mother moaned. 'If I have to hear the purple-breasted sapsucker, I'll start screaming.'

'All right, then, which one *do* you want to hear?'

'None of them. I'm trying to watch Dr Welby, all right?'

'How about the bobolink? That was always your favourite when you was a girl.'

'How about the loon? At least that would be appropriate,' she said.

'Well, here's the bobolink for anyone who wants to listen.'

'Pap, have mercy! You know whistling sets my teeth on edge.' She put her hands over her ears, but carefully so as not to disturb her hairdo.

Unconcerned, Pap whistled the bobolink call. He ended, paused, and said, 'Wait a minute, let me try that again. I'm getting rusty – haven't done my calls in a good while.'

'In a good while! Pap, you did them last night! We sat right in this room and had our television disrupted for forty-five minutes while you whistled your head off. Isn't that right, Alfie?' She patted her hair. It was a new shade – golden wheat – and she was proud of it.

'Yes.'

'Well, let me do just one more to make sure I remember. How about the whippoorwill?'

'*Pap!*'

As the call of the whippoorwill filled the small crooked room, Alfie's mom got up and crossed to the television. She turned the volume up loud. Then she came back and flopped angrily on the sofa. The springs protested.

Alfie sat between the two noises – the television and the bird-calls. He closed his eyes. In his mind he went over the drawing of the giant. Suddenly he knew what he had done wrong – he had tried to show too much of the giant. Just the head would be enough, with the ring held right at the front of the picture.

He smiled to himself. Tomorrow . . .

3

'HEY, Lizabeth!' Tree Parker yelled. 'Take my picture. Take a picture of me and Alfie.'

Alfie said, 'Oh, come on, Tree, will you? I've got to get home. I've got to study.' It was after school, and Alfie was eager to get to his drawing.

'Well, can't you wait just one minute? I want Lizabeth to take our picture. Oh, Liz-a-beth!'

Alfie and Tree were standing on the sidewalk in front of Elizabeth Elner's house. Elizabeth was posing her cat on the front steps. The cat had on a doll's hat and sweater. Elizabeth was spending a lot of time getting the angle of the hat just right. She ignored Alfie and Tree.

'All right, Lizabeth, we're going to leave,' Tree warned. 'This is your last chance to take our pictures.' Tree loved to have his picture taken. The people he envied most in the world were the people at football games who managed to jump up in front of the TV camera and wave.

Elizabeth stepped back and took a long critical look at the cat. 'Now, don't you move,' she warned. She looked through the lens of the camera and got the cat in focus.

'Watch this,' Tree whispered to Alfie. He began sneaking up the front path.

Tree had got his nickname in second grade when he had taken the part of a weeping willow in an ecology play. Not until the class saw him standing there, wrapped in brown paper, artificial leaves in his hair, did they realize how much like a tree he was. Now no one – not even the teacher – called him anything else.

Slowly, his long arms and legs angling out, glancing back to see if Alfie was watching, Tree moved closer to Elizabeth and the cat.

Apparently unaware, Elizabeth said, 'Because if this picture comes out, I'm going to enter it in the Purina cat contest.'

Tree slipped closer to the steps. Then just as Elizabeth was ready to snap the picture, he jumped forward, arms out, and said, 'Scat!' He was like a bundle of sticks in motion.

The startled cat jumped to the sidewalk and disappeared in the bushes.

Elizabeth spun around. Her face was red. 'Now look

what you've done, Tree. If that cat snags my sister's good doll's sweater, you're going to get it.'

'Oh, am I scared,' Tree said. His limbs trembled.

'I mean it, Tree Parker.'

'Come on, Tree,' Alfie said. 'I've got to get home.'

Elizabeth advanced. 'If that cat comes back without his outfit – my sister only let me use it because I promised nothing would happen to it – and if he comes home without it, Tree . . .'

'What you going to do?'

'Let's go,' Alfie said.

'Well, I want to find out what she's going to do. What you going to do, Lizabeth?'

'Just wait and see.'

'Come on.' Alfie grabbed Tree by the sleeve and pulled him away. Reluctantly Tree began to walk down the sidewalk.

'I wouldn't let her take my picture now if she got down on her knees and begged,' he said. He spun around. 'You're not taking my picture now, Lizabeth,' he said.

'Then quit posing,' she called back.

'I wasn't posing! Alfie, you saw me. Was I posing?'

'No,' Alfie lied.

'Anyway, why didn't you help me? You never want to do anything any more.'

'She wasn't going to take your picture, Tree.'

'I know, but if you'd have helped, we could have got the camera away from her and taken pictures of each other and of her trying to get the camera away from us. It would have been fun. Listen, let's go back and I'll distract her while you grab the –'

'I've got to get home,' Alfie said.

'I know. You've got to *study*.' The way he said the word showed what he thought of studying. 'If you want my opinion you'd do better not to study so much. Look at me. I never study and I get all A's and B's.' He broke off and turned to Alfie smiling. 'Hey, did I ever tell you about Lizabeth in kindergarten?'

'Tell me while we walk.'

'You'll love this, Alfie. Her mom sends her to this special kindergarten, see, so she could get into first grade early – her birthday's in February. And in this kindergarten they have red day and yellow day and purple day and orange day and green day. And on red day, Alfie, you get red Kool-Aid and red stars for good work. On yellow days it's yellow Kool-Aid and yellow stars. So Lizabeth takes this test, see, to find out if she's ready for first grade, and the first question they ask is to name the days of the week. Lizabeth knows that. It's the one thing she's really sure of. "The days of the week," she says – you know how important her voice gets when she knows the answer – "The days of the week," she says, "are red, yellow, purple, orange and green!" That's why she flunked the test, Alfie, and ended up in our grade. That's why – Hey, let's double back and ask her what day it is. I'll say –'

'I gotta go, Tree. This is my corner.'

'Oh, all right. Come up later if you get through with your *studying*.'

They parted and Alfie walked towards his house. The house looked even stranger from a distance. A house made without a plan. Alfie liked the idea. Three men started building a house. 'You two start at those corners. I'll start over here.'

They'd begin. They'd hammer and saw and raise beams

and lay bricks, and when they finally met in the centre, they'd step back to admire their work. Their mouths would fall open in surprise. 'Hey, are we building the same house?'

'I'm working on the Mason house.'

'I'm on the Kovac job.'

'Well, I'm doing the new Pizza Hut.'

They'd consult their blueprints. 'No wonder it looks so weird,' they'd say, and leave, dragging their tools behind them. 'If that don't beat all.' It would make a nice animated cartoon, Alfie thought. Someday he'd do it.

He glanced down at his turned-in feet. His shoes were eating his socks as he walked.

He had once said he could make a cartoon about anything. Life was very close to cartoons, he had said, whether you liked it or not. That's why they were funny. Cartoons took life and sifted out the beauty, the sweetness, the fleeting moments of glory and left you as you really were.

He could do a cartoon about himself, he thought, about his turned-in feet. That was the stuff of cartoons, no beauty or sweetness, no moments of glory in turned-in feet.

In the first scene he'd be walking down the sidewalk with his turned-in feet and he'd meet a man with regular feet. The man would say, 'Turn those feet out, son.'

In the next scene he'd meet a woman. She'd say 'Better turn those feet out, sonny.'

In the next scene he'd meet a group of children. They'd yell, 'Hey, turn your feet out like us. Look at our feet. See how they turn out!'

In the last scene he'd meet a duck and a pigeon. They'd

say, 'Your feet look all right to us.' And the three of them would waddle off into the sunset.

He smiled.

He came to the front door of the house and paused before entering. The smile left his face because he was afraid he couldn't get to the attic before his mother caught him.

'What happened at school?' she'd ask, eyes shining. She loved gossip, even about people she'd never heard of.

'Nothing.'

'Oh, come on. *Something* must have happened.'

'No.'

'Come *on*. I've been sitting in this house with nothing but Pap and TV for company. What happened?' Sometimes she would make him tell her at least one thing before he could go to the attic. 'Well, we had a substitute teacher in World Studies.'

He opened the front door quietly. There was no one in the living-room, but he could hear the rattle of dishes in the kitchen. Quickly, silently he climbed the ladder and pushed open the trapdoor. The warm attic air felt good against his face. He thought of this door as an escape hatch, like the kind they had on a submarine.

Long ago, when his father was alive, he had felt like this about the junkyard. His father, starting from nothing, had built up a wrecking business. He called himself the Wreck King of West Virginia. His junkyard covered seven acres. On top of the concrete building where his father conducted business was a huge crown made of hub caps.

To Alfie, the junkyard had been as good as Disneyland. Car after car, some brand new, some rusted and old, an ocean of cars that would never move again. To crawl into those cars, to work controls, to sit and dream was as good as a ride on a roller-coaster.

Alfie especially liked the old Dodge sedan because every window in it was cracked and splintered, so that if you sat there when the sun shone through, it was as beautiful as being in church. And the Chrysler Imperial – its windows had a smoky distortion, so that, beyond, figures seemed to float through the junkyard like spirits through the cemetery.

His last memory of the junkyard still hurt him. It was the day the yard was sold at auction. Alfie had sat on a wrecked Ford pick-up truck, on the fender, where a dent made a perfect seat, and had watched the junkyard go to a man named Harvey Sweet. For a long time after that, Alfie had been as lost as a bird without a nest. Then he had found this attic.

Suddenly he heard his mother's voice in the kitchen. She was complaining to Pap. 'Oh, I wish Bubba was here, don't you, Pap?'

'What?'

'Don't you miss him?'

'Who?'

'Pap, put down that paper!' Alfie heard her crumple it. 'I'm talking about Bubba. Don't you miss Bubba?'

'No.'

'Don't you ever miss anything?' she asked in exasperation.

He took the question seriously. 'I miss the junkyard,' he said after a moment.

Slowly Alfie let the trapdoor close. He knew what Pap meant about missing the junkyard. It was possible to miss a place more than a person, if the place was where you felt at home. And Pap had been more at home sitting on an old Coca-Cola crate in the shade of the hub-cap crown than he had ever felt in his chair in front of the television.

He also understood why Pap did not miss Bubba. He himself was glad Bubba was gone – working at a gas station in Maidsville, married to a girl named Maureen. There was something about Bubba that overshadowed everyone, like the walnut tree in their old yard whose leaves were so thick nothing could grow beneath. Its shadow had been as black at noon as it was at midnight.

'Well, I do miss him,' his mother said loudly below. She had come into the living-room and was standing right below the trapdoor. 'Something was always happening when Bubba was here. It was like all the life and all the fun went into Bubba, and the other children, well . . .'

Alfie wished suddenly there was an easy way to close the ears. He could hear too much in the attic. You could shut your eyes, he thought, block out everything you didn't want to see, but the ears . . .

Alfie sat down quietly at his table. He did not turn on the lamp. A little light filtered in through the slits in the eaves, a soft dusty light in very old paintings.

'Oh, I'm going out,' his mother said below.

'Where to?'

'*Out!*'

'Well, if you're going to the beer hall, wait for me.'

'You got any money, Pap?' she sneered. 'They don't take food stamps.'

'They take Social Security money, don't they? The government ain't made a law about how we spend that, have they?'

Alfie heard the front door close. He reached out and

turned on the light. He looked up at his cartoons, his comic strips, his drawings.

With one hand he reached for a pencil, with the other a fresh sheet of paper. A slight smile came over his face. He was home.

4

ALFIE lay in his bed. He was staring up at the ceiling. He did not see the sheets of pale plywood or the dark nail heads, because in his mind he was looking beyond the ceiling into the attic.

Alfie squinted his eyes. He tried to imagine the house without ceilings, with only the rafters. He imagined his cartoons, Sellotaped, pinned, tacked to the underside of the roof, hanging down, enlivening the whole crooked house. He imagined people dropping by the house to look up at his drawings the way they went into the Sistine Chapel to see Michelangelo's.

Some day the attic would be famous. 'This is where he began his cartoons,' they'd say. There would be people filing through, climbing, one by one, up the ladder to the attic. There would be a souvenir stand where copies of his comic strips could be bought and machines where his cartoons could be viewed for a quarter.

He shifted and sighed. He was restless. He could not fall asleep. He knew this was because of the comic strip he had drawn after supper. He had been so pleased with it that he had taken it down to show his mother.

'What's this?' Squinting, she had turned it first one way

and then another, as if it were a modern painting.

'Like *that*,' he had said, putting it right. He looked over her shoulder with a pleased, expectant smile. It was the strip about his turned-in feet, and she would *have* to laugh at that. When he was little, she had laughed about his feet all the time and called him 'Duck' and 'Pigeon'. For the first time he had felt secure about pleasing her.

'What is this thing?'

'It's a comic strip. I drew it.'

She held it at a distance to see it better.

'It's about me,' he went on. 'Don't you see the feet?'

'What feet? Turn up the light, Pap.'

'It's up high as it can get,' Pap said. 'Forty watts is forty watts.'

She tried turning the strip of paper sideways.

'Never mind,' Alfie said angrily. He snatched it from her. The paper tore.

'I *want* to see your drawing,' she said, offering to take it again.

'Never *mind*.'

'Well, just 'cause I can't tell which way is up, that's no reason to get mad, is it, Pap?'

'Getting mad runs in our family,' Pap said, leaning back, getting ready to start a story. 'Did I ever tell you about the time Cousin Cooley and me –'

'Yes!'

'I've got to study,' Alfie said.

'Leave your drawing or your cartoon or whatever it is, honey, and I'll look at it in the morning.'

Holding the comic strip to his chest, he went quickly to the ladder.

'Well, the way it started was that Cousin Cooley had

got himself what he called an antique can opener, bought it off –'

'Pap!'

'– bought it off Jimmy Hammond at the hardware. Well, soon as I seen it, I knew that . . .'

Alfie slammed the trapdoor shut, and he sat in the attic until they were all in bed. He had heard the water in the basin as Alma washed her hair, the brushing of teeth, the flushing of the toilet, the dropping of hair pins, and then finally the snores.

He pushed aside his blanket. They were all snorers. Pap was the loudest. Alma was the quietest, with just a lady-like wheeze. He had told her that once as a compliment and she had erupted like a volcano. 'Don't you ever say I snore! I do not snore!' His mom snorted every once in a while as if she had thought of something funny.

Alfie closed his eyes. He suddenly found himself thinking, as he had earlier, of the one and only time he had made his mother laugh.

He and Tree had been coming down Elm Street one evening on their way home from the Fall Festival at school. Tree had been talking about the general sorriness of the booths. 'Did you go in the Haunted House, Alfie? It was in Mrs Lorensen's room.'

'No.'

'Well, some girl in a witch suit – I think it was Jenny DeCarlo – said, "And now you have to feel *eyeballs*", and I knew it was going to be grapes, but, Alfie, these grapes weren't even *peeled* –' He broke off abruptly. 'Hey, what's going on at the corner?'

Ahead they could see two people pushing a car down the street. Alfie and Tree edged closer, sensing the two people were not just trying to get the car started. Moving from the shelter of one tree to another, they got closer. When they were almost at the corner, Tree said, 'Hey, that's your brother! That's Bubba! What's he up to?'

Alfie ran forwards in his concern. 'What are you doing, Bubba?' He glanced over his shoulder at the deserted street behind him.

Bubba, smiling, turned to Alfie. The other boy was Goat McMillan.

'Is this your car, Goat?' Tree asked. He was standing apart, keeping himself separated from what might be trouble.

'No, it's not his car. Goat wouldn't have a car like this, would you, Goat?' Bubba said.

'Not if I could help it.'

'But whose car is it?' Alfie asked.

'It's Perry Fletcher's.' The sound of the name on Goat's lips caused Bubba to double over the fender with laughter.

'Who's he?'

Bubba and Goat were laughing too hard to answer. Alfie reached out and touched the sleeve of Bubba's football sweater. 'Who's Perry Fletcher?'

Bubba straightened. 'Perry Fletcher's this boy, see, and all he can do is talk about his car and his boat and his stereo and how wonderful everything he owns is. So me and Goat see Perry Fletcher park his car in front of Maria Martini's house and go inside. We know the car's brand new, see. We know this is the first time he ever drove it.'

'But why are you pushing it down the street?' Alfie asked in a worried way.

'Because we're going to hide it in somebody's driveway,' Goat explained.

'Yeah, and then we're going back to sit on Goat's porch, see, and watch Perry Fletcher come out and find his new car gone.'

Goat broke in with, 'If I know him, he'll call the fuzz first thing. "Officer, Officer, come at once. I've been robbed!"'

'Hey – hey –' Bubba was laughing so hard he could barely speak. 'Hey, let's hide it in *Big Bertha's* driveway!' Big Bertha was their algebra teacher.

'I don't think you ought to be doing this,' Alfie said. Again he glanced up and down the deserted street.

'Yeah, we'll put it in Big Bertha's driveway,' Goat said. 'Hey, this is better than Friday.' He turned to Alfie and Tree. 'See, last Friday we let the brakes off Ted Copple's Buick and pushed it into a tow-away zone because Ted Copple wouldn't let me copy his maths, and then we went in a phone booth and called the police and pretended to be irate citizens – Morrie Hutchinson was the irate citizen – and he demanded that the police do something about illegal parking in front of the high school. Ten minutes later Brant's tow truck arrived. It made my day.'

'I gotta go,' Tree said.

'Me too,' Alfie said. They turned together and began running up Elm Street.

'Wait, you can help us,' Bubba called.

'Yeah, Alfie, we may need help getting up Big Bertha's driveway!'

At the top of the hill Alfie and Tree separated without a word. Alfie cut through the park. The swings were moving slightly in the wind from the river. He ran around them. He stumbled over his feet and fell.

On his knees in the dust by the swings he remembered that

when Bubba had played in this park, he could swing higher than anybody. And at the peak of his swing he could slide off the seat, easy as grease, fall through the air and land, cat-like, on his feet. Another boy who tried it landed so hard in a stoop that he had bitten a piece out of his knee.

Alfie got to his feet. Running again, he left the park and ran through the Lanley's yard. A dog barked. He entered the apartment building where they lived at the time.

He looked so wild as he entered that his mother asked him what was wrong. Gasping for breath, he broke into the story of Bubba and Perry Fletcher's car.

Half-way through the story he faltered. He realized his mom would be furious with Bubba. She would probably throw on her coat and go looking for him. Bubba would never forgive him.

Instead he saw that his mother was beginning to laugh. He hesitated, puzzled.

'But, Mom, this could be car theft.'

'Not if he doesn't get in the car,' she said. 'Anyway, go on.' She reached forward and turned off *I Love Lucy* so she could get a real laugh. 'Now, start from the beginning and tell me every detail.' Her eyes were shining. 'Don't leave out a thing.'

He told it again, slower, standing as rigid as if he were in front of his class giving a report.

She laughed so hard at this second telling that she had to have a tissue. When she dried her eyes, calm at last, she said, 'Do me a favour.'

'All right.'

'Don't let Bubba know you told me.'

'All right.'

'I want to hear him tell it too. Can't you just imagine

them sitting on Goat's porch? Can't you just imagine the expression on Perry Fletcher's face when he – Hey, get me Bubba's annual. I want to see what he looks like.' The picture of Perry Fletcher in the annual set her laughing again. 'I *knew* he'd look like that. He's the only boy on this page who's got a tie on.'

Alfie shifted in his bed again. On the ceiling the lights of a car passing on the street below reflected, moved, disappeared. In the next room his mother snorted in her sleep.

Maybe he could do a cartoon about it, Alfie thought. That was what artists were supposed to do – turn life's painful experiences into art.

He imagined two boys pushing a car down the street. It was too real. He imagined an old man and a woman pushing a funny-looking car down the road. That was better. They would be hot and sweaty. The old woman's hair would be flying out from her head. The old man's shirt-sleeves would be rolled up. The old woman would be snapping at the man. 'Sure you invented the car! I want to know when you're going to invent the *engine!*'

Maybe his mother would laugh at that, but he didn't think so. Planning a better cartoon, he fell asleep.

5

AT his school desk Alfie was drawing a comic strip about a dog. The rest of the class was working on maths problems.

Alfie had had the idea for his strip that morning during breakfast. Alma was talking about an article she'd read. 'It said you shouldn't buy this kind of cereal, Mom.'

'Why not?'

'Because it's got additives in it. Look on the box – artificial colouring, artificial flavouring – just read what we're eating.'

Pap said, 'It's better than hot dogs. There's rat hairs in them.'

'Not at the table, please, Pap,' Alfie's mother said.

'And where there's rat hairs, there's probably rat –'

'Pap!'

'– droppings.'

'*Pap!*'

'Let *me* buy the cereal from now on, all right, Mom?' Alma said, getting up from the table.

Alfie was dipping his spoon into his soggy cereal, thinking up a comic strip about artificial flavouring.

'Alfie, are you going to sit there all morning or are you going to school?' his mom said finally.

'Don't bother me right now.'

'Well, you're lucky to have somewhere to go, isn't he, Pap? Don't you wish you could go to school?'

'No.'

Now Alfie had finished his comic strip. He had intended that as soon as he finished, he would begin work on his Maths problems, but now he sat admiring his work. His Maths was forgotten.

In the first square a large dog was reading the label on a can of dog food. 'Artificial flavouring.'

In the second square the dog was reading the label on a box of dog biscuits. 'Artificial colouring.'

In the third square the dog was reading the label on a dog collar. 'Artificial fibres.'

In the fourth square he was howling, 'Is everything artificial these days?'

In the last square a little sign comes up from the dog's fur. 'Fleas are still real!'

Alfie was very pleased with it. He wanted to take it up immediately and show it to his teacher, but she would know he had done it during Maths.

'All right,' the teacher said, 'time's up. Change papers with your partners and we'll check our work.'

Alfie looked up, startled. He glanced at Tree. Dutifully Tree was holding out his paper to Alfie. 'Go easy,' he said. He waited a minute with his hand outstretched and then he said, 'Come on. Give me your paper.' He snapped his fingers with impatience.

'I didn't do mine,' Alfie whispered back, hiding his comic strip under his notebook.

'Why not?'

'I just didn't.'

'But then I don't have anything to check!' Tree complained. He was upset. He loved to grade papers. It gave him a feeling of power. Grading papers made him want to become a teacher when he grew up.

'What's wrong back there, Tree?' Mrs Steinhart asked.

'Nothing.'

'Alfie? Anything wrong?'

'No.'

'All right then, we'll go over the first problem.' Mrs Steinhart began to put the problem on the board. All the class bent over their papers.

Tree leaned forward too, hunched miserably over his bare desk. He shot Alfie a resentful look. Alfie did not glance at him. He was going over Tree's first problem.

Tree punched Alfie to get his attention. Then he acted out the difficulty of grading an invisible paper.

'Tree?' Mrs Steinhart called.

He looked up.

'Is anything wrong?'

'What could be wrong, Mrs Steinhart?' This was what he always said when something was wrong that he was not free to discuss. He had got this from his sister, who had got it from soap operas.

'Whose paper are you grading?'

Tree looked down at his bare desk, the pencil in his hand. He sighed. 'Alfie's.'

'Bring it up here, please.'

Tree's mouth fell open. He stared down at his desk. Finally he looked up at Mrs Steinhart. 'I can't find his paper, Mrs Steinhart, that's what we were muttering about.'

Alfie cleared his throat. 'The reason he can't find my paper, Mrs Steinhart, is because I didn't do it. My mind was on something else.'

'Oh.' There was a pause, and then Mrs Steinhart said, 'Well, then we'll continue without Alfie. Tree, give your paper to Maurice and you can grade Elizabeth's paper.'

Tree's face lit up with delight. 'Yes, *ma'am!*' He snatched his paper from Alfie and made the exchange. He took Elizabeth's paper with a flourish. 'Revenge,' he whispered happily. He pantomimed making big X's beside every one of her problems. 'Is she going to be sorry she didn't take our picture yesterday!'

Alfie sat without moving. He thought about going up to Mrs Steinhart after class and explaining why he didn't do his Maths, but he knew he didn't have a good enough reason. Not comic strips. She wouldn't buy that. Maybe he could say he had an attack of something. He sat silent and miserable.

Tree punched him. 'She missed number three,' he whispered, his voice rising with delight, 'subtracted instead of added.' He bent over Elizabeth's paper again, pencil poised for action. He began to whistle through his teeth. Alfie slumped lower in his desk.

Beside him Tree straightened abruptly. His hand shot into the air. 'Oh, Mrs Steinhart,' he called, 'is that a two or a three on the second line?'

'It's a three.' She went over the number with her chalk.

'That's what I was afraid of!' Tree said, singing the words in his joy. He made an elaborate X beside the problem. To Alfie he hissed, 'She's missed two out of five. Bet she's really sorry she didn't take our picture!'

Alfie nodded by lowering his head. He lifted his notebook and glanced at his comic strip of the dog. He pulled it into view. It made him happy when one of his cartoons came out just right, but now he didn't smile.

Tree's long arm was waving in the air again. 'Oh, Mrs Steinhart?'

She sighed. 'Yes, Tree.'

'How many can you miss and still pass?'

'This isn't a test, Tree.'

'I know, but if it *was* a test?'

'Well, there are ten problems. Everyone should get at least seven, though I would like to see everyone have a perfect paper.'

'Too late for *everyone* to get a perfect paper, Mrs

Steinhart,' Tree said cheerfully. Tree nudged Alfie. 'If she misses one more she's —' He made a down gesture with his thumb.

Alfie nodded without enthusiasm. He took his comic strip and slipped it carefully in the back of his notebook in a pocket for special papers. When he got home he would put it up on the rafters in the attic. It deserved a place of honour, he thought, even though it couldn't cheer him up now.

Also in the pocket was a comic strip he had done the day before during English. He pulled it out and looked at it. 'Super Giant.'

In the first square the giant was destroying a forest, ripping trees from the earth, crying, 'I love violence.'

In the second square the giant was destroying a village. 'I *love* violence!'

In the third square the giant was destroying a farm. '*I love violence!*'

In the last square the giant was flattened on the ground, being attacked by the villagers, the farm people, and the forest animals. He was saying, 'It's things like this that take the fun out of violence.'

The strip hadn't come out the way Alfie had wanted it to, and although he had spent most of English and Science trying to correct it, he had not succeeded. He saw now that he had failed because he had tried to put too much into each square. Perhaps if he . . .

Beside him Tree was desperately going over Elizabeth's paper one more time.

'Give me my paper, Tree,' Elizabeth said. She tried to snatch it from him.

'In a minute, in a minute.' He waved her away with his

long arms. 'I just want to make sure there aren't any more mistakes.'

'Tree, give me my paper. Mrs Steinhart, Tree won't give me my paper.'

'Tree.'

'I'm just trying to be thorough, Mrs Steinhart, like you taught us. I know there's another mistake here. I just can't find it.'

Elizabeth snatched her paper from him. 'I'm rechecking this whole thing, Tree, and you better not have made any mistakes either.'

'Me? Make mistakes?' Tree said. He looked as lofty as if he were in the forest, glancing down at a mere sapling. He took his own paper from Maurice. He fell silent.

'By the way, how many did *you* miss, Tree?' Elizabeth asked scornfully.

Tree didn't answer.

'All right, class,' Mrs Steinhart said, 'pass the papers to the front of the room, and, Alfie, I want to see you after school for a few minutes.'

Alfie closed his notebook. He shook his hair out of his eyes. 'Yes'm,' he said.

6

'WHAT'D she want?' Tree asked. He had been waiting for Alfie. He was leaning against the lone schoolground tree, his foot propped on a root. He seemed part of the landscape.

'Nothing,' Alfie said.

A line of boys and girls were waiting to board the school bus. One of the boys called, 'What'd she do to you, Alfie?'

'Nothing.' He kept walking. All the grass had been worn off the schoolyard, and the dirt was packed as hard as concrete.

Tree fell into step with Alfie. 'What *did* she want?'

'If you *must* know –'

'I must.'

'– she wanted to tell me I'm flunking Maths.'

'That's supposed to be news?'

'Also she wants a conference with my mom.'

'She must not know your mom.'

Alfie kept walking, watching his feet.

'Nothing against your mom,' Tree went on. 'I just can't imagine anybody wanting to have a conference with her.'

Alfie said nothing. He had made a terrible mistake in his talk with Mrs Steinhart, one he regretted deeply. In the middle of the talk, he had abruptly decided to take her into his confidence and show her his comic strip about the dog. This had been for two reasons. First, he really liked Mrs Steinhart, and, second, he did not want her to think he was just goofing off during Maths.

'Wait a minute,' he had said.

He had hurried back to his desk and got his notebook. He had carried it to her, opened it, and carefully pulled out the comic strip. He had laid it before her like a fabric salesman.

'What's this, Alfie?' She put on her glasses.

'It's a comic strip, Mrs Steinhart. I drew it myself.'

'This is what you were doing instead of your Maths problems?' she asked.

'Yes.'

She looked at the strip. Alfie watched to see if a smile would come over her face. It did, but it was too faint to count. When she looked at Alfie the smile was gone. 'You like to draw, don't you, Alfie, cartoons and things?'

'Yes.'

'But –' She got even more serious. She took off her glasses. 'But don't you think, Alfie, that there are times to draw – we do have Art, you know.'

'I know,' he said quickly. The week before they had cut out and coloured Indian symbols. School Art was as different from cartoons as Science was from recess.

Mrs Steinhart was still talking. 'And then there are times for Maths and for English and for Science.' She made it sound as exact as sorting mail.

He picked up his drawing and slid it back in the pocket of his notebook. 'Yes.'

'Your cartoon is really very good, and I think there's a lot of humour in it.'

'Thank you.'

'And you've made a good point about the way we live today. There *are* too many artificial things. I myself have started reading the labels on everything I buy.'

'Thank you.'

'Only you're going to have to do your cartoons after class.'

'I know.'

'I don't want to see you drawing again.'

'You won't.'

'Good.' She smiled at him, a big smile now, the one he had wanted to see earlier when she had first looked at his comic strip. 'You're a smart boy, Alfie, and I want you to do as well as I know you can.'

139

'That's what I want too.' He paused. 'Can I go now?'

He had stumbled over his feet as he left the room. All the time he had been drawing his cartoons, he had secretly felt that they were touched with genius. He had known that if he had shared them with other people, they would have been as delighted as he. Now he *had* shown them – to his mother, Pap, Mrs Steinhart – and nothing had happened.

Beside him Tree was talking about a conference he had had with Mrs Allen in first grade. 'I didn't know what I was doing, Alfie. I loved to make letters, see, but they didn't have any meaning for me. Little *b* and little *d* were my favourites, but even they were just circles leaning against sticks.

'Anyhow, the way Mrs Allen found out I was copying off other people – you'll love this, Alfie – was because I'd *copy their names too*! I didn't know it was their names. It was all just a bunch of circles and sticks to me but –'

Suddenly Alfie stopped. He said, 'I've got to go back. I left my notebook on Mrs Steinhart's desk.' He didn't know how he could have done such a thing.

'Aw, you can get it tomorrow,' Tree said. 'Anyway if you go back in there, she'll say, "Oh, I'm glad you're back because there are a few more points I'd like to make about your conduct." '

'I've got to go back.'

'I'll lend you some paper if that's –'

'I've got to have my notebook!'

Tree stopped and looked at him in disgust. 'What've you got to have – your *pictures*?' He made a scornful sound as he said the word *pictures*.

'What?' Alfie stopped walking.

'Your *pictures*. Those things you draw all the time. What are those things anyway?'

'I don't draw.'

'I see you. Today you were drawing a dog. Yesterday it was a giant. Last week it was an octopus.'

Alfie stood without moving. He felt sick. He didn't know anyone had been watching him. He said angrily, 'I was not drawing a giant.'

'I saw you! Look, this is me, Tree. I can see everybody in the class.'

'You didn't see me drawing a giant!'

'Well, all right,' Tree said, bending. 'Maybe it was a picture of a huge enormous man.'

Alfie said nothing.

'Which, I may point out, *is* a giant.'

Alfie stared up at Tree. There was a hard moment between them. They had been friends since second grade, and yet the friendship had suddenly gone sour. They seemed to move apart, even though no footwork was involved.

'And today,' Tree went on in the same loud tone, 'I guess you weren't drawing a picture of a dog.'

Alfie said nothing.

'So, all right, maybe it was a picture of a *canine*.'

Alfie said nothing.

'Which, I may point out, *is* a dog!'

Without a word Alfie turned and started for home. When he got to the corner, Tree relented and called to him. 'Oh, come on, Alfie, I'll go back with you to get your notebook.'

Alfie kept walking.

'I was trying to keep you from going back for *your* sake.

One conference a day is enough. Listen, I was thinking of
you!'

Alfie did not turn around. He kept walking at the same
pace like a robot. There was a silence. Alfie was almost to
the next block when Tree called, 'All right, be that way!'

7

ALFIE walked slowly up the front path to his house. He
stopped at the steps because he could hear his mother and
Pap arguing in the living-room. He knew there was no way
he could get to the attic without being drawn into the
fight.

'Well, I'll tell you what you can do,' Pap was saying in a
hurt, angry voice, 'just get rid of me. That's what you're
driving at. Send me to the poor-house!'

'They don't have the poor-house any more and you
know it.'

'The government's even took that away from us,' Pap
said. He was mournful now.

Alfie stood with his toes touching the bottom step. He
looked down at his turned-in feet.

'Well, then send me to the Nursing Home for Christian
Gentlemen,' Pap said.

'Whoo, you think they'd have you?' his mom snapped.
'You do not *quite* qualify. Besides, that place costs over two
hundred dollars a month.'

'Well, what do you want me to do then – just
disappear? Want me to go off like some tired elephant to
the burial ground and –'

'Pap, don't start in on the old-elephant routine now. I just can't take it.' His mother's voice changed abruptly. 'All I want you to do,' she went on slowly, 'is help me.' She was wheedling now, trying to get Pap in a good mood.

'I ain't cutting no hole in no wall.'

'Aw, Pap.'

Alfie sat down on the steps. He looked at the ground.

All the other houses they had lived in had had bushes by the door, hiding places. On Tenth Street there had been a regular tunnel behind the shrubbery. Alfie could duck through the low branches at the front door and come out by the back door without anybody seeing him. He missed that now. He would have liked some place to crawl into, a place to wait out the storm.

His mother was saying, 'You just don't know how important this is to me, Pap.' Her voice sounded louder. Alfie imagined that she was close to the window now, perhaps ready to look out and see him sitting there. 'Well, here's Alfie,' she'd cry. 'We'll let him decide.' She loved to have a referee.

Alfie got up quickly and ran down the dirt path to the street. He hesitated a moment and then turned towards town. He had no plan, but as he walked it occurred to him that this would be a good time to check with Logan's Printers and Binders to see if they had any more scrap paper for him.

The thought made the air feel suddenly fresh and good again. He breathed deeply. His shoulders relaxed. A box of new paper, all different sizes and kinds, some sheets thin enough to trace through, others thick as cardboard – that was all he needed to bring back his good feeling. He imagined himself in the attic, sorting out the paper, putting it into piles, cutting off the letterheads and smudges. He began to walk faster. He remembered that the man had promised to save all the scrap paper for him. By now there was probably a mountain of it. He imagined himself falling into the mountain of paper the way farm people fell into haystacks. He –

'Hey, Alfie, where are you going?'

He turned and saw Alma coming down Grant Street. She had a bag of groceries in one arm and a carton of Cokes in the other. Her long hair was tied back with a scarf.

'I've got to go downtown,' he called back. He wished he had thought to borrow a wagon from the little boy next door. He would probably need a *truck* to carry all the paper they'd saved for him.

'Did you hear the wonderful news?' she called.

Alfie could tell from the way she said the word *wonderful* that the news was very bad indeed.

'What's happened?' He waited, toes touching, while she walked towards him. She set down the Cokes and shifted her bag of groceries to the other arm.

'Bubba's coming home.'

'What?' He leaned forward a little.

'Bubba,' she repeated slowly, 'our *wonderful* brother, and Maureen, his *wonderful* wife, are coming to live with us.'

'But that couldn't be,' he sputtered. His words went too fast, like a speeded-up tape-recorder. 'Why would they be coming to live with us? They've got an apartment in Maidsville. Bubba's job is there. He –'

'He got fired.'

'But how could that happen? What's going on? I thought the man at the gas station really liked Bubba.

That's what Mom said. She said the man wanted Bubba to be like a son to him. She said he was going let Bubba buy into the station. She said Bubba might even inherit the station when the man died.'

'Bubba took one of the cars at the gas station – borrowed it, he said – because he had to drive over and pick up Maureen at the doctor's office. She's going to have a baby, by the way. That's another *wonderful* surprise. And coming back to the station in this *borrowed* car, he ran a stop-light and hit a police car broadside.'

'A police car?'

'Yeah, trust Bubba to go for the spectacular.'

'But if he borrowed the car . . .'

'Borrowing without asking, Alfie, is stealing.'

'But how could he do such a thing?'

'With Bubba it just comes naturally.' She sighed. She shifted the groceries again as if they were getting heavier. 'Anyway, they're going to live with us until Bubba can find another job, which is not going to be easy. It took him seven months – if you recall – to get the job in Maidsville, and it was only because of Maureen's dad that he got that.'

'But if he hit a police car, maybe they'll arrest him,' Alfie said, speaking in a rush. 'After all, a crime against a policeman is supposed to be worse than anything.'

Alma shook her head. 'All he's charged with is ignoring a stop-light and reckless driving.'

'But he stole the car from the station, didn't he? That's a crime.'

'The owner of the station is covering that up because he doesn't want the bad publicity. He says that if Bubba pays for the damage – though what Bubba's going to pay for it *with*, nobody has said.' She gave Alfie a hard look. 'If you've got any money, hide it.'

'I haven't.'

Alma looked past Alfie to the river, where some coal barges were moving slowly. 'We're never going to be free of Bubba,' she said in a low voice.

Alfie turned and looked at the barges too. He felt close to Alma for the first time in years. It was like on the *Titanic*, he thought, or the *Hindenburg*, where perfect strangers suddenly became best friends. Mutual tragedy did bring people closer together. He reached out to take her groceries.

'Well, I've got to get home,' she said, moving away before he could do it.

Suddenly Alfie's mind turned to the crooked house – the two bedrooms, the living-room, the bathroom, the kitchen. That's all there was, he thought. The sofa in the living-room didn't even make into a bed.

'But where are they going to sleep?' Alfie asked, following her. He went over the sleeping arrangements. He and Pap shared one bedroom, Alma and his mother, the other. There was no room for Bubba and Maureen. His hopes rose. 'There's nowhere for them to sleep!'

'Mom's going to fix up the attic.'

For a moment he felt as if he had been hit over the head with a hammer. He was paralysed.

'The attic?' he muttered.

'Yeah, she's got it all planned. She's getting a window from Mr Wilkins, and she's talking Pap into cutting a hole in the eaves and installing it. Then she's getting a double bed from Hill's Used Furniture and *my* dressing table and –'

'But the attic belongs to me.' He stammered for the first

time since he was three. His knees felt weak. In his mind the attic wavered like a desert mirage.

He had once watched an old apartment building on High Street being demolished. A huge ball had pounded into the walls, and they had crumbled. As the dust settled, Alfie could see pieces of people's lives shimmering in the air – the old faded wallpapers they had chosen, the linoleum they had walked on. An old curtain had flapped from a third-storey window. Finally everything had sunk into a mound of dust. His attic crumbled now in the same way, his cartoons fluttering down through the dusty air like autumn leaves.

'The attic *used* to be yours,' Alma corrected.

'No, it's *mine*.'

'As soon as I get home with the cleaning stuff, Mom's going to start on it, and tomorrow – if she can talk Pap into it – the window will be installed, and by noon it'll be Bubba's bedroom.'

'Mom wouldn't do that to me.'

'Alfie, Mom would do anything for Bubba. Haven't you learned that by now?'

'It's *my* attic.'

'Nothing has ever been yours and mine, Alfie, not since the day we were born, not if Bubba wanted it. Do you remember the time Mom took my baby-sitting money to pay Bubba's fine? Well, you probably don't remember because it was two years ago, but I'll never forget it. I was saving my money so I could go to Florida with the band, and my bank was almost full. I was so proud. And then I came in one night and put on the light and started over to put my baby-sitting money in the bank – remember I had a great big bank shaped like a globe? And I saw that it had been broken open. Pieces were all over the floor. I stopped. I couldn't move. I thought a burglar had done it. I was getting ready to go next door and call the police. And then I saw Pap standing in the doorway, and he said, "Your ma had to have some money for Bubba. He's in trouble with the police." '

'Well, I just stood there. I couldn't move. I could see Mom's shoe by the bank – she had cracked it open with the heel. And all of a sudden I went over and I took that shoe and I beat the rest of my bank until it was dust. Everything was dust. The Atlantic Ocean, the Pacific, Russia, Africa, the Fiji Islands.' She gave a sad laugh. 'I guess I would still be there beating the world to dust if Pap hadn't stopped me.

'Do you remember now? I think you cleaned up for me. And you have to remember me crying. I cried so hard Pap wanted to take me to the University Hospital. He thought I was cracking up.' She sighed. 'I guess I *was* cracking up in a way because, Alfie, that really was the world to me in those days.'

'They're not taking my attic.' His face looked so pale and strained that Alma shifted her groceries to reach out and touch him.

'Hey, it's not the end of the world,' she said. 'It wasn't for me. I admit it took a long time to get over it. I still feel bad about it sometimes but –'

'They're not going to take my attic.'

She shook his shoulder gently. 'Hey, look, it's –'

He glanced at her without seeing her. 'Nobody's going to take my attic.' Twisting away from her hand he turned and began to run for home.

'Wait, Alfie,' Alma called. 'Wait!' Clutching the groceries, she hurried after him.

8

As he ran past the Hunters' house, his mother stuck her head out the door and called to him. 'Alfie!' He didn't look at her. 'Alfie, stop. Wait a minute! I've got some wonderful news.'

Alfie kept running. He took the steps in one bound, went down on his knees, got up, lunged for the screen door, pulled himself up by the knob, and entered. It was all one long awkward motion.

His mother started after him and called back to Mrs Hunter, 'I'll send Alfie and Pap over for the chest of drawers after supper.' She paused to adjust her thong sandal. 'And Bubba and Maureen will take real good care of it.'

Alfie plunged across the living-room. He grabbed the ladder as a man being swept away in a flood grabs for a tree. He swayed in the current.

Pap loomed up in the kitchen doorway, filling it. He held a coffee mug in one hand, a jelly doughnut in the other. 'Did you hear the news?' He paused to lick some jelly from the side of his thumb.

Alfie started up the ladder. He felt the pull of gravity for the first time in his life. His feet were lead. His pants were nailed to the floor. He would never reach the attic.

'Bubba's coming home,' Pap said.

Alfie struggled for the next rung of the ladder. He swayed with the unseen current. He struck his head on

149

the wall.

'Bubba *and* Maureen.'

Alfie reached up with one shaking hand. He pushed at the trapdoor. It was heavy. Usually it sprang open at his touch. Now it wouldn't budge. He went up another rung of the ladder. He put his head to it. Goat-like, he began to shove the door open.

'I don't mind him coming so much as I do her,' Pap said, sitting on the sofa. 'I don't know why Bubba had to marry a girl that pops gum all the time.' He licked his thumb again. 'And she'll leave it anywhere. One time I found a big wad of bubble gum in my tooth-glass. It scared me. I thought my teeth had shrivelled.'

Heaving as if he had climbed a tall mountain instead of a ladder, Alfie pulled himself into the attic. He crawled forward. He let the trapdoor shut behind him. The slam was like a cannon firing, the first shot of a long and difficult war.

'Alfie!'

He lay stretched out on the dusty attic floor, completely spent. Faintly he heard his mother call him as she came in the front door.

'Alfie, don't go up in the attic. I want to talk to you. I've got some great news.'

'I done told him the great news,' Pap said from the sofa.

'And guess what, Pap? Mrs Hunter's got a chest she's going to let me use. She just covered it with contact paper – red and orange pansies – and it's going to really brighten up the attic. I'm getting so excited. Look at me, Pap. My hands are trembling.'

In the attic Alfie's hands were trembling too. He got slowly to his knees.

When he had first started doing his cartoons in the attic, he had worked out a way of locking the trapdoor so nobody could come up and catch him unaware. Now he took the board and slipped it over the trapdoor and under the floor-boards on either side.

'Alfie, what are you doing up there?' his mother called. 'Come on down. I want to talk to you.' She said to Pap, 'Is there any coffee left?' She went into the kitchen.

On his knees Alfie stared blankly at the trapdoor. The board was in place now. No one could open it.

He heard his mother walk back into the living-room. 'Alfie, do you hear me? Listen, Bubba and Maureen are coming home. They called this morning. It's going to be like old times around here. We're going to make a little apartment up there in the attic. Alfie?'

There was a pause while she blew on her coffee and took a loud sip. She raised her voice. 'Alfie, do you hear me? Now listen, you and Pap and Alma are going to have to help me or I'm not going to be able to get everything done.'

Alfie heard the front door open and shut. He heard Alma say, 'Where's Alfie?'

'He's up in the attic and I can't make him hear me. Did you get the 409 cleaner?'

'Yes, Mom, but Alfie –'

'Because that attic is going to need a real scrubbing. I know it is.'

'Mom –'

'And I'll need you to fix supper for me. I *know* you've got to go to work but –'

'Mom, will you listen to me for a minute?'

'Not now, Alma. Alfie, will you come down?'

'Mom, will you listen to me! Alfie is very upset about this. I just –'

'Upset about what?'

'About Bubba coming home and taking his attic.'

'*His* attic? Since when has it been *his* attic? I'm the one who pays the rent.'

'Mom, the attic has been his ever since we moved in here and he's got all his stuff up there and –'

'What stuff? I didn't see anything but an old card-table and a bunch of papers.'

'Well, those are his special things, Mom and –'

'All right. He can move them into the bedroom, can't he Pap?'

'Not in my half.'

'Well, we'll make space. Anyway, once he realizes Bubba's coming home – why, he worships his brother, Alma, he always has, and he'll have fun helping with the arrangements. He can paint the headboard for me and –'

'Mom, Alfie doesn't even *like* Bubba, much less worship him.'

'Alma, that's an awful thing to say.'

'It's the truth.'

'My half of the room ain't even got room for a postage stamp,' Pap said.

'Pap, will you shut up? And, Alma, if I wasn't so busy, I'd give you a good talking to. Alfie has looked up to Bubba all his life.'

'Mom, Alfie does not like Bubba. That is a fact. Here's another fact. I don't like him either.' Alma spoke very clearly, pronouncing each word separately so she could not be misunderstood.

There was a long pause. 'You still hold it against Bubba,

don't you?' his mother said finally in a low, flat voice.

'What exactly do you mean? I hold so many things against him, Mom, that I don't know which one you're talking about.'

'I'm talking about the time I used a tiny little bit of your precious baby-sitting money to –'

'I don't want to hear about that, Mom.'

'– a tiny little bit of your precious money to keep your brother out of trouble. I should have thought you would have been glad to help, but I see that you still begrudge him that money.'

'Mom, I said I don't want to talk about it.'

'It doesn't matter at all to you,' his mother went on, 'that Bubba was just having a little fun after the football game. He *won* the game for them that night, you know. It was *his* touchdown that won the game, and afterwards he deserved a little fun.'

'It wasn't a little fun,' Pap said. 'Giovanni don't call the police for a *little* fun.'

There was a silence. Alfie rose. His knees cracked as he got to his feet. He could hear his mother set her coffee cup heavily on the TV. He heard her sigh.

'All right,' she said in a cold, hurt voice, 'I will see that your precious money is paid back, Alma, every penny of it. I didn't know that you still *begrudged* . . .' She made begrudging sound like the worst thing a person could do.

Alma said nothing.

'Just don't bother me about it now and I will pay every single penny back!'

There was another longer silence. Alfie stared down at the barricaded trapdoor. There was no expression on his face. He felt strange now, as if he were looking through the wood, seeing the three of them – Alma, his mother, Pap. They were as small and distant to him as figures seen from an aeroplane.

When his mom spoke again, her voice was trembling. 'All my life, it seems like every time I need people, they all of a sudden turn against me.'

Alma sighed. 'I haven't "all of a sudden" turned against you, Mom.'

'Well, you won't help me. You're bringing up old stories that hurt me and make me feel bad. Look how my hands are trembling.'

'I didn't bring up anything, Mom. Anyway, I *am* helping. I went to the store, didn't I?'

'Yes,' she admitted.

'And I'm going to fix supper before I go to work. That's helping.'

'I know, Alma, and I appreciate it.' His mother's voice softened. 'I knew I could count on you. You and Pap always stick by me.'

'I'm not putting in no window,' Pap said. 'Last time I used a saw I was fifteen years old and I done *that*.' Alfie knew he was holding up the finger with the missing tip.

'I'll saw the hole, Pap,' his mom said soothingly. 'All you have to do is go over to the Wilkins, get the window. It's been stored in the garage for five years so it's bound to need a washing. Maybe you can borrow their hose.' She broke off, raised her voice. Alfie knew her face was turned to the ceiling. He knew her expression. 'Alfie, will you come down out of that attic?'

He did not answer.

'Alfie, you come down this minute or I'm coming up after you.'

He remained silent, staring at the trapdoor.

'Alfie!' It was a command now. 'Come down this minute!'

Slowly he turned and eased himself down onto his chair. He was trembling a little. He breathed deeply of the warm attic air and sighed.

9

ALFIE was still sitting in the attic. His arms were stretched out across the table. His hands were flat on the worn plastic top. It was beginning to get dark.

Below, the family was in the kitchen, eating supper.

'Alfie, you hear me?' his mother had called just before they went in. 'Supper's ready. It's on the table.'

He had not answered.

'Alma fixed it and she's going to be real hurt if you don't come down. What'd you fix, Alma?'

'Liver.'

'Won't be no additives in that,' Pap mumbled.

'It's something real good, Alfie, something you like,' his mother lied.

She had paused and then she had started thumping on the trapdoor with the handle of a broom. It was something she used to do in anger when they were living in an apartment and the Nolans made too much noise upstairs. Alfie remembered how angry her face had looked when she did it.

She had given him three more loud thumps with the broom handle and then, abruptly, had given up. 'You try,

Pap,' she said.

'Try what?' He sounded startled.

'Getting him down.'

'Well, how am I going to get him down if you can't? You're his *mother*.'

'You can force the door open, can't you? You do that and I'll get him down.'

'He's got that door fastened somehow,' Pap said in a worried voice. 'I went up and pushed on it. Alma saw me. I didn't want to push too hard lest he was standing on it. I didn't want to topple him.'

'Pap, get up there and force that door open. I don't care if you topple him from here to China. This has gone on long enough.'

'Forcing a door ain't like it is in the movies,' Pap warned. 'Doors don't just spring open with one kick. I had to force a door in a New Orleans hotel one time and I know. Me and two men worked on that door the best part of fifteen minutes. Never did get it open. The bellboy finally had to go in through the transom. And that was a regular door in a *wall*. How am I going to force a door that's in the ceiling?'

'With your hard head!' Abruptly her tone changed. 'Oh, I don't care what you force it with, Pap. Just get it open, please.'

'Give him a count of three,' Pap begged, playing for time. He had always believed, Alfie knew, that if you waited long enough, everything would turn out all right by itself. 'Don't be too hasty' was his lifelong motto.

Alfie glanced over at the barricaded door. He could imagine Pap standing at the bottom of the ladder, his worn face turned up to the task ahead.

In a strained voice Pap said, 'Alfie, this is Pap speaking.

Your ma's going to give you a count of three, and if you come down, why, then everything'll be all right. We'll go in the kitchen like nothing happened and enjoy whatever Alma's cooked and not a word will be said about the attic or any locked doors. We'll –'

'Quit stalling,' his mother said impatiently.

'Your ma's going to count now, Alfie. She'll give you till three, and if you don't come down, well, then she's going to make me force the door open. I don't want to. I'm seventy-eight years old, but she's going to make me. All right, Alfie, your ma's going to count. Go ahead, Lily, he's ready.'

'One . . .' his mother began.

Alfie could imagine them standing together at the foot of the ladder, both faces turned upward. In his mind they were as unimportant as ants.

Pap burst out with, 'She's counting, Alfie.'

'Two . . .'

Alfie turned his head. He stared at the end of the attic where the window would be if he let them come up and install it. The last of the afternoon sun slanted between the boards.

'Three!' There was a silence, and then his mother snapped, 'I knew it wouldn't work. Now get up there and open that door.'

'Alfie,' Pap called, 'she's making me come up the ladder, me who don't even like to get up on a chair to change a light bulb. Come on down, Alfie. For Pap.'

There was a creaking noise below as Pap took the first rung of the ladder. 'I'm coming,' he said wearily. It sounded as sad as the beginning of an old spiritual. 'I'm nothing but an old tired elephant anyway who's no more use to –'

'Pap, *please* don't start on the old tired-elephant routine.' His mother was all but screaming with frustration and anger. 'I simply cannot stand it. Just get up there and get that door open!'

'Well, I can't go but one rung at a time. You want the door forced open so bad, *you* come up and do it. I'm seventy-eight years old.'

'All right, Pap, just get him down at your leisure,' his mother said in a voice of forced calm. 'Take all evening going up the ladder if you want. I'll serve you supper on the ladder. I'll bring your pipe and slippers to the ladder. Only *get him down!*'

Pap reached up with one hand and knocked at the trapdoor. 'Alfie, you up there?'

'Pap, we *know* he's up there,' his mom said. She was still trying to be patient . 'We saw him go up there. If I wanted someone to knock politely at the door. I'd have sent for Amy Vanderbilt. Alma, get the crowbar. It's under the sink.'

'I'm not having any part of this,' Alma said in a quiet voice.

'Well, get out of my way then,' his mother said.

'Your ma's gone for the crowbar,' Pap said. His mouth was almost touching the side of the trapdoor. 'She's going to make me pry it open, Alfie. You might as well come on down. Once I get that crowbar . . .'

Alfie glanced at the trapdoor. The door was an inch thick. It fitted tightly except for the hole at the side where the light cord went downstairs. Pap, weak as he was, would never work it open.

'Here, Pap,' his mother said.

'I've got the crowbar,' Pap said. 'This is your last chance.'

There was a silence while everyone waited, without hope, for a sound from the attic.

Pap sighed heavily. 'Well, hold me steady,' he said. 'Somebody get a grip on my legs. If my feet slip off the rungs, I'm done for. An old elephant with a broke hip ain't –'

'Pap, I warned you!'

'– worth much.' There were scratching noises at the side of the trapdoor. 'It won't go in,' Pap panted. 'The door fits too tight.'

'You aren't trying, Pap.'

'Well, old arms is old arms.'

'Pap!'

'It's true, and my arms always have trembled when I held them over my head for a long time. That's what kept me out of the army.'

'Pap, you didn't get in the army because you cut your trigger finger off with a saw. Now get that door open.'

There were more scratching noises at the side of the trapdoor, feeble sounds as Pap tried to work the crowbar into the wood. 'This is hard wood,' he complained. 'Feels like mahogany.' The sound of splintered wood crackled at the door. 'There, well, I done *some* good.'

'Three splinters, Pap. Wonderful!'

'I'm doing what I can. I feel weak, though, and it's not just my arms. Maybe if I had my supper . . .'

'All right!' His mother gave in with a shout. 'We'll eat supper.' She paused and lifted her head. 'You hear that, Alfie? We're going in to eat. You stay up there and starve.'

'He's not going to starve.' Pap said. 'He's got crackers up

159

there and peanut butter, Kool-Aid, a regular pantry. He could stay up there a month if he'd a mind to.'

'Well, he's not going to stay up there a month. I guarantee that. I'm getting him down.'

'How?' Pap lowered his voice, but Alfie could still hear him. 'To tell you the truth, Lily, I got as much chance of forcing that door as I have of picking up a mule. They don't retire old people for nothing. If them people at the plant had thought I was strong enough to force a door . . . but they didn't. That's why they let me go.'

'*One* of the reasons.'

'Anyway, the truth is I'm too old to be forcing doors.'

'All right then, I'll call the fire department.' She started into the kitchen. 'Junior Madison works there, and I went with him in high school. Firemen are used to chopping down doors.'

And now the house was quiet. The family was eating supper in the kitchen, and here he was at the card-table, sitting in the darkness, staring at the end of the room. He had not glanced up once at his cartoons. He couldn't.

There were some things in old folk tales and myths he remembered, that you *couldn't* look at. If you looked, you would be turned to stone or a pillar of salt.

He knew that if he looked up at his cartoons, if he looked at his drawings, pale ghosts of happier days, he would be struck in the same way. When the firemen broke into the attic, they would find him changed to stone or salt, face turned to the ceiling, eyes blank, mouth open a little.

'He was like that when we found him, Lily,' Junior Madison would say. They'd stand around sadly, and then one of the firemen would try to comfort his mother. 'One thing, ma'am, he'll make a real nice statue. Any park would be proud to have him.'

10

'YOUR show is on,' his mother called to Alfie. 'The one about international cartoons.' It was Alfie's favourite programme, but his mother's voice had a flat, hopeless sound, as if she knew he would not come down.

He did not answer. He had not moved for hours. His face had a hard set look, like clay.

The only change at all in Alfie had come with his mother's threat of the firemen. The more he thought of that, the more trapped he'd felt. The security of being in his own attic, locked away from the world, had been broken.

Firemen *could* stream in from all directions, he had thought as the minutes ticked slowly past. They could chop their way through the roof, the eaves, axe down the door. He imagined them swarming into the attic, hale and hearty as hornets in their yellow slickers. This would be the kind of assignment they would really enjoy, he thought. They could practise their techniques without any risk.

It was Alma who had saved him.

'Mom, you are not going to call the fire department,' she had said as they came into the living-room after supper. Alfie could hear their voices much clearer up here than he had heard them below. Maybe sound rose like heat. 'I mean what I'm saying, Mom,' Alma said sternly. 'Alfie has got to come down by himself. It's important.'

'What do you know about it? You've never locked yourself up in the attic. You and Bubba had too much sense for that.'

'No, I've never locked myself in the attic, but there have been other things that I've had to accept and work out for myself, and that's what Alfie's going to have to do.'

There had been a pause. Alfie sagged a little in his chair. He knew there was no way he could work this out, alone or with the firemen's help. He could never come down the ladder into the harsh light of the living-room, no matter what happened. It was impossible. He had gone into the woods like Hansel, turned, and the breadcrumbs were missing. There was no way back.

Maybe when he was very old, he thought, eighty or ninety, when there was nothing left of the boy he had been, maybe then he could come down. He would be an old man, straggly beard, long grey hair, as thin as a skeleton, bent with arthritis and malnutrition. He would lift the trapdoor at last, trembling with effort, shaking in every limb, and slowly climb down the ladder.

There, in the faded living-room, he would discover that his family – Mom, Alma, and Pap – had moved away years ago. A new family lived in the house now, a family who hadn't even known he was up there. He would stand bewildered and lost, blinking in the light, as frightened and confused at seeing the strangers as they were at seeing him.

Below, his mother said to Alma, 'Yes, but he could be dead up there, Alma, or unconscious. That's why I wanted to call the firemen.'

'He's not dead.'

'Well, sulking then. That's just as bad.'

'Look, I've got to go to work – I'm late as it is, but you are *not* to call the fire department. I mean that, Mom.'

'The only reason I'm not calling them,' she said, 'if you want the truth, is because I do not want Junior Madison, who I went with in high school, to know I have a son who goes around locking himself in attics!' She slammed something down on the television. 'The last time I saw Junior Madison was at the Morgantown-Fairmont football game which Bubba *won*, and Junior Madison told me he knew how proud I must be of Bubba because his son had bad ankles and couldn't even run across the family room.'

Alfie could hear the music of the international cartoon. His mother called, 'Alfie, this cartoon from Yugoslavia is real interesting. It's about cities that keep building until they turn into atomic explosions.'

'I don't know why they make cartoons like that,' Pap complained. 'Atom bombs ain't funny.'

'It's not supposed to be funny. If you'd listen to what the woman said –'

'Well, *cartoons* is supposed to be funny.' He got up from his chair. It creaked as he rose. 'I'm going out back and see what the Governor's up to.'

'He's gone to Pittsburgh, Pap. Don't you remember?'

'Oh, yeah.' He sat again, heavily.

'You've started over there four times. I thought *old elephants* never forgot.'

'Well, old brains ain't like new ones.'

Alfie heard the music swell. He thought the city must be exploding in the cartoon now, spreading crayon radiation over the land.

'Hey, Miss-es Ma-son!'

Alfie lifted his head. It was one of the Finley twins calling his mother from the sidewalk. He recognized the high nasal twang.

'Hey, Miss-es Ma-son! We hear Alfie's in the attic!'

Alfie stretched his arms out on the table as if he were trying to reach the eaves.

'Is Al-fie in the at-tic?'

Somehow they made it rhyme. Alfie closed his eyes. He imagined himself as part of a jump-rope rhyme. Years from now thin-legged girls would be reciting his saga as they jumped.

'Al-fie's in the at-tic
Doing his car-toons.'

'Miss-es Ma-son! Is Alfie being pun-ished?' Both twins were calling now in perfect unison. 'Is Al-fie being punished?'

The Finley twins had always had a special sense for trouble in the neighbourhood. They never missed an ambulance or a police car. They sensed when and where a fight was going to break out, and they knew when a child was going to be punished. They would be leaping up at the window, like dogs after a bone, in time to see the first blow.

'What'd he do, Miss-es Ma-son? What'd Al-fie do?'

Alfie heard the front door thrust open. It banged against the porch wall. 'Get away from here!' his mother shouted. 'Get away from here before I turn the hose on you.'

'But Miss-es Ma-son,' they persisted. They inched closer to the steps. They wanted to be gossip columnists when they grew up. 'But, Miss-es Ma-son, *why* is Al-fie in the at-tic?'

'Scat!'

'What'd he –'

'Scat! Shoo! Get away from here!'

There was a clanging noise. His mother must have thrown something at them, possibly the framed picture of himself that sat on the TV.

Alfie's head sagged. He knew his mother must be very ashamed of him, and yet he didn't understand it exactly. She had not been embarrassed at all when Bubba had been arrested after the football game riot. She had told that over and over, to anyone who would listen. And the time Bubba stole a car to drive the cheerleaders to a game in Clarksburg – she had told that next morning in the grocery store. And Bubba's running into the police car and losing his job – she would make a good story out of that one day too, Alfie thought.

'Miss-es Ma-son!' voices called from the porch.

'Ignore them,' Pap said.

'I *knew* Wanda Wilkins would spread it all over town about Alfie. I should never have . . .'

Alfie could hear his mother's voice fade as she went into the kitchen. She drew a pot of water. She crossed the living-room, opened the door, and flung the water outside.

Alfie heard the splat, the two screams. The Finley twins must have taken a direct hit.

'We're telling our mom,' one of the twins threatened as they retreated. 'Miss-es Ma-son, we're telling Mom.'

'And also tell *Mom* you were up on my porch trying to look in my door. Tell her *Miss-es Ma-son's* going to call the cops the next time you come poking around here!'

She sat down on the sofa. Immediately she got up. The springs creaked. She turned off the television. 'Oh, I'm going to bed. I've had all I can stand for one day.'

Alfie laid his head on his arms. The house was quiet now and he missed the noise. The sound of the television was a natural sound of the house, like the heater in winter or the wind from the north blowing through the eaves.

He lifted his head. Suddenly he actually felt like a statue. Maybe, he thought, he had turned to stone, even though he hadn't looked up at his cartoons. He felt like stone.

He imagined himself in a park, high on a pedestal, far above the world. No matter what happened around him he would remain unmoving at his table, hands folded. Pigeons would flap around his head, alight on his shoulders. Children would throw stones at them, hitting him. The statue would remain perfect. Muggings would take place in his shadow. Babies would teeter, fall, and cry. Girls would play games of tag around him. Only at night, like this, when the world got quiet, would the statue begin to soften.

He closed his eyes. He became stone again.

11

'HEY, Alfie!'

Alfie's eyes snapped open. He blinked. He lifted his head, turtle-like, and looked around the dusky attic. It was morning and there was no sunlight. The attic was as empty and cheerless as a stage waiting for props.

'Alfie, you ready for school?' Tree called. Alfie knew he was outside, standing at the edge of the steps. *'Hey Alfie!'* he called again, louder.

Alfie waited with his hands folded on the table as if he were holding a small bunch of invisible flowers.

'Tree, would you come in the house a minute, please,' Alfie's mother said at the front door. She had just got out of bed, and Alfie knew she would be standing in the doorway clutching her peacock-blue bathrobe around her.

'Isn't Alfie ready for school?' Tree asked anxiously. 'I can't be late again, Mrs Mason, because I've already been late nine times, and if you're late ten times you have to write a composition.'

'Just step inside for a second, Tree.'

'Compositions aren't my thing.' He entered, feet dragging. He looked around the living-room. 'Where *is* Alfie? He's not still in bed, is he? Look, Mrs Mason, if he's still in bed –'

'Tree, Alfie's up in the attic,' his mother said in a serious voice, 'and I want you to help me get him down.'

'*Where* is he?'

'In the attic.'

Alfie could imagine his mother pointing up to the trapdoor, holding her bathrobe closed with one hand. He could see Tree's face lifted, puzzled, looking at the square door.

'He went up yesterday,' his mother explained, 'and he won't come down.'

There was a pause. Then Tree said in an awed voice, 'That's weird, Mrs Mason.'

Alfie recognized that as one of Tree's greatest insults. 'He's weird, Alfie, sang a solo in the Christmas pageant. Oh, Holeeeeeee night!' Or, 'She's really weird, Alfie, toe-dances.' Or, 'Yeah, but somebody told me he plays the fife. He's *weird*, Alfie.'

167

And now he, Alfie, had joined the group. Drawing cartoons was bad enough, he thought, but locking himself in the attic, really clinched it. 'He's weird.' Tree would tell everyone, 'locked himself in the attic.'

'Well, you know how he is, Tree,' his mother said. 'He just does things without thinking. Anyway, I thought maybe if you called to him, he'd come down and you could walk to school together.'

'Well, I don't know. I could try.' Tree cleared his throat. 'Alfie, you want to walk to school with me?' He waited, then said in a lower voice, 'I don't think he wants to, Mrs Mason.'

'Call again . . . please.'

'Alfie, you going to school?' He paused, and then his voice began to pick up speed with his enthusiasm. 'Listen, the reason I came by this morning is because Lizabeth and me are having a kind of war – it's not going to be anything violent, Mrs Mason,' he added quickly, 'it's just going to be one of those boys against the girls things – like *Challenge of the Sexes* on television. Anyway, Alfie, we worked it all out last night. It's going to be five different contests. And it's you against Zeenie in – get this! – bowling! And Zeenie's lousy too, Alfie. Half the time her ball never even gets *to* the pins. I mean, if it goes all the way down there, she's *proud*. Gutter balls are her speciality.'

Tree swallowed, almost choking on his enthusiasm. 'And, Alfie, here's the really good news. It's me against Lizabeth in *basketball*. I still can't believe she agreed. I mean, free throws are my speciality, Alfie. Everybody knows that. I can do them blindfolded, but she said, "All right, fine with me," and so we each get ten shots from the free-throw line – she takes one and I take one – or rather she *tries* to take one, right, Alfie?'

'And then – more good news – it's Willie against Beth Ann in a race. He looks slow because he's fat, right, but you and me know he is *fast*. Remember when he stole my adenoids? Remember the doctor put them in a little jar for me and we chased him for seven blocks? Anyway, you've got to come down. We need to make plans. And, Alfie, if I'm late to school one more time I have to write a composition!'

There was silence. In the attic Alfie could imagine Tree and his mother with their faces turned up to the trapdoor. There were sounds as Tree climbed up the ladder. He slapped his hand against the trapdoor. 'Alfie, hey, come on down. This sex challenge is going to be one of the biggest things Morgantown's ever seen. We may get on TV!'

Alfie's mother let her breath out in one long sigh. 'He's not coming, Tree.'

'But he's *got* to. He's got to be in the challenge, Mrs Mason. I already promised Zeenie he'd bowl her.' He raised his voice. 'Alfie, I *promised* Zeenie. She won't bowl anybody but you!' He went up another rung on the ladder and lowered his voice. 'Look, if you're mad about what I said yesterday, forget it. That's over with. I didn't mean it. This is too important for us to stay mad. This is *war*!'

There was another long silence while Tree realized slowly that Alfie was not going to come down. 'Mrs Mason, are you sure he can hear me up there?' he asked.

'He can hear you.'

'But then why doesn't he come down? This is important.'

'I know, Tree.'

'We've got to make plans.'

'I know.' Her voice had a cold, ringing sound. 'Alfie has upset a lot of plans.'

In the attic Alfie shivered.

'Well, when he comes down, Mrs Mason,' Tree went on, 'tell him about the war – he may not have heard all the details through the ceiling. And tell him to come on to school. We can't put this war off. We're *up* for it, you know, Mrs Mason? We don't want to lose our momentum. Tell him I'm going against Lizabeth after school today – three o'clock in the gym. I know he'll want to be there for that. Did you hear me, Alfie? It's me against Lizabeth at three o'clock. And tomorrow, Alfie, it's you against Zeenie. Now she's lousy, Alfie, but she's also the niece of a man who runs the bowling alley – Red Cassin is her uncle, Alfie, and he'll probably get some pro to coach her. Alfie, are you listening?' Tree stepped down from the ladder and started for the door. 'Is that clock right, Mrs Mason?'

'I think so, Tree.'

'Then I'm late.' His voice sank.

The door slammed, and Tree ran down the sidewalk towards school. Alfie heard his footsteps fade in the distance.

Alfie's mother went into the kitchen, plugged in the coffee-pot, and sank down into one of the chairs. In a few minutes the scent of coffee reached Alfie in the attic. He glanced over at his own supply of food. He looked away. He wasn't hungry. Hunger seemed now to be one of those things he would never feel again. Like thirst. Or sorrow. Or happiness. He just didn't think he would feel anything again ever.

A raindrop fell on the roof. It made a loud sound as if the room material were stretched, drum-tight, over the rafters. Alfie had never been in the attic when it rained. He put his head down on his arms.

The rain began to come down hard now, splattering against the roof in waves. It was a rhythmic thing, Alfie thought, like the ocean he had never seen. He closed his eyes and drifted back to sleep.

12

'ALFIE, do you hear me? This is Pap speaking.' Pap's voice sounded as clear and pronounced as a radio announcer's.

Alfie lifted his head. The rain had slackened and was now a steady drumming on the roof. It gave Alfie a drowsy feeling. His eyelids drooped.

'Alfie?'

His eyes opened.

'Alfie, your ma's gone over to the Wilkins to use the telephone. She's calling to tell Bubba and Maureen to come over as soon as they can get their things together. She's not letting on that you've locked yourself in the attic. She's telling them the attic is all fixed up like something out of a picture.'

Pap pulled his chair closer to the trapdoor. Alfie could hear the chair legs scraping on the floor. Pap sat down heavily. He sighed, scratched his chin. Alfie could hear his whiskers bristle.

'There's something I want to say before she gets back,' Pap went on. 'Now, Alfie, I don't want Bubba and Maureen staying here any more than you do. I wish I could lock myself somewheres. I'd do it if I thought it would do any good. Only it wouldn't. There's not much an old man can do to get noticed without them sending him to the asylum.'

Pap cleared his throat and leaned back in his chair. Alfie knew Pap was looking up at the trapdoor now. He could hear the back cushion creak.

Alfie opened his eyes wide, trying to stay awake. He didn't know why he was so sleepy. It was mid-morning – he knew that from the television programmes – and yet he felt as tired as if it were midnight. Maybe it was because of the bad dreams, he thought. All night long he had had nightmares in which cars crashed together and the ceiling cracked like a jigsaw puzzle and fell on him.

'So here's what I was thinking, Alfie.' Pap said, his voice rising with his enthusiasm. 'I was thinking maybe you and me and Bubba could get the junkyard back. Harvey Sweet's let it run down. I was out there the other day – took the bus to the end of the line and then walked five miles just to see how things was – I miss that place, Alfie – and things was bad. Sweet hadn't got a new wreck in three months. And the crown – remember the hub-cap crown your dad made? Wreck King of West Virginia? Well, it's gone – blew down in the wind, Sweet said – and the whole place is looking run down. I got a catch in my throat when I saw it.'

He shifted in his chair. Then Alfie heard him get to his feet and begin lumbering around the living-room like a bear just learning to walk erect. Alfie remembered that last day when the junkyard was being sold. Pap had walked among the ruined cars like a dazed, defeated general.

'Things could be the way they used to be, Alfie, when your dad was alive. You remember them days?'

In the attic Alfie looked down at his empty hands.

Slowly he closed them into fists.

Below, Pap had reached the wall. Alfie heard his footsteps stop, then begin again as he returned. Alfie imagined him touching pieces of furniture as he had long ago touched fenders and windshields. 'We had someplace to go then, something to do. Remember how we used to sit out there on a summer evening? People would come shopping for parts after supper, remember? That was our busiest time. And I'd sit there on an upturned Coke carton, greeting people, and you – you was as good at tracking down car parts as your dad. And when you got tired you'd take a rest in an old blue Dodge sedan you was fond of. You *got* to remember the Dodge, Alfie!' He sighed.

'Well, Alfie,' he went on, 'it could be like that again. I know it could.' Pap stopped walking, and Alfie heard the ladder creak as Pap leaned against it. 'I know how you feel up there, Alfie. I have give up a time or two myself. I think about the government rotting away like an apple and senators using our money for trips to China – did I tell you, Alfie, *twenty-seven* senators is going to London, England, to pick up a copy of the Magna Carta? Which they could *mail*, Alfie! And you know who is paying them twenty-seven senators' way, don't you? You and me!' He snorted with disgust. 'I think about things and about us giving money to countries that hates us and arms to countries that wants to shoot at us. Well, it makes me want to go somewheres too. Stick my head in the sand. Lock myself in a closet. Get where I can't hear no more.' His voice lowered. 'Only if we had the junkyard again, Alfie, well, it would make up for everything. Come on down and we'll talk about it. I got a little money saved up –

don't tell your ma. It's not much, but we could use it for a
down payment, get a loan for the rest. And Bubba – well,
if he's good at anything, it's wrecking cars, and between
the three of us –'

Pap broke off. 'Your ma's coming back. She looks mad
too. Come on down, Alfie. No need to rile her any more.'

Alfie could hear his mother running up the walk, taking
the steps. She came in the door, shaking water off her
raincoat. 'It's pouring, Pap,' she said, 'and I couldn't get
anything but a busy signal. Twenty times I dialled. You'd
think they'd stay off the line when they knew I was going
to call.'

'Maybe they'd took if off the hook. A busy signal don't
always mean busy.'

She ignored him. 'Maureen stays on the phone all the
time. I suppose we'll have to have one installed to keep her
happy. Is Alfie down yet?'

'No.'

'It figures. When one thing goes wrong, everything goes
wrong.' She looked up at the ceiling and yelled, 'Did you
hear that, Alfie? You are now just *one* of the things going
wrong. You are one of the two thousand and ninety-nine
things going wrong!'

'Alfie and me was just talking about starting up the
junkyard again.'

'Oh, Pap, you know that'll never happen.'

'We could do it.'

'Forget it.'

'How can I forget it when every time I see a dented
fender I get a pain over my heart?'

Alfie closed his eyes. The junkyard seemed so long ago
to him. He couldn't go back. It was as if someone had

taken him by the hand and said, 'Remember how much fun being five years old was? Let's go back to kindergarten and make flowers out of pipe-cleaners and masks out of paper plates.' You couldn't double back.

Alfie raised his head and looked at the end of the attic. Water was dripping through the eaves, and a puddle had formed on the floor. Around him were the sounds of other drips. Alfie did not look up, because he did not want to see his cartoons.

There was an old game he played long ago with Alma. 'Heavy, heavy, hangs over your head,' she would say, and he would have to guess what the object was.

'Is it made of wood?'

'No.'

'Is it made of metal?'

'No.'

'Paper?'

'Yes.'

'Is it – cartoons?'

Alfie let his head drop heavily on the plastic table-top. His pencils in their glass jar trembled. Pointing up, they reminded him of what he could not forget.

13

ALFIE heard the opening music of his mother's favourite soap opera, and he knew it was three o'clock. Tree would be going into the gym now. Maybe he was already there at the free-throw line, practising. Alfie knew just how Tree would look, one foot slightly behind the other, one hand on either side of the ball. He would bounce the ball three times for luck. His eyes would be riveted on the basket. He would shoot. Elizabeth wouldn't have a chance.

Alfie sighed. For a moment he wished he were in the gym with them. If he could have got there without going down the ladder and walking through the living-room, he would have done it.

If only, he thought, he could move from one attic to another, walking through tunnels over everyone's head, unseen, unheard. He would stroll to the game, listen to Tree beat Elizabeth, walk home through the tunnel, sit down at his desk. He would never have to see anyone. That was the way he wanted his life to be – a series of attics.

He laid his head on the table. The rain had stopped, and everything seemed clearer, as if the rain had cleaned the air. Sun was slanting through the leaves.

He imagined that by now Tree was probably half-way through the shoot-out. The score was probably five to nothing, Tree's lead. The boys would be counting every time Tree's ball went in the basket. *'Five!'* *'Six!'*

Below all was quiet. His mother had been to the Wilkins two times to call Bubba and Maureen, but she had got a busy signal both times. Now she was watching her soap opera, sipping a cup of coffee. The programme ended in a burst of music, and his mother turned the channel to a game show.

Suddenly he heard Tree's voice. 'Mrs Mason, can I see Alfie?'

'Tree, he's not down from the attic yet.'

'Well, that's all right. I just want to tell him something.'

'Be my guest.'

Tree paused, cleared his throat. 'Could I speak to him in private, Mrs Mason?'

'I'm watching television, Tree,' she said. 'Oh, well, I can hear it in the kitchen, I guess.'

She walked out of the room, and Alfie heard Tree climbing up the ladder. Tree reached up to the trapdoor with one hand. He drummed his fingers against the wood. 'Alfie, can you hear me?'

Alfie didn't answer.

'Because, Alfie,' Tree went on. He swallowed loudly. 'Alfie, I've got bad news.'

Tree paused a moment to see if Alfie was going to answer. Then he cleared his throat. He said, 'You're not going to believe this.' He swallowed again as if forcing down a large and bitter pill. He moved up one rung on the ladder. 'Lizabeth beat me.'

The silence stretched out, long and painful.

'I just don't know how it happened,' Tree went on in a rush, 'because I was really up for it, you know? That's supposed to count for a lot in sports – being psyched up.'

He sighed. 'Here's the way it was, Alfie. I came into the gym, all psyched up, and there were a lot of people there. It was packed. It had spread all over school about our war – even Mrs Steinhart was there – and I felt real good, Alfie, that's what makes it so unbelievable. If I'd been nervous and uptight – if I'd had a virus – but I never felt so good. It was like the time I fought Richie Davis, remember?'

There was a pause while he got into a better position on the ladder. 'Anyway, we got out on the floor, Lizabeth and me, and I clowned around a little – you know me, and everybody was laughing, and in the middle of all this

Lizabeth goes up to the free-throw line and without any warning – I mean, she doesn't even bounce the ball for luck – she *flings* the ball at the basket, *flings* it, Alfie. It's the worst looking thing you ever saw. It's like she's throwing a Frisbee, and it goes right in. All the girls go, '*One!*' Then they start yelling and clapping. Naturally all the boys are booing.

'Now I step up. I bounce the ball three times and I feel good, Alfie. I'm ready. I throw, and Alfie,' he sighed, 'I miss.'

There was another pause while Tree got the strength to continue. 'I don't know how it happened, Alfie. It was *my* shot. I did everything right, and –'

He broke off as Alfie's mother came in from the kitchen. She said, 'Oh, I'm sorry, Tree. I thought you were through.'

'No, I'm just getting started.'

'Who won on *Match Game*? The water was runnning and I didn't hear.'

'I didn't hear either, Mrs Mason.'

'Well, don't fall off that ladder.'

'It wouldn't matter if I did,' Tree said. He waited until she went back into the kitchen. Then he said, 'So now it's one to nothing, her lead. Only, Alfie, I'm still not worried, because I know she just had a real lucky break. She could fling that ball a thousand more times and she'd be lucky to even hit the backboard.

'Now the principal comes in – *Mr Harrington*, Alfie! I haven't seen Mr Harrington since I cheated on those history dates. Mr Harrington is like Howard Hughes, Alfie, he never comes out, and here he is strolling in to see me beat Lizabeth! It's the biggest thing our school has ever had!

'I figure I've got it made now. I always do good under pressure, and Lizabeth will fall apart – remember when she had to sing that solo in the pageant, started too soon, and threw the whole chorus off? She steps up to the free-throw line, flings the ball – you won't believe how she does this – get her to show you when you come down – and the ball goes in.

'"*Two!*" yell all the girls.

'Now I *am* worried. Sure, free throws are my thing, but even Wilt Chamberlain can have a bad day. I bounce the ball three times, throw, and, Alfie, it goes in. I never saw a sweeter sight in my life. The boys go crazy. Everybody's yelling but the girls, and they're booing. It really made me feel good.

'Lizabeth comes up now. She flings and – I knew it would happen sooner or later – she misses.

'I come up. I bounce three times, throw, right through the old hoop.

'Now the score is two to two, a tie which I figure I'm about to break. I can't wait till my turn. I'm hot now. She gets up there, throws, misses. I get up there and I'm too eager, Alfie. I forget to bounce three times for luck. I miss. The score is still two to two.

'She gets up, flings, hits. The score is now *three* to two, her lead.

'I get up there, miss.

'She gets up there, flings and – real bad news – she hits. The girls go *"Four!"* real loud, Alfie. I felt like crying because, Alfie, now I'm down by two. I'm good, but being down by two is bound to affect my performance. I've never been known as a catch-up player. My way is to get in front

179

and stay in front. You can't lose that way, and now I'm down by two!

'I get up, throw a bad ball, but it goes in anyway. Four to three. The boys are yelling so loud now I can't even hear myself think. They figure I'm closing the gap.

'She shoots, misses.

'I shoot, miss.

'She shoots, scores.

'I shoot, score.

'Now it's five to four, Alfie, and we each have one more ball. If she hits, I'm done for. It's all over. She gets up there and I'm praying, Alfie. Every boy in the gym is praying. It gets real quiet. There's not a sound. She flings. She misses! Now I've got a chance. I'm still alive. I figure I'll score and we'll go to sudden-death overtime. I can't wait. Sudden death is my thing. I get up to the line, bounce three times, throw, and, Alfie, it's the most beautiful throw I ever made in my life. It goes right for the basket. It rolls around the rim like it's going in – you know how golf balls do – it rolls around the rim like it's going in and then, Alfie – you won't believe this – it pops out! Alfie, it *pops out*!

'I just stood there and, Alfie, my mind went blank. It's a merciful thing that happens sometimes to people who've been in accidents and stuff, their minds just go blank, and that's what happened to me. I mean, I *must* have walked out of school and I *must* have walked to your house because here I am. But I don't remember one single thing from the time that ball popped out of the hoop until I climbed this ladder.'

'Oh, Tree, are you *still* here?' Alfie's mother said, coming into the room again.

'I was just getting ready to leave, Mrs Mason.'

'Well, don't go on my account. My shows are over. Anyway, I've got to go next door and make a call.'

'I was through.'

Alfie's mother paused at the door. 'Don't tell me *you've* got troubles too, Tree.'

'Yes,' he answered.

Her voice got louder to reach Alfie. 'Too bad you don't have an attic to lock yourself in.'

'Yes.'

'That's the trouble with this world,' she snapped. 'There aren't enough attics to go around.'

'You can say that again, Mrs Mason.'

Tree climbed slowly down the ladder, crossed the room, and left. The screen door slammed shut behind him.

14

ALFIE sat in the attic, hands folded in front of him. He was tired – no, *weary* was the word for how he felt. His English teacher was always urging the class to find just the right word for their feelings, and now he had found it. He was weary. He had to make an effort to hold his eyes open.

Since Tree had gone, the house had been quiet. Pap was probably outside reading yesterday's newspaper, Alfie thought, looking for things to blame on the President. His mother had not returned from borrowing the Wilkins' telephone.

The sunlight showed the dust in the air. Alfie thought that this floor had never been swept, not since he'd lived here anyway. There was enough dust, Alfie imagined, to make a man, like in the Bible. Or a boy. A dust boy could be made and sent downstairs while he, Alfie, stayed in the attic for ever. His family would notice the difference, but they would excuse it by saying, 'Alfie has never been the same since he locked himself in the attic.'

He lowered his head to his arms. He closed his eyes. He remembered hearing that in seven years a person became entirely new. It was the first happy thought he'd had. Every cell was replaced. Maybe in seven years, pink and shiny and new, he could come down the ladder.

'Why, Alfie, you look marvellous. Come look at Alfie. He's brand new.'

'Alfie, are you still up there?' Alma called from downstairs, breaking his thoughts. 'Are you all right?' He had not heard her come in. He lifted his head. It seemed heavy.

'Alfie, I was hoping you were going to be down,' she called. He did not answer.

'Because I've been thinking about you all day. In typing I got my hands on the wrong keys and typed for two minutes without noticing.'

Alfie heard her drop her books on the TV. 'Listen, want me to fix you something hot to eat? I'll slip it up when nobody's looking, because I remember how cold I felt that time Mom took my money. I felt like I'd never get warm again. How does hot chocolate sound?'

Suddenly the front door slammed. 'Pap, where are you?' It was Alfie's mother and she sounded upset. 'Where's Pap?'

'He's out in the backyard,' Alma said. 'Is anything wrong?'

'Is anything wrong? Is anything *not* wrong?'

'What's happened?'

'Alma, I am so mad. I am furious! Do you know what Maureen's parents are doing?'

'No.'

'They are now trying to get Bubba and Maureen to live with *them!*'

'I'm surprised they want them.'

'Well, they probably didn't until they found *I* did. I could never stand that eely little woman. I *knew* she'd pull something. I told her I had the attic all fixed up. I told her all the plans I had. Alma, I could hardly get a word in. It was like trying to talk to a parrot. *She* had Maureen's old room all fixed up. *She* had Maureen's dressing-room for the baby. She! She! She! And Piggie – don't forget that awful husband of hers. *Piggie*'s getting Bubba a job at Quaker State. Piggie's doing this. Piggie's doing that. I tell you I could have smacked her – it was a good thing all this was happening over the telephone or I would have.'

'Did you talk to Bubba? What did he say about all this?'

'You think she'd let me to talk to Bubba? To my own son? Oh, no! And I know he was there. I heard his voice in the background at one point saying, "I wish everybody would get off my back."'

'Well, maybe it's the best thing, Mom.'

'Best thing for who? Not me! Not me who just put a ten-dollar down payment on a double bed at Hill's.'

'Mom –'

'I wish you could have heard the conversation, Alma. Everything I said, she turned it around. I mentioned, just mentioned, that I was going to replace the ladder, and as soon as I said the word *ladder*, she said, "Oh, Maureen could *never* go up a ladder. Maureen's afraid of heights. Maureen once froze on the diving-board ladder at Marilla Pool, and four firemen had to get her down."'

'Mom –'

'That did it for me. I said very sweetly, "Only four firemen? I should think, considering Maureen's size, it would have taken at least *six*." Then she said, not so sweetly, "Maureen's size is none of your business." And I said – I was really furious now –'

'Mom!' Alma interrupted.

She broke off. 'Oh, where's Pap? I want to see Pap.'

'He's probably outside.'

'Pap. I've been had!' she called. She stopped suddenly in the doorway to the kitchen. She said, 'Although I realize I cannot expect sympathy from any of you. You have all been against me from the start. You, Alma, have been very clear about your feelings. And Alfie up there in the attic –' She raised her voice without turning around. 'Did you hear the news, Alfie? You can come down now. Maureen and Bubba aren't coming. Your precious attic is saved. You've won!'

Alfie did not move. His mother's words rang in his ears. He had won. This was victory. He remembered an old cartoon he had seen of a soldier slumped forward, tired beyond caring, worn down, eyes that had seen too much staring straight ahead at nothing. It seemed to Alfie the cartoon had been called 'Victory'. Alfie felt too flat and wound down to remember exactly.

Pap came lumbering into the house. His mother said, 'Pap, did you hear the news?'

'Me and everybody else on the block.'

'Oh, it is so infuriating! And that awful Piggie! During

the whole conversation, Pap, he was babbling in the background. Tell her this. Tell her that. I could have wrung his neck.' She raised her voice even louder. 'Well, are you getting the message, Alfie? You can have your attic. You can go up there any time you want to now.'

'*If* he comes down.'

'Pap!'

'Well, he can't go *up* if he don't come *down* first.'

'If you start in now, I just cannot take it.'

'It's the simple truth. He can't –'

'Well, I don't feel like hearing any simple truths now, if you don't mind. I want to hear some good old comforting lies.' She raised her voice again. 'Did you hear, Alfie? You have won.'

'He heard you, Mom.'

Alfie's shoulders sagged a little more. He hurt without being able to put his finger on what really was hurting. It was like the time Bubba had teased an old cat that lived with them. He had clamped a clothes-pin on its ear, and the cat had crouched down, cringing, but not shaking his head or scratching at his ear. It was as if he couldn't locate the hurt.

Suddenly Alfie wondered if Bubba had felt this way the first time he had done something wrong. He tried to remember the first of Bubba's deeds. Maybe it was the fire-crackers he had set off in Cinema I.

Would this become a family joke too, Alfie wondered. Would his mother laugh and make this *funny*? 'Did I ever tell you about the time Alfie locked himself in the attic? You'll die laughing at this.'

Anguished, he shook his head from side to side. He remembered the time he had gone to the zoo with Pap and his mother. In a cage painted arctic blue, a polar bear had sat, shaking his head from side to side, just as Alfie was doing. He had been the picture of despair.

At once Alfie had wanted to leave. He could feel the bear's hopeless anguish too clearly.

'Let's go to the monkey house,' he had pleaded. Monkeys could always make him laugh. They chattered and picked each other's fleas and screeched at people as if the people were trying to get into their cages.

Also, he knew his mother loved the monkeys. She had had one as a pet when she was a girl. Pap had bought it from a gas station attendant. It had had seven outfits, and they were washed and ironed with the family's clothes. The monkey was dressed every day, and he had run away wearing a two-piece pink play-suit. Alfie's mother had never seen the monkey again, even though they ran ads in the newspaper for a month.

Whenever his mother visited the monkey house, she talked about what kind of outfits they'd look good in. 'I'd get the gorilla a sailor suit, Alfie, pale blue with a straw hat to match.'

But even in the monkey house, with his mother happily clothing the monkeys, he had remembered the silent, despairing polar bear.

'Alfie, are you coming down?' Alma asked from below.

He didn't answer. He didn't know. All his life it had seemed to him that things would go on as they were. If he was happy, he would always be happy. When he hurt, he could never see relief. The way things were, that was the way they would always be. He could not see beyond this chair, this attic, this flat misery.

'Because you didn't *win*, Alfie. Mom was wrong. It

didn't have anything to do with you really. Bubba and Maureen decided on their own to live with her parents. They didn't even know about you.

'I didn't win when I threw a fit and smashed my bank and almost had to be driven to the hospital. It was just something I did because I couldn't stand what had happened to me. But even if I had got my money back by doing what I did, I still wouldn't have won. And you didn't win either.'

Alfie waited. He shut his eyes. He felt as it he were getting a cold. His eyes burned with tears.

'So don't feel like you've won,' she said. 'Did you hear, Alfie? Don't feel like you've won!'

I don't, Alfie said, so softly the words didn't actually leave his mouth. He cleared his throat. He spoke for the first time in twenty-four hours. 'I don't,' he said.

15

'WELL, come on down then,' Alma called. 'Supper's ready.'

He kept sitting at his table in the attic. He felt swept away by emotion. Like those people caught in *The Wizard of Oz* tornado, whirling past Dorothy's window, sitting normally in rocking-chairs or pedalling bicycles, all the while being carried away. Alfie felt himself circling closer to something.

Suddenly a fly buzzed around his head. It landed on his ear. Alfie brushed it away. He felt irritated at the intrusion.

The fly must have been here all along, he thought, resting on a beam and had chosen this moment to fly down and irritate him. It was like the fly in a television studio who waits until an actor is on camera, in his most moving scene, and then comes down and buzzes around his made-up lips. He swatted the fly away again.

'Is Alfie coming down for supper?' his mother called from the kitchen. 'Tell him it's Sloppy Joes.'

'He's coming,' Alma said.

'Well, if it's Sloppy Joes,' Pap groaned, 'I'm *going*. Them things is not fit for human consumption.'

'Then they should be just right for *you*,' his mother said.

Alfie leaned back in his chair. The fly had left as quickly as it had come. It had been strange, like a touch from a wand. He thought of those old stories where the fairy godmother waves her wand and in a shower of sparkles changes evil to good and ugliness to beauty. Only *his* fairy godmother, he thought, was old; her wand, weak. She had noticed him in trouble here in the attic and had waved her wand over him with all her strength, really wanting to change the whole world for him. But instead of magic sparkles, her wand had given off one tired fly. He had buzzed down, touched Alfie's ear, and been whisked back up.

His fairy godmother was waiting above him now, holding her wand anxiously. To the fly she'd be saying, 'Well, it's up to him now. We did our best, Igor.'

Igor would buzz in agreement, perched on her shoulder, anxious too.

Alfie let the air go out of his lungs in one long sigh. He remembered what was really waiting over his head. Slowly he turned his face to the ceiling. He lifted one hand as if he were going to shield his eyes. Through his tears he saw his cartoons.

They hung pale and still in the warm, dusty air, 'Super Caterpillar.' 'Super Bird.' The boy with the turned-in feet. The chicken. The children. The old man and woman with their car. Super balloon . . .

He rose from the table the way Pap got up from a chair, as if he weren't sure he would make it, as if he feared his bones were going to give way. He stood. He stepped back from the table, stumbling a little on the uneven boards.

Then slowly, as if he were picking fruit, he began to take down the cartoons. Sellotape pulled off with a sigh. Drawing-pins gave. Paper tore. One by one the cartoons came off. The pile grew in his hand.

He pulled the last one, 'Super Caterpillar', from the rafters and put it with the others. For some reason he felt a little easier, as if the clothes-pin had been taken from his ear without his knowing it. He rolled the cartoons up like an awkward diploma.

Holding them under one arm, he slid the board from the trapdoor. He opened it. He looked down into the room below. For a moment it looked wrong, like a negative. Black was white; white was black. Then everything got normal.

He started down the ladder. He could hear the family in the kitchen. Pap was saying, 'Don't nobody care what I want to eat anyway. You get old – it's like in the jungle – the old elephant can't reach the good leaves no more, and nobody'll pull them down for him.'

'Pap, if you start in on the old-elephant routine now, I really will scream.'

'All right, Pap,' Alma said, 'what do you want to eat? Tell me and I'll fix it for you.'

'Anything I want?' he bargained.

'Yes.'

'I want a souse meat pie.'

'A souse meat pie?' his mother said. 'Are you loony? Where's Alma going to get a hog's head?'

'I'll get one, Mom.'

Alfie paused on the ladder. Suddenly he thought that maybe it was possible to make a cartoon even of this. The idea surprised him. He leaned his cheek against the wood. Not a cartoon of himself – he wasn't ready for that yet. He could do a comic strip about a *man* who had taken himself away from the world. He was better at drawing men anyway. In a balloon, he thought. Balloons were better than attics in a comic strip. He warmed to the idea.

In the first square a man would be suspended over the world in a balloon. He'd be saying, 'Nobody can make me come down!'

In the second square he'd be saying, '*Nobody* can make me come down!'

In the third square he'd be saying, '*Nobody can make me come down!*'

In the last square he'd be saying, 'But somebody could try.'

Alfie smiled. He was glad there would still be cartoons. He climbed the remaining rungs of the ladder. He stepped on the living-room floor. He felt jarred for a moment, as if he had stepped on something unexpectedly hard. He put one hand on the ladder to steady himself.

He set his cartoons on the television. They unrolled, and he put Alma's books on top to hold them. He walked into the kitchen. 'I'm down,' he said.

THE TV KID

1

LENNIE was in front of the motel washing down the walk with a hose. He directed the spray on a chewing-gum paper and some grass and twigs. He watched as the trash went down the drain.

A truck passed on the highway, building up speed for the hill ahead. Lennie glanced up. He watched until the truck was out of sight.

'Aren't you through yet?' Lennie's mother called. 'You've got to do your homework, remember?'

He turned off the hose. 'I'm through.'

He started towards the office. At that moment his mom turned on the neon sign and it flashed red above his head. THE FAIRY LAND MOTEL – VACANCY.

Lennie paused at the concrete wishing-well. There was a concrete elf on one side and, facing him, Humpty Dumpty. With one hand on Humpty Dumpty's head, Lennie leant forward and looked down into the wishing-well. On the blue-painted bottom lay seven pennies, one nickel and a crumpled Mound wrapper.

Lennie walked on to the office. As he went inside he paused in front of the TV.

A game show was on, and there were five new cars lined up on a revolving stage. The winning contestant could pick one of the cars and if it started, he got to keep it. Only one of the cars was wired to start.

'It's the Grand Am,' Lennie said instantly. He felt he had a special instinct for picking the right box or door or car on shows like this. 'I *know* it's the Grand Am.'

'Lennie, are you watching television?' his mother called from the utility room.

'I'm looking for a pencil,' he called back.

'Well, there are plenty of pencils on the desk.'

'Where? Oh, yeah, I see one now.'

Lennie was hoping to stall until he could see if it really was the Grand Am as he suspected.

The contestant said he wanted to try for the Catalina. 'No, the Grand Am, the Grand Am!' Lennie murmured beneath his breath. He found the stub of a pencil on the desk and held it against his chest like a charm.

'Lennie, I meant what I said about no television,' his mom called.

'I know you did.'

'No television at all until those grades pick up.'

'I know.'

A commercial came on. 'Doc-tor Pep-per, so mis-un-der-stooooooood.'

'Me and Doctor Pepper,' Lennie mumbled. He knew he had sixty more seconds to stall now. 'Where did you say those pencils were?' he called.

'On the desk.'

The commercial ended, and the contestant was walking across the stage to the Catalina. He was getting into the car, fastening his seat belt. At that crucial moment Lennie's mother appeared in the doorway.

'The pencils are –' She broke off as she saw him. She said sternly, 'Lennie, go into my room right now and start studying.'

'I will, just let me find out if it's the –'

'Now!'

In one incredibly swift move – it was like something out of an old-time movie – Lennie's mother stepped in front of him. She turned off the television. As the picture faded to one small dot, she and Lennie looked at each other.

'You didn't have to do that,' Lennie said. He was hurt. He felt as if his mother had slapped him. 'Now I'll never know if it was the Grand Am.'

'You've got to do your homework.'

'Well, will you watch for me?'

'If you go right now.'

'I'm going. I'm going.' He started from the office. 'Only turn the set back on or it won't warm up in time. You'll miss it.'

Once outside the room Lennie stood in the hall and waited. 'I wish I was on TV,' he said to himself. 'I wish I was getting in the Grand Am.'

His mother came through the doorway. She took his shoulder and started him into her room. 'It was the Firebird,' she said.

'Oh.' He was strangely disheartened. 'Then I wish I was getting in the Firebird.'

'Well, you won't be getting in anything till those grades pick up,' his mom said.

'If you're thinking I'm too dumb to be on TV, well, half the people you see on those shows are drop-outs. Most of the contestants are out of work.'

'Len, will you please go into my room and start studying,' his mom said tiredly. 'I simply cannot argue with you this way every night.'

'I'm going.'

As he went, he thought of himself getting in the Firebird, fastening the seat belt, turning the key. He thought of his face lighting up as the engine started.

However, he thought, walking slower, if he could go on just one game show, it had better be something like *Let's Make a Deal* where knowledge didn't count. He would dress up like a pizza, and if he got in the Big Deal of the Day, he would go for curtain number two.

'Don't stall, Lennie.'

'I'm not stalling.' He walked into his mother's room. His mom had set up a card table in the corner, and Lennie had to study there these days. It was the only place in the motel where there was nothing to do and nothing to look at. He couldn't even see out of the window without getting up and walking round the bed.

His mother was still standing in the doorway. Lennie glanced at her. He said, 'If you're thinking that I'm too ugly to be on television, well, you don't have to worry about that either. The uglier you are these days, the better. Ugliness is in.'

'Start with Science.'

'Mom, have you ever had a look at that kid on all those meat-spread commercials? I know I look as good as him, and they say he makes thousands of dollars.'

'Lennie.'

'He gets three hundred and twenty dollars for every one of those commercials. Think of it. The kid is sitting at home, probably watching himself on TV and he is making three hundred and twenty dollars.'

'Lennie –'

'And if you get on a soap opera, Mom, if you just walk in front of the camera, which anybody could do, for that you get fifty-one dollars. If you have five lines, you get ninety dollars.'

'Lennie, stop this and get to your work.'

''Course five dollars goes to your agent and twenty goes into a trust fund for when you get too old to perform. I read that in *TV Guide*.'

'Lennie!'

'All *right!*'

They stared at each other for a moment. Then with a sigh Lennie flipped open his Science book. He turned to the chapter on plants. There was a pencil hole in the page where in anger he had stabbed the book.

With his mother watching he stared down at the cross-section of a plant. To give the illusion that he was serious about studying, he put his finger on the first part of the leaf. Slowly he moved his finger down the page, round the pencil hole.

His mom watched a moment more, and then she turned and went back into the office.

Lennie kept his eyes on the page. As he got to the picture of the stem, his eyes began to close. His mind drifted to more pleasant things. He saw his own face on TV, a close-up.

He would make the perfect contestant, he thought. In the first place he was eager and enthusiastic. In the second place he was a little dumb, so the audience would identify with him and be glad when he won. And third, he was such a good sport he would go along with anything.

As the parts of the plant grew dimmer in his mind, his own face on TV grew sharper and clearer. The announcer's voice, hushed with urgency, replaced the sound of the trucks on the highway.

He dreamed.

2

'AND now, Lennie, you have won over three thousand dollars in cash and merchandise and, more important, you have won the chance to spin our Vacation Wheel. How do you feel about that, Lennie?'

'Real good, sir.'

'Then join me over here at the Vacation Wheel. Now, Lennie, I don't have to remind you that up there on the wheel are twenty, all-expense paid vacations to places all over the world, do I?'

'No, sir.'

'That's twenty, all-expense paid vacations! You can go to Rome, to London, to Paris. You can go to beautiful Hawaii, exotic Mexico or sunny Spain. All in all, there are twenty, wonderful, all-expense paid vacations up there on the wheel. But, Lennie, as you know, there are also what we call our zonk trips. How do you feel about those, Lennie?'

'Well, I hope I don't get one.'

'And that's what we're hoping too, aren't we, folks? Hear that applause, Lennie? They're all with you. Now step up close to the Vacation Wheel. That's right. The three zonk trips, as we call them, are here and here and here. Try not to land on them.'

'I will, sir.'

'All right, put up your hand now, Lennie, right here on the Vacation Wheel, and Lennie, *give it a spin!*'

'Here goes!'

'Good boy! The wheel is spinning, folks. Lennie really gave it a good spin, didn't he? Where do you want to go, Lennie?'

'Any of those places is all right with me.'

'Except the zonk places, right?'

'Right.'

'It's still spinning, and now it's beginning to slow down. Watch the wheel, folks. Where is Lennie going? To Paris? Rome? London? It's almost stopped, It looks like *Egypt*! No! *Rio*! No! Oh, *no*! Look at that! Lennie, you have landed on number thirteen, one of our zonk trips, and I don't have to tell you what that means.'

'It means I'm going to have to take a zonk trip.'

'Right.'

'Where?'

'Well, let me look at my zonk envelope. Oh, Lennie.'

'What?'

'*Oh*, Lennie.'

'What? What is it?'

'*Oh, Lennie!*'

'What? I want to know. What is it?'

'Lennie, you are going to have to spend one full night, all-expense paid, in a *haunted house!*'

'A what?'

'Yes, Lennie, you heard correctly, you are going to Haunted House Number Thirteen located right on the outskirts – that's the dark, scary outskirts, I might add – of beautiful downtown –'

'But I don't want to spend the night in any haunted house.'

'Of course you don't, but you take your chances, Lennie, just like all the other contestants. Remember that paper you signed when you came on the show?'

'Yes, but I didn't – I mean I couldn't – I mean –'

'Oh, all right, Lennie, I'll tell you what I'm going to do. You go to the haunted house, spend one night there, and if you survive – I say, *if* you survive – then you come back next week and we'll let you spin the Vacation Wheel again. How about that?'

'But, sir, couldn't I just take my three thousand in cash and merchandise and –'

'How many want to see him take the cash and merchandise and go home?'

Silence.

'How many want to see him go to the *haunted house?*'

Wild applause.

'But, sir –'

'See, the audience is with you. Hear that applause? Well, it's time for a commercial break now, but stay with us, folks, for the second half of *Give it a Spin*, the show where *you* pick your prizes and *we* see that you take them.' . . .

3

'LENNIE?'

His eyes snapped open as quickly as a puppet's. He said, 'Yes'm.'

'Have you finished your Science?' His mother was standing in the doorway, her hands in her jeans pockets.

'Practically.'

'You know all the parts of the leaf?'

'I think so.'

'And the stem?'

'I think so. I get mixed up on some of them.'

'Which ones?'

'These.' He made a circular motion that took in the entire page.

'Well, as soon as you're sure of them, Lennie, you bring your book into the office and let me call out the questions.' She sighed. 'I wish that man was still in 314, the one from Decatur, remember? Now, that was a smart man. He could have helped you with your Science.'

Lennie didn't answer.

'And that man was a slow starter just like you, Lennie. He told me he didn't learn a thing until he was eleven years old. He said people thought there was something wrong with him.'

Lennie didn't answer.

His mom paused. Then she said, 'I don't want you getting another bad grade in your test tomorrow.'

'I don't want to get one either,' he said.

His last Science grade had been 23 out of a possible 100. Staring down at that 23 – it had been written in red pencil and circled – Lennie had for the first time felt the real meaning of numbers. His arithmetic teachers had been trying to get that across for years – numbers *mean* something. Well, the arithmetic teachers were right, he had thought. A number, just a *number*, could ruin a person's whole day, week maybe.

Lennie had not started feeling like himself again until he was home watching a re-run of *The Lucy Show* in which Lucy thought Mr Mooney had turned into a monkey. When Lucy came back from lunch, saw the monkey sitting at Mr Mooney's desk and staggered back with her mouth open – that was when Lennie had smiled for the first time since Science.

As Lennie's mother went to the office Lennie rested his chin on his hand and stared at the pictures. The leaf, like something in a dream, moved farther away. Slowly Lennie closed his eyes. His mind, like an unmoored ship, drifted to other shores.

The interruption by his mother was like a station break . . . 'And now', the announcer said in Lennie's mind, 'back to *Give it a Spin.*'

'Ladies and Gentlemen, this is Dink McLeod again. Now that our young contestant is gone, I want to let you in on a little surprise we have planned for him.

'See, our staff has concealed in that haunted house – the haunted house where Lennie will be spending the night – thirteen of the scariest, most terrifying movie and television monsters of all time. We have Dracula and Frankenstein's monster. They're in the living-room. The werewolf is in the kitchen. The mummy is in the sewing-room, and out in the back yard, folks, will be Godzilla, Mothro, Scorpo and a Giant Behemoth! How about *that* for a scary quartet?'

Applause.

'We'll have hidden cameras in every room of the house to catch Lennie's reactions so you won't want to miss our next show. Remember now, tune in next week to see what it's going to be like for young Lennie in Haunted House Number Thirteen.'

'Lennie?' his mom called from the motel office.
'Yes'm?'

'I'm taking some extra towels to 316. I'll be right back.'

'Yes'm.'

'I'll call out the questions then.'

'Right.'

He didn't open his eyes. He didn't want school books and Science and his unfortunate position at the card table to intrude on his dream.

He smiled to himself. He was thinking of entering the living-room of the haunted house. What a sight he would be! His knees would be trembling, his heart pounding. His eyes would be rolling round in his head like marbles. He would be holding out his hands in a blindly terrified way. He would bump into Dracula.

'Gut e-ven-ing!'

Lennie would glance up. He wouldn't have seen Dracula because of the black outfit. Now he would see the white face.

'Velcome.'

Lennie's eyes, bulging almost out of their sockets, would see that Dracula's fangs were bared. His black cape was raised. Dracula would bend low, aiming for Lennie's neck.

Lennie would scream, turn, run for the door and crash right into Frankenstein's monster. Before the huge, un-matched hands could close round Lennie's throat, Lennie would scream again and make a headlong dash for the safety of the kitchen.

He would lean against the wall, eyes closed, catching his breath. His hands would be clutched over his pounding heart. Suddenly Lennie would feel something furry beside him. He would open his eyes. At that moment he would look out of the window and see the full moon. A werewolf's moon. And the something furry beside him had to be ... Very slowly, making no sudden moves, Lennie would ease over to the door. Then, abruptly, he would rush into the sewing-room and slam the door.

'I'm back, Lennie. Are you ready for me to call out the questions?'

'No, leave me alone for a few more minutes.'

'But –'

'I'm almost through.'

He began speeding up his dream. He thought of himself running out of the back door of the house into the yard. It would be dark despite the full moon, and in a panic Lennie would dash straight into Godzilla's big toe.

He thought of himself falling back, gasping with fright. He would stagger round Godzilla's instep, uttering incantations and cries for help, and plunge straight into Mothro's wings.

After narrowly escaping being fluttered to death, he would have a long, panic-stricken dash to Scorpo, the scorpion as big as a Boeing 747. Lennie would cringe there, too scared to move, awaiting the fatal sting.

At that moment a voice would come on the loud-speaker concealed in the trees. 'Lennie! Lennie, can you hear me?'

He would be too frightened to recognize his own name. 'No, no, not Scorpo!' he would be sobbing. 'Anyone but Scorpo. I'm allergic to stings.'

'Lennie, can you hear me? This is Dink McLeod and I'm here with our *Give it a Spin* audience and, Lennie, we have had hidden cameras on you ever since you got to Haunted House Thirteen.'

'You've had cameras on *me*?'

'That's right, Lennie.'

'The whole time?'

'Lennie, we got the whoooooole thing.'

He would realize then what a pitiful sight he must be. Here he was cringing on the ground, sobbing at Scorpo's feet like an infant. He would raise his head. He would give a shaky laugh. He would dry his eyes on his shirt.

'Did you have hidden cameras in the house too?' he would ask.

'That's right, Lennie.'

'In the – er – sewing-room too?' He would remember how he had come into the sewing-room and tried to hide behind the mummy, which in the dark had looked like a ragged sewing dummy.

'The sewing-room too. We're just sorry you didn't go upstairs, Lennie, because upstairs we had the Son of Frankenstein, and the Blob, and the Creature from the Black Lagoon.'

'Gee, I'm sorry I didn't get up there too.'

'And now, Lennie –'

'Lennie!' It was his mom. 'Bring the book out on to the porch. These two schoolteachers from Wilmington checked in and they say they'll help you.'

'In a minute.'

'They haven't got all night, Lennie.' She sounded impatient.

'I'm on my way.'

He sat with his eyes closed, speeding up his dream even more.

'And now, Lennie, we have a car waiting to bring you

back to our studio to collect over three thousand dollars in cash and merchandise. How does that sound to
you?'

'Real good, sir.'

'And, more important, you get another spin of the
Vacation Wheel.'

'Oh, well, never mind about that, sir. I'll just take my
cash and –'

'We'll leave it up to the audience. How many want to
see Lennie come in and take his cash and merchandise?'

Silence.

'How many want to see him spin the Vacation Wheel?'

Wild applause.

'See, the audience is all with you, so come on in, Lennie,
and *give it a spin!*'

'Lennie! These schoolteachers are leaving for Nashville
at seven o'clock in the morning!'

'Yes'm.' Lennie rose. He picked up his book. As he
carried it through the motel office to the porch, he went
over the strange words for the first time . . . petiole . . .
stipule . . .

4

LENNIE leant over his desk, pencil in hand, waiting for the Science tests to be passed out. He always got a worried feeling when he was waiting to take a test. Even if he knew everything there was to know about a subject – something that had never happened – he knew he would still be worried.

He erased a mark on his desk and then pencilled it back. He beat out a rhythm from *The Adams Family*, snapping his fingers when he got to the two clicks. He jiggled his leg. He turned to the boy sitting next to him and said, 'Hey, Frankie, is the petiole the stem or is the stipule the stem? I'm mixed up.'

Frankie shrugged.

He turned round. 'Letty Bond, is –'

'The petiole is the stem,' she said in a bored voice, 'the stipules are extra leaves.' She clicked open her ballpoint pen.

Lennie turned back to the front of the room and raised his hand. 'Miss Markham?'

'Yes, Lennie.'

'Can we take our tests in pencil or do we have to have a ballpoint pen?'

'Pencil's fine.'

'But can we use pen if we want to?' He asked this on behalf of Letty Bond who he thought might be growing anxious.

'Either one is fine.'

Lennie's throat was dry. The tests were coming. He put down his pencil, wiped his hands on his shirt and picked up his pencil. He took the tests from the girl in front of him, selected the top one and passed the rest to Letty Bond.

'Well, here we go,' he said with false liveliness. He glanced at Letty Bond. She had already written her name at the top of the page and was ready to take on the first question.

Lennie turned back to his desk. The test was mimeo-graphed in purple ink, and for a moment Lennie had a vision of another red 23 at the top of his. He let out his breath in one long unhappy sigh. He felt like writing the 23 there and saving Miss Markham the trouble.

Glancing down the page he decided to skip the first part which was fill-in-the-blanks and go on to the second part which was a plant with all the parts to be labelled. He had done that last night for the schoolteachers – twice.

Very carefully he printed the word 'petiole' on the line opposite the stem. Then he looked at the word. It looked wrong. Quickly he turned his pencil and erased the word. He wet his lips. He wanted to turn round and ask Letty Bond if she was sure the petiole was the stem. It seemed to him . . . Nervously he printed 'petiole' back in the same space.

He printed in four more words and then he got up. With his eyes on his paper he went to the teacher's desk. 'Miss Markham?'

'Yes, Lennie.'

'Is that word spelt right?'

'I'm sorry but I can't give you any help after the tests are passed out.'

'Oh.' He stood there for a moment staring down at the word he had written. 'Stupile.' He had never felt more miserable in his life. He gave Miss Markham a weak smile. He said, 'I feel kind of stupile myself today.'

'I do believe though,' Miss Markham went on kindly, smiling back at him, 'you should look at what you've written *very* carefully. There may be something wrong.'

'Thank you, Miss Markham.'

As Lennie hurried back to his desk Miss Markham said, 'Remember, spelling counts, class.'

Lennie erased the word and respelt it. He filled in two more blanks and erased one. His test now had a worked-over look. He had worn through the paper in two places. He thought that anyone who thinks school isn't hard ought to take a look at his paper.

He bent over his desk, wet his pencil-point and filled in another blank. He went on to the multiple-choice section and filled in three of those. He glanced again at the word 'stepile'.

'Time's up, class,' Miss Markham said.

Lennie looked up, startled. He turned to Frankie. 'Are you through?'

Frankie shrugged.

'Are you through, Letty Bond?'

'I've been through since ten thirty,' she said. He glanced at her desk. She was writing a note to someone named Anne. It started: 'Am I bored!'

Lennie spun round and glanced in desperation at his test. Only half of the blanks were filled. Quickly he began filling in the rest, guessing, putting anything down so that Miss Markham would see a full, completed sheet when she got to his test. That was bound to make a better impression.

'Lennie.' It was Miss Markham.

'Yes'm.' He kept writing. He did not have time to look up.

'I have to have your test now.'

'Yes'm.'

'The next class is coming in.'

'One more word.' In desperation Lennie kept writing. Cammie Hagerdorn was standing by his desk, waiting to take Lennie's seat. Lennie looked up.

'Hard, huh?' Cammie said.

'Hard for me.' Lennie sighed. He got up, dropped his test on Miss Markham's desk and went out into the hall. Shoulders sagging, he went slowly to World Studies.

5

'How'd you do on your Science test?' His mom didn't glance up as he came in the office door. She was looking at the guest register. She was going over the names carefully, as if she were hoping they would multiply like amoeba and fill the page.

'Oh, all right.'

'Really?' She looked up, smiling.

'I think so.'

'I *knew* you'd do well.' She leant forward on her arms. 'And it wasn't the schoolteachers either – it was all that studying you did.'

He glanced at the TV set. Farmer Fred was on. He was yelling, 'Pull up your milking-stools, boys and girls, and get set for Farmer Fred and his cartooooons!'

Slowly Lennie started back to his room. The sounds of the first cartoon washed over him. It was Tweetie Bird and Sylvester. Tweetie Bird was crying, 'I *did*! I taw a *putty tat*!'

His mom called, 'Oh, Lennie, would you take a rollaway bed to 314.'

'Yes'm.'

As he came back through the office, pushing the bed, he saw Sylvester was sawing a hole in the ceiling over Tweetie Bird's cage. Lennie walked slower.

'The bed, Lennie.'

'Just let me see him fall to the floor.'

Sylvester finished his circle in the ceiling and fell with a crash to the floor. He pulled himself up in the shape of a round paper doll.

'I'm *going*,' he said before his mother could remind him again.

He pushed the bed out of the door. There were three rooms occupied at the motel that afternoon. A farmer with a station wagon of roosters was in 310. A salesman was in 316. A family of five had just checked into 314.

Lennie knocked at the door. 'Here's the bed,' he called out.

'Come in.'

Lennie opened the door and pushed the bed into the room. The television was on, and Lennie glanced quickly at it to see if he could catch the ending of the Sylvester cartoon.

On the screen a man in a chef's suit was teaching the number three by juggling three pizzas. '*Three*,' he said.

A girl of about five was sitting on the edge of the bed, watching the chef. Her mouth was open a little. 'Cartoons are on Channel Seven,' Lennie said as he unfolded the bed.

The chef took another pizza and started juggling. *'Four,'* he said.

'Will that be all ?' Lennie asked formally.

The woman nodded, and Lennie turned to the door. The chef cried, *'Five!'* and the woman said, 'See what else is on.'

Lennie turned. He said, 'We get *Farmer Fred's Cartoons, Gilligan's Island, Bonanza* and Mike Douglas.'

'Oh. Thank you.'

'Sure.'

Lennie started back to the office. His mother was sitting in one of the webbed chairs on the porch. It was her favourite time of the day – when she could sit out and chat with the guests. Now she was talking to the salesman in 316.

'I delivered the bed,' Lennie said.

She turned to him, her face bright. 'Lennie, guess what this man sells?'

'I don't know.'

'Encyclopedias!'

'Oh.'

'Why, you should have been here last night.' She turned back to the salesman. 'We had a regular school going on out here, didn't we, Lennie?'

'Yes.'

She looked at him. She said, 'Listen, you go on in and watch TV if you like.'

'I thought I wasn't allowed.'

'You deserve it for doing so well on your Science test.'

'Oh, all right.'

Lennie went into the office and sank down on the

plastic sofa. He reached for the TV knob. He began to feel a little better. He said to himself, I think I'll see what Hoss and Little Joe are up to. He leant back on the plastic. It felt good and cool. He put his feet up on the plastic coffee table. He sighed with contentment.

6

LENNIE came out of the back door of the motel. Here lay the broken Fairy Land figures – the dwarfs and fairies that had been out in front of the motel until they crumbled. Lennie stepped round an armless Red Riding Hood and a headless fairy godmother.

He climbed down the hill behind the motel and crossed the field. It was a Saturday, a bright October morning, and he had finished his chores at the motel. Usually he sat in the office on Saturday mornings and watched cartoons, but this morning he felt the need to get away.

The day before he had gotten his Science test back and he had made a 59. The thought of that 59 still made him feel sick. Only 11 more points and he would have passed like everyone else.

As soon as he had seen that 59 he had thought there should be some kind of patent medicine for moments like this. This had to be worse than acid stomach and sinus headache and low backache all rolled into one.

'For that uncomfortable feeling that comes when you fail your Science test, take Fail-Ease, the tablet that eases failure and makes you less afraid to fail the next time.'

He would be on the commercial, sitting right at his desk

in Science class, pale and sick. He would drop two Fail-Ease tablets into a glass of water, drink, and a wonderful feeling of relief would come over him. The lines of tension in his face would relax. Colour would come back to his cheeks.

The teacher would walk back to his desk. She would lean down, smiling, and say, 'I hope you've learnt, Lennie, that with Fail-Ease you never have to feel the pain of failure again.'

'Yes,' he would say, 'for relief from the nagging pain of failure –' and then he and Miss Markham would smile at each other and say together – 'take Fail-Ease, the failure reliever that requires no prescription.'

The thought had raised Lennie's spirits for a moment. Then Miss Markham had rapped on her desk and said, 'I want these tests signed by one of your parents, students, and returned on Monday.'

Lennie had brought his test home and stuck it in his sock drawer. His mom had been too busy to ask about it – they had seven rooms occupied at the motel that night – but sooner or later she would. And even if she didn't, Lennie would have to get her to sign it.

It was something he couldn't bear to do. When he disappointed his mother with his school work, her mouth got as sad as a clown's.

'This is our big chance, Lennie,' she had been saying ever since she had inherited the Fairy Land Motel from her father. They had been heading for the motel on a Trailways bus the first time she had said it. 'This is our big chance, Lennie. All a person can hope to get in this life is one good chance.'

He had nodded, smiling at her. He had been as pleased

about inheriting the motel as she was.

'Now we can live like other people,' she had said. She had begun to hum. Her favourite songs were about home and going home. Now she was humming *Country Roads*. She stopped humming long enough to say, 'You'll go to school regularly and make good grades – no more of this moving around.'

They looked like people who moved around, Lennie thought, both in jeans and tee-shirts, his mother's hair frizzled and his own uncut. But no more.

'And I'll make a success of the motel. I promise you that.'

'And I'll be a success in school,' he'd said.

As he sat there on the bus, he saw himself as the end of a TV show. All his problems and troubles were over. The last crisis had been passed. He and his mom heading for home and happiness. It was as perfect as the ending of a Lassie show. He saw himself smiling while the credits rolled past his beaming face.

Only that was the trouble with life, Lennie had found out later. He had expected things to change as quickly and dramatically as they did in bad-breath commercials – one gargle and a new life. It hadn't worked that way.

In real life, Lennie found out, problems didn't get wrapped up neatly between commercials. In real life you moved, and all the things that were wrong with you moved with you. If you couldn't pass Science in Kentucky then you wouldn't be able to pass it in Tennessee either.

Lennie wondered if this happened to other people, like Presidents of the United States or famous TV stars. Did they get their lifelong ambition, thinking life would be perfect when they got to be President or when they got their own series, and then find out that all the things wrong with them were still wrong?

Lennie walked quickly down the hill. He had come this way so often that there was a faint path in the deep grass. He came to the maple trees – the leaves were solid gold now, and he walked up the next hill. At the top were the ruins of two old camp fires, black circles like a puff of breath from a dragon.

The first time Lennie had seen the old fires, he had paused and planned a TV show about a dragon. Only one person, himself, knew about the dragon. He had trailed the dragon to his cave by following these double camp fires, and the dragon and he had become friends.

The highlight of the programme came when the townspeople arrived at the cave to kill the dragon, thinking him responsible for the recent slaughter of sheep.

'Get out of the way, son. We're going in.'

'But the dragon's my friend. He wouldn't kill anything!'

'There's seventeen sheep dead in the valley. Somebody killed them.'

'Well, *he* didn't do it. He couldn't.'

'Get out of the way, son. We got no quarrel with you.'

'But he *couldn't* have killed the sheep I tell you! He doesn't even have any *teeth!*'

'What?'

'He's over two hundred years old and all he eats is bananas and tomatoes and once in a while a real ripe apple.'

'Listen! The boy might be telling the truth! Seems to me my gran'daddy said there was a dragon around here when he was a boy.'

'Your gran'daddy Amos?'

'My gran'daddy Amos, and I recall him saying that dragon never hurt a fly.'

'Well, then maybe it was *wolves* that got them sheep. If, as the boy and your gran'daddy says, the dragon's harmless, we'll let him be.'

That had been one of Lennie's favourite dreams. It had re-run for days. But now he stepped between the old fires without noticing and went down the hill beneath the red beech trees. Here the grass was as soft and green as official grass. Then he came to the lake.

He stood for a moment looking at the water, at the places where the reflection of trees turned the water red and gold. He looked at the houses. Each of them was closed for the winter. The lake was really his now.

Lennie went into the weeds and, pulling hard, brought out his boat. He eased it into the water.

The boat was old and heavy. Someone had abandoned it long ago because the seats were half rotten and the boards leaked. When Lennie had first seen the boat, weeds were growing inside. Purple flowers were poking up over the sides as if they were waiting for a ride.

Lennie got into the boat. Old and rotten as it was, it was still sturdy enough to get Lennie across the lake. The first time he had pushed off in the boat he had half expected to sink. He had imagined himself going down the way Coyote and Bugs Bunny and Sylvester did in old cartoons, just standing there, sinking, with a comical expression.

That was one thing he particularly liked about cartoon characters. When they walked out on a limb and the limb cracked, or they ran out on the air and then realized nothing was under them, they looked into the camera in such a comical way. If he had a camera on him, he could do the same thing.

For a moment he wished he were back at the motel watching the Saturday morning cartoons. Then, leaning on his oar, he pushed into deeper water. He began to row.

Lennie was not supposed to be here, because this was a private lake. It had been dammed up and filled for the benefit of the people who had houses here. No one else was allowed. But as long as nobody saw him – and there was nobody to see him now, he thought – it was all right. He kept rowing.

Lennie knew more about this lake and these houses than anybody. There was not a house here that he had not entered at one time or another. Sometimes he went in through a window, sometimes through a door if he knew where the key was hidden. But however he got in, Lennie never took anything or did any damage. He just liked to look at other people's things.

There was something about strange people's houses that fascinated Lennie. Perhaps that was because he had never lived in a real house himself, only in apartments and trailers and motels.

Lennie's favourite house was the stone one with the willow trees in front. His finest hours had been spent in the tiny back room of the stone house, sitting on the floor, warmed by the sun coming in the window, playing with twenty-five-year-old Tinker Toys or dealing out games of Circus Old Maid or Animal Rummy or looking through shoe boxes of stringless yo-yos and stones as smooth as birds' eggs.

In the centre of the lake he suddenly wished he were back at the motel again. He tried to lose himself in his thoughts.

What if the Partridge family's bus had broken down and they were stranded and while he was rowing across the lake he started singing and they heard him and asked him to join the group and gave him his own electric guitar? While he was imagining himself in a white fringed suit on the stage with the Partridges, he lost interest.

He shifted thoughts.

What if he were the last person on earth? He had seen that the week before on *Thursday Night Movie*. A plague had come and disintegrated everyone but one person. Now Lennie imagined himself that person, rowing across the lake wondering what had happened to everyone else.

He rowed more slowly. His oars dragged in the water. He felt as lonely as if he really were the last person on earth.

To change his mood, he imagined a commercial. 'To help that lonely feeling,' the announcer would say, 'buy Friend, the doll that's as big and as real as you are.'

He brightened. He imagined the announcer's voice saying, 'Yes, with Friend, you'll always have someone to talk to.' There would be a shot of him and Friend talking and laughing on a park bench.

'With Friend, you'll never have to go to the movies alone.' There would be a shot of him and Friend entering a movie theatre. The announcer would say quietly, 'And remember, Friend comes with a special ID card that lets him enter all movie theatres and sports events for half price.'

Lennie smiled. He began to row again. He felt better. He imagined the end of the commercial with him and Friend strolling along a country road. The announcer would say, 'Yes, take Friend everywhere you go and – '

then a choir of a hundred voices would sing – '*You'll never be a-lone.*'

Lennie was close to the shore now, and he eased up on his rowing. He drifted the rest of the way. When his boat touched shore, Lennie got out quickly. He pulled his boat up under the long waving branches of the willow tree. He started for the house.

7

LENNIE was on the front porch of the stone house now. He peered through the window.

In his mind the announcer reminded him, 'Whenever you enter an empty house, take Friend along. Yes, remember, no house is ever empty with Friend.'

He imagined Friend peering through the window too, glancing at Lennie, waiting.

'Let's go in,' Lennie would say. Friend would nod in agreement. 'Follow me.' Another nod and Friend would fall in behind.

'Remember,' the announcer would say, 'with Friend there's never an argument. He does what *you* want, goes where *you* go.'

The key to the front door was on top of the door-moulding, and Lennie took down the key and put it in the lock. He liked to enter with the key because it gave him a feeling of belonging. Going in through the window wasn't as good.

His hand was on the doorknob when he heard a car on the road. He was startled. He had thought everyone at the lake had gone back to their regular houses. He stood deerlike for a moment, one hand on the key ready to turn, the other on the knob.

Then his tension eased. It's just somebody who made a wrong turn, he told himself. He took a step backward and caught sight of the car. It was a blue sedan, four houses away. Lennie could just see a glimpse of it shining through the trees, but he could see that the car was moving slowly up the road, pausing at each driveway.

Lennie glanced over his shoulder at the lake. He saw the willow trees. He saw the bow of his boat poking through the leaves. Then he glanced back at the car. It was at the A-frame now, three houses away.

Silently Lennie closed the screen door, leaving the key in the lock. Bending low, he crawled to the steps. Here he hesitated again. He didn't think he could make it to his boat. And if he did, he knew he couldn't row across the lake without being spotted.

In a crouch, he went round the porch. The car was two houses away now. It was behind the house with the artificial-brick siding. And for the first time Lennie got a good look at the car. It was a police car.

His fear flared. He dodged quickly round the side of the house. He stood there a moment, flattened against the stones.

Lennie had never heard that the police patrolled this area. Maybe they didn't as a usual thing, he thought. Maybe somebody had complained that their houses had been bothered. Maybe they had asked the police to keep an eye out. Maybe he was going to be arrested.

The car was next door now, pausing at the driveway. Lennie was afraid he had waited too long. He glanced around, panic-stricken.

Then in one fast move he fell to his stomach and wriggled into the crawl space under the house. It was damp and musty here, a maze of discarded items and old tools and unused building materials. A cold air moved under the house, and Lennie thought he heard something scamper.

Pulling himself along with his elbows, he scooted round a pile of shutters, a box of Mason jars and a watering-can with the bottom rusted out. He was cold, and his jacket was back at the Fairy Land Motel, hanging on a hook in the office.

Lennie struck his head on a low water pipe and ducked. He was rubbing his head when he caught sight of the police car through the gap between some old plastic milk bottles and a tipped-over-barrel. The police car slowed down and came to a stop at the driveway.

To calm himself, Lennie thought of Friend. It really wasn't a bad idea, a product like Friend. Girls would always have someone to dance with at parties. Old people would never be caught talking to themselves. Right now he would feel a lot better with Friend sitting beside him.

'Whenever you feel afraid, reach for Friend. His hand is always there in a plastic so lifelike you can hardly tell it from the real thing.'

Lennie would touch the plastic hand, not for comfort, but to get Friend's attention. 'You go out,' he would whisper to Friend, 'let them catch you.'

One nod and Friend would crawl out, willingly surrendering, his arms outstretched for the handcuffs.

Against his will Lennie's mind turned from Friend. He could see the policeman now. He was standing by the car.

He leant down and spoke to the other policeman who was working on the radio. Lennie couldn't hear what they were saying.

He inched forward so he could see the policeman a little better. He was a big man. He had probably been strong once, but he had started going downhill. Everything about him sagged – his arms, his stomach, his neck. The other cop – Lennie could see him now too – looked like Tiny Tim with a haircut.

It was so much like a television show that for a moment Lennie half expected to see the two cops framed in an eleven inch black-and-white set. He wished suddenly it *was* a television programme and that a commercial was about to come on. All Lennie would need would be sixty seconds to get away.

The two policemen spoke again. The big cop looked up at the sky.

Lennie waited. He crossed his fingers for luck.

The policeman looked down at his shoe. Lennie thought for a moment he was getting ready to step back into the patrol car. Lennie's breath began to ease out in a long sigh of relief.

Then, abruptly, the policeman turned and headed straight for Lennie.

8

LENNIE inched closer to the large pile of stones by the chimney. He crouched behind it. He couldn't see the policeman now.

The stones he was leaning against were as round and smooth as cannon balls. These stones were what had first impressed Lennie about the house. He had felt that only very particular people would choose stones like this. Ordinary people would just settle for rough stones blasted out of a quarry. These stones – if Lennie knew anything about stones – had been hand-picked out of some creek where they had been worn smooth by about a thousand years of rippling water.

Lennie still couldn't see the policeman, but he could hear his footsteps coming closer. The policeman tried the back door, paused, took two steps to the right. He was probably looking in the kitchen window now, Lennie thought, and then the policeman came down the steps and went round the right side of the house. Lennie pressed closer to the pile of stones and put his hand on one of them for comfort.

Slowly, as if he were pacing off a distance, the policeman walked to the front of the house. Lennie could see his legs now, the crease in his pants. His shoes were as shiny as Christmas ornaments. If Lennie crawled closer, he could see his face in them.

The policeman stopped, and for one terrible moment Lennie expected the policeman to drop down on all fours and peer past the trash to where Lennie crouched. Lennie's face would shine in the darkness like a lightbulb. 'I see you, son, come on out.'

But the policeman moved on to the steps. He stood there a moment, shielded by the ferns. Then, one by one, he took the stairs. He went up as slowly as a trained bear.

Lennie was almost under the porch, so he could hear every move the policeman made. The policeman looked in the living-room window, peering in for a long time like a beggar. He took in the deer-head over the mantel, the faded sofa, the big oilcloth-covered table, the electric motor somebody had left on the daybed. Lennie knew that room by heart. And if the policeman wanted to, if he bent to the left he could see into the back bedroom, Lennie's room. He could see the chest where all Lennie's favourite things were stored.

The policeman moved to the front door. He opened the screen.

There was a silence, and Lennie knew the policeman was looking at the key in the lock, wondering what it was doing there.

'Hey, Bert,' he called, 'look here a minute.'

The second policeman got out of the car. He walked round the house and took the steps to the porch two at a time.

'Looks like somebody was going in.'

'Yeah, or trying to.'

'People ought not to leave their keys just lying around, careless like.'

'Yeah, there ought to be a law.'

Lennie rubbed his hand over the smoothest of the stones. It was so smooth it could be an old dinosaur egg,

Lennie thought. Here, under his hand, fossilized for a million years, could be an embryo dinosaur that had never even had a chance at life. The idea appealed to Lennie. In good faith some dinosaur had laid this egg, expecting a tiny bright green miniature of herself to pop out, and instead it had wound up as an imitation rock under somebody's lake house.

It would make a nice television show, Lennie thought. The show would open with a shot of the rock under the house and then very slowly the rock would begin to crack open and out would come the little dinosaur.

'Could be somebody inside,' the policeman said. His foot moved and a little dust shifted down through the cracks in the boards.

'We'd better take a look.'

The policeman turned the key in the lock and pushed on the door. He didn't know that you had to turn the knob, Lennie thought. Then, abruptly, the door opened and the two policemen entered the house.

Lennie couldn't hear them as clearly now, but every now and then a board would creak, and Lennie would know they were in the kitchen, looking behind the hot-water heater. Or they were in Lennie's bedroom or climbing the stairs to the second floor.

'Looks like everything's in order,' Lennie heard the policeman say as he came out on the porch.

'Better take the key though.'

'Mr Wilkins was right, I guess, about somebody going in these houses.'

'Yeah.'

'Probably some kids.'

'Nothing's been taken, though. It doesn't look like

it anyway.'

'Not much to take, if you ask me.'

In the crawl space Lennie lifted his head in surprise and almost hit the water pipe again. How little those policemen understood! Why, the objects in this house were as valuable as the contents of a museum – to him, anyway. He would give anything to have the contents of the drawers in the chest. To Lennie they would be like a mummy's possessions, special chosen things to be saved for a later life. Lennie would settle happily for just the old marbles and the Parcheesi set and the worn dominoes.

The policemen came down the front steps. 'If it was me, I'd rather have a place over on Paradise Lake,' one said. They walked round the left side of the house. They were as perfectly in step as drilling soldiers. 'That's a real nice place. You can't build a house at Paradise Lake that don't have metal siding.'

They paused at the corner of the house. Lennie could see their legs perfectly now.

One of them said, 'Look at that. The drain-pipe's busted. The steps'll be rotten by summer.'

Then they walked, still in step, to the patrol car. They got in and the little cop started the engine. Slowly, as Lennie reclined against the smooth stones, the car pulled away from the drive and moved on down the road.

9

FOR a moment Lennie could not move. He was weak with relief. He had been spared, saved, let off the hook. A fish probably felt like this, Lennie thought, when he was caught by Marlin Perkins for *Wild Kingdom* and then was mercifully thrown back into the water because he was too little.

'Although some fish are too little, *you* are never too little to be insured by Mutual of Omaha,' Marlin Perkins would say later with a quiet smile.

Lennie thought of the rejected fish hitting the sparkling water, sinking, dropping down where the water was dark and cold and lying there, taking himself for dead. Then Lennie thought of the fish realizing that life was still there and in a burst of power going straight up, breaking the surface of the water like one of those trick porpoises at Sea World.

The fish had good reason to be relieved, Lennie thought, especially since in the next scene Marlin Perkins would have arranged for a baby bird to be caught on camera being devoured by a boa constrictor.

'Even though this bird was caught by a boa constrictor, *you* will never be caught by unexpected trouble if you are insured by Mutual of Omaha.'

Lennie rested a moment more because his legs felt weak. Fright took a lot out of a person, turned the legs to rope and the heart to a caged bird.

And also Lennie was waiting. The police car had moved

on round the lake, but this could be a trick. At any moment the car could make a U-turn and come back. If the policemen were suspicious, that's exactly what they would do. Lennie decided he would stay where he was for at least another fifteen minutes.

He rested against the stones. To pass the time he began to think of himself as part of TV shows. He could see the listings in *TV Guide*:

The Rookies: The cops are called to investigate a breaking and entering at a lake house. Making his TV debut is Lennie in the role of the criminal.
Medical Centre: A young boy faces permanent injury when he is tear-gassed by the police in an attempt to get him out from under a lake house. Making his TV debut is Lennie in the role of the tear-gassed boy.

He smiled to himself. Now that his fear had lessened, now that he was sure everything was all right, the danger from the cops didn't seem real. Actually his only real worry had been about his mom. If they'd caught him . . . If they'd driven him to the Fairy Land Motel . . . If they'd taken him into the office and said, 'Ma'am, we just placed your son under arrest.' That *would* have been terrible.

He remembered that only the evening before his mom had said she was proud of him. A family of four had driven into the motel at dusk and Lennie had taken two cots to their room. He had taken ice to the couple in 316, extra linen to 304 and he had made up 311 and 313 without being told. It was, he admitted, mostly to make up for the bad grade he had gotten on his Science test, but his mom hadn't known that.

'I'm really proud of you,' she had said. 'All that studying

the other night on your Science – it will pay off too. I know it will – and all the help you're giving me tonight. We're going to make it, Lennie, I know we are.'

For a moment Lennie lay there staring up at the cobwebs that had formed between the boards of the house. He was thinking about his mother.

Then out of the corner of his eye he caught sight of movement. He straightened.

The police car was coming back. So silently Lennie hadn't heard it, moving in that slow, first-gear way, the car came to the driveway of the stone house and turned in.

10

LENNIE waited. When he did not hear the car door open, he slipped forward until he had a better view. The policemen were not getting out of the car. Perhaps they were sitting there having a smoke, Lennie thought. Maybe a late lunch. The big sagging cop was probably downing a couple of Twinkies. Lennie smiled. He imagined the cop taking a bite, looking at the other cop, saying, 'Freshness never tasted so good.'

The smile faded. What were the cops *doing*? Anyway, Lennie thought, it was lucky that he had stayed under the house, that he hadn't scrambled out right away. If he had, he would have been yanked up by the heels like a newborn baby. 'Got you! All right, kid, tell us who your parents are.'

Lennie was lying on his side now. A cobweb beneath the flooring touched Lennie's cheek, but Lennie didn't even raise his hand to brush it away. He kept his eyes on the blue strip of the car. There was still no sound or movement.

'Come on, come on, *leave!*' Lennie begged beneath his breath. He crossed his fingers, then uncrossed them. *'Leave!'*

Then, abruptly, Lennie heard the engine start. He couldn't believe it for a moment. The wheels spun a little in the dust of the drive and then the car backed up. It was moving fast.

The car backed on to the road, moved forward and drove out of Lennie's vision. It took the first curve in the road so rapidly that Lennie could hear the squeal of tyres. He smelt dust. He did not move. He waited.

Five minutes later the car got to the highway and Lennie heard the high wail of the siren as the car headed for Bennetsville.

Now Lennie relaxed for the first time since he had seen the car. It really is over now, he thought. An emergency somewhere – an accident perhaps, a criminal on the loose, and the police were called to duty.

He could crawl out in peace now. He turned on to his stomach and got set to scramble out. His left leg touched the pile of stones, and Lennie pushed himself forward.

The pushing started a small slide. The rocks shifted. A few tumbled to the ground and rolled away like balls. Mixed with the sound of the shifting, rolling stones was another sound. A rattle. No sooner had Lennie heard it than he felt the sharp stab of fangs on his ankle.

He jerked his head round, and in the shadow of the crawl space he saw a snake. It was so nearly the colour of the ground that it seemed for a moment to be the ground itself set in motion.

Instantly Lennie twisted away. He rolled over twice. When

he stopped and glanced back, the snake was moving behind the tipped-over oil drum. It disappeared in the shadows.

Lennie drew his leg up to his chest and yanked up his
pants. There was a yellow stain on his sock. Slowly, as
carefully as if he were unwrapping something, Lennie
pulled down the sock and looked at the two tiny holes in
the inside of his ankle.

Drops of blood oozed out, and instinctively Lennie bent
down and sucked the wound and spat out blood and
venom. He did this a second time, a third and then he
drew back again and looked at the wound.

A cold chill went up his spine. He said to himself: the main
thing I am not supposed to do is panic. He remembered that
from when Little Joe got a snake bit on the Ponderosa. But he
knew he already had panicked. Just the sight of those two
holes in his ankle had caused his heart to pound like a
hammer. Blood rushed through his body with the force of
Niagara Falls. His throat had tightened up. Suddenly he
couldn't see because tears were in his eyes.

It seemed to Lennie then that this was the secret of life
– the thing man had always been afraid of. Even when
man thought he was afraid of the Russians or the atom
bomb or some new virus, what he really feared was that he
would wind up bitten by a snake – two holes in his ankle.
Lennie tried to see the wound through his tears.

It was man's first fear, Lennie seemed to remember,
way back in the Bible, and the Bible knew how to scare a
person. Lennie almost felt that this was the same snake. It
had slithered down the tree in the Garden of Eden,
tempted Adam, wound through deserts, round pyramids,
stowed away on a banana boat, come to the United States,
crossed ditches and parks and burning asphalt roads and

come here to wait for Lennie beneath the stone house.

Lennie blinked, and the two holes came into focus again. 'I got to get out of here,' Lennie said.

Then, using the same side-to-side motions the snake had used going behind the oil drum, Lennie pulled himself out of the shadow of the crawl space. He slid into the sunlight. He sat up.

And there in the dappled sunlight, beneath trees that were solid gold, Lennie rolled up his pants' legs and took off his shoe. He stripped off the stained sock. He looked again at the two small holes in the pale flesh of his ankle.

11

LENNIE'S ankle was bleeding freely now. The blood was streaming down his foot, dropping on to the dry dusty earth. The pain had increased.

Lennie hunched over his foot. This sharp stinging pain made him even more afraid. His heart started beating harder. His mouth got drier. He kept saying over and over, 'I got to keep calm. I got to keep calm.' But this seemed only to make him more frightened.

He reached into his back pocket for his knife. It was there tangled in some string and a red bandana. When he got it loose, he tried to open it one-handed as he always did, but his fingers were trembling too much.

Fumbling, using both hands, he got the knife open. Then it dropped in the dust. In a panic now, Lennie wiped the dusty knife blade off on his pants. He knew what to do but he hesitated a moment. He felt physically sick now. Then he bent quickly and cut little x's over both the fang marks.

He moaned. For the first time in his life he wanted to be in a hospital among people who knew what they were doing. Doctors and nurses had always frightened Lennie before, but now in his mind they took on the beauty of painted pictures.

He took three deep breaths. Then he bent down and began to draw out the blood. He spat it into the dust.

Suddenly he thought of a tourniquet, and he wrapped the bandana round his leg and tied it tight. He sucked hard at the snake bite, drawing a mouthful of blood. He spat it out.

His ankle really hurt now. It was a burning pain, sharp and stinging, as if his leg was being slashed by razor blades.

The telephone! Lennie thought. He got up and, hobbling on one foot, made his way round the house and up the steps. The key was gone, but Lennie went straight to the window by the sofa and pulled it up. Lucky that he had known about that latch being broken.

Carefully he swung his leg over the sill. The telephone was on the far wall, and Lennie kept his eyes on it as he struggled across the room. Rainbow-like, it seemed to get farther and farther away.

Lennie held on to one piece of furniture after another – the overstuffed chair, the end-table, the floor lamp. He had once thought this furniture must have come from at least twenty different people.

'Well, I can get along without this chair, I reckon,' someone had said.

'I got no more use for this table.'

'I was going to give this rug to the Sunday School, but if you can use it . . .'

Lennie had liked that. At the time he had thought that

if he ever had a house, that's the way he would have wanted to furnish it – one piece of furniture from everybody he liked.

With a swimming motion, weaving through the furniture, he got to the phone at last. He lifted the receiver. Silence. He jiggled the piece up and down. Silence. He dialled O. Silence. As he stood there on one foot, he seemed to get smaller in size. The phone had been disconnected for the winter.

Slowly Lennie let himself down into the first chair he came to. It was the brown overstuffed armchair, and he sank as slowly as an old rheumatic man. He didn't think he would ever get up again. He lifted his leg as gently as he could and rested it on the green plastic footstool. His ankle was turning purple.

He had so wanted to hear the voice of the operator saying, 'Number, please.' He had so wanted to reply, 'Get me the Fairy Land Motel.'

He laid his head back against the chair. There was a picture hanging on the opposite wall. Lennie had never noticed it before. He would not have noticed it now except that the sunlight from the window was falling on it, lighting it up as if it were in a museum.

The picture was a barnyard scene painted by someone who had never been in a barnyard. No pigs were that pink. No rooster was that red. No cow went around with four golden straws in the side of her mouth.

Tears came to Lennie's eyes. They spilt over on to his cheeks and rolled down his face. He caught the first one with his tongue. He tasted the salt. Then he gave up and let the tears flow.

It would take a miracle to save him now, he thought. He

couldn't walk. Any movement at all was terribly painful. The police wouldn't come back. No one knew where he was. He needed a real miracle, a twitch from Samantha's nose or a visit from the Flying Nun or a nod from Jeannie.

He had always loved those shows. When things went wrong – when Darren got changed into an elephant, Samantha would just twitch her nose and make him a man again. When Jeannie's master was accidentally sent into space instead of a rhesus monkey, Jeannie would nod him back again. That kind of magic was what he needed.

Slowly he reached down, loosened the tourniquet, let the blood flow back into his leg for a moment. Then he tightened it again.

Suddenly he thought of his mother. He knew how sad she would look when she found out. All the trouble he had caused her – all the vaccinations and school lessons and tooth fillings. She had even signed him up for safety lessons one summer at a municipal pool. She had taken him with her through seven states – and all for what? To have him sink down into an overstuffed chair and die.

Wincing with pain, Lennie got to his feet. Outside the sun went behind a cloud and it got dark in the room. For a moment Lennie was terrified. He thought the end had come. He began to shuffle across the room. In a panic he grabbed the sofa and as he reached for the table, the sun came out again. The room got bright.

By accident, as he leant there, he saw his face in the mirror by the front door. It scared him. He looked as wild as a man marooned twenty years on a desert island.

Lennie swallowed. He took a deep breath. Then slowly, his shoulders hunched forward, his chest heaving with unspent sobs, he started for the door.

12

LENNIE struggled out on to the front porch. Every step killed him. He could not even touch his wounded leg now.

He moved so slowly and carefully it almost seemed that he was not moving at all. Inch by inch he made it across the warped floor boards and caught the porch railing. He hung there for a moment, bent forward, staring down into the ferns below.

He raised his head then and looked across the lake. The sun was lower in the sky. Could it already be setting? How much time *had* passed, Lennie wondered. The lake was shining with the red sun and the reflection of the beech trees. Probably not more than a half-hour since he had first felt that piercing sting on his ankle.

The redness of the lake seemed like a bad omen to him, a prediction of terrible things to come. It was like a prophecy. When the waters of the earth turn red . . .

Someone he knew had believed in omens. Who was it? His Grandmother Madison probably. When the caterpillars were thick, a bad winter was coming. When an owl cried in the night, somebody was going to die. What would she say about this? 'When the waters of the earth turn red . . .'

Or maybe it was his Grandfather Madison. No, his Grandfather Madison had been an old man who ran motels and in his spare time worked at making concrete figures to adorn them.

The thing his Grandfather Madison believed in was not

complaining. One time when Lennie had broken his arm and was crying because the cast itched, his Grandfather Madison had told him that there was an old legend that said birds were created without wings. When their wings were put on their bodies as a punishment, the birds complained, but as soon as they stopped complaining the wings grew to their bodies and lifted them into the air.

Lennie had been so puzzled about what this had to do with the cast on his arm that he had stopped crying at once. He still didn't understand it.

Lennie's leg jerked again. The pain was so sharp and sudden that Lennie threw back his head like an animal. He felt like howling, but instead he yelled, 'Does anybody hear me?'

He waited, listened to the silence and then tried again.

'Will somebody please help me?' Pause. 'I'm over here at the stone house!'

Nobody answered, and the silence frightened Lennie. It was a total silence. He couldn't even hear any birds or crickets. The leaves had stopped turning in the trees.

It was as if he really were the last person on earth. Even Friend couldn't help him. Remember, Friend had surrendered to the police. In a flash a picture came to Lennie of Friend sitting in a cell at the station, his batteries gradually getting weaker. ('Don't forget, kids, to keep spare batteries handy so you'll never be without a Friend.') By the time the police got around to questioning him, his voice would be too faint to hear.

'Speak up, son, tell us your name in a good loud voice.'

Hmmmmmm.

'I said for you to speak up! If you don't, we're going to have to take some action.'

Hmm.

The silence continued. Even the water no longer lapped at the shore.

Lennie glanced down at his leg. It was swelling now, the skin tight and shiny, and as hot as if it were on fire. His leg twitched again, frog-like, and the pain almost made him faint.

His strength was leaving him rapidly. He was so weak now that he had to sit down or he would collapse. Moving his leg as little as possible, Lennie eased himself down on the top step. With a sigh, he reclined against the porch railing.

After a moment, even weaker, he let himself lie on the porch. He sagged. All his strength was gone. His leg felt like a sausage in a frying-pan.

He looked up at the porch ceiling. Rain had seeped through the tar and shingles of the roof and stained the boards. Lennie saw it all in a kind of blur because he had started crying again.

All of a sudden Lennie found himself remembering a poem. Lennie only knew one poem. He had had to learn it for a school assignment.

'If everyone else can memorize a poem, you can too, Lennie,' his teacher had said.

'But why can't I substitute a TV jingle? They're poems. They rhyme.'

'No, Lennie.'

'But listen to this. Why isn't this a poem?

> *Hold the pickle, hold the lettuce*
> *Special orders don't upset us*
> *All we ask is that you let us*
> *Serve you —'*

'No, Lennie, that's not poetry.'

'Well, here's another one. What's wrong with this?

> *Hotdogs, Armour hotdogs,*
> *What kind of kids like Armour hotdogs?*
> *Fat kids, skinny kids, kids who —'*

'Lennie, for the last time, you are to learn a *poem*. Advertising jingles are not poetry.'

Lennie could no longer remember the teacher's name — he had had twenty-three different teachers in all that year — but he could still remember his poem and how bright the sun had been, slanting into the room, as he said it. It was as if the audience were lit up for the occasion instead of the stage.

> *The July sun is gone,*
> *The August moon.*
> *September's stars are dim,*
> *October's bright noon.*

'I am curious,' the teacher had said when he had finished. 'Why did you select that particular poem, Lennie?'

He had selected it because all the months of the year were in it, and that would make it easier to memorize. He already knew the months. 'It just appealed to me,' he had said.

'Why, Lennie?'

'I don't know.'

'What do you think the poet had in mind when he wrote the poem?' The teacher, interested in Lennie for the first time, crossed in front of her desk.

'Let me think.' Lennie had put his hand to his chin at

this point to give the impression of deep thought. Lennie had always had a hard time arranging his face in the right expression. Looking interested or studious was especially hard for him. He sometimes thought he needed acting lessons on being a person.

'Do you think he was just talking about *one* year passing?' the teacher went on. 'Or do you think, Lennie, that the poet was seeing his whole life as a year, that he was seeing his whole life slipping past?'

'I'm not sure.' Lennie's hand was still on his chin as if ready to stroke a long grey beard.

'Class?'

'*His whole life slipping past,*' the class chorused together. They had had this teacher so long that they could tell, just from the way she asked a question, what they were supposed to answer.

'I was just getting ready to say that,' Lennie mumbled into his hand.

And now, two years too late, Lennie knew what they were talking about. The poet *had* meant his whole life. Lennie knew because he saw his whole life slipping away too. In exactly the same way. July's sun. August's moon. September's stars. October's noon.

He closed his eyes and the tears came again, hot and fast. He couldn't remember the rest of the poem. What was it he would miss about November and December? He squeezed his eyes shut tighter in determination. He stuck out his jaw.

Then his body went slack. He sighed. He realized that he would miss everything about the world. He would miss all the re-runs of *Bonanza* and *Star Trek*. He would miss shows that hadn't even come on the air, midwinter replacements he didn't even know about. He would miss shows that hadn't even been thought of yet. He would miss his mother.

Lennie sighed again. And his mother would miss him. That was the worst thought. To get his mind off it, he tried to think of something he had seen on TV. All the programmes were a blur. He couldn't even remember what dangers Mannix had faced last week, or Columbo. And Kojak had been in real trouble. What was it?

He groaned, feeling again the pain of separation from his mother.

All Lennie's life his own feelings had been as hard to get to as the meat in a walnut. His feelings were there – Lennie was sure of that – somewhere inside the hull, probably just as perfectly formed as the rest of the things nature put in a shell.

Lennie remembered that one March morning he and his mom had been burning trash behind the motel. His mom had said, 'Why, Lennie, look at this.'

Lennie had come over to where his mom was standing by some bushes. 'What is it?'

'It's an old cocoon. We'll take it in and cut it open and you can see where a butterfly grew.'

His mom had broken off the twig and, forgetting the trash fire, had gone into the motel. She had taken her onion knife and sawed through the cocoon. 'There,' she had said.

For a moment Lennie and his mom had stared at the cut-open cocoon in silence. Then his mom had said in a sad voice, 'Oh, dear. It wasn't empty. I cut through a butterfly.'

Lennie had stared silently at the two halves, the pale

wet centre.

'It was the first cocoon I ever saw. I'm sorry, Lennie.'

He could see that it really bothered her and he'd said, 'That's all right.'

'I just didn't know.'

Lennie felt that his own feelings had suddenly been laid bare in the same way. Now that it was too late, he found that – he broke off. He had just remembered the last part of the poem.

> And November's morn
> White with frost
> And December's snows
> Are melted and lost.

Anyway, it was something like that.

13

TRYING to remember the lines of the poem had helped Lennie forget his pain for a moment. It seemed to him then that if you knew enough poems to say to yourself, you could get through anything. He tried to think of something else to divert him. He went back to TV. TV jingles maybe.

> 'I'd like to teach the world to sing
> In perfect harmony
> I'd like to hold it in my hands
> And keep it company.
> It's the reeeeeal thing, Coke is –'

Lennie moaned. They weren't as good as poetry.

> *'Quaker State your caaaaaaar,*
> *To keep it running young.'*

Maybe they were too easy to remember.

> *'Oh, Log Cabin makes it thicker,*
> *As thick as anyone can.*
> *On your pancakes or —'*

Abruptly his leg jerked and he couldn't think of anything but the pain. He raised up and looked at his leg. Grimacing with the pain, he looked down the slope to the willow trees. He could see the edge of his boat through the trees. He took a deep breath.

> *'Double your pleasure, double your fun*
> *With double —'*

It wouldn't work. He looked again at his boat. He thought: maybe if I can reach the boat I can float across the lake. Then maybe I can crawl real slowly through the field. Then maybe I can . . . He saw it as if it were happening on television. It seemed possible.

He leant up on one elbow. He hesitated, struggling with himself. Lassie would make it, he told himself. A rattlesnake bite wouldn't stop Lassie. A shark bite wouldn't stop Flipper. Gentle Ben would drag a bear trap for a hundred miles to save himself.

Lennie took a deep breath and tried to push himself into a sitting position. He fell back on his elbow. He tried again. He couldn't make it.

He was very weak now, but he wanted desperately to be in his boat floating towards home. He could almost feel himself floating over the gentle waves. He tried to push himself up again. He failed. He lay back on the porch.

246

The silence around him was awful now. It wasn't only the silence that bothered Lennie. It was the terrible feeling that everything had stopped moving. The sun wasn't dropping in the sky. It was still hanging in the sky in exactly the same place. The wind wasn't blowing. The clouds weren't moving. The trees were as still as plastic arrangements.

He closed his eyes. He had lost track of time. He didn't know how long he had been lying here. It seemed like days. Years. Centuries.

He felt as if he had been lying here long enough to have been frozen in a glacier or petrified by burning lava. He had been lying here long enough to be preserved and sent to some museum as the main display.

He would be more popular in the museum than the mummy or the fossilized whale. 'Hey, did you guys see the preserved kid?'

'No, where's any preserved kid?'

'Around yonder. He's ten million years old – the card says so, and he's got a snake bite in his ankle. You can even see the holes.'

'Where? Show me.'

'Come on if you don't believe me.'

He would be so popular that they would make a whole educational TV programme about him, Lennie thought. They would reconstruct his life, his last day. The show would be called *This is the Way We Think it Was* and as the young actor lay stretched out, imitating Lennie's pain, imitating Lennie's dying, the announcer's voice would say, 'Yes, this is the way we think it was, ten million years ago today.'

Lennie raised his head. The only bit of movement left in

the world was his pounding heart. And now even that seemed to be slowly winding down.

Lennie stretched out flat on the porch. His mind drifted back in time. He thought of a friend he had had in Nashville. Nashville was the only place he and his mom had stayed long enough for Lennie to get a good friend. The other places they had lived, by the time Lennie got people used to him and to stop picking on him, right then he and his mom had moved.

This friend in Nashville was Carl Lee Norton, and he and Lennie used to walk home from school together through an old cow field. They both lived in side-by-side trailers in Pineview Trailer Court. And sometimes when they got tired, they would lie down in the field and just look up at the sky.

One day as they were lying there in silence an airplane flew overhead, a small plane, white and red, single-engine. Lennie, watching the plane, began to will it to fall from the sky. 'Fall! Fall! Fall!' he was saying to himself, not really wanting the plane to fall, just testing his ability to make things happen.

At that very moment, as Lennie lay there with his brain powers trained on the airplane, Carl Lee sat up and said, 'Hey, I bet that's my uncle.'

'Where?'

'Up there in that airplane. You know, Uncle David. It looks like his Cessna.'

'Oh.'

Lennie lay back and closed his eyes. He felt weak. He realized he had been willing one of his most admired people – Carl Lee's Uncle David, the man who had let Lennie sit in the cockpit of his glider and promised to take him up in an airplane – *this* was the man he had been willing to fall from the sky.

'I got to go home,' he said after a moment when he felt he could stand. He got up slowly. The plane was out of sight, still flying, he hoped.

'Me too,' Carl Lee said.

And the two of them walked towards their trailers with the matching plastic sofas and the plastic sliding doors and the carpets of miracle fibres. As he entered his trailer, Carl Lee called, 'I'll ask Uncle David if we can go up in his Cessna this Sunday.'

Lennie nodded, but he wasn't so eager to go up any more. Going up in the airplane was ruined now. Because maybe, just maybe, there would be some other person in some other field looking up at the sky saying, 'Fall! Fall! Fall!' to Lennie's plane. Sure, he, Lennie, didn't have any power, but maybe somebody else did.

But now, lying on the porch, dying, he sent out a mental signal to the world. 'Come! Come! Come!' Silently he willed the invisible people with all his might. 'Anyone within range of my mind, come! Help me! Help!'

His leg jerked again and he cried out. He put his fists up to his eyes.

'You have to keep hold of yourself,' his mom had told him once. It was just after her boyfriend Sam had died. Lennie had been sad too. Sam was his favourite of his mother's boyfriends. Sam had owned a diner and was so big and strong he flattened hamburgers like he was swatting flies. He was always saying, 'Hit me, kid, go ahead and hit me hard as you can.'

Lennie would hit and hit until his arms got tired, but it was like trying to hurt a mattress. Lennie liked it when he couldn't hurt Sam. It was nice to know that there was one person in the world who could not be hurt no matter what you did.

And then Sam had died. He died right at the diner while he was shovelling snow off the parking-lot. His heart, it turned out, was not as strong as his body.

Lennie had sat in the last booth with his mom while she warmed her hands round a cup of coffee.

'You always have to keep hold of yourself,' she said.

Lennie had a young-looking mother. People were always mistaking her for his sister. Now for the first time she looked old enough really to be his mother.

She wrapped her arms round herself. 'Never let go, Lennie.'

'I try not to.'

'No matter what happens.'

'Will we have to leave the diner?'

She nodded.

'But where will we go?'

'I don't know, but if we just keep hold of ourselves we'll be all right.'

'I'll try to.'

Now, as if to keep his word, Lennie hugged himself. One arm was on each shoulder, but his fingers were like icy claws. There was no comfort. He wished for dream arms that would grow long on command and wrap him like soft fleshy hoses.

Holding himself tighter, he sent out the message again. Somebody, anybody, come.

14

A SOUND broke through the stillness of the front porch. Lennie couldn't place the noise at first, but he waited. He held his breath and listened.

Maybe the sound hadn't been real, he thought. It was puzzling. It was like the time his mother had taken him to the wax museum in New Orleans. The wax museum had been a substitute treat because they hadn't been able to find Midget City. 'All right,' his mother had said finally, 'we'll just go to the wax museum. You want to see wax people, don't you?'

They had gone in, and Lennie had been really surprised at how real the people looked. Lennie could see the pores in their hands. Their eyes looked right at him.

Still and all, there had been something wrong, something so wrong that Lennie couldn't really be scared no matter how hard he tried, not even in the Chamber of Horrors. It just wasn't real somehow.

That was the same feeling Lennie had now as he lay on the porch, thinking back on the sound he had heard. He listened. Now he couldn't hear anything at all.

It seemed to him that maybe the sound had been a car door slamming, but he wasn't sure. Maybe it was just because that was what he wanted it to be. He tried to pull himself up on his elbow.

'Help me,' he called out. 'Is anybody there?' He waited. 'I'm here on the porch. I'm dying.'

His hopes went up and down like a pop fly. He sank

back to the porch. He didn't have the strength to hold his head up any more. He called again, but his voice seemed to be no more than a sigh.

'Somebody help me,' he begged. For a moment his hopes were all mixed up with the wax figures in New Orleans, and he imagined that Napoleon and Huey Long and Flip Wilson were drawing round him.

Abruptly he turned his head from side to side as if to clear it of a bad dream. He wet his lips. He murmured, 'No,' to the wax figures. 'No!'

Then he grew still. He had heard another sound. It was real. Someone had spoken to him.

'Son?'

Lennie's eyes snapped open. He tried to rise up again. The big sagging cop was standing at the bottom of the steps, tall as a tree.

Lennie blinked. He saw the policeman clearly now. Lennie drew in a breath of air. His heart rested a moment. He said, 'Help me.'

'Sure, son, what happened to your leg?'

'Snake bite.'

'What kind of snake, son, do you know?'

'Rattler.' Saying the word made him shiver. His leg jerked again and he cried out.

The big cop straightened. 'Hey, Bert,' he called, 'get the hospital on the double.'

'My leg's on fire,' Lennie moaned.

'Tell them a kid's been bitten by a rattlesnake,' he yelled. 'We're bringing him in. Then get over here and help me.'

'My mom –' Lennie began.

'Yeah, son, who is your mom?'

'She runs the Fairy Land Motel.'

'We'll get your mom – now you just lie quiet. When did it happen, son, can you tell me?'

'It was right after you drove off the second time.'

'We knew you were there. We saw your wet footprints on the front porch.'

Lennie nodded. The boat leaked, his sneakers were wet, he had left his footprints.

His leg twitched again, and the hot pain shot through his whole body. He began to cry.

'Don't cry, son. We're going to get you to the hospital. Won't take us five minutes.'

'I can't help crying.'

'I know. A buddy of mine got bitten by a snake – we were on a picnic down at Wandover Falls – and my buddy was reaching in the grass for a baseball, and the snake caught him on his little finger, right there, by the nail. My buddy cried too, and he was a grown man, forty years old.'

Lennie groaned.

'Give me a hand here, Bert,' the big cop said. 'I'll steady his leg.' They got Lennie into lifting position. 'Here we go.'

Lennie cried out as they picked him up – his leg couldn't stand the slightest touch now – and then he felt himself being rushed to the car.

'Can you get the door?' the big cop asked.

'Yeah.'

As they struggled with the door, Lennie stared up through the golden leaves of the trees. He saw a moon in the late afternoon sky. It was white. A children's moon they called it when it came out like that in the daytime. Lennie's grandfather had told him so. There was a story connected with it, but Lennie didn't feel like remembering it. He moaned as they slid him into the back seat.

'Now, you just stretch out there and try to relax. You all right?'

'I don't know,' Lennie groaned.

'I'll stay back here with you,' the big cop said. 'Bert, you drive.'

He crawled in and sat on the edge of the seat. He said, 'I wish we'd found you the first time we came by. Then this wouldn't have happened.'

'I do too,' Lennie said.

'Where were you?'

'Under the house.' Lennie turned his head away. 'I didn't know snakes stayed under houses.'

'I reckon they do.' The car started. 'Here we go,' the big cop said.

15

LENNIE glanced out of the car window, and he got one last look at the stone house. It was just a grey-and-brown blur now. It had nothing to do with him. It wasn't *his* house, no more than a theatre he had watched a movie in was his theatre, or a café he had had a meal in was his café.

It was strange the way objects could be valuable one moment and worthless the next. It was the way coloured Easter eggs seem like real gold when you're on a hunt, running through the grass with an empty basket swinging at your side. And then the next day, one of those same coloured eggs can be just a cracked smelly object.

'How're you doing, son?' the big cop asked.

Lennie closed his eyes as if to shut out the question. 'I

don't know.'

'You just hang on there.'

'That's what I'm trying to do.' Lennie wet his dry lips. Without opening his eyes he said, 'What happened to your friend that got bitten by the rattlesnake? Did he die?'

'Naw, he didn't die. That was old Hank Thompson, Bert, you remember him. Big fellow. Used to coach Little League. He missed two weeks of work, as I recall it, and he never has stuck his hand down in deep grass again.'

'I'll never crawl under another house,' Lennie said, moaning a little as they went over a bump.

'They used to tease him about it. "Get the ball, Hank," they'd call. "It's right over there in the *grass.*" ' He smiled. 'Hank would back up a mile to keep from touching a clump of grass. He'd always say, "One rattlesnake bite'll do me for the rest of my life." '

'That's true,' Lennie moaned.

As they got to the highway, the siren started up. It sounded different, Lennie thought, when it was *you* inside the car, when it was *you* that the trucks and cars were going to pull over to the side of the road for. He tried to raise his head and see if it was happening. He was too weak.

'You all right, son?'

Lennie opened his eyes. He looked at the big cop. He nodded.

'Well, just hold on.'

Lennie kept looking at the big cop's face. Suddenly he thought of the time his mom had taken him down the street in Nashville to see a man who was buried alive. The man was buried in a special box and there was a green awning over it. For a dime you could look down a tube and speak to the man who was buried below.

Lennie would never forget looking down the tube. He had had a million questions he wanted to ask, but as soon as he saw the man's face below him, he couldn't say a word.

'Ask him how long he's going to stay down there,' his mother prompted.

'How long are you going to stay down there?'

'As long as the people of Nashville want me to,' the man had answered.

'Ask him how he eats.'

'How do you eat?'

But the woman taking up the dimes had said, 'Move on now, these girls want to see too.' And Lennie had to move on and make room for three girls who were already arguing over who would have to look first.

Lennie had moved on, but it had left him with a funny sensation, looking at a stranger through a tube like that. Because for a moment the stranger's face had blotted out the whole world. It had just been the stranger and Lennie.

Lennie had thought everybody should have to look at everybody else at least once through a tube. You could see them so much clearer.

Now Lennie could see the big cop in the same clear, one-to-one way. Lennie said, 'Tell me about your friend some more, your friend that got bitten.'

'Well, let's see. He lost his fingernail, I remember that.'

'What did they do to him at the hospital?'

'Well, they gave him some shots, as I recall it, and something to take away the pain. He was real happy to be in the hospital –' He broke off. 'Pull in here, Bert, this is the emergency entrance.'

The big cop turned back to Lennie. 'We'll get you inside and you'll be fine.'

In Lennie's mind the big cop suddenly got mixed up with Sam. Maybe it was because they were both so big. Lennie half expected the big cop to turn round and say, 'Hit me in the stomach, kid.' Lennie put out his hand and held tightly to the cop's sleeve. 'I want you to carry me, not him.'

'All right.' Bert opened the door. Awkwardly the big cop climbed out and reached back to help Lennie. 'Let's go.'

16

'ANTIVENOM test was negative,' a voice was saying.

Lennie was lying with his eyes closed. He was sobbing to himself. He opened his eyes once to see if the big cop was still standing in the doorway. The big cop lifted his hand and said to Lennie, 'Your mom'll be here in a minute. Bert's gone to get her.'

Lennie turned away. He closed his eyes. His body shook with sobs.

'Just hold on,' the cop called.

Lennie felt himself being given shots all over his body. It was just another pain. Then they were making slits in his leg, and just when he thought it was all over, he got two more shots, one in the ankle and one in the thigh, then two more in the hip. He lost count.

Somebody said, 'We gave you something to ease the pain. You should be feeling some relief soon.'

They rolled him out of the emergency room, down the

green hall and into the elevator.

'I'll stay with you till your mom gets here,' the cop said.

Lennie nodded. He reached out and took the cop's hand. He was beginning to relax a little now.

'The doctors say you're going to be just fine.'

'I don't know,' Lennie murmured.

Two people lifted him on to a bed. Lennie reached out for the cop's hand again. He ran his free hand over the sheet like a small child comforting himself with a favourite blanket. He felt sleepy.

'Here's your mom,' the big cop said.

She was standing in the doorway in blue jeans and a tie-dyed shirt. She came over to the bed and started to cry.

Lennie said, 'I'm sorry.'

'You don't have anything to be sorry about,' she said. 'You just get well.'

'I shouldn't have tried to hide.' His lips were dry. It was getting hard to talk.

'Don't say anything. You just rest and concentrate on getting well. You are very important to me.'

His mom kept patting his arm. His mom used to play the piano long ago, but she had been taught by an aunt who could only play hymn chords, and now she was patting him with all her fingers, the same chord over and over.

Lennie felt confused. He said, 'Am I still in the hospital?' The room was blurring. The green walls were moving closer.

His mom said, 'Now, you just keep hold of yourself.' She kept patting his arm, the same chord.

Lennie thought of his arms rising and winding round his body like ropes. He ran his fingers back and forth on the sheet.

'Try to sleep.'

'I got to tell you something first,' Lennie began through his dry lips, but before he had a chance to speak, he had forgotten what he wanted to say.

'No, don't talk. I understand.'

Lennie sighed. It was easier, if she really did understand, not to have to tell it, whatever it was. He couldn't remember.

'What time is it?' he asked.

'Four thirty.'

'When was I bitten?'

'Well, they said it must have been about an hour and a half ago. You were lucky to get help that fast.'

'I know.'

'Now you just lie back and rest. Get well. That's all that matters. Want me to close the blinds?'

Lennie opened his eyes and saw the sun. It looked like it was setting. It didn't seem possible. He couldn't remember what day it was. Maybe, he thought, this was the longest day on record. They would put it in a book. The longest day ever recorded was on an afternoon in early October, the day a boy was bitten by a rattlesnake under a stone house at a lake.

His mother got up and closed the blinds. 'There, is that better?'

'I can still smell the lake.'

'No, hon, the whole hospital's air-conditioned,' she said. 'The window's shut tight.'

'I can smell it, Mom, I tell you. I can smell it. Don't you believe me?'

'Yes, yes,' his mother said, playing three quick chords

on his arm. 'Don't get upset, Lennie. Just lie there and try to sleep. I think I can smell the lake too.'

Lennie remembered suddenly what he had wanted to tell her. 'I failed my Science test,' he said. 'It's under my socks.'

'That's all right.'

'You have to sign it.'

'I will.'

'It's the Science test you thought I was studying for so hard.'

'That's all right.'

'It's the Science test you said you were proud of me for passing.'

'It's all right.'

'It doesn't matter to you?'

'No.'

Comforted, Lennie sighed. His mother kept patting his arm, and in a few minutes he slept.

17

'HE'LL be all right, ma'am. They've made a lot of progress in snake-bite treatment.' It was the big cop talking to Lennie's mother. Lennie heard him, but he didn't open his eyes for a moment. The pain was back now, as bad as before.

'I hope,' his mom said.

'Folks who talk about the world going to the dogs forget all the progress we've made.'

'I know,' his mom said.

260

'Why, I read the other day that there's McDonald Hamburger places in Japan now and shopping-centres in India.'

'We all have a lot to be thankful for.'

'And your boy's going to be just fine. Living in modern times has its advantages, and one of them is that your boy's going to be all right.'

'Mom,' Lennie said through dry lips.

'I'm right here, Lennie.' He could feel her leaning over him. He could smell her clean lemony smell.

'What time is it?'

'It's –' She paused and looked at her watch. 'It's eleven forty.'

'At night?'

'Yes.'

'Oh.'

Lennie moaned. He hadn't known pain could be this bad. The worst pain he had suffered before today was the digging out of a splinter at Sam's diner and the setting of a broken arm in Nashville. This was a total, all-out pain.

'I don't think I'm going to get through the night,' he said, more to himself than to his mom.

'Yes, you will, Lennie. It'll get better. Just hold on to yourself.'

'Can't they give me something for the pain?'

'They already have, hon.'

'Are you sure?'

'They've given you all they can. It'll ease up soon.'

'I know it won't.' He began to cry. 'Pain like this doesn't ease.'

'It *will*.'

He lay with his eyes closed for a moment, tears rolling

down his cheeks. Then he said, 'What time is it?'

'It's –' she paused – 'eleven forty-one.'

'Oh.' He lay without moving. He was trying to last just five more minutes. He could no longer think of getting through the whole night. Five more minutes was the best he could do. 'What time is it *now*?'

'It's eleven forty-two.'

'Oh.' Three more minutes to go.

The big cop – Lennie had forgotten he was in the room – said, 'I'll go speak to the nurse. Maybe she can do something.'

'I'd appreciate it.' After the cop left the room, his mother said, 'You want to talk, Lennie? Maybe it would help you get your mind off the pain.'

'I'll try.'

'Want me to tell you about the time I was in hospital? I was just about your age.'

'All right.'

'It was an accident.'

'Car?'

'No, I was climbing a tree behind the motel –'

'Our motel?'

'No, this was a different one. It was in Kentucky and it was called the Kosy K. We lived in one of the cabins. Kosy K Kabins was the full name. Anyway, I was out climbing an old oak tree and I fell. I landed in the crook of the tree on my knee and then I fell on the ground and broke my arm.'

'Oh.'

'And they took me to the hospital in the back of an old pick-up truck. I can still remember how scared I was because I had never even spent a night away from home.'

'Oh,' Lennie said. He paused, wet his lips. 'What time is it now?'

'It's –' pause – 'eleven forty-four.'

One more minute to go, Lennie thought.

'You want to hear the rest about my arm?'

'Yeah, go on.'

'Well, the knee wasn't too bad, but the arm got infected. See, the bone had poked through the skin, and they thought I was going to die, Lennie. I was in the hospital for two and a half weeks. It almost caused me to fail fifth grade.' She broke off as the cop came back into the room.

'The nurse'll be in in a minute,' he said.

'Did you hear that, Lennie? Hold on to yourself because the nurse is coming.'

'What time is it now?' Lennie asked.

'It's eleven forty-six.'

He had made it. Five minutes. And he was already one minute into the next five.

His mom said, 'Officer Olson was just telling me while you were asleep, Lennie, that a friend of his got bitten by a rattlesnake on his little finger.'

'Oh.'

'I told him about it, ma'am.'

'And, Lennie, he says he'll get the man to come and see you tomorrow if it'll make you feel better.'

Lennie nodded. He waited as long as he could stand it and then he said, 'What time is it now?'

18

THAT was how Lennie got through that first night – five minutes and then five minutes more. It seemed to Lennie that the whole night, separated into those five-minute periods, was longer than the rest of his whole life. He would never have believed that five minutes could be longer than a year, but now he knew it was true.

In the morning when the doctor came in to look at Lennie's leg and to change the dressing, Lennie was past caring. He didn't even want to get well any more.

'How are you feeling?' the doctor asked.

Lennie just shook his head.

'Well, let's see that leg.'

Lennie closed his eyes and moaned. His leg hurt so badly he could even feel the doctor's breath on his knee. It was like a blowtorch.

'Don't get near my leg,' Lennie murmured as he fainted.

He didn't remember anything else about the rest of the morning except that it was one terrible pain after another.

In the afternoon the big cop came in. He leant on the foot of the bed. 'Remember me telling you about my friend that got bitten by a snake?' he said. 'Well, here he is!' The cop sounded as cheerful as if he'd done a feat of magic.

Lennie tried. He opened his eyes. He blinked to clear his vision. He made an effort to see the man beside his bed.

'There's my finger that got bitten,' the man said, leaning over Lennie's bed. 'See? You can still see the scars and here are the slits they had to make in my hand to relieve the swelling. Here, here, here, here and here. And my fingernail's gone.' He wagged his little finger. 'See? No fingernail!'

Lennie tried to focus his eyes on the finger and the slits, but he didn't care any more. Nothing mattered. He closed his eyes.

'He would be real glad to see you if he wasn't feeling so bad,' his mother said.

'Well, we'll come back, son, don't worry 'bout it. Tomorrow or the next day I'll bring him back,' the cop said.

'He'll feel more like looking at the finger then,' his mom said. She turned to Lennie. 'And Lennie, did you see what Officer Olson brought you? It's a clock! Now you won't have to ask for the time so much. It's an electric clock and you can read it as easy as a sign.'

There was a silence while everyone waited for Lennie's reaction.

Then his mother said, 'I'm sure he'd thank you if he was feeling better.'

'Why, that's all right. He don't have to thank me,' the cop said.

'Well, I'm sure he would if he could.'

Lennie glanced at the clock. It *was* nice. Any other time it would have pleased him. The numbers rolled into view on a special dial. The numbers said 3:45. Then, slowly, 3:46 rolled into view.

'Thank you for coming,' his mom said.

'Ma'am, I wouldn't have missed it,' the man said. He was still holding out his little finger liked he was drinking tea. 'I know what it's like to be bitten by a snake, believe you me.'

Lennie didn't remember anything else about that afternoon except that after supper the doctor came in and changed the dressing and had to make some more slits in Lennie's leg.

'I'm going to give you something for the pain, Lennie, but it's going to hurt. You're going to have to be a brave boy,' the doctor said.

'He will be,' his mother said.

Lennie was already crying. Just the mention of any more pain than he was suffering now was more than he could bear.

'Now, Lennie, get hold of yourself please, honey,' his mother said. Then she turned to the doctor, 'He's usually real brave about everything. The time he had his arm set he never even moaned.'

But bravery didn't seem important to Lennie now. Nothing was. He yelled and cried and hollered. He hit at the doctor until the nurse had to hold his hands. He cursed. He screamed. He sobbed as if he would never stop.

'Now, it's all over,' the doctor said. 'That wasn't so bad, was it?'

His mother was coming back in the room. 'See, hon, it's all over. Things will be better now. I'm just real sure things'll be better.'

'The nurse will give you something to help you sleep now,' the doctor said. 'In the morning you should be feeling better.'

The only thing Lennie remembered about the next morning was that he saw his leg for the first time. It scared him so much that for a moment even the pain stopped.

His leg no longer even resembled a leg. It was a huge

swollen object, shiny as glass. 'Oh, no,' he moaned. From his thigh to his toes, his leg was twice as big as normal, and it was every colour in the rainbow.

Lennie fell weakly back on his pillow. 'I told you not to look,' the nurse said. 'Now you lie back and relax.'

'Where's my mom?' Lennie asked weakly.

'She stepped out into the hall for a minute.'

'I want my mom.' The sight of his leg had made him weak and sick and scared. 'Mom!'

'She'll be back in just a minute, soon as the doctor gets through. Your mom just felt a little dizzy and needed some air.'

'Oh.' The nurse pushed him back against his pillow. Lennie knew that the sight of his leg had been too much for his mother too. He remembered she went out into the hall every time it was uncovered.

'It's beginning to look better,' the doctor said.

'Not to me,' Lennie moaned. 'I never want to see my leg again.'

But to everyone else, the leg was a fascinating sight. That was what Lennie remembered most about the next two days – showing his leg. Nurses from other floors, doctors, patients who were allowed to walk about, visitors, all came in to have a look at Lennie's leg.

'Haven't they ever seen a leg before?' he kept asking the nurse.

'Not like that one,' she said. 'You couldn't get any more colour on that leg with a paintbrush.'

'Will it ever go away?'

'Oh, sure.'

'When?'

'Oh, by next week probably.'

'Next week?' Lennie moaned. It seemed a lifetime. Turning his head to the window, he began to weep.

19

IT was Friday before Lennie felt he really wanted to live. That happened about four o'clock in the afternoon. Lennie's mom had rented a TV set for him to watch, and she had just rolled up the head of his bed so he could see. A re-run of *Bonanza* was on.

And as Lennie lay there watching Hoss win a Chinese girl in a poker game, he suddenly felt hungry. The hunger surprised him for a moment. Up until now he hadn't wanted a thing to eat. They had had to feed him through a tube in his arm.

He said, 'Mom, I'm hungry.'

His mom was watching Hoss, smiling because Hoss had thought he was winning a *horse* named Ming Lee. Now he was afraid to take the *girl* Ming Lee back to the Ponderosa and show her to Pa. His mom turned her head to Lennie and got up at the same time. 'I'll get you something to eat,' she said quickly.

At the door she turned, still smiling, and said, 'The nurse will be so pleased. She has been trying to get Jell-O and broth down you for days.'

'I know, Mom, but I don't want that stuff.'

'What do you feel like eating then? I'll go out for something if the doctor says you can have it.'

'I want a hamburger.'

'Oh, Lennie, I don't think –'

'And a chocolate shake.'

'Well, I'll try, but I really don't –'

'And if they won't let me have that, then I'll take a pizza.'

'I'll try, Lennie.'

He lay back down. He already knew he wasn't going to get the hamburger or the pizza. His mom was going to come back with Jell-O and broth, but it didn't much matter. He felt hungry enough to eat anything.

A commercial came on the screen. A little girl was swinging, and a solemn voice announced that the little girl had skinned her knee yesterday, and was about to fall on the same knee today.

Lennie looked at the girl's knee. There was a mark the size of a dime. He glanced down at his own huge, discoloured leg. He thought that the people who made television commercials didn't know anything about real life, not the way he, Lennie, did.

It seemed to him suddenly that every TV person he had ever seen wasn't real, not the girl in danger of skinning her knee again, not the women who had just given up their soap for an experiment in white clothes, not the man who had eaten enchiladas and gotten an acid stomach.

Lennie went on, even including his favourites. Not Hoss who had just won a Chinese girl in a poker game. Not Lassie who had rescued a colt from a burning barn. Not Gentle Ben who didn't really kill the chickens. Not the Brady Bunch who had to go on a talent show and sing a rock song to get money for their parents' anniversary gift.

That wasn't life. It was close enough to fool you, Lennie thought, if you weren't careful, and yet those TV characters were as different as a wax figure is from a real person. Lennie imagined you had to come up against life hard to know what it was all about.

He looked at the TV. He smiled slightly. On the screen Hoss was saying, 'But, dagburnit, Pa, how was *I* to know Ming Lee was a girl?'

Lennie watched Pa for a moment. Pa Cartwright was the kind of father that would make you think – if you had a father – that your father wasn't good enough. Or Lassie pulling a new-born colt from the burning barn made you think your dog wasn't good enough. Or Mother Nature-type forests ruined real forests for you, made them seem dirty and empty. Or the Waltons or the Brady Bunch made you think there was something wrong with your family, when really, Lennie thought, his own family – just him and his mom – was a hundred times realler than the Bradys or the Waltons or the Cleavers or any other TV family you could name.

Lennie shifted on his hospital bed. After his mother brought his supper, he thought, he would turn off the TV for a while and work on his report. It was the only thing that really interested him. His teacher, Miss Markham, had come to see him in the hospital and had suggested that he do a report on rattlesnakes and rattlesnake bites. She would, she had said, give him extra credit for it. It would make up for his last Science test.

He had wanted to start the report right away, but he hadn't felt like it. Now, suddenly, he did.

Lennie looked at his clock. He decided he would work on his report during *Let's Make a Deal*. For a second he had a feeling of betrayal. All those people in their farmer suits and banana costumes would be in place, waiting.

Monty Hall would be coming down the aisle. A great cheer would go up. Signs would wave. People would beg Monty to choose them. And Lennie would dial them all down to a small dot and start working on his report.

And after that, he would betray the celebrities on *Hollywood Squares* who were waiting with their funny answers.

And after that . . .

Lennie's mother came in with a tray. She was smiling. 'The nurse says no hamburgers or pizza today.'

'What is it?'

'It's Jell-O and broth, but she says you can have something else tomorrow if you're feeling better.'

'A hamburger?'

'We'll see.' She sat by his bed, spooned up some broth and fed it to him. She said, 'What happened to Hoss while I was gone?'

'I don't know,' Lennie said. 'I was thinking.'

'Oh?' She fed him some more broth. She dabbed at his face with a napkin. 'What about?'

'My report.' The broth felt good and warm inside him. 'I'm going to work on it after supper.'

'Now, the doctor says you shouldn't do anything you don't feel like doing.'

He nodded, took another spoonful of broth. 'I feel like it,' he said.

20

LENNIE stood in front of the Fairy Land Motel. He was beside the wishing-well. One hand was on Humpty Dumpty's head. He leant forward and looked down at the painted water below. There were still seven pennies and one nickel but the Mound wrapper was gone.

Lennie eased himself down on the edge of the well. His grandfather had made this well, Lennie thought, and painted all the fairyland figures. Lennie could remember how proud his grandfather had been. He glanced around. Now there were only three figures in good enough condition to be in front of the motel – one elf, Humpty Dumpty and Hansel. But once the whole lawn had been covered. People had had their pictures taken there as if it were Disneyland.

'Mom, get a shot of me with the dwarfs.'

'Dad, take me with the Wicked Witch.'

Lennie ran his hand over the rim of the well. It was odd how different things looked to him now. The motel was more a home to him now than any house he could imagine. Driving up to the door after he had left the hospital had made him understand why his mom was always singing songs about home. It had given him such a peaceful feeling to go in his room and lie down on his own bed.

Lennie straightened. He imagined that if he went back to the stone house by the lake, that would look different too. Maybe some day he would do that, go back the way other people returned to look at their old high schools or the places where they had been born.

Using his crutches, Lennie got up and walked across the driveway. He passed the cold-drink machine. Behind him the red neon sign flashed on. FAIRY LAND MOTEL – VACANCY.

Lennie's mother was watching him through the picture-window of the office. She had just turned on the sign, and she came to the door. 'Lennie, are you all right?'

'I'm fine, Mom.'

'Well, you're supposed to take it easy.'

'The doctor said I could do anything I felt like doing,' he called.

'Well, I want you to take it easy. You're a very lucky boy. Everyone at the hospital says so.'

'I know.'

'Don't undo all the doctor's good work now and have a relapse.'

'I won't.'

A relapse was the last thing he wanted to have. By the time he got out of the hospital he had been jabbed with needles and stuck with thermometers and had his blood pressure taken enough times to last him for ever.

A truck passed on the highway, building up speed for the hill ahead, and at the same time a car turned in the motel driveway. Lennie glanced round.

It was a policeman's car, and the big cop who had helped Lennie – Officer Olson – was behind the wheel. The car pulled up by Lennie.

'Well, how are things going today?' the policeman asked.

'Lots better,' Lennie said. 'I'm still sore from all those

shots, though.'

'How many did you have – did you ever find out?'

'Sixty-one. The nurse counted them for me from my chart.'

'That's a lot. How's the leg?'

Lennie held it out. 'I can walk around on it now. I don't even use my crutches in the house.'

'Well, that's fine. You'll be ready to go on that fishing trip with me before long. I haven't forgotten my promise.'

Lennie nodded.

'Your mom around?'

'In the office.'

The policeman parked his car in the slot for room 316 and got out. His jacket was open and his stomach hung over his belt. He stood for a moment, looking over the grounds. 'Grass could use a cutting,' he said.

'That's my job,' Lennie said. 'I'll probably be back at it next week the way I'm going.'

He nodded. 'You know, you folks got a nice place out here, real peaceful.'

'Homelike,' Lennie said.

The policeman went into the motel office, and Lennie hobbled across the walkway. He sat down in one of the plastic webbed chairs. He stretched out his leg. He looked at the empty chair across from him.

Suddenly he thought of Friend. 'Yes, with Friend – the doll that's as big and as real as you are – you'll never be alone again.'

He shifted in his chair. Only a few weeks ago, he recalled, Friend had seemed like a pretty good idea. The way toys like G I Joes seem great when you see six kids playing with them on TV, laughing, having a wonderful time with about a hundred dollars' worth of extra equipment and perfectly formed little hills and cliffs and sand dunes. You don't even realize that you'll be playing on the sidewalk, probably by yourself, with no extra equipment at all. Or the way games on TV seem so much fun because they're being played by one of those TV families that do nothing but laugh together.

Why, if he had seen Friend advertised on TV, he would probably have sent off for one himself. Television could make you believe anything – it was their business.

'Only ten ninety-eight in cash or money order for Friend. And remember, Friends also come in the Multi-Pack, which consists of three Friends in assorted sizes and colours so, overnight, you can become the most popular kid on your block.'

Lennie would send off his money and wait. He would check the mailbox daily. He would come running in from school every day gasping, 'Anything for me?'

'Not yet, Lennie.'

Then when he couldn't stand it another moment, the box would come. He would tear it open, eager to have Friend as soon as possible, eager to get on with the good times, the picnics, the long walks down country lanes, the movies.

He would lift the box-top, fold back the tissue paper and there would be Friend. Lennie would be too excited to notice anything.

He would struggle with Friend, trying to get the arms and legs bent in the right position. He would get Friend on his feet. He would drag him outside. He would sit him in the other plastic webbed chair. He would begin telling Friend a joke.

A car would pass on the highway and Lennie would imagine how he looked sitting there, laughing and joking with Friend, just like on the TV ads.

Then a little boy in the car would stick his head out of the window and cry, 'Hey, look, that kid's talking to a *doll!*'

Looking at the empty chair, Lennie smiled.

21

LENNIE could hear the policeman and his mom talking. The policeman was saying, 'After I go home and change, I'm going to come back and cut the grass. The boy shouldn't be pushing the lawn mower till he's a lot stronger.'

The policeman had come to visit Lennie every single day he was in the hospital – some days he even came twice, his mom had told him.

'Did he say anything about me?' Lennie had asked when he felt good enough to worry about being caught by the police.

'Nothing bad.'

'Nothing about me going in all those houses?'

'No.'

'He's probably waiting till I get well.'

'No, he is a very nice man, Lennie, and he's taken a real interest in you. He and his wife never had any children so you be nice to him.'

'I'll try.'

'It was he who got your picture in the newspaper.'

Lennie *was* grateful for that. It was the first time he had ever been in the newspaper, and he had had twenty-nine get-well cards from people he had never heard of. And every single person in his English class had written him a note. And the Mayor of the city had sent him good wishes in a letter.

A Mercury sedan turned into the motel driveway and stopped just in front of where Lennie was sitting. Lennie could hear the car radio. John Denver was singing about nature in Colorado.

The man said, 'I'll check and see how much the rooms are,' and he got out of the car.

There were two girls in the back seat fighting over a *Young Love* comic book. The older girl was saying, 'Mom, I'll have you know I bought this comic with my own baby-sitting money, and I don't have to share it with anybody if I don't want to.'

'Mom,' the smaller girl whined, 'I told her she could look at my Porky Pig but –'

'Who wants to look at Porky Pig? Anyway, you make me sick. Everything *I* get, *you* want. Mom, she copies every single thing I do.'

'It's flattering to be copied,' the mother said in a tired voice.

'Not by *her*.'

'Now, Faye.'

'I mean it. You *made* me let her wear my good pink top, and look! She's got chocolate all over it! I hate her!'

'Will you please stop it, girls? You've been arguing all the way from Tuskaloosa. Look, over there's a wishing-well. Go make a wish, why don't you? I think I've got some pennies.'

They took their pennies and walked to the well. The little girl looked up at her sister and said, 'What are you going to wish for, Faye?'

'I'm not telling you.'

'Why?'

'Because you'll wish for the exact same thing, that's why!'

They stood at the wishing-well for a moment. Lennie watched them. Then silently they made their wishes and dropped their pennies into the well. The coins clanged faintly against the bottom of the well.

The man came out of the office with a key. 'We're staying,' he said. 'Drive down to room 302.'

The policeman came out of the office right behind the man. He paused and said to Lennie, 'Well, I'm taking over your job for the evening.'

'What's that?'

'Grass cutting.'

'Oh.'

'Probably this'll be the last time it has to be cut before winter.'

'Yeah.'

He got in the patrol car and drove off. Lennie continued to sit in his chair.

'Hey, what's wrong with your leg?'

Lennie glanced up. It was the smallest of the sisters.

'Oh, I got bitten by a rattlesnake.' Lennie never said those words without a feeling of great importance coming over him. He could hardly wait to get back to school to give his report. 'You want to see it?'

'Yes.'

He pulled up his pants and showed his wounded leg. It was still colourful enough to startle.

'See all those little slit marks?' he said.

'Yes.'

'They had to cut those to keep my leg from bursting open like a sausage.'

'Oh.' The girl's eyes got a little bigger. Her tongue came out and touched her upper lip. 'Hey, Faye,' she called, straightening, 'he got bitten by a rattlesnake. Come look.'

Lennie kept his pants' leg raised so that he wouldn't have to do it twice. Faye bent forward, then she turned away, one hand over her mouth. 'Oh, I can't look. It must have been awful!'

'It was pretty bad.'

'I used to think I wanted to be a nurse but every time I see something like that, I know I couldn't. Let me see again.'

'If they hadn't made those slits in his leg,' the little sister said, 'it would have burst open like a sausage.'

'I hate snakes,' Faye said, shuddering a little as she sat in the chair next to Lennie. 'I think they're the awfullest things.'

'You ought to read my report,' Lennie said. 'It's real interesting, even if I did write it myself.'

There was a silence and then the little sister said, 'Hey, you want to look at my Porky Pig comic book?'

'Yeah, I guess so.'

'I'll go get it. It's in the car.'

Faye was still looking at him. She said, 'I never met anybody who got bitten by a rattlesnake before.'

'I've only met one other person myself,' Lennie said.

'I wish I had some film in my camera. I'd take your picture.'

'Oh, well,' Lennie said. He leant back in his chair. He drew the evening air into his lungs. On the highway a truck passed, building up speed for the hill ahead.

'Here it is.'

Lennie held out his hand for the Porky Pig comic book. He began to flip through the pages. He glanced up and said, 'You know in my report – my report about the rattlesnake – I even tell how many shots I had to have.'

'How many?' the little sister asked.

Lennie looked closely at the first page of the book. Porky Pig was having to take care of the neighbour's baby. Lennie glanced up. 'Sixty-one.'

'*Sixty-one!*'

He nodded. He bent back over the comic book. A very small bank robber had dressed up in baby clothes to escape the cops and, without Porky Pig's knowing about it, had taken the place of the baby. Porky Pig was trying to get him to take his bottle.

'When you get through with that,' Faye said, 'you can read my *Young Love* comic.'

Lennie looked up at her. '*If* I have time,' he said. He paused. 'You see, I have to go over my report on rattlesnake bites one more time. I'm going to give it in Science class for extra credit.'

'I'd like to hear your report,' the little sister said.

'You would?' Lennie said. He had thought they would never ask. He'd begun to give up hope. 'If you really want to . . .'

The girl nodded.

'Well, all right.' Lennie got up quickly. He started for the motel office. He turned on his crutches. 'In a lot of ways,' he said, 'my report is better than the stuff you see on television. It's –' He paused, searching for the right word. 'It's *realler*,' he said.

Both girls nodded.

'I'll be back in a minute,' Lennie said, and he went inside to get his report.

THE
CYBIL
WAR

1

Being Ms Indigestion

SIMON was at his desk, slumped, staring at the dull wood. Someone had once carved 'I hate school' in the wood, and over the years others had worked on the letters so that now they were as deep as a motto in stone.

Simon sighed. His teacher, clipboard in hand, was choosing the cast of a nutrition play. She had already cast Tony Angotti as the dill pickle which meant that he, another of her non-favourites, would probably be the Swiss cheese. The thought of himself in a yellow box full of holes made him miserable. He had never been one for costumes – even at Hallowe'en he limited himself to a mask – and now this. Well, he would just have to be absent that day.

Miss McFawn cast Laura Goode and Melissa Holbrook as the green beans.

'Good casting,' Tony Angotti said. 'You guys look like green beans when you turn sideways.'

Simon smiled.

'Frontways you look like spaghetti.'

Simon laughed, and Laura Goode hit him on the arm with her music book.

'I didn't say it,' Simon protested.

'You laughed.'

He turned away. 'Violence is not characteristic of the green bean,' he said coldly. His arm hurt but he refused to rub it.

He waited, without hope, while Miss McFawn cast Billy

Bonfili as the hot dog, Wanda Sanchez as the bun. Slowly he realized that the entire play had been cast. Bananas, tacos, onions, pecans surrounded him. He alone had no role.

'Let's see,' Miss McFawn said, 'who can we get to be Mr Indigestion?'

Mr Indigestion! Simon couldn't believe it. This was the lead role. She could only be doing it out of spite, he knew that, but still he really wanted to be Mr Indigestion. He who had walked along in misery last Hallowe'en in his Jimmy Carter mask while Tony Angotti romped beside him in his mother's dress stuffed with balloons, *he* now actually wanted to put on a black cape and moustache and twirl on stage as Mr Indigestion. He was surprised at himself.

'Oh, yes,' she said. 'Simon can be Mr Indigestion.' She made a note on her clipboard. 'Simon will be the perfect indigestion.'

'It takes one to know one,' Tony Angotti muttered.

Everyone around Tony snickered and Miss McFawn looked at him. Miss McFawn could stare down a cobra. In three seconds Tony's eyes were on his desk.

In the pause that followed, Cybil Ackerman called from the back of the room. 'Miss McFawn?'

Miss McFawn's eyes were still on Tony Angotti in case he was fool enough to look up again. He was not and Miss McFawn's eyes shifted to Cybil.

'Miss McFawn?'

'Yes, Cybil, what is it?'

'Well, every time we have a play the boys get all the good parts. When we did the ecology play, the girls had to be trees and flowers while the boys got to be forest fires and coal mines and nuclear waste. And when we did the geography parade, the boys got to be countries like Russia and China, and we had to be Holland and the Virgin Islands. It's not fair.'

'What do you suggest, Cybil?'

'I think we ought to have a *Ms* Indigestion.'

Simon swirled round in his seat. He felt as cheated as a dog deprived of a sirloin steak. His mouth was open. He tried to give her a McFawn stare-down, but she was looking over his head.

'We could vote on it,' she said nicely.

'That's not fair,' Simon said. There were seventeen girls in the room and fourteen boys. He turned back to Miss McFawn. 'All the girls will vote for Ms Indigestion.'

'We will not!' the girls said in chorus. They were used to voting in a bloc.

'All right, that's a good idea. We'll vote,' Miss McFawn said. Simon thought she looked at him with satisfaction. 'How many would like to have a Ms Indigestion?'

Seventeen girls raised their hands.

'How many for Mr Indigestion?'

Fourteen boys raised their hands. Tony Angotti had two hands up, one positioned to appear to be Wanda Sanchez's, but Miss McFawn was not fooled.

'Ms Indigestion it is,' Miss McFawn said in a pleased voice. She crossed out Simon's name on her list. 'Let's see. Cybil, would you like to be Ms Indigestion?'

'Yes!'

'So what's Simon going to be?' Tony Angotti asked. He was not going to be the dill pickle unless everybody else was something.

'He can have my part,' Cybil offered.

287

'Or mine,' Tony said. 'I have the feeling I'm going to be absent that day.'

'No, Tony, I especially want you to be the dill pickle.' Miss McFawn checked her list of players and foods. 'Let's see, we could do with another starch. All right, Simon, you can either be a macaroni and cheese pie or – what were you, Cybil?'

'A jar of peanut butter.'

'Or be a jar of peanut butter.'

Simon kept his eyes on his desk. He stared at the phrase 'I hate school' so hard that he expected the words to catch fire.

'I'll have to have your decision, Simon.'

He did not move. He felt betrayed. For the first time in his life, he had actually been willing to put on a costume, come out on stage, twirling his moustache, even saying, 'I am the dreadful Mr Indigestion,' only to have it taken away.

'Simon,' she prompted.

He mumbled something without taking his eyes from the letters on his desk. Now he was actually willing them to catch fire, like Superman.

'I'm sorry, Simon, I didn't hear you. You'll have to speak up. What do you want to be?'

'*A jar of peanut butter!*'

'Violence is not characteristic of peanut butter,' Laura Goode sneered.

Simon struck at her, hitting his hand on the back of her desk. Pain shot all the way up to his shoulder.

'Miss McFawn, Simon hit me,' Laura called happily.

'Simon, I'm not going to have violence in my classroom.'

Simon looked up at Miss McFawn. He stared at her

with the same intensity and hatred he had stared at the letters on his desk.

For the first time that anyone could remember, it was Miss McFawn who looked away.

'Rehearsal Friday,' she reminded them as she shifted the papers on her desk.

2
Arbor Day is for the Birds

SIMON, eyes on his book, felt his face burn. He had made a fool of himself, and over nothing. Over being Mr Indigestion, which nobody in their right mind would want to be.

'Tony, will you explain what the poet means?' Miss McFawn was asking.

'He means,' Tony said slowly, stalling for time, 'he *means*, now, wait a minute . . .'

'Wanda?'

'He means that things are not what they seem.'

'Very good!'

And what really hurt, Simon told himself – he was sitting with his eyes on the wrong page, finger marking the wrong poem – what really hurt was that Cybil Ackerman had a part in his humiliation. And he was in love with Cybil Ackerman, had been for three years.

He had fallen in love with her in the room right below this one. It was Arbor Day, and their teacher Miss Ellis made a big thing out of it. She gave every student a little tree to take home and plant, and the celebration was capped off with the writing and reading of tributes to trees.

Simon had been careful with his baby tree. Some of the other boys were using theirs in whip battles and trying to see how high they could throw them. Not Simon. He was taking his home in the crook of his arm, like a real baby, so his father could help him plant it. It was the first time he had something he was sure his father would want to do.

He went into the house, and his mother was standing in the kitchen. He said, 'Look, I've got this baby tree and Dad and I are going to plant it and watch it grow and . . .'

'Your dad cannot help you plant that tree,' his mother said tiredly. 'Your dad's gone.'

'Well, I'll wait till he gets back. I'll put the tree in a little bucket. I'll water it. I'll . . .'

'Simon, look at me.' She sat down on a chair so that their heads were level. 'Now, your dad's gone. We've been over this and over this. No, don't turn away. Your dad is gone and I do not know where he is or when he's coming back. Do you understand me?'

He tried to look away, but she held his head in place with her hand. He blinked uneasily. He was aware his mother had been talking to him about his father's absence, probably for days, but for the first time he realized what she was talking about.

'When will he be back?'

'I don't know.'

'Well, where has he gone?'

'All I know is this. He has gone. His clothes are gone. The car is gone. The camping equipment is gone. Half the money in our bank account is gone.'

'It's business . . . it's vacation . . .' he stuttered.

'No, he's gone.'

It was more than he could stand – that his father, the

only person he could not live without, could actually
decide to live without him. The earth seemed to tremble
with a terrible inner quake.

'Maybe he's dead,' he said, his voice reflecting the
quivering world.

'He's not dead.'

'How do you know? He could be. People die. Their
bodies are never found.'

'It turns out he's been talking to Mitch Wilson about
leaving for months.'

'What did he say?'

'Oh, he talked about solitude and about getting away
from the confusion and corruption of the world and going
back to the simple way of life and about living off the land
and about . . .'

'It has to be more than that. It has to be!'

Suddenly Simon turned, pulling away from his mother.
He looked down. He was clutching the baby tree in both
hands as if he were trying to choke it. He ran from the
room.

'Simon, he'll be back some time. I know he will,' his
mother called. 'It's just something he's going through and
we'll get along.' She followed him to the back door. 'Simon,
I can't give you answers because he didn't give them to
me!'

Simon ran into the backyard and threw his baby tree as
far as he could. He didn't see it land because his hands
were over his eyes, but in his mind that baby tree went so
high and so far nobody ever saw it again.

When it came to the reading of tributes to trees, Simon
was the first to volunteer. He read in a loud, hard voice:

'I hate Arbor Day, I hate trees.

I'm going to chop down every tree I see.'

He had to lean close to read his writing. He had pressed down so hard with his pencil that he'd gone through the paper in three places.

There was a gasp from Miss Ellis. 'That is enough!' She made her way to the front of the room in three steps. She took the paper from him so violently that she tore off the corner. Then she ripped the rest into pieces and threw them into the trash can.

'Sit, Simon,' she said.

He had heard kinder tones used on dogs. He walked back to his desk with his head held so high he stumbled over Billy Bonfili's foot.

In a voice still trembling with rage, Miss Ellis called on Wanda Sanchez. Wanda made a lot of noise walking to the front of the room because she, too, was outraged about Simon's tribute to trees.

Her composition went:

> 'The tree is a gift from God, It
> gives us shade. It gives us wood. It
> gives us food. Thank you, God, for trees.'

'Thank *you*, Wanda,' Miss Ellis said.

'You're *welcome*, Miss Ellis.'

When all the children had read their tributes, Miss Ellis announced that they would have a vote on whose paper was the best. Wanda Sanchez, the favourite, got nine votes. Tony Angotti got five. He had written a comic tribute to trees, pointing out that if there were no trees, birds would have to build nests on top of people's heads.

'Oh, Miss Ellis,' Cybil Ackerman called from the back of the room when the voting was over.

'Yes, Cybil?'

'You forgot to call Simon's name.'

There was a pause while Miss Ellis inhaled and exhaled. 'I don't think anyone wants to vote for Simon's paper,' she said, 'do they?'

She sounded as if she was asking if anyone wanted to vote for a fungus infection.

Simon put his hand up so high his arm hurt.

There was another icy pause. 'Simon Newton – two votes.' It was as if the North Pole had spoken.

Simon swirled around in his seat. He could not believe he had got another vote. Who would dare risk Miss Ellis's displeasure?

Cybil's hand was in the air. As Simon looked at her, she grinned and crossed her eyes.

Love washed over him with the force of a tidal wave. He turned back to the front of the room. He lowered his hand and put it over his chest. He had not known it was possible to love like this.

His eyes blurred. His heart was beating so hard he expected to look down and actually see it pounding, like in cartoons.

He glanced back once again at Cybil Ackerman and knew he would love her until the day he died.

'Simon! *Simon!*'

He looked up. 'What?'

'Would you like to tell the class the meaning of the next poem?'

Simon was sitting with his hand on his chest, over the very spot that had pounded so hard years ago. He was surprised to see it was Miss McFawn in front of the class instead of Miss Ellis.

'Would you like to tell the class the meaning of the next poem?' she repeated.

He looked down at the blurred image of his English book. He decided to tell the truth. 'No,' he said.

3

Popsickle Legs and Tub of Blubber

It was after school, and Tony Angotti and Simon were standing at the drinking fountain. Tony had forgotten the insult of being cast as a dill pickle, and he was telling Simon that today was his sister's birthday and he couldn't go home until five o'clock. He began imitating his sister. He could do this perfectly.

'Tony spoils eeeeeeverything. He spies on us and he copies what we say. I don't even want to have a parttttttttty if Tony's going to be here. He spoils eeeeeeeverything.'

He was warming to the imitation when Harriet Haywood came up. 'Cybil wants to know if you're mad at her,' Harriet said to Simon.

Simon raised his head from the drinking fountain. Before he could answer, Tony asked, 'What would he be mad at Ackerman for? What'd she do?'

'*You* know,' Harriet said, 'for taking his part in the play, for getting to be Ms Indigestion.'

'Oh, that.' Tony was plainly disappointed.

'Well, *is* he mad?'

Simon stood to the side, hand still on the drinking fountain, watching Harriet and Tony Angotti. He felt like a patient being discussed by a doctor and nurse.

'Well, sure he's mad, Haywood,' Tony decided. 'What'd you think? You think anybody in his right mind wants to be a macaroni pie?'

'A jar of peanut butter,' Simon corrected.

'Whatever.' Tony warmed to the discussion. 'Listen, Haywood, you go back and tell Cybil Ackerman Simon is mad. Tell her he's plenty mad.'

'Well, I'll tell her what you said,' Harriet began slowly, but Tony cut her off.

'You tell Cybil Ackerman he is so mad he said she ought to be a double popsickle in the play with them legs of hers.'

Harriet gasped.

'Wait a minute. I didn't say that.'

'Listen, this is between me and Haywood.' Tony had recently learned the pleasure of quarrelling with girls and he didn't want to be interrupted.

'I will tell Cybil *exactly* what he said.' Harriet's eyes had become smaller. 'And don't think I won't either.'

She turned so fast it was like a move out of a pro basketball game. She started to walk down the hall. She was so upset over this insult to her best friend's legs that her whole body was trembling.

'And you know what he said about you?' Tony called after her.

She slowed down but did not glance round.

'He said it's too bad there isn't a tub of blubber in the play because that part would be perfect for you!'

Simon watched Harriet draw in a breath so deep he thought she was going to inflate herself. 'Wait a minute, Harriet,' he called. Tony was laughing so hard he had to put one hand on Simon's back to steady himself.

Harriet went directly to the girls' rest-room. She pushed

the door open with such force that it swung back and forth five times, a school record.

Tony slapped Simon on the back. 'I love it,' he said. 'Old popsickle legs and tub of blubber.' Again, he leaned on Simon's back for support.

Simon shrugged him off. The weight of his friend on his back seemed, unexpectedly, enough to send him to his knees. 'Get off!'

Tony raised his hand. 'I'm – Oh, here she comes, Pal, and she has not forgotten and forgiven.'

Harriet came out of the rest-room like a missile. There were two girls with her, and the three of them, in tight formation, seemed like an attack force out of *Star Wars*.

Simon and Tony stepped back against the wall to avoid injury. Tony was silenced for a moment and then he stepped back into the middle of the hall as they passed and watched them.

'Hey, Haywood,' he called. 'You know what Simon just said? He said them girls with you ought to be sacks of potatoes in the play.'

The sacks of potatoes stiffened, ruining the tight formation.

'Wait a minute,' Simon said. 'I didn't say any of that.'

Tony grinned with satisfaction as the girls attempted to go through the school door at the same time. 'You can't get three hamburgers in one bun,' he called cheerfully. Harriet turned. Her eyes were so slitted with anger that they were invisible.

'Now, I did not say *that*, Harriet,' Simon called. 'I couldn't have. I –'

'He's just being modest. He thinks of these things and then doesn't want credit. You be sure to tell Ackerman what he said about them legs.'

'I will,' Harriet called back. She slammed the door and went down the steps.

'She'll tell too,' Tony said happily. 'She loves to blab. Remember that time I put the trash can upside-down on Miss Ellis's desk and Miss Ellis came in and before she even noticed the trash can, Harriet jumped up and said, "Tony Angotti did it! Tony Angotti did it!"' He jumped up and down on the pavement to demonstrate. Then he said, 'Course I don't have the flab she's got. When Haywood jumps up and down, windows all over the school slam shut.'

'Why do you –' Simon began, but Tony interrupted.

'And then came victory. Miss Ellis said, "What did Tony do?" And then she notices that there is a trash can upside-down on her desk. Oh, horrors! And before anyone can stop her, she picks up the trash can and trash falls all over her desk!'

In the silence that followed Tony's laughter, Simon asked his question again. 'Why do you do stuff like that?'

'Like what?'

'*Lie!*'

'Oh,' he said, shrugging. 'Everybody in my family lies. You know that.'

'Well, quit lying about me!'

'Even my mom lies. The first thing she ever said to me that I can remember was a lie. She told me chocolate-covered cherries were medicine.'

'That's different, Tony. That's –'

'My mom would make a real bad face every time she ate one. It took me three, four years before I'd even try a chocolate-covered cherry. She also told me that if I made

297

ugly faces my face would freeze like that and that if I sat too close to the TV I wouldn't be able to see anything but black and white.'

Tony Angotti went on, happily listing his mother's lies. Simon walked beside him in silence. His long friendship with Tony, which had brought him such pleasure in the early grades, seemed this year to be bringing him only discomfort. He walked slower. He had the uneasy feeling that he had been led, half-willingly, like a blinded horse, into a stream and abandoned. And now, blindfold lifted, he had to face the current alone.

'And my grandmother – talk about lies! My grandmother told me that if I wore my cousin Bennie's shoes – which were two sizes too little – see, we were out in Wheeling and my uncle died and we all had to go to the funeral and I didn't have any dark shoes. So she told me that if I wore my cousin Bennie's shoes, something nice would happen because they were magic shoes. Can you believe that! And I put them on – can you believe *that*? And off I go to the funeral in my magic shoes – I could barely walk.' He began to limp comically. 'The toes were pointy, Simon – they were like real little old men's shoes!'

Simon smiled despite himself.

'And when I got home, I had blisters, them things were that big and my grandmother – you know what she told me? She told me they were magic blisters and that if I didn't pop them, they would turn into silver dollars!'

'Did you pop them?' Simon asked.

'No! – well, yes, but only after Annette laughed at me. Anyway, *that* was lying.' Pride in the family trait showed in his face and voice. 'I could never think of anything that good.'

Simon glanced at him and then back at his own feet, dragging along in his torn sneakers. His smile faded. 'Yes, but you're just getting started,' he predicted in a low voice.

'That's true.' Tony nodded. 'That is sooooo true.'

4

Let My Dad Kidnap Me

SIMON entered the house and sighed with relief at being rid of Tony. Then he picked up the mail.

When there was a letter from his father – and there had only been four – he felt worse. In the first two letters, his father was living on a boat off the coast of California; in the next two, in a forest in Oregon. The letters were Robinson Crusoe descriptions of what he was eating and how he gathered wood and built fires and mended his clothes.

The letters made Simon hate the outdoors in the way he would hate a rival. And it seemed to Simon that Nature had sensed his hate, just as a dog senses fear, and had sent poison ivy and wasps and pollen to retaliate.

He could imagine a Mother Nature who had thought up hurricanes and tornadoes pointing in his direction, instructing her plants and insects with a smile. 'Sickum!'

Today there was no letter. I should stop hoping for letters, he told himself. It was as useless as trying to get kidnapped in second grade. He had finally learned to smile about that now.

It was the first awful winter without his father and Simon had seen a TV special about a father who had left, just like his father, and then the father had come back and kidnapped his own son!

The idea had almost made Simon stop breathing. Maybe at this very moment – the possibility made him put his hand on his chest, right over his pounding heart – maybe at this very moment his father was planning to kidnap him.

It was like suddenly learning there's Christmas or television. There's kidnapping.

It was odd. He could remember how in first grade they had had long lessons on the dangers of being kidnapped. Mr Repokis had given them an oral quiz about it.

'Now if someone offered you an ice-cream sundae with marshmallows, nuts, bananas *and* decorettes, would you get in the car with them?'

'Noooooooooo.'

'And if someone offered to give you a Barbie doll with a majorette suit and a light-up baton, would you get in the car with them?'

'Noooooooooo.'

'And if someone offered to give you a Matchbox car with real headlights and a real engine, would you get in the car with them?'

They were all collecting Matchbox cars then, and Bennie Hoffman, overcome, had cried, '*I* would!' and they had to start all over again, because kidnapping was such a terrible thing.

Now it became Simon's dream. Let my dad kidnap me, he prayed as he played dangerously near the road at recess. Let my dad kidnap me, he pleaded as he stood at the edge of the driveway. Let my dad kidnap me, he begged as he slowly passed a strange van parked down the street.

He was always at the edge of the street in those days, waiting for the feel of his father's arm as he was lifted into the waiting van and driven away.

It was December before he finally gave up. It was such a cold month that his mother would not let him sit outside without his Yogi Bear face mask. Even he, with all his dreams, had to admit that it was unlikely he would be kidnapped in that attire.

A voice at the door said, 'I forgot, I can't go home till after the partttttty.' It was Tony, speaking in his sister Annette's voice.

'I'll come out,' Simon said quickly, but before he could open the door, Tony was inside.

Tony came through the house like a pickpocket, opening drawers, picking up objects, glancing in envelopes, pulling out letters. He paused to glance through the Newtons' mail.

'Nothing from your old man?'

'No.'

Tony looked with interest at a Reader's Digest Sweepstakes Entry. 'He must not have got his head together yet,' he commented.

'No.'

'Do you mind if I take this? I'd like to win some of this stuff – that boat, for instance.'

'There's no lake around here.'

'Well, do you mind if I take it?'

'No!' He paused, then said calmly, 'Let's go outside.'

They went out and sat on the steps. Tony put his Sweepstakes Entry in his back pocket. 'It's not fair,' he said. 'Why am I – a member of the family – kept out of my own home so that strangers can come in and eat cake?'

'Because you imitate your sister and her friends and spy on them,' Simon answered with unusual bluntness.

'Come on. When did I spy?'

'Last week.'

'Name two other times.' He broke off and sighed. 'Oh, never mind.' Suddenly he straightened. 'Hey, here comes Haywood. What's the Tub doing walking past your house?'

'Don't call her that. Maybe she's on her way somewhere. Lay off, will you?'

'Huh, she's walking past your house for one reason. She wants to see you.'

'After what you said this afternoon, I would be the last person she'd want to see.'

'Listen, I know about walking past people's houses. My sister Annette does it all the time. When she wants to see Rickie Wurts, she walks past his house, reallllll slow, just like Haywood's doing. Sometimes she pretends to be looking for something she's lost. That way she can walk past ten, fifteen times until he comes out of the house.' He broke off to yell, 'Haywood, where are you going?'

Harriet turned her head and looked surprised to see them. Then she exhaled, giving the impression that the two of them were giving off an unpleasant odour.

'Come on,' Tony said. He grabbed Simon's shirt and pulled him down the sidewalk to where Harriet was waiting at the edge of the street.

'Well, I didn't expect to see *you*,' Harriet said. She lowered her eyes with the coldness of someone recently called a tub of blubber.

'It's his house,' Tony said. 'Why wouldn't you expect to see him?'

'I just thought,' she was colder than ever now, 'that after what you said today, the two of you would have the decency to stay out of my way.'

'We want to stay out of your way, Haywood,' Tony said, 'only how are we going to do that when you come looking for us?'

'I was *not* looking for you!'

'She wasn't looking for us, Tony,' Simon said.

'Listen, I know what's happening here. I've got experience in these things.' Tony put up his hands. 'Okay, Haywood, so while you weren't looking for us, what were you going to tell us when you found us?'

'Nothing, except that I told Cybil what you said about her legs.'

Harriet was glancing from Simon to Tony now, including them both in the responsibility for the insult.

'Well, I'm glad to hear that, Haywood,' Tony said. 'You keep things like that to yourself, you'll end up in the funny farm.'

'And you know what she said about you?' She was looking right at Tony Angotti now, but Simon felt she was talking about him too.

'No, I don't know what Popsickle Legs said about us and I don't want to know.'

Simon said, 'I do.'

Suddenly Harriet hesitated. She glanced from Tony to Simon. Simon could see that she wanted to tell them, indeed, she had walked all the way over here to tell them, but his eagerness made her change her mind.

'I'm not going to tell you,' she said and started walking away.

Tony yelled, 'Haywood, you mean you come all the way over here to see us, walk fifteen, twenty blocks, and we take pity on you and come down on the porch and then you won't tell us what Cybil said?'

'You've got it,' Harriet said over her shoulder.

Simon and Tony watched her until she turned the corner. Then Tony said in a surprised voice, 'I wonder what Cybil did say about us.'

'I don't know.'

'It had to be an insult of some kind.'

'Of course.'

'But there's nothing to insult!' He held out both hands to show he was hiding no flaws.

'Well, we're not perfect,' Simon said.

Tony was silent while he went over a mental checklist of his body. 'Really, there's nothing to insult!'

'Maybe she said we're lousy baseball players.'

'What kind of insult is that? We call her legs popsickle sticks and she comes up with, "Well, you play poor baseball." Come on, if I know Cybil Ackerman, she said something a lot worse than that.'

'Yes, she could.'

Tony stood for a moment, looking up the street where Harriet had disappeared. Then he turned abruptly and said, 'I'm going home.'

'It's not five o'clock yet. Annette's party isn't over. You . . .'

'Right. I've got . . .' he checked his watch '. . . exactly twenty minutes to spoil eeeeeverything.' He started down the sidewalk for home, then he turned. 'And I'll let you know tomorrow what Ackerman said about us.'

5
Tears and Ravioli

SIMON went back into the house and looked in the kitchen. His mother sometimes left notes for him. 'Put the casserole in the oven. Clean the celery.' Today the message was 'Defrost the chicken.' He took the package from the freezer. He was like a robot kitchen helper, he sometimes thought, who performed acts without understanding what he was doing.

He went back to the living-room. The television was broken so he sat doing nothing, hands dangling at his sides.

Simon and Tony were known as best friends. Their friendship had been sealed in second grade when the entire class was asked to write essays on their fathers.

Simon refused to write one, and Tony could not because his father had died when he was one year old. Tony could not even remember his father. So they had sat in their desks, both miserable, both staring at their dirty fingernails while other children went to the front of the room and read happily, 'My father is a dentist. He plays golf. He plays tennis. He has a new car.'

When the voting was held on the best paper – Billy Bonfili won because his father was the high school football coach – only Simon and Tony did not vote.

'You don't have a father?' Tony asked after school. He had waited at the door to ask this, his long face intent.

'I have one,' Simon said carefully, 'but he's gone.'

'Where?'

'I don't know.'

'I had one but he's dead.'

'Oh.'

And thus sealed together by a mutual loss rather than mutual interest, their friendship had begun. They walked together to Tony's house.

'Do you like ravioli?' Tony asked at the edge of the driveway.

'I don't know.'

'You've never had ravioli?'

'No.'

'Well, come *on!*'

They went into Tony's house, and Simon sat at the kitchen table. He watched while Tony heated the ravioli. He was looking down at his steaming plate, at the strange, soft squares, when Tony's grandfather came in.

'You want some ravioli, Pap-pap?' Tony asked at the stove.

Pap-pap nodded, pulled out his chair, sat heavily. When the three of them were seated, plates full, Tony said, 'He doesn't have a father either.'

Pap-pap looked over at Simon. His eyes, blue as a baby's, began to fill with tears. 'You got no papa?'

'I have one but he's gone.' Pap-pap pulled out his handkerchief. It was old and faded because it was used all the time. 'Your papa left home?' he asked.

'Yes.'

'He comes to visit?'

'No.'

'He writes?'

'We had one letter.'

'One letter,' Pap-pap said sadly. He shook his head.

Tears spilled on to his wrinkled cheeks. He wiped his eyes and blew his nose.

'He cries a lot,' Tony explained to Simon.

Simon nodded. He looked from Tony to the weeping Pap-pap. Simon had not seen his mother cry when his father left. He himself had not cried. And here, across the table, from an old man he had never seen before, were tears for his father. He felt the first stirring of tears in his own eyes.

'Sometimes he cries just because the moon's full, you know, because it's beautiful,' Tony explained as he chewed. 'And sometimes he cries because he sees a picture that reminds him of home and sometimes – well, he just cries all the time. It doesn't mean anything.'

Simon nodded again.

'That's not true,' Pap-pap said. 'It means something.' He peered at them over his handkerchief. 'It means I get so full, I spill over.' He made a gesture with his handkerchief as if it were water pouring over a dam. Then he wiped his cheeks again, and, sniffling, began to eat.

Simon ducked his head, cut a piece of ravioli in half with his fork and put it in his mouth. The tears in his own eyes, the tightening of his throat made him unable to swallow, but there was something in the soft warm food, the weeping sympathetic man across the table that would make him feel sentimental every time he ate ravioli. Even in the school cafeteria, where ravioli came straight from a can, he would feel tears in his eyes when he ate.

Simon got up and went back into the kitchen. He opened the refrigerator. His mother's taste ran to yoghurt and natural foods and fresh vegetables and bran muffins. He selected a cup of yoghurt and ate it slowly with a spoon, feeling nothing at all.

Then he went back into the living-room, sat in his same seat and turned his thoughts to Cybil Ackerman.

6
At Cybil Ackerman's House

CYBIL Ackerman was practising the piano. This was so that she could play trumpet in the band when she got to junior high school. It was a deal she had made with her father. She was playing intently, eyes darting from the music to her hands. There was a carrot in her mouth. The doorbell rang.

'Cybil, open the door please,' Mrs Ackerman called.

Cybil removed the carrot from her mouth and stuck it in a jar of peanut butter beside her music. 'I'm practising,' she called back.

'Cynthia?'

'I'm studying.'

'Clara?'

'I'm in the bathroom.'

There was a rule in the Ackerman house that whoever was least busy had to answer the door and the phone. Mrs Ackerman made the decision. 'Cybil.'

'Oh, all right.' Cybil got up. 'But I was just about to get that part.'

She dipped her carrot into the peanut butter as she went to the door. She saw through the screen that Tony Angotti was standing on the porch. His hands were in his pockets. A slight smile of anticipation was on his face.

'Who is it?' Clara and Cynthia both called.

'Nobody!' Cybil called back.

'What do you want?' Cybil asked. She took a bite of peanut-butter-covered carrot.

'Nothing. I was just passing by, and I figured I'd find out what you said about Simon. *I* don't want to know but he – well, you know how *he* is – he . . .'

'I didn't say anything about Simon.' Crunch, crunch. 'I like Simon.'

'Well, sure, but after Harriet told you he said you had popsickle legs . . .'

'I do have popsickle legs.'

'No.' The conversation was not going as Tony had anticipated. 'I mean Harriet said you said something bad about Simon and maybe,' he gave an improbable laugh, 'about me.'

'Oh, I said you were juvenile.'

'What?' He leaned forward as if he had been struck a light blow on the back of the neck.

'Juvenile,' she repeated.

'Me juvenile? Or Simon?'

'You.'

'Who's at the door, Cybil?' Mrs Ackerman called.

'*Nobody.*'

'Then get back to your practising.'

'That's what I'm trying to do!'

Tony said, 'But why would you say that about me?' He was genuinely puzzled. 'Simon's the one who acts like he's still in kindergarten. If I told you some of the stupid stuff he does, you wouldn't believe me. One time he . . .'

'I've got to go.'

'Wait a minute, Cybil, give me a chance. Just let me tell you one stupid thing that Simon Newton did, just one thing and then you can decide which of us is juvenile.'

Cybil sighed, stuck her carrot in the peanut butter jar and waited.

'Okay, Simon was going to this funeral, see. His uncle died while he was visiting his grandmother and he didn't have any dark shoes. And so his grandmother told him that his cousin Bennie's shoes were magic shoes, and that if he wore them something good would happen. And so, believe it or not, he puts on the magic shoes and limps off to the funeral. They were two sizes too little, they were like tiny little men's shoes and . . .'

Clara stuck her head around the door to see who was on the porch. 'Mom,' she called, 'Cybil's talking to a boy! And if she can talk to a boy before she finishes practising then I can talk to Tommy before I finish studying. Tommy's been sitting in the garage for fifteen minutes and –'

'Girls!' Mrs Ackerman warned.

'I was not talking to a *boy*,' Cybil explained, 'I was talking to Tony Angotti!'

As Cybil turned away and shut the door on him and his unfinished story, Tony Angotti could see that she was grinning at her sister and that her eyes were crossed.

7
In the Bushes

SIMON Newton heard this conversation from the bushes where he happened to be hiding.

That night, after supper, he had decided to walk over to Cybil's house. He would just walk up the sidewalk slowly, perhaps pretending to have lost something and then, when

Cybil came out of the house he would tell her that it was Tony, not he, who had thought up the unfortunate similarity between her legs and popsickle sticks. 'I like straight legs,' he would tell her.

He would then go on to say that he was glad she was going to be Ms Indigestion. This was true. Now that he had had a chance to realistically imagine himself in costume, his peanut butter sign and his one line – 'I am rich in protein and blah – blah – blah –' – did seem like a reprieve from public humiliation.

He was going over this in his mind, practising it, when he turned the corner and saw Cybil's house.

Simon had walked past Cybil's house many times since that Arbor Day when he fell in love with her, and he never tired of doing so. Cybil had four sisters – all had red curly hair and looked alike, and so he had the pleasure when the youngest – Clarice – came running out, of seeing what Cybil had looked like in first grade. And when the oldest – Cynthia – came out, of seeing what Cybil would look like in high school.

Tonight, for the first time, when he looked at Cybil's house, he got a nasty shock. Tony Angotti was standing on the porch. Tony Angotti was ringing the bell and straightening his jacket. Tony Angotti was smirking.

Keeping low, Simon had made his way behind the hedge, up to the shrubbery, and behind the bushes to the side of the porch. He had been here before too. Once he had sneaked up to look in the window so he could see what Cybil's living-room looked like, and at that exact moment Mrs Ackerman had come out to cut some oleanders for a party she was having. Simon had crouched there, head against his knees, while Mrs Ackerman snipped blossoms around his head with a pair of shears.

This time he crouched in place just in time to hear Cybil ask, 'What do you want?' and to hear the crunch of her carrot. And now, only minutes later, with every word of the conversation between Cybil and Tony burning in his brain, he watched through the leaves as Tony Angotti made his way down the driveway.

Simon was stunned by what he had heard. 'Simon's the one who acts like he's still in kindergarten . . . Just let me tell you one stupid thing that Simon did . . . Simon was going to this funeral, see . . .'

A funny lie – that was how he thought of Tony's attributing the tub of blubber and sack of potatoes similes to him – a funny lie was one thing. He had survived dozens of those over the years. What he had just heard was character assassination. He could sue.

Simon watched with slitted eyes as Tony paused at the edge of the street. Simon was breathing through his mouth, the way he did when the pollen was bad.

Tony lifted his head as the opening notes of 'Under the Golden Eagle' floated through the window. He scratched his head, a sure sign of thought. He adjusted his jacket. He turned his face towards the window as alert as a listening bird.

Tony Angotti was having a hard time believing that Cybil had called him juvenile. Him, Tony Angotti, who looked like Donny Osmond! He paused, head turned to the music, trying to find an answer.

Tony's head shifted with another thought. Tony could not keep his head still when he was thinking. Sometimes during a science test, his head would snap up as quickly as if he had a sudden toothache.

Cybil Ackerman was trying to make him jealous by pretending to like Simon Newton who, everyone knew, really was juvenile! That was it! At this very moment, Tony thought, she was probably watching him through the window.

He turned. With studied nonchalance, he made his way to the hedge. Quickly, head low, he ducked behind the hedge and walked in a crouch to the bushes. Holding his hands over his face to protect it from scratches, he squirmed through the bushes to a place beneath the window. Cautiously he lifted his head.

Simon watched all this with an awful fascination. Seeing Tony come closer and closer, knowing a showdown here in the bushes was inevitable, he still made no effort to get away or hide. He waited, his eyes bright with anger.

Tony straightened and peered into the window. His face reflected his disappointment. His mouth hung open.

He had somehow expected to see Cybil Ackerman standing behind the curtain, peering out, trying to see him as he walked away. That was what Annette did when Rickie Wurts left. Instead here she was, playing the piano with a carrot stuck in her mouth.

It was hard for Tony to believe. Cybil Ackerman was not even pretty. Her legs really were like popsicle sticks.

And yet here she was treating him, Tony Angotti, the image of Donny Osmond, as if he were an ordinary person. No, worse – as if he were nothing. He was glad no one was round to see this humiliation.

'Cybil!'

One of Cybil's sisters rushed into the living-room. Cybil's hands stopped playing, hovered over the keys.

'Quick, play "The Wedding March" while Clara goes

down the steps to meet Tommy. Hurry, she's leaving.'

'I don't know the music.'

'Fake it!'

Cybil's hand twitched, hesitated, then struck.

Dum da-da-da. Dum da-da-de. Dum da-da-daaaaaaaaa-da-da dadadadada-deeeeeee.

'Cybil! Cynthia! That's not funny!' Clara yelled. She spun around on the porch and glared back at the open window.

Tony Angotti crouched so quickly his knees popped. He bowed like a Moslem.

Clara waited, eyes on the window, until she was sure Cybil was through with 'The Wedding March'. Then, as the laboured strains of 'Under the Golden Eagle' floated through the window again, she went down the steps to where Tommy was waiting.

'Excuse my sisters,' she said, 'they think they're soooooo funny.'

Tony Angotti lifted his head. He brushed dirt from his brow. He pulled his T-shirt from his stomach where it had stuck with his sweat. He was now doubly grateful that no one could see him here on his knees.

It was then that he turned his head and saw Simon Newton.

8

The Spies and the Lies

'I DIDN'T know you went around hiding in the bushes, spying on your friends,' Tony Angotti said as soon as they were safely on the sidewalk. After that one long, hard moment in the oleanders when their eyes met and locked, they had not glanced at each other. They were now walking, eyes down, towards Simon's house.

'May I point out,' Simon said, 'that you were in the same bushes?'

They kept walking. Each was torn by the feeling that the other's crime was worse, and yet unable to put that proof into words.

'That doesn't count,' Tony said. 'I had a reason.'

'Maybe I had a reason too.'

There was a silence, awkward and long, while each searched for another accusation. Then Simon brushed his hair from his forehead and said with a faint smile, 'Anyway, did you find out what Cybil said about you?'

'You didn't hear?'

'No,' he lied, 'I got there right after that.'

'You didn't hear what she said?'

'No.'

Tony glanced at Simon, quickly, then away. 'Well, she didn't say anything about me, Pal. She said you were juvenile.'

'What?'

'You heard me – juvenile.' Tony would like to have spelled the word out for emphasis, but he wasn't sure if it started with a 'j' or 'g'.

'Oh.'

Tony sighed, partly from relief, partly from being on safe territory – lying. 'I tried to tell her you weren't, but she wouldn't listen. Right in the middle of a long story about you – I was really pouring it on – she just went back in the house.'

'What story were you telling?'

'About the time you broke your arm,' he said swiftly, happy he came from a family where lying was an inborn gift. 'And that when they set it you didn't take any ether and . . .'

'I never broke my arm.'

'Oh, I thought you did. Well, anyway, she wouldn't listen. She went in the house and started playing the piano. You heard that?'

Simon nodded. 'Well, I've got to go in.'

'Sure.'

Their eyes met again, a questioning look, but both of them turned away before anything was revealed. Tony kept watching Simon as Simon walked up the steps. Then he shrugged. 'Ahh!' He made the motion of pushing Simon and the whole stupid business away as he turned to go home.

'Did you and Tony have a fight?' Simon's mother asked as he came in the door.

'Why do you ask that?'

'Because you always have that look on your face when you have a fight.'

'I don't have any "look" on my face.'

'Yes, you do. Your face gets red and . . .'

'Maybe I've been running. Maybe I've been in the sun.' He resented the fact that his emotions showed on his face. 'Just leave me alone.'

He was aware that his mother was watching him closely. Ever since his father left, she had been doing this. How are you? How do you feel? Is there anything wrong? Talk to me. It was as if she never wanted to be taken by surprise again.

'I'm not going to run away and live in a forest, if that's what you're thinking,' he had said once in exasperation. 'May I remind you of my allergies and my magnetic ability to attract wasps?'

'I know you're not going to run away,' she'd said, but the fact that he'd put the thought into words only seemed to make her worry more.

'Simon . . .'

'Oh, leave me alone,' he said again. He sometimes had the feeling that when he died, if people would just leave him alone, he could come back to life.

She sighed and smiled. 'Then tell me what *isn't* wrong, tell me something, anything.'

He paused, his red face turned towards the blank television set. The TV had broken three months ago, during a re-run of 'Bonanza', Simon's favourite serial, and Mrs Newton had not had it repaired. From habit, Simon still watched the blank screen when he wanted to be diverted.

'Tell me something that happened at school today,' she suggested.

He looked at her. 'And then I can go to my room?'

'Yes, *if* it's about you. Don't tell me about somebody throwing up in the cafeteria.'

'That happened yesterday. Well, let's see. Oh, here's the big news of today. We are having a nutrition play. This is because Miss McFawn used to teach first grade where they did nothing but put on plays. I have been selected for a lesser role – the peanut butter, but I shall try to bring dignity and character to the part. Can I go?'

'What's Tony?'

His face did not change expression. 'Dill pickle.'

'Go on.'

'Well, that's basically it. One of the green beans – Laura Goode – hit me because I laughed when Tony said she actually resembled a green bean from the side.'

'Aw.'

'*Hard*, Mom. Look.' He found a small bruise above his elbow and showed it to her. 'And then I was falsely accused of calling two other girls sacks of potatoes and one girl a tub of blubber which, incidentally, she does resemble. The tub of blubber did not hit me, fortunately, or I would be in hospital.'

He looked at her, keeping his face bright and cheerful so she would know he was fine and leave him alone. 'Is that enough?'

'Yes.'

'Can I go now?'

'Simon, you are not a prisoner. I just like you to tell me things.'

'That's all there is to tell.'

As he left the room she called after him. 'Simon.'

'What?'

'Don't let Tony take advantage of you.'

He stopped where he stood. He sighed with irritation. 'That is not the problem.'

'What is the problem, then?'

His shoulders sagged. With his back to her he said, 'Everything is just so complicated.'

'How?' she asked quickly, sitting forward on the edge of the sofa.

Fathers desert you, he told himself, friends lie about you, teachers humiliate you – and those are supposed to be the good guys. He sighed. 'Oh, nothing,' he said.

'I *want* to know.'

'Forget I said anything.'

He went into his room and shut the door. As he flopped down on the bed he remembered that was something his father used to say, 'Everything's just got so damn complicated.'

9
Good Things/Bad Things

THAT night as Simon lay in bed he decided to try and think of the good things about Tony Angotti. This was because he now hated Tony so much he could not understand why they had ever been friends. He also, at this point, wanted to conceal from Tony how he felt and that now seemed impossible, not unless his hatred was somehow diluted.

He started thinking as soon as he got into bed and it was ten o'clock before he thought of the first thing.

GOOD THING NO. 1

At times Tony Angotti would say the right thing. Like, one time in third grade, he and Tony decided to bore a small hole in the school wall. Tony was in room 104 that year and Simon was in 106. It was the first year they had been separated and they wanted this hole so they could pass secret code messages to each other.

Simon brought a drill from home, hidden under his jacket, and during recess they began to work on the hole. Just when Simon was getting started, Mrs Albertson came in.

'What are you doing?' she asked. She was right behind Simon.

He was so startled that he dropped the drill. Mrs Albertson picked it up.

'Boring a hole,' he stammered.

Just then Mrs Albertson and Simon heard a tapping on the wall. Simon knew it was Tony Angotti, directing the drill so the hole wouldn't go through the blackboard.

Mrs Albertson walked out into the hall and down to room 104. There was Tony, waiting to see the drill come through. He was so excited that he didn't see Mrs Albertson until she touched his shoulder. Then he screamed.

'Come with me,' she said.

She sat them down and gave them a talk about respecting school property and made them promise not to drill any more holes. They promised even before she finished the sentence. When they were leaving the room, Tony turned and said, 'Could we have his drill back? It's borrowed.'

'After school,' Mrs Albertson said.

Only a good friend, Simon reminded himself, would have asked about the drill.

Simon had no sooner thought of this when, against his

will, he remembered a bad thing.

One time in second grade Tony told Miss Ellis that Simon had licked the icing off one of the Christmas cupcakes when he had only pretended to do that to be funny, and then Miss Ellis had made him take the cupcake that looked like it had been licked!

It was ten-thirty before Simon was able to think of another good thing about Tony Angotti.

GOOD THING NO. 2

At times Tony Angotti could be nice.

Like one day Simon was over at Tony's house and Pap-pap was crying. This day everybody was busy and so nobody was paying any attention to him.

Finally Tony's mother said, 'Tony, go and see what's wrong with Pap-pap.'

'Why can't Annette do it? I've got company.'

'Who?'

He pointed to Simon.

'Go and see about Pap-pap.' Mrs Angotti raised her hand. Mrs Angotti had a ring with a stone as big as a bird's egg, and she could – Tony claimed – thump you on the head with it from ten feet away.

'All right!' Tony got up and backed out of the room.

He and Simon went outside and sat on the bench by Pap-pap, who was crying harder now, wiping his eyes with an old faded handkerchief.

'Is anything wrong?' Tony asked.

Pap-pap shook his head.

'Do you hurt?'

Again Pap-pap shook his head.

'Well, I'm supposed to find out what's wrong!'

At last Pap-pap managed to speak. 'I've got too good a

memory, that's my trouble.'

'What?'

He mopped his eyes. 'I was standing by the fence, see, over there by the bushes, and I smelled my mama's apron.'

'What?'

'I used to be a puny little kid, see, and the big kids would pick on me and I would run home crying and hide my face in my mama's apron. I never forgot the way her apron smelled.' He started crying again. 'Over there.' He waved with his handkerchief. 'Over there, that's my mama's apron.'

'Show me,' Tony said in a nice voice.

The three of them got up and walked over to the fence. They stood there in a gush of warm air. Simon realized they were standing by the vent from the Angottis' stove and Mrs Angotti was cooking peppers in olive oil.

'That's it?' Tony asked.

Pap-pap wiped his eyes, nodding.

'Nice,' Tony said, breathing deeply.

Pap-pap nodded again, smiling a little now, happy to be sharing the smell of his mama's apron with them. Simon was smiling a little himself.

And the three of them stood there together, inhaling, until Mrs Angotti had finished frying peppers.

Then again, right away, Simon remembered another bad thing about Tony Angotti.

When they were in first grade they used to play the game Simon Says on rainy days. Since Simon was the only student named Simon, Mr Repokis let him start the game a lot. Those were his happiest moments in first grade.

'Simon says, "Stoop down,"' he'd yell, as happy as a

dictator. 'Simon says, "Hands on your ears."' He could have gone on like that for hours.

Then one day, after one of his best games in which even Wanda Sanchez had been tricked, Tony said, 'You should stop doing that.'

'What?'

'Leading that stupid game.'

'Why?' Simon had been genuinely surprised. He had thought he was the envy of the class.

'Because you lisp.'

'What?'

'You lisp!' he said. 'Thimon thays thtoop down!'

'That's — that's because of my teeth,' he said, both lisping and stuttering now.

'Well, it still makes you look *thtupid!*'

After that, Simon did not try to think of any more nice things about Tony Angotti.

10
T-Bone's Invitation

CYBIL'S sister Clarice was out on the roof of the porch. She had been there twenty minutes, sitting like a Hindu, facing out over the front yard.

'Come in off the roof, Clarice,' Mrs Ackerman called.

'I'm not coming in until Cybil apologizes for calling me Boney!'

'Cybil!'

'Well, Mom, she *is* boney and you told us always to be truthful.'

'Cybil!'

'All right, all right. I apologize . . .'

Clarice got up and crawled to the window. As her foot went over the sill, Cybil added, '. . . to *Skinny!*'

Clarice bounced back on to the porch roof. 'Mom, now she's calling me Skinny!'

'Cybil!'

'Listen, Mom, she's on the roof and you told us we couldn't play on the roof because it made us look like the monkey house at the zoo.'

'Cybil!'

'All right! I apologize to *Glamorous!*'

'That's more like it.' Clarice began climbing in the window again.

Cybil started to say something else, but she caught sight of Simon across the street. 'Oh, Simon, wait a minute. Don't go away. I'm coming out.'

Simon had been standing beneath a tree, in the shadows, watching the house. He had intended to walk by slowly, pretending to have lost something, but he had become so interested in the sight of Clarice sitting on the roof that he had forgotten his plan.

He waited dutifully until Cybil came running out of the house. 'Guess what? Harriet's having a pet show and she wants you to come and bring your dog.'

'T-Bone?'

'Yes.'

Simon was caught by surprise by the invitation; he knew Harriet would not want him at anything other than a hanging.

'T-Bone's not much for shows,' he said.

'That doesn't matter.'

'And also I don't think Harriet would want me to come. She has it in her mind that I called her a – well, that I called her something unattractive.'

'A tub of blubber?'

'Yes.'

'She's forgotten about that.'

'I don't think so. I know the sacks of potatoes haven't. They keep hitting me with their books in the hall.'

'I *want* you to come.'

He hesitated, decided to level with her. 'My dog – look, we got him at the pound. And the day mom and I went over there, well, it was on a Friday and they put all the dogs that are left to sleep on Saturday and he was the only dog left.' He swallowed. 'So we didn't choose him, you know, because he was real beautiful or cute or spotted or anything like that. We chose him because he was left.'

'But I like dogs that are just dogs. I want him to come. And, listen, there's a prize for the best costume. He could win that.'

Simon shook his head. If T-Bone was anything like him – and Simon often felt the kinship – then he wouldn't want to wear a costume either.

'I want you to come. Tony's coming.'

His head snapped up. 'Tony Angotti?'

'Yes.'

'Tony doesn't even have a dog.'

'He's going to borrow his aunt's poodle, and it can pop balloons and open its own Gainesburgers and say its prayers. Guess what its name is?'

Simon shook his head.

'Miss Vicki!' She grinned and crossed her eyes.

Normally this would have turned his knees to jelly, but

the news about Tony alarmed him.

'When did you see Tony?' he asked.

'Just about fifteen minutes ago. He was walking by the house looking for something he'd lost.'

'Oh.'

'At first I said, "No." You can't *borrow* a pet, because somebody could go out and *borrow* Lassie and win all the prizes. But he said it was a *family* dog that belonged to the whole family, so anyway he's coming and he thinks Miss Vicki can win Best Behaved and Best Costume and Best Trick. I suppose I shouldn't give this away, but guess what Miss Vicki's costume's going to be?'

'I don't know.'

'A baby cap and diaper!'

There was a pause while she grinned. In the pause Simon said, 'You know, I believe I will come to the pet show. If Tony's going to be there – I mean, well, if my *friend*'s going to be there, I want to be there too.'

'Great! It's tomorrow afternoon at two o'clock.'

'T-Bone and I will be there.'

11
The Love Quiz

SIMON walked to Tony's house with his face set. He was furious. He felt somehow like a character in that fairy tale where the little pigs tell the wolf to meet them at six o'clock and then they go at five and get all the apples. He had no idea what he would do when he actually saw Tony, but he knew he had to confront him.

He rang the bell, and waited.

'Come on in. I want to show you something,' Tony said. He pulled Simon in by the shirt.

'I understand you were over at Cybil's this morning, that you *lost* something and were looking for it,' Simon said in a voice carefully drained of emotion.

'I didn't *lose* anything. I was doing an errand for my mom, and Cybil comes running out on them popsickle legs of hers. "Wait a minute, Tonnnnnnnny." Guess what she wanted? She wanted me to come to a pet show. I said, "I ain't got no pet." She said, "Borrow one." I thought she was going to get down on her knees so I finally said, "All right, I'll borrow my aunt's poodle." Come on.'

He looked both ways and then slipped into his sister's room. 'I've got to show you this,' he said.

'What is it?'

'It's a quiz – a love quiz – you do it to find out if you're in love.'

'Why would you be doing a quiz like that?' Simon asked in the same flat voice.

'*I'm* not doing it. It's my sister. Annette's doing it to find out if she's in love with – guess who?'

'I don't know.'

'Bubsie Frasure!' He laughed. 'Bubsie Frasure – you know he led our school patrol last year. If we got out of line, he'd stamp his foot? Well, look at this. You'll love it, Simon. Question One: Do you think about this person (a) occasionally (b) often (c) most of the time (d) all of the time?' He looked at Simon. 'And, Simon, my sister – I'm ashamed to tell you this – my sister has ticked (d). My sister thinks about Bubsie Frasure *all of the time*.'

Simon sighed.

'Simon, all the time! That don't leave room for

arithmetic, nuclear energy, world affairs – nothing!'

He shook his head in disbelief. 'Question Two: When you are not with this person you are (a) happy (b) content (c) unhappy (d) miserable. My sister once again has gone for the big D. Simon, she is *miserable* when she's . . .' Suddenly he lowered the notebook. 'Hey, want to spy on them?'

'No.'

'They're on the back porch. We just have to crawl into the living-room and hide under the picture window. Come on.'

Tony gave Simon a tug on his T-shirt and they left the room. Simon, eyes cold and unsmiling, followed. They crouched beneath the window in time to hear this conversation:

Annette: What are you thinking about, Bubsie?

Bubsie: Nothing.

Annette: Really, what are you thinking about?

Bubsie: Nothing!

Annette (getting kind of desperate): But they say we're always thinking of something.

Bubsie: Even when we're asleep?

Annette: Yes, isn't that wild?

Bubsie: Then I guess I must be thinking of something.

Annette: What?

Tony punched Simon to get his attention. Then he grinned a Groucho Marx grin and crossed his eyes.

Bubsie: I guess I was thinking about what I'm going to be doing tomorrow.

Annette: What are you going to do tomorrow?

Bubsie: Oh, just mess around.

The conversation on the porch continued, but Simon

did not hear it. He was stunned. He had never seen Tony Angotti cross his eyes before. He had never known he could cross his eyes – and Tony was not one to keep a talent like that hidden for four years. He felt confused, suspicious, betrayed. His face started to burn.

'Let's go. This is boring.' Tony mouthed the words.

They straightened, walked into the hall and through the kitchen. Simon stumbled over the doorstep and on to the porch in time to hear Annette say, 'Bubsie, what are you thinking about *now*?'

'I have to go,' Simon said quickly. He did not look at Tony. He knew all his emotions – even the ones he didn't understand – would be revealed in his red face. Then he added defiantly, 'I'm going to the pet show too and I have to find a costume for T-Bone.'

'You're taking T-Bone to the pet show?'

'Yes.'

'*T-Bone?*'

'Yes!'

'No offence, Pal, but T-Bone unless they're giving a prize for the dog who looks like he swallowed the most rotten bird – well, he hasn't got a prayer.'

'I'll see you there,' Simon said. He kept his hands in his pockets so he would not smash Tony Angotti in the face.

12
The Pirate

'WHAT on earth are you doing?' Simon's mother asked from the doorway.

He jumped as if he had been caught committing a crime. 'Nothing,' he said quickly. He snatched the pirate's hat from T-Bone's head and attempted to hide the eye-patch under his knee.

'Are you making a costume for the dog?' she asked. She moved into the room.

'What if I am?' he said, trying for dignity.

'Well, it just seems so odd. I cannot imagine *you* making a dog costume.'

'We're going to a pet show,' he said calmly. He waited, hoping she would go back to the kitchen so he could work on the eye-patch.

His mother burst out laughing. He looked back at her. She was leaning against a chair, holding her waist.

'There's nothing funny about that,' he said.

She laughed harder. 'It wouldn't be funny if it were anybody but you. I mean, you're so odd about costumes and never wanting to be noticed. And here you are dressing T-Bone up like Moshe Dayan!'

'He is a *pirate*, Mom.'

'Well, all I saw was the eye-patch.' She laughed again, and then tried to stop. She said, 'Look, I'm sorry. It's just been such an awful day. I had to type four reports and Mr McBee came in and . . .'

'No, don't apologize. I'm delighted to be the object of

such hilarity.'

'Now, I'm not laughing at *you*. I'm laughing at . . .' She paused to think of the object of her laughter.

'At what?' T-Bone nudged his knee, and the eye-patch, a flimsy item made of cardboard and black elastic, fluttered into view.

His mother looked away. 'Oh, I don't know. I'd better get back to the kitchen.' At the door she paused. 'May I ask one favour?'

'You can *ask*.'

'Let me see T-Bone before you go, when he's all in costume. Just let me see!'

'No, Mom, you'll laugh.'

'I won't. I promise.'

'You always promise and then you laugh.'

'This time I won't.'

'It's a terrible thing when a boy cannot believe his own mother.'

He glanced back at her. She was in the doorway, watching him with a faint smile on her face. She ran her hands through her short hair.

Once, in the year after his dad left, Simon would have said, 'Did you laugh at Dad like this? Isn't that really why he left?' But somehow he had grown beyond that. He liked it when his mother laughed and his dad probably had too.

He looked down at T-Bone and pulled out the pirate hat. He straightened it.

'I want T-Bone to look better than Tony's dog. I want T-Bone to beat him,' he admitted.

His mother came back into the room. Her smile was gentler now. 'Well, put it on and let me see.'

He worked the eye-patch over T-Bone's ears and into

place. He opened the hat, set it carefully on his head. He glanced back at his mother.

She was watching with her head cocked to one side. 'He'll win,' she predicted.

13
Two for the Show

THAT afternoon Tony and Miss Vicki and Simon and T-Bone made their way to Harriet Haywood's. Tony was in a mood of great optimism. It was the sight of his aunt's poodle in costume that did it.

Simon was trying to think of this as a period of truce and to take pleasure in the fact that T-Bone was wearing his eye-patch as nicely as if he really had a bad eye. Simon was not going to put the pirate's hat on him until the last moment.

'Miss Vicki could get Best Trick, Simon, if – and I admit this is a big if – if she will stop pulling at her diaper long enough to sit up and bark two times when I say, "How much are one and one, Miss Vicki?" Have you ever seen her do that?'

'I never saw the dog until five minutes ago, Tony.'

'I keep forgetting you don't know my aunt. Well, watch. How much are one and one, Miss Vicki? How much are one and one?'

Miss Vicki was twisted round pulling at her diaper. Tony tugged her leash and she looked up and whined. She couldn't get the diaper off by herself because Tony had made a hole in the diaper for her tail.

'She's not going to do it.' Tony leaned down and yanked

up the sagging diaper so hard Miss Vicki's back feet left the ground. 'Leave your costume alone.' He started walking again. 'Man, I don't ever want to be a mother.'

As they crossed the street, Tony's spirits lifted again. 'Maybe there'll be a balloon-popping contest. She's good at that. Or a praying contest.' He glanced at Simon. 'But if she's not in the mood to pray, Simon, she won't pray.'

Simon was silent. He reached down and scratched T-Bone behind the ears. T-Bone raised his head and gratefully licked the air.

'There it is,' Tony said cheerfully.

They were now approaching Harriet's house. It was a scene of confusion. Cats were mewing sadly in tight-fitting dolls' clothes. A parrot was screaming. A cocker spaniel was trying to get in a position to wet on someone's leg.

Harriet met them at the end of the driveway, her hands on her hips. She looked from Tony to Simon. 'You two better not cause any trouble. I mean it.'

Tony held up his hands to show he was hiding no bad intentions. 'We came to win prizes, Haywood, not to cause trouble.'

'That means you too, Simon.'

'Would Simon cause trouble?' Tony asked innocently.

'Yes.'

Tony made a face behind her back as she turned away. 'She's got your number, Pal – Hey, there's Bonfili. What you got, Bonfili?'

Billy Bonfili held up a turtle.

'Bonfili, you brought a turtle?' Tony called in disbelief. 'What kind of prize d'you expect to win – Slowest? Man, I thought this was going to be a show for dogs and cats. I didn't know they were going to let reptiles in.'

333

Billy lowered his turtle and moved behind two girls with cats.

'Hey, Bonfili,' Tony called, 'is that the same turtle you brought to school for Show and Tell in second grade? Remember that, Simon? Teacher, teacher, I'd like to tell about my little friend Snappy.'

'Lay off,' Simon said.

'You bring a turtle to a pet show, you've got to expect turtle jokes.' Tony looked around. 'You seen Ackerman?'

'Attention, everybody!' Harriet called from the steps. 'We're going to select Best Costume first because some of the dogs are ruining their outfits. First contestant will be Paw-paw Ackerman.'

'There she is,' Tony said. 'She's brought a cat!' He sounded as delighted as if she had brought a unicorn. 'Let's get closer.'

He pushed his way to the front and stood, eyes glowing, while Cybil displayed Paw-paw in a grass skirt and lei.

'Her cat's got them same legs,' Tony said to Simon. Then, louder, 'Hey, Ackerman, you know what Simon just said. He said your cat's got them same –'

Simon lunged forward and jabbed Tony so hard in the ribs that he choked off the rest.

'What d'you do that for?' Tony demanded. He rubbed his side. 'That hurt!'

It was the first time Simon had ever physically attacked anybody. He was stunned at the fury that had sent him, like an out-of-control car, into Tony Angotti. 'I slipped,' he said.

'Well, watch where you're stepping.'

Simon nodded.

Cybil was twisting Paw-paw so that the lower half of his

body was doing the hula. Paw-paw's slitted eyes reflected, Simon thought, the same helpless fury he himself felt.

'Second contestant – T-Bone Newton.'

Simon managed to get the pirate's hat on T-Bone and lead him forward.

'He should get a prize,' Cybil whispered as they passed. 'He looks just like Long John Silver.'

'Thank you,' Simon muttered.

He led T-Bone to the steps and back into place. 'I wish I'd thought to bring a little baby bottle,' Tony said. 'That would clinch it for me.' He bent down to straighten Miss Vicki's cap, and it was then that he noticed Miss Vicki had wet her diaper.

He straightened abruptly. 'I've got to get out of here.'

'Next contestant – Miss Vicki Angotti!' Harriet called from the steps.

'Miss Vicki's withdrawing,' Tony called quickly. He said to Simon, 'She's wet her diaper. Let's get out of here.'

'Nobody will notice,' Simon said loudly. He counted on the sharp eyes of Billy Bonfili to catch the accident. 'Go on!' He shoved him forward.

'Hurry *up*,' Harriet called. 'We've got seventeen contestants in this event.'

Billy Bonfili stepped over to see what the trouble was. 'Hey, he can't come because his dog wet her diaper,' he yelled happily.

Simon sighed, stepping back slightly to avoid being involved in the incident.

'Shut up, Bonfili,' Tony said.

'Anybody got an extra diaper?' Billy called. 'Tony needs one baaaad. His dog has had a little accident.'

'Lay *off*, Bonfili,' Tony said.

335

'It does make the costume authentic,' Cybil commented. She grinned and crossed her eyes.

Tony turned from side to side like a bear beset by dogs. Then he yanked Miss Vicki up beneath his arm. 'Let's get out of here,' he said to Simon.

'I don't want to. T-Bone might win a prize.'

'No way. These things are rigged. Harriet's going to give the prizes to her friends. It was stupid of us to come. Let's go.'

'I'm staying.'

Tony glared at him. 'Suit yourself,' he snapped.

Tony shoved his way through the crowd. He went behind a bush and removed Miss Vicki's diaper and cap. Then he came out pulling her by her leash.

'Hey,' Billy called, 'you forgot something behind that bush. Why, it's a little, tiny wet dog diaper.'

Now that her clothes had been removed, Miss Vicki – perhaps out of gratitude – was trying to say her prayers.

Tony glanced behind him to see what the trouble was with Miss Vicki. 'You are *not* praying.' He jerked the leash as she again tried to put her head between the paws. 'No praying!'

The crowd around Harriet's porch watched in pleased silence as Tony Angotti, head down, walked out of sight, dragging the prayerful Miss Vicki behind him.

14
That was Cybil Ackerman

SIMON was sitting in his living-room after the pet show. He was slumped on the sofa, staring straight ahead. His emotions were so strong that he was surprised his mother was not questioning him about them. He felt he must reek of pleasure like an onion. He could not wipe the smile off his face.

Simon felt, he decided, a little like that prehistoric fish must have felt, millions of years ago, when he noticed he had tiny legs and decided to try and step out of the water. That first weak step which probably left him jammed in the slime on his belly must have seemed at the time like a useless and stupid thing. Just as his own step today seemed useless and stupid, childish even.

'So much for walking,' the fish probably said, writhing back to the sea.

'I will not writhe backwards,' Simon said to himself. His smile broadened. He felt better than he had felt in a long time.

Suddenly Cybil Ackerman appeared at the screen door. The sight of her there caused Simon to leap up like a puppet. His feet actually left the floor.

'Good news!' She opened the door, came in and saw Mrs Newton. 'Oh, you must be Simon's mom. Hi!'

Before Simon's mother could nod, Cybil turned back to Simon. 'Guess what? Miss Vicki got first prize for Worst Behaved!' She looked delightedly from him to his mother. 'It was between her and the cocker spaniel who bit the peekapoo, and we voted. This was after you left.'

Simon nodded. After Tony's disgrace, Simon had waited a while and then slipped away too. He hadn't thought anyone noticed. The fact that Cybil had, gave him another pang of pleasure.

'Miss Vicki won by a landslide! It would have been unanimous except for the peekapoo's owner. I'm going over to Tony's house to tell him.'

'I'll do that,' Simon offered quickly. He was half-way across the living-room, no longer smiling. It came over him in a rush how much he did not want Cybil to go over to Tony Angotti's house. 'I was going over there anyway,' he lied.

'No, I want to see his face when I tell him.'

'But I . . .'

Cybil turned to Mrs Newton. 'Did Simon tell you what Miss Vicki did to get Worst Behaved?'

'No.'

'Wet her diaper.' Cybil grinned. 'You'd have to know Tony to appreciate it.'

'I appreciate it,' Mrs Newton said with a smile.

It came over Simon that he *had* to prevent Cybil from going over to Tony's. He had to keep her *here*. He made a desperate offer. 'You want a Coke?'

'No, I've got to go.' She swirled. 'Say good-bye to everybody, Paw-paw.' She made Paw-paw wave to each of them.

Mrs Newton waved back. It was the first time Simon had seen his mother wave to a cat, but that, he thought, was the effect Cybil had on people. Swinging Paw-paw under her arm, she went out of the door.

Simon stood in the middle of the rug as Cybil's

footsteps faded into the distance. His thoughts went with her as she crossed Brock Street, turned down Oak, went up the Angottis' driveway. As he thought of her ringing the bell, his face twisted with misery.

'Who was that girl?' Simon's mother asked.

Simon looked at her. It sounded like the end of 'The Lone Ranger' shows when somebody asks in an important voice, 'Who was that masked man?' and somebody answers in an equally important voice, 'That was the Lone Ranger.'

Simon answered in an equally important voice, 'That was Cybil Ackerman.'

He did not move. He was overcome by how quickly tides could turn in love and war, how quickly up could become down, victory, defeat.

'That was Cybil Ackerman,' he repeated to himself.

And it was not like there were dozens of Cybil Ackermans, he realized. There was only one. And in the world that swirled in confusion and conflict around him, she was an oasis, a patch of fresh air, a circle of peace.

He started for his room, stumbled over the rug and missed a step. 'Are you all right?' his mother asked quickly.

'I'm fine,' he said with careful cheer.

'Your face looks flushed.'

'I'm hot.'

'Simon . . .'

'Let me alone.'

He closed the door behind him.

15
The Saddest Sentence

When Simon was in third grade the teacher Mr Romano asked the class to write in twenty words or less the saddest sentence they could think of.

Billy Bonfili's sentence was: Last summer I almost drowned in front of my cousins and they laughed.

Cybil's was: My cat Paw-paw has been missing for three weeks and I think he's dead.

Simon's was: Last summer my mom sent me to Camp Okiechobie to make up for the fact that my dad left and on my third day I got the worst case of poison ivy the counsellors had ever seen and finally it reached my eyes and I had to be led blindly to the toilets by a boy named Mervin Rollins who refused to tell me if there were any Daddy-long-legs on the toilet seat.

Simon's sentence was way too long, of course, but Mr Romano gave him an A anyway because he admitted it was hard to condense that much sadness into twenty words.

After that, Simon had often tried to create the saddest sentence in the world. He knew he had it with 'My father has gone,' but he still kept writing. So far he had written twenty-seven.

Now he tried for twenty-eight.

'I was a jar of peanut butter in the class play and I stepped out and said my line perfectly (peanut butter is a nutritious food and good in sandwiches or on crackers), but when I stepped back into place, I bumped into Billy

Bonfili who shoved me back so hard that I pushed Harriet Haywood who was unsteady in an ill-fitting cottage cheese carton and who sat down on the stage and couldn't get up until me and the green beans helped her and Cybil looked at me and the whole thing made me wish I had never seen, heard of or tasted peanut butter.'

Way too long, Simon decided, too tiresome, too many who's, and anyway nobody cares about the feelings of a jar of peanut butter.

He was sitting at his desk as he wrote the sentence, waiting for the bell to ring. The sign 'Peanut Butter' which he had worn in the play was on the floor under his feet. The dusty prints of his tennis shoes had blurred the letters.

Simon re-read his sentence and then folded it to take it home. One day he would have a collection of sad sentences worthy of being donated to a library. They would have a special room – The Simon Newton Collection – and people would pass through and marvel at the sadness of the sentences in the glass cases.

The bell rang, startling him out of his thoughts. He got up, sighing, and picked up his books.

The sacks of potatoes jostled him as he went into the hall. He barely felt the jabs of their elbows.

He had the eerie, crystal-ball feeling that there would be another, newer, sadder sentence in the very near future. It was such a strong feeling that he could almost hear the sympathetic sighs of the viewers as they looked into the last case and read –

It was just as well, he thought, that he didn't know what.

16
The Newer Sadder Sentence

IN the week that followed, Simon sometimes felt he was a yo-yo he went up and down so quickly. In school he could not concentrate because he had to keep watching Tony Angotti who was watching Cybil and then watching Cybil to see if she was watching Tony. His neck began to ache with all this unnatural straining.

'Eyes front,' Miss McFawn said again and again.

Sometimes to Simon's surprise she would add, 'Tony', and Simon would know Tony had been looking at Cybil and he hadn't caught him. Then he would glance back quickly himself. Cybil would be writing or looking for something in her notebook, and Simon would feel instantly better.

One day after school when Simon and Tony were walking home, Tony said, 'Everybody likes me but Cybil Ackerman,' in a depressed way.

Tony's genuine dismay made Simon feel wonderful. His steps quickened with pleasure. But then he began to analyse that statement and he slowed down. Everybody did *not* like Tony. He himself could name at least ten people who didn't like Tony, starting with Simon's mother, Miss Ellis, Mr Repokis, Annette, Harriet Haywood, Billy Bonfili . . . And if Tony could be wrong about that, then he could also be wrong about Cybil not liking him.

'What makes you say that?' Simon asked carefully.

'Oh, I don't know. Do you think she likes me?'

'I don't know. She's the kind of person who likes everybody.' He paused then added, 'No matter what they're like.'

'Yeah, there's no reason why she *wouldn't* like me.' He held up his hands as if he were testing for rain. 'She probably does like me. Thanks, Pal.' And he walked on, obviously feeling much better.

Behind him, Simon followed, feeling much worse. 'What do I know,' he said, but his target was out of range.

But even with all these ups and downs, he was not prepared for Thursday.

Thursday had been an ordinary school day, one of those days so boring that when his mother would ask him to tell her one thing that had happened, he would not be able to. He would have to make up something that had happened another day to satisfy her.

Not once had he caught Tony looking at Cybil or Cybil looking anywhere but at her papers or through her notebook, and he had been lulled into a feeling of warm security.

He was walking home, whistling happily under his breath, when the blow fell. Tony Angotti said, 'Cybil Ackerman *does* like me.'

Simon stumbled over a root. He looked up to see a smirk on Tony's face. 'What?' He felt his cheeks begin to burn.

'Cybil Ackerman *does* like me.'

'Yesterday you said she didn't.'

'That was yesterday.' Another smirk.

'But what happened? I didn't see her even look at you. What makes you think she likes you?'

'She must. She's going to the movies with me.'

'What?' Simon stumbled again. 'What? You asked Cybil to go to the movies with you?'

Tony nodded.

Simon kept staring at Tony. He could not believe it. He had known that some time in the future, all of them would be taking girls to movies and maybe even to dances, but that was years in the future. It was as unthinkable now as their joining the army.

A runner passed them. Simon heard the man's rasping breath, felt a spray of sweat, heard the slap of shoes against the pavement.

Sometimes it seemed to Simon that the whole world was running, that someone had yelled, 'Fire,' and everybody had started running, with his father leading the pack. And he, like the prehistoric fish, couldn't take a step without plopping belly-down in the mire.

'There's just one catch,' Tony said.

'What?'

'She won't go unless you and Haywood come too.'

Simon stopped as abruptly as if he had run into a brick wall. 'What?'

'You and Haywood have to come to the movies with us.' Tony spoke as slowly and carefully as if he was speaking to someone with concussion.

'Wait a minute. Do you mean I would have a date with Harriet Haywood?' Simon's voice was higher than he had ever heard it.

'Well, it's not actually a date,' Tony explained. 'We aren't going to pay their way. I was careful about that.' He touched his forehead. 'I told them we would meet them *inside, beyond* the candy counter. How's that for planning? We won't even have to buy them pop-corn!'

'I'm not going to the movies with Harriet Haywood,' Simon said flatly.

'You have to.'

'I don't.'

'But I've already set it up. I've told Harriet you wanted to make up for overturning her in the play. You made a fool of her, Simon. I should think you'd want to . . .'

He kept shaking his head.

Tony sighed with disappointment. 'Then I'll have to get Bonfili.'

'What?' Simon looked up. Tony's face, honest and open, looked back at him with regret.

'Harriet said she would go with either you or Bonfili and so since you won't go . . .' He shrugged.

Simon moaned beneath his breath. He put one hand to his forehead. It was one of those moments in a war, he decided, when the first inkling of failure comes, when that first sickening awareness that the war can be lost, that *you* can be defeated, comes and stays and grows. Grown men must tremble, he thought, deep inside them like volcanoes. He himself felt sick.

'I'll go,' he muttered.

Tony clapped him on the back, almost sending him to his knees on the sidewalk. 'I'll tell them it's all set.'

'Yes, tell them that.'

Tony hurried off, leaving Simon alone. Simon kept standing there. All week he had been trying to prevent Cybil from looking at Tony – just from looking at him, and while he was congratulating himself on his success, he learned that somehow, without those looks, they had arranged a *date*. It was like the enemy taking the castle without the moat.

He turned around on the sidewalk like a person starting a game of Blind Man's Bluff.

Slowly he began to make his way home. He walked like an old man trying to get used to new glasses. He tripped over kerbs, tree roots, blades of grass.

It was, he decided, like Camp Okiechobie again, being led blindly to the toilets by Mervin Rollins. He could almost hear Mervin calling in his clear, young voice, 'There are no Daddy-long-legs on the toilet seat.'

And when he got home at last and sank down on the front steps, he even thought he heard, once again, the silken sigh of crushed Daddy-long-legs.

The fact that he had now, without even trying, written an absolutely perfect sad sentence – I have a date with Harriet Haywood – was no comfort at all.

17
An Hour of Misfortune

Simon stood by his bed looking out of the window. It was dark, but he had not turned on the light.

On this, the evening before his date with Harriet Haywood, darkness seemed appropriate. All day, as he had sat in school with his head down – never looking up once to see if Tony was looking at Cybil or Cybil looking at Tony or – worse, if Harriet Haywood was looking at *him*, he had wished for darkness.

Now that the miracle had happened, he could not enjoy it. There had been a letter from his father that afternoon. He was in Arizona in a deserted mining town. He and some friends were working the mine, digging out turquoise. When they earned enough money, his father said, they were going to build a raft and sail to South America.

'He's obsessed,' his mother said when she finished the letter. She let it drop to the table as if it were heavy. 'He's digging for turquoise when every single person in the world has as much turquoise as they can possibly wear.' She shook her head. 'And what will he do in South America? Can you tell me that?'

He shook his head. The letters upset them both, only they reacted differently. His mother asked question after question, one after another, questions that had no answers. Even a week later she would interrupt his studying to say, 'And why on earth would he . . .' Simon had asked the questions at first too, only now he had stopped.

The image he had of his father was getting blurred, altered by all the pictures he'd seen of hermits and wild men, miners now, and men who let the ocean sweep them away on rafts. He could not remember his father's face at all.

Once he had believed he would be like his father when he grew up. It was more than a matter of genes. He wanted to be like him.

He would wear old woollen jackets and patched jeans and let his hair grow and protest against nuclear power. He would no longer fear wasps and poison ivy and would genuinely care about the natural habitat of the snail fish. He would eat mostly beans and rice.

But this afternoon, sitting at the table, looking at the letter that lay between him and his mother, he no longer believed it.

It wasn't just that he could not imagine himself digging for turquoise in a mine hundreds of feet below ground or living in a forest. It was that he was still trying to go forward somehow, fighting through the confusion and complications, against all biological odds, and his father had gone so far backward that he wanted to go to South America on a raft.

He sighed, watched the street below where a dog was checking out the garbage cans. The dog found a piece of meat paper and went away.

And in his date with Harriet Haywood, Simon thought, the first terrible social obligation of his life, an event so complicated and awful it made him feel sick, in this was the final proof of his difference. It had never once occurred to him to run.

It was odd. The original reason for accepting the date was so that he could be there to keep an eye on Cybil and Tony. But this was no longer true. He didn't want to see what they did. And yet here he was, going on the date as bravely as Daniel went into the lion's den.

But then maybe his father had done this too, he thought, gone on dates he didn't want to go on, done things he didn't want to do, until one day . . .

He turned abruptly and walked into the living-room. T-Bone was lying on the hearth.

Simon lay down beside the dog with his cheek against the cool slate. 'T-Bone, I've got some unfortunate news. I have a date with Harriet Haywood.'

He was pleased that his voice was calm, normal, nothing in his tone to alarm the dog.

T-Bone opened his eyes but did not lift his head. He thumped his tail once on the hearth.

'She's as big as a woman, T-Bone.'

Thump.

'A grown woman.' He paused. 'Make that an *overgrown* woman.'

As he said that, a picture of Harriet Haywood came into his mind, bigger even than life and with the kind of stern authority of an adult. He remembered her, hands on her hips, saying, 'You'd better not cause any trouble,' at the pet show. It was like having a date with Miss McFawn, he decided, and shuddered.

At almost the same moment he thought of Cybil. He remembered her running out of her house once with Clara's diary. It was during second grade, the peak – he thought then – of his love.

And Clara had come after her and Cybil had scooted up in the mimosa and, legs dangling in the sunlight, pretended to read from the diary.

'Mom! Cybil's got my diary.'

'Cybil!'

'Mom, you ought to read this yourself, especially Saturday, September ninth!'

'Cybilllll!'

'Oh, here's your old diary,' Cybil said, dropping it. 'Anyway, if it makes you feel any better, I can't read cursive writing yet.'

Then she had seen Simon standing at the edge of the street. 'Simon, come on up!'

He had climbed up, feeling better and stronger with each climb as if the air itself was getting cleaner, rarer, less polluted. When he got there at last she said, 'I don't like Miss Ellis, do you?'

'No.'

'You know what my sister calls her?'

'No.'

'Devilled Egg.'

That alone – the perfect assessment of Miss Ellis – would have made the climb worthwhile.

'Your sisters,' he said, paying them his highest compliment, 'remind me of you.'

'Yes, we all look alike, and d'you know what? My mom is beautiful. Have you ever seen her?' He shook his head. 'Well, she's *beautiful*, only she has very weak genes. We've got my father's eyes, my father's skin, my father's hair, my father's legs, everything. Guess what we've got from my mother?' He shook his head again. 'Skimpy ear lobes. Look!' She lifted her hair. 'None of us can ever wear earrings.'

He had been so charmed that he almost fell out of the tree like a drunken bird.

Simon glanced over at T-Bone who was asleep again. He said, 'I had a nightmare about my date with Harriet, T-Bone. I was on a TV show called "Take Your Pick" and I had to decide whether I would go on a date with Harriet or with a gorilla and I couldn't decide and the clock was ticking and they were in glass booths – Harriet and the gorilla – and I was running back and forth, from one booth to the other, and by accident the gorilla's door opened and Harriet thought I'd picked the gorilla and she came out and hit me over the head with an umbrella.

'Well, my mom came in then and woke me up and said, "Simon, you were having a nightmare." And I said, "Yes." Then I said, "Oh, by the way, I have a date this Saturday," in a normal voice as if I had been dating all my life. She said, "Oh, with that nice little girl who was over here last week – Cybil Somebody." And I said, "No, with the tub of blubber." End of conversation between me and my mom.'

Suddenly Simon put his arms around T-Bone and buried his face in the fur of T-Bone's neck. He hadn't done this in a long time, but the dog smelled exactly the same, felt exactly the same. He himself felt compelled to act as he used to.

'Oh, T-Bone, I don't want to go,' he said, feeling the childish words coming in a comfortable rush. 'I don't want to go on a date with Harriet Haywood. I don't want to have dates. T-Bone, help me, bite me, do something, anything. Give me a dog disease. T-Bone, do something!'

Lick.

Simon sat up and looked at the dog. 'T-Bone, I must say that you have been a real help and consolation in my hour of misfortune. Thank you.'

Thump.

18
A Date with Harriet Haywood

THE day of Simon's date was beautiful and mild, and Simon made his way to the Mall under a cloudless sky.

He began walking slower when he got to the Mall parking lot. His determination, which he now estimated to have the size and permanence of an ice cube, began to grow even smaller as he crossed the warm pavement. He stopped beside a van.

This would be, he thought suddenly, the absolutely perfect moment for his father to kidnap him. His father could leap from the van, beard flying, snatch him up, toss him inside and roar off to ancient forests and turquoise mines, or wherever real day-to-day living didn't exist. Only

Harriet Haywood, cheated out of her date, would mind. Hands on hips, eyes narrowed, she would say, 'I *knew* he wouldn't behave!' He shuddered slightly as he left the shelter of the van.

Suddenly Tony Angotti burst through the Mall doors. He ran across the parking lot, dodging cars like he was on the football field.

'Disaster,' he gasped when he got to Simon. The force of his movement caused them to swing round like children on the playground.

'What happened?' Simon asked. His voice rose with sudden hope. 'Harriet didn't come?'

'Worse! They're waiting *outside* the movie theatre.' He grabbed Simon's shoulders and shook him to get the meaning to go down. 'I told them *inside*, you know, so we wouldn't have to *pay!*'

'Well –'

'And now they're *outside!*' His eyes shifted to Simon's pocket. 'How much money have you got?'

'Three dollars.'

'Well, it's two dollars to get in, and that's what I've got – two dollars! And even for that I have to stoop down and pretend I'm a child!'

'That won't work for Harriet. She's big, Tony. I was thinking about that last night. She's –'

'Shut up and think!'

'Maybe we should just go home,' Simon said while Tony wrung his hands. 'Forget it.'

'We are not going to forget it,' Tony said firmly. He began pulling Simon towards the Mall by the front of his shirt.

'Well, if we haven't got the money –'

'We'll tell them to go on inside,' Tony said with sudden inspiration. 'How does this sound? We'll tell them you have to buy something in Penney's for your mother. We'll tell them to save us some seats. All right now, let's go in and try it.'

Cybil and Harriet were waiting – Tony was right – outside the theatre. They were both wearing skirts and blouses. This alarmed Simon. He thought the only time girls wore skirts and blouses was to church and special occasions. He did not want anyone to think of this as a special occasion. He began to walk slower.

'Now back me up,' Tony said. He approached the girls and stood by Cybil. 'Look, Simon's got a little problem. Me and him have to go into Penney's for a minute and get something for his mom. You go on inside and we'll be right with you.'

'We'll wait for you here,' Harriet said firmly. She looked so big in her skirt and blouse that she seemed to block the whole front of the theatre.

'Inside, *inside*.' Tony pushed them towards the ticket seller. 'You'll have to save the seats.'

'But we're the first people here,' Harriet said. She turned and faced them. Her hands were on her hips. 'The whole theatre is empty.'

'Yeah, but me and Simon like to sit in the front row, don't we, Pal?'

This time Tony spun Harriet round with such force and skill that she found herself directly in front of the ticket booth. 'How many?' the woman asked in a bored voice.

'One – child,' Harriet said through tight lips. She glanced back with fury at Tony and Simon as she bent her knees.

'One,' said Cybil.

Tony pulled Simon towards Penney's. 'Don't look back,' he said. 'It might be a trick.' He shook his head. 'If they don't buy those tickets, well, we'll just have to keep on going.'

They went into Penney's and hid in the shoe department. Tony peered around the display of high heels. 'They've either gone in or they've gone home,' he reported.

'They've gone in,' Simon said pessimistically.

'Let's go then.'

They walked back to the theatre and Tony said, 'Did two girls buy tickets and go inside a minute ago?'

'Were they wearing skirts and blouses?' the woman in the booth asked.

'I didn't notice what they were wearing,' Tony said. 'One's redheaded and one's fat.'

'They were wearing skirts and blouses,' Simon said quickly.

'Then, yeah, they're inside.'

'Did they buy popcorn and candy?'

'No.'

'Bad news,' Tony said as he bent his knees. 'One – child.'

Simon bought popcorn and they made their way into the theatre. They did not have any trouble spotting Harriet and Cybil because they were the only two people there. They were sitting in the front row, talking to each other over two empty seats.

Harriet looked back and said, 'Here they come and look! They didn't buy anything at Penney's. I told you they just didn't want to pay our way.'

'Penney's was all out of unmentionables in his mom's

size,' Tony explained quickly, slipping into the seat beside Cybil.

Simon sat by Harriet. 'Popcorn?' he asked.

'Thanks.'

She took the box and began to eat. Simon watched as the top pieces, yellow with butter, disappeared into her mouth, then the dry middle pieces. When she got to the bottom where the crumbs were, she offered the box back to Simon.

He shook his head.

'You're sure you don't want any?'

He nodded.

'Well, if you're sure.' She turned up the container and drank the crumbs. Then she said, 'I'm thirsty, aren't you?'

Simon got up dutifully. He made his way to the back of the theatre and bought a small Coke with the rest of his money.

'Thanks,' Harriet said. 'Did they have any Jujubes? Now I've got my braces off I can eat anything.'

'They didn't have any.'

'How about Milk Duds?'

'No.'

The lights went down at last and Simon sat staring up at the screen like a sick dog.

'You want some Coke?' Harriet asked.

He shook his head.

She polished it off and began to chew on the ice. Simon's eyes misted over, either from the nearness of the screen or the fact that his whole adult life was stretching ahead of him as a series of dates, one Harriet Haywood after another.

Tony nudged him. Simon looked over in time to see

Tony reaching for Cybil Ackerman's hand. He turned his eyes quickly to the screen and watched the images waver in the mist.

'The scary part's coming up,' Harriet told him. 'My sister's already seen this. She says to keep your eyes on the door because that's where the monster's hiding. She says the door bursts open just when they reach the cages and the monster comes through. She says it'll really scare you if you're not expecting it.'

'I'll be expecting it,' Simon said.

'Oh, listen, don't let me ruin the fun for you!' She nudged him with her elbow.

The chances of ruining something that was non-existent seemed slight.

'You won't,' he promised, shifting to the far side of his seat where he would, he hoped, be out of range.

19
His Own Worst Enemy

HARRIET walked Simon home. This, he felt, was the equivalent of being marched home by the principal. He only spoke two words. Twice Harriet asked him what he was thinking about, and twice he answered, 'Nothing.'

When they got to his house Harriet said, 'You know, I think Cybil's feelings were hurt.'

'What?' He had already started to turn into his driveway, but now he paused. This was the first interest he had shown in anything, so Harriet looked pleased.

'You know, because you wanted to be with me.'

'What?'

'Oh, you know.' She gave Simon a playful poke, and he put his hand over the spot to protect it. 'Cybil thought she was going to be with you at the movies and then this morning Tony called me and said that you wanted to be with me, that you would not come unless you could sit by me, and for me to tell Cybil when we . . .'

'What?'

'Well, Cybil had agreed to go to the movies with you because she didn't like Tony. It was all set – you and Cybil, me and Tony. I don't like Tony either, but I wanted to see the movie. Only then, Tony said you wanted to be with me and . . .'

She continued, but Simon no longer heard her. This was like something out of a soap opera – lies and plots and misunderstandings. Rage began to burn in his chest like a hot coal.

'Good-bye,' he told Harriet.

'Wait. I'm not through.'

'Good-bye.'

He went into the house, walked through to the kitchen and waited for his mother to ask what was wrong. His face had to be so flushed she would go straight for the thermometer. She glanced up and then back down at a cake she was icing.

'How does that look?' she asked, turning the plate around on the table.

'Fine,' he snapped.

'I'm going to a supper tonight – it's Parents Without Partners – and I want my cake to look, you know – edible.' She smiled.

He waited, then said, 'Is this Parents Without Partners like a *date*?' He wanted to remind her that he had just come from such an event himself. For the first time in his life he actually wanted to talk.

'No, it's just people getting together.'

'Oh.' He waited again, and then said in a rush, 'Aren't you going to ask me how my date was?'

'Yes, how was it?'

'Terrible, awful, horrible, miserable, sickening and infuriating.'

She made a face. 'I'm glad you had such a good time.'

'Thanks.'

'What went wrong?'

'Everything. I was supposed to be with Cybil and Tony tricked me into being with Harriet. Mom, she poked me all during the movie. I *hate* Tony!'

'Don't be too hard on him.'

'Mom! When I used to like Tony you were always putting him down and wanting me to get new friends, and now that I hate him, you're defending him!'

'No, what worried me when you and Tony were friends was that he took advantage of you and you seemed to always get the short end of the stick and take the blame – and you never seemed to know what he was doing. Now that you see Tony for what he is, well, I feel better about your being friends.'

'We *aren't* friends.'

'Tony is his own worst enemy.'

'No, he's got me now.'

She looked at him. 'Do you remember when you were in first grade and Tony moved here and he sat behind you and that whole year he claimed he had got an unlucky desk?'

'I don't remember that.'

'Every time he got a bad grade, he would start hitting his desk – you told me this, and you told me that one time you went home with him and he had his report card and it was bad and his mother thumped him on the head with her ring and he burst out crying and said, "What d'you expect? I told you I'd got the unlucky desk."'

'I remember his mom hitting him.'

'Well, anyway, that, to me, is Tony. Tony is probably going to go through his whole life without knowing what he's like or why things happen to him or why things don't happen to him or what other people think or feel. It's sad.' She looked at him, waiting.

'I still hate him,' he said.

She smiled. 'Okay, hate him.' She glanced down at her cake and picked it up. 'Now, I am proud of that cake,' she said. 'I've got out of the habit of cooking and I bet I haven't made a cake in –' She paused, remembering the exact day she had lost interest in cooking.

'In two and a half years,' Simon said.

'Two and a half years.'

Simon got off the stool and walked into the living-room. 'I hope you didn't fill up on popcorn and candy,' his mother called after him.

'That is not possible on a date with Harriet Haywood,' he called back.

'Because your supper's ready.'

'Good, I've got to go somewhere tonight.'

'Not over to Tony's. Not till you cool down.'

'No, not over to Tony's.'

20
The Victory

SIMON stood at the edge of Cybil's yard, waiting respectfully with his hands behind his back. Cybil's sister, Clarice, was having a Miss America pageant on the front lawn. It was the talent portion of the production, and Clarice was dancing to 'God Bless America' which someone was playing on the piano inside.

Simon had come there right after supper. He had decided that this time he would not pretend to be looking for something. There had been enough lies and pretences. He would walk straight up to the door like an adult, ring the bell and ask to speak to Cybil. He would try to explain the confusion of the afternoon by uttering the understatement of the year. 'I did not really want to be with Harriet Haywood at the movies.'

His intention had been stalled by the Miss America pageant, but as soon as it was over he would proceed to the front door.

Clarice finished her dance. She said loudly, 'I want to be Miss America so that I can bring peace to all the world through my dancing.'

Applause. Clarice went back and stood proudly on the front steps with the other three candidates. Simon shifted restlessly. He wondered if he could slip past the candidates without disturbing the whole production.

Too late. A baton-twirling routine to 'God Bless America' began. Simon continued to stand respectfully on the sidelines.

He looked up at the house, listened to the music. The Ackerman house was like a commercial for living, he thought, an advertisement to show how zestful ordinary, day-to-day life can be.

As he stood there he began to realize that it was Cybil at the piano. He could not see in the window, of course, and never intended to try to do so again, but somehow he was sure it was Cybil, willingly, energetically playing 'God Bless America' again and again. A warm feeling came over him.

The baton routine ended. Now the decision of judges – Clarice is the new Miss America! Simon broke his respectful stance long enough to applaud.

'Why do *you* get to be Miss America?' the baton twirler snapped. Her hands were on her hips. Simon thought this was the way the losers would really act if the TV cameras weren't there.

'Because the judges picked me,' Clarice said coolly.

'The judges are your sisters!'

'I can't help that!'

'Well, I better get to be Miss Congeniality or I'm going home!'

Simon slipped past them, up the steps, and to the front door. He rang the bell.

It was Cybil who came to the door. 'Oh, hi,' she said.

His plan, which had seemed so sensible, so adult on the way over, now seemed stupid. Finally he managed to get out his statement. 'I just wanted to tell you that I didn't really want to be with Harriet that afternoon.'

'Oh, I know that.'

'You do?'

'Tony told me. He got mad and said I didn't know how

lucky I was to sit by him. He said most girls would consider it an honour. And you know who he thinks he looks like?'

'Donny Osmond.'

'Yes! And you know what he did? He tried to hold my hand in the movies. And you know what I did? I pinched his hand right in the palm where it really hurts. Didn't you hear him gasp?'

'I was watching the movie.'

Clarice stormed by. 'Just because I got to be Miss America everybody's gone home!' She turned back to Cybil. 'And you were supposed to play 'There She Is, Miss America' so I could come down the steps and – everything is *ruined*. Mom, Cybil ruined my Miss America Pageant!'

'Cybil,' Mrs Ackerman called tiredly from the living-room.

Cybil grinned and crossed her eyes. 'You want to go bike riding?' she asked suddenly.

Simon felt a stab of despair. 'I don't have a bike.'

'You can borrow Clara's. Clara! Can Simon borrow your bike?'

'If he's careful and puts some air in the front tyre,' Clara called back.

'We'll stop at the gas station,' Cybil told Simon as she led him to the garage.

As they started out of the driveway Simon glanced at Cybil and paused. Her red hair was streaming behind her in the wind. It made Simon think of flags and banners and bands. She looked back. 'Are you coming?'

'Yes!'

He had a brief struggle with his pedals and his knee hit the straw basket which was tied on the handlebars. Then his feet and legs got straightened out, and he pedalled after Cybil.

They rode down the hill in silence. As they turned the corner in a wide arc, Simon suddenly thought that his father was missing a lot out there in that turquoise mine. It was the first time he had felt sorry for his father rather than for himself. Because in this world, with all its troubles, even if you had to sit by Harriet Haywood in the movies in the afternoon, you could still be riding beside Cybil Ackerman in the evening.

He thought again about that prehistoric creature who finally got on his legs in the slime, stepped forward and found himself not bellied down but – miracle! – on a bicycle, cool wind in his face, going thirty miles an hour with Cybil Ackerman at his side. Millions of years of evolution bypassed in a moment. It seemed so clear a transformation that the whole process flashed through his mind, with himself the final glorious frame.

'We better stop at the gas station,' Cybil said over her shoulder. 'Clara's real particular about her things. Let's cut through here.'

It was Oak Street – Tony's street. Simon felt his heart beat faster. 'All right,' he said quickly. He steered to the right beside her.

He glanced up as they approached Tony's house. He braked slightly when he saw that Tony was sitting on the front steps with Pap-pap. He wanted to give them time to see him. Pap-pap was getting ready to cry about something. He already had his handkerchief out, twisting it into a rope. But Tony was staring at the street.

When Tony saw the bicycles, and who was riding them, he got quickly to his feet. His mouth was hanging open in surprise.

Risking an accident, Simon lifted one hand in a half wave. Then he clutched the handlebars again. The thought of wrecking Clara's bicycle made him decide not to even glance at Tony again.

'Wait a minute,' he heard Tony yell. 'Hey, come back. Wait a minute. I'll come with you guys. Hey, wait! I'll get Annette's bike!'

Simon pedalled faster again and he and Cybil rode down the hill, around the corner, and down Elm Street. Simon's smile was so broad that his teeth were getting dry. He felt he had had his victory. That wave – just a lift of the hand without wrecking the bike – that was all he needed to acknowledge it.

He felt he had seen something like this in an old newsreel. It was so clear he had to have seen it. A victorious general came riding through a war-torn city, and he graciously – just like Simon – lifted one hand to the crowd. The crowd waved flags, shouted, wept. There was none of that celebrating for Simon's appearance, and yet the result was the same, he thought. The war was over.

Simon glanced at Cybil. He wondered if she would like to ride past Harriet Haywood's and lift *her* hand. No, he decided, she was bigger than that. He watched as she made a left hand signal to turn into the gas station. He did the same.

'Do you know how to use this?' Cybil asked as they stopped in front of the air hose.

'No,' he admitted.

'I'll show you.'

Her red head bent over the tyre. Her curls blew in the wind. She glanced up at Simon.

Abruptly he abandoned his pose as the triumphant general. After all, the war was over. This was the real world, and he better learn how it worked.

He knelt beside her and watched.